PRAISE FOR THE WRAITHWOOD TRILOGY

"Alyssa Roat gives new life to Arthurian legend."

— PORTLAND BOOK REVIEW

"Immersive, atmospheric, and brimming with magic... A treasure for any booklover."

— CAROLINE GEORGE, AUTHOR OF *DEAREST JOSEPHINE* (HARPERCOLLINS)

"Irresistible."

— *FOREWORD REVIEWS*

"A magical and notable retelling of Arthurian legend."

— READER'S FAVORITE 5-STAR REVIEW (*WRAITHWOOD*)

"An instant classic."

— HOPE BOLINGER, AUTHOR OF THE BLAZE TRILOGY

"A perfect summer read!"

— LINDSAY A. FRANKLIN, AWARD-WINNING AUTHOR OF *THE STORY PEDDLER*

"An emotional journey of coming-of-age."

— READER'S FAVORITE 5-STAR REVIEW (*MORDIZAN*)

"A thrilling sequel to Wraithwood."

— LOREHAVEN MAGAZINE

CASTELON

Also by Alyssa Roat

The Wraithwood Trilogy

Wraithwood

Mordizan

Castelon

The Dear Series

Dear Hero

Dear Henchman

Dear Hades

CASTELON

THE WRAITHWOOD TRILOGY

BOOK THREE

ALYSSA ROAT

Vista, CA

Copyright © 2026 by Alyssa Roat

All rights reserved. Torchflame Books supports copyright. Copyright fuels creativity, encourages diverse voices, promotes free speech, and creates a vibrant culture. Thank you for buying an authorized edition of this book and for complying with copyright laws by not reproducing, scanning, or distributing any part of it in any form without permission, except by a reviewer who wishes to quote brief passages in connection with a review written for insertion in a magazine, newspaper, broadcast, website, blog or other outlet. You are supporting independent publishing and allowing Torchflame Books to publish books for all readers.

NO AI TRAINING: Without in any way limiting the author's [and publisher's] exclusive rights under copyright, any use of this publication to "train" generative artificial intelligence (AI) technologies to generate text is expressly prohibited. The author reserves all rights to license uses of this work for generative AI training and development of machine learning language models.

ISBN: 978-1-61153-620-1 (paperback)

ISBN: 978-1-61153-621-8 (ebook)

ISBN: 978-1-61153-622-5 (large print)

Library of Congress Control Number: 2026934730

Castelon is published by: Torchflame Books, an imprint of Top Reads Publishing, LLC, 1035 E. Vista Way, Suite 205, Vista, CA 92084, USA

Previously published in 2023 by Mountain Brook Ink under the Mountain Brook Fire line, White Salmon, WA U.S.A.

Scripture quotations are taken from the King James Version of the Bible. Public domain.

Cover Design: Indie Cover Design, Lynnette Bonner

Interior Layout: Jori Hanna

The publisher is not responsible for websites or social media accounts (or their content) that are not owned by the publisher.

This is a work of fiction. Names, characters, places, and incidents are either the product of the author's imagination or used fictitiously, and any resemblance to actual persons, living or dead, business establishments, events, or locales is entirely coincidental.

To the end of journeys
and the start of new adventures.

CHAPTER ONE

M*ordred's bane, his final doom.*

"You can do it. One foot in front of the other."

The heir of Arthur doth supply.

"Don't stop. We're so close."

With sword Excalibur in hand.

"Stay with me, Brinnie. Stay with me."

His magic to destroy.

Snow crunched under her feet. Bare feet, wrapped in rags. She left steaming footprints behind her, each step melting the snow. So hot. Too hot.

She clutched Marcus's arm, grateful he was resistant to heat, even the magical sort. She'd burned through the thick padded fabric of his sleeve, scorched the front of his chain mail when he'd carried her until he took it off and cast the mail aside.

With sword Excalibur in hand.

She would destroy Mordred. Burn him to the ground.

Mordred's bane, his final doom.

This heat would not consume her.

Not before she killed Mordred.

CHAPTER TWO

Brinnie repeated her name to herself. *Brynna Gwynneth Lane.* Or was it Brynna Ludovic-Drakon now? *Doesn't matter. Brinnie. I'm Brinnie.*

With each step she and Marcus had taken the past few hours, she'd faded in and out of consciousness. The magic swirling in her veins threatened to consume her, erase all but the most important thoughts, which she repeated in her mind.

Her name, the prophecy, Excalibur. Her name, the prophecy, Excalibur.

"We should reach the border in half an hour." Marcus kept his left arm wrapped around her, supporting her, while he held her right arm over his shoulders with the other hand. "You should let me carry you until then."

"The portal couldn't have . . . dropped us off just . . . the *slightest* bit closer." She gasped out the words, attempting a smile.

"The wizard who made it probably intended for a sneaky approach." He stopped. "Are your eyes open?"

"No," she admitted. She forced her eyelids apart, wincing at—well, everything. The overwhelming onslaught of refracting light and slumbering earth and bare trees pulsing with inner life and rocks and water and snow and air and . . . She wobbled.

"Okay, keep them closed." Marcus gripped her tighter, keeping her upright. She slumped, and he caught one arm behind her knees, lifting her and striding onward. "Sleep if you need to. Just . . . only sleep."

"Not planning to die," she mumbled into his chest. *Sleep. Maybe? So much pain.*

"I believe you a little more now than a few hours ago."

Fair.

The moment they had stepped out of the portal fleeing the scene of Mordred's conquest of the final stronghold, she had looked Marcus in the eyes, stated, "His bane is Excalibur, and I'm the one who has to wield it," and promptly keeled over. Which definitely killed the dramatic mood.

She curled her arms in close with a shiver. Great, now she was cold? *Make up your mind, magic.* She squinted up at him. "You're absolutely sure my dad is in charge of Dirklon?"

"Positive. Mordred and my father have been furious, but there was nothing they could do while the protection spells were active." Marcus paused. "Of course, now that all the strongholds have fallen, his borders will be open."

"So, we should be able to walk right in."

His boots crunched a comforting rhythm as he looked down at her, brown eyes worried. "Kind of." *"More like the guards on the walls will be on high alert and hopefully won't shoot on sight."*

His voice echoed in her mind. Again. For the past few hours, ever since the portal, she'd been hearing strangely. As if parts of his speech rang through her ears, and parts entered only through her mind.

His gaze turned ahead. "I see it."

She lifted her head and sucked in a breath.

A rocky hill loomed ahead of them, crags dusted with snow. Walls rose from the solid rock, forming concentric rings around a fortress of beige sandstone. In front of them, the outer walls jutted to two points, flanking the one part of the hill that sloped rather than falling away to cliffs, and the only entrance to the fortress—an uphill trek through the narrowing bare expanse between the walls, forming a gauntlet for any would-be attackers.

She searched for words. Only one thing came to mind. "Excellent castle design."

Marcus snorted, then laughed. "Said like a true Drakon. You come from a line of talented architects."

I do? She hadn't thought much about being a Drakon, other than to refuse to acknowledge Goran Drakon as any relation. To be ashamed of the name and the bloody history.

"When it comes to fortresses and sadistic ways to destroy enemies, of course," Marcus added. "Not pretty, but extremely effective."

Ah. There it is.

As they approached the looming castle, Marcus set her on her feet. "Best to keep my hands free."

As if he could do anything against the shapes of a dozen soldiers now visible stationed on the walls. Brinnie could make out crossbows that would surely cut them down before Marcus could ever shoot fireballs their way.

Her breath came in heaving gasps as they ascended the slope. Marcus put his hands up in a gesture of peace.

"State your business." The shout came from a man positioned at the apex of the left-hand wall, the Drakon serpent crest visible on his armor. His crossbow remained trained on Marcus—probably because Brinnie didn't look like much of a threat as a skin-and-bones waif tottering along next to Marcus's brawny form.

"We're here to see the Master of Dirklon."

"State your identities as well," called a woman on the right wall in a position mirroring the man.

Marcus hesitated, glanced at Brinnie. *"Eh, what's the harm."* "Marcus Vorath and Brynna Drakon, here to see her father."

The wall loomed too high for Brinnie to determine what the soldiers said, only their sharp gestures. One gave a quick salute and ran for a guard tower, presumably to descend with the message. Finally, the first guard called, "Drop any weapons and make your way toward the gate, hands up."

"Does it look like we have any weapons?" Brinnie muttered. Her legs shook, and her eyes burned as they traced the upward slope to the gate. She raised trembling hands, her arms quaking at the exertion.

Marcus shot her a worried look. "We're close. You can do it." *"Probably not, but if she keels over, at least they'll see we aren't a threat."*

"Thanks for the encouragement. Maybe I'll just keel over now and spare us the trouble."

His brow furrowed. "I didn't say anything about . . ."

"No talking!" The woman on the wall hefted her crossbow. "Keep five paces apart."

Brinnie focused on her breathing as they ascended the slope toward the entrance, which consisted of both a portcullis and a timber gate several feet back reinforced with iron. She shuddered, remembering the screams of wizards trapped in the no-man's-land of the stronghold's fortress, where they had been shut in and slaughtered.

Because of her.

Spots swam in front of her vision. Stone sizzled beneath her feet.

Here we go again.

The ground rose up to meet her.

It was soft. Like a cloud.

I'm in heaven. But there wouldn't be pain in heaven. She wouldn't be burning.

She forced open eyelids that felt as heavy as the portcullis of Dirklon. She blinked, but her vision remained blurry. Warm forest green above her, something red and orange crackling in her peripheral.

She turned her head, her hair rustling against a soft pillow. A thick bedspread covered her, the same color as the forest green above. Ah, a bed with a canopy.

Her eyes adjusted, making out the heavy drapes around the bed, the stone walls, the wooden beams across the ceiling, and the wide stone hearth, where a fire danced.

A form slumped in an upholstered chair beside the bed, arms draped over the armrests and head bowed. Dad's dark hair hung over his eyes, longer than he kept it before. His embroidered doublet and white shirt fit him well, as did the pants tucked into high boots. He looked like a well-dressed nobleman, his broad shoulders accentuated in a way that suggested he could wield a weapon as well as a turn of phrase.

Perhaps that was part of why his fashion choices had always looked so awkward and dorky in the human world—modern clothing didn't quite suit him.

She reached out a hand, revealing a white, long-sleeved nightgown someone had dressed her in. "Dad," she croaked.

His eyes shot open, shoulders straightening. A grin spread across his face, even as moisture collected in eyes rimmed with dark circles. "Brin. It's good to see you awake."

"I assume I'm alive." Her voice rasped.

"By a miracle." He reached for a pitcher on the bedside table. "Do you want water? Anything? I'll call for the healer."

"I'll take water."

He poured her a glass, then helped her sit up slowly. Once she was sitting, he handed her the cup before crossing to the door. He cracked it open, said something with an authoritative gesture, then closed it and returned to her side.

The glass cooled her burning palms while she took careful sips. "I don't think I need a healer, Dr. Lane," she teased. "What's your prognosis?"

His usual humor didn't light his eyes. "I know human medicine. Anything magical is beyond me."

She sobered. "How long have I been out?" From the way her back ached, she had a feeling she'd been in the same position for a while.

"It's been two days." His jaw tightened as he watched her like she might disappear.

"Wow." She blinked, holding onto the glass with both hands until a shiver ran through her. She attempted to lighten the mood. "How many sets of sheets did I burn through?"

He did offer a slight smile at that. "Only three." He sat again. "Brin . . . magical overload is deadly—and rare. The little research we have of survivors is from ancient texts. More recent cases have all been fatal."

"And yet, here I am." A shudder caused her hands to quake until water sloshed over them.

Dad took the cup, setting the glass on the end table. "Yes. And if the old texts are correct, if you survive the first few days, you should live. But the magic will be very volatile, and you could kill yourself by using too much magic or being exposed to more." He fixed her with a stern Dad Look. "I need you to make sure you don't use any magic, at least for the next few days. For anything. Got it?"

"Got it." Spots flashed in front of her vision. Dad adjusted the pillows, lowering her again. "What's the status on Mordred?"

"Absolutely not. You need to rest. You're safe in Dirklon and that's all that matters."

Before she could respond, the door cracked open and Marcus slipped into the room, hugging the wall. His gaze landed on her and his countenance flooded with relief. Their eyes met. His lips didn't move, but almost audibly, she heard him say, *"Praise God you're alive."*

She raised an eyebrow. *Piety is a new look on you.*

His eyes widened. *"You heard that?"*

Yes.

"But I didn't say anything."

Neither did I.

They stared at each other. *What on earth is going on?*

Dad cleared his throat. "You could knock."

Brinnie rolled her eyes. What did Dad hate more, Marcus being a guy near her age who seemed close to her, or Marcus being a Vorath?

"My apologies, my lord." Marcus bobbed his head. "I heard a healer had been sent for and was worried."

"I'm fine, everyone." A chill sweeping through her along with a spurt of pain through her veins attempted to contradict her words, but she kept her expression neutral. "Marcus, did you tell him about the bane?"

"As much as I knew." Marcus stepped forward. "I don't know all parts of the story—only about Excalibur and some lines of the prophecy you were repeating as we walked."

"I have my most trusted scholars looking for information as we speak." Dad patted her hand, sending pins and needles into her nerves. She flinched, and he retracted his touch. "Sorry. For now, our walls are secure, and you don't need to worry."

Yeah, right. "Wraithwood?"

"Your mom and the others are there, safely guarded by the Maze." He shot Marcus a look, as if warning him not to say more.

She attempted to sit up. "I need to get back to Wraithwood. It needs a Master's protection now that the strongholds have fallen."

"It will be fine for a good while," Marcus said as Dad placed a hand in front of her shoulder, preventing her from rising. "Mordred's forces are attacking easier targets than Wraithwood."

"How many have fallen?"

He darted a look at Dad. "Two estates so far."

She squeezed her eyes shut. *My fault, my fault, my fault.* She could almost feel the warm, sticky blood coating her hands.

A knock at the door interrupted her spiraling thoughts.

"Enter," Dad said.

A gray-haired wizard with a long beard stepped through the doorway. Brinnie squinted. Something about him looked familiar. *Wait.* She'd met him two summers ago, at Wraithwood. He was a healer traveling with Mordred's invading party and had revived her after she nearly drowned in quicksand-like mud. "Dolphus?"

He chuckled. "I suppose I'm not allowed to call you a ninny anymore, my lady." The old man shut the door behind him.

Dad's brow furrowed. "What?"

"We've met." Dolphus shuffled forward. "Under less pleasant circumstances."

Brinnie narrowed her eyes. "You were working for Mordred."

"I was a healer and I was available." He shrugged. "I didn't have much of a choice in getting sent along on the mission."

"Dolphus was a healer at Dirklon when I was a boy," Dad explained. "He returned once I claimed the Mastership."

"Making me feel old, my lord." Dolphus stopped at the side of the bed. "May I?"

Brinnie stilled while he put a hand to her forehead and closed his eyes, sensing her ailments, his brow furrowed in concentration. Her gaze roved the room as she waited and tried not to shiver or shrink away from the pain prickling at even his light touch.

Finally, he opened his eyes. "Some internal damage still. Extremely malnourished. Multiple injuries that have been magically healed and are luckily holding up under the pressure. Quality work, there." He turned to Dad. "I suggest small meals, easy on the stomach to begin with, to regain mass. A slow regimen of physical therapy to rebuild muscle—"

"Yes, I know those things." Dad sighed, running a hand through his hair. "I want to know about the magical element. What is the magic doing to her?"

Dolphus fiddled with his beard. "That would be the internal damage, my lord. Even with the enhanced healing abilities of wizards, that much magic running unchecked is . . . well, it's like radiation to humans, I would imagine. Wreaking havoc on cellular structures."

The books she'd read on nuclear disasters flashed through her mind, and she took a shaky breath. Many of the images had given her nightmares. "Radiation poisoning can cause complications weeks, months, even years later," Brinnie interjected. "I thought the ancient texts said if you survive the first few days, you're good?"

"Those texts are based on wizards being exposed, not *absorbing* the magic." Dolphus fixed her with a stern look. "*If* you can get it under control, the same logic as that in the texts should apply. Your cellular structure will recover in ways a human's won't, once the magic is contained. But if you can't—it would be like wandering around Chernobyl for days after the incident. The magic is coursing through you unchecked."

"So I need to get it under control." *I did it with my shadow magic. I'll do it with this too.* "Got it."

Dad clasped Dolphus's hand in a firm shake. "Thank you. If you have any dietary supplements for regaining weight . . ."

Dad and Dolphus moved toward the doorway, discussing fattening her up in medical terms. She closed her eyes briefly, exhaustion dragging at her limbs. Her time in Mordizan's dungeons hadn't helped her constitution.

Marcus moved to the bedside with a slight smile, but she caught the worry beneath his expression. "While they swap expertise for the next twenty minutes . . . how are you really?"

She blew out a puff of air. "I don't know, I managed to help Mordred conquer the last stronghold and open the way for him to attack the estates, so I feel pretty good about myself."

"Brinnie—"

"How's it going with Excalibur? Any information?" She didn't need comfort right now, she needed action.

He looked like he might protest, but instead he sighed. "They contacted Castelon about the bane. No one knows the location of Excalibur. That's what your father has his scholars looking into day and night."

Of course. She bit her lip. "Any clues?"

"Not really." He hesitated, attention wandering toward the door and the hall beyond where Dad and Dolphus stood talking. "It was a well-guarded secret, kept only by Arthur's heirs."

"The Masters of Wraithwood." She squeezed her eyes shut. "And the last Master died without passing that information along."

"I'm sorry."

As she opened her eyes again, she saw his fingers twitch, as if he had been about to reach out in comfort, but stopped himself. Good. Even if touch wouldn't hurt, she might come undone. She had no space for emotions.

She firmed her jaw, glancing at Dad and Dolphus. "Well, we know where the Masters of Wraithwood like to keep their secrets. The Wraithwood Scrolls." She fixed her gaze back on Marcus. "You up for a road trip?"

"It's never boring with you, is it?" The corner of his mouth quirked up. "As soon as you're feeling better, count me in."

CHAPTER THREE

"A portal. Anything. I'll take a bicycle at this point."

Dad frowned, leaning on his hands on the oval table, and barely looked up from the maps. "You're not ready."

She clenched her fists and resisted the urge to lean against the opposite side of the table. That would just prove his point.

A few wizards circled the work surface along with Dad, moving pieces, making notes. Most likely advisors or military leaders—probably not people she should be questioning his judgment in front of, but what choice did she have?

"I'm walking, I'm standing—"

"You're hobbling and wobbling." He straightened and waved a hand at a young man standing at attention along the wall of the office-like space. "Take her back to her room, please." He gave her a stern look, accentuating the dark circles under his eyes, no doubt caused by the weight of bad news no one would tell her. "I'll come see you in an hour. Where's Marcus?"

"I don't know." Her tongue took over with more impertinence than she'd ever leveled at him before. "I imagine he has better things to do in the middle of this war than make sure I don't leave my room."

A few of the wizards shot each other uncomfortable looks. Dad sighed. "One hour, Brin. You can survive that long."

She followed the stiff young man back to her room, trying not to pant too much from the simple exertion of walking through the halls.

Two days of consciousness had made for two days of monotonous pain heightened by the urgency stirring in her gut. She had to get back to Wraithwood. She had to find Excalibur. She had to stop this war, this slaughter, the destruction she had caused.

When Marcus wasn't hovering over her like an anxious mother hen, he'd been spending every moment in Dirklon's—admittedly limited—library. Finding nothing. But Dad banned her from accompanying Marcus even there.

"You go book crazy," Dad had said. "I'll find you climbing some shelf or forgetting to eat for a whole day in a research frenzy."

She wanted to protest that she didn't do that. Except that she definitely did, and had, done that. More than once.

So instead of book crazy, she went stir crazy, with nothing to think about but pain.

Sometimes the magic in her veins ran hot, sometimes cold. Sometimes it seemed to push against her skin, threatening to explode. She dared not explore the deep, roiling mass within her like an acidic sea.

"Here you are, my lady." The young man gave a jerky bow.

She focused, only now realizing they had stopped. "Thank you." She pushed open the wooden door and shut it behind her, slumping against the surface, her scant muscles feeling like gelatin.

"I thought we agreed you wouldn't wander."

She scowled at Marcus where he leaned against the bedpost, arms crossed.

He pushed to his feet and scanned her face. Unlike Dad's, his expression was soft. "Brinnie. Please. There's nothing we can do right now."

"So much for agreeing to a road trip." She winced at her own sharp tone.

"I'm still on board." His tone remained even, unaffected by hers. "*After* you take time to rest and heal."

Tears formed in the corners of her eyes. She blinked them away. "I need to do something. Something to keep my mind—" She didn't finish. *To keep my mind out of that dark place. To keep it from returning to the dungeon, the battlefields, the screams . . .*

He placed gentle hands on her shoulders. *"I know."*

She took a shuddering breath. His unexplained voice in her mind, another mystery, should have concerned her, but it soothed her thoughts. She sighed and leaned against him for support.

"Should I tell her?"

Her head snapped up, almost knocking him in the chin. "Tell me what?"

"Whoa." He steadied her, expression sheepish. "You weren't supposed to hear that. How about you sit down first?"

She eased herself into the bedside chair. If she sat on the bed, she would be sucked into sleep. And she didn't have time for that. "What do you know?"

He sighed. "Things aren't . . . great at Wraithwood."

She shot to her feet, then wobbled and almost fell over sideways, prevented only by Marcus's steadying arm. "What's going on? I knew Dad was lying." Her vision faded in and out.

Marcus eased her back into the chair. "It's okay. Nothing urgent. Basically, no one can leave due to the Maze—not if they want to be able to get back in afterward. They could leave by door, but with how volatile magic has been these days, the humans shouldn't try going through the door even to abandon Wraithwood altogether."

"Okay." Maybe if her brain didn't throb every time she tried to think, she could figure out why this was a concern. "So they stay, in the protection of the Maze."

"Er, yes." He rubbed his neck. "Problem is, supplies are low. Food is running out, firewood . . ."

Finally, the issue clicked. "They're running out of time. And even if they could risk the door, they would end up somewhere completely random. Possibly in the middle of danger." Brinnie massaged her temple. "This *is* urgent. You're telling me my family is starving, and we're doing nothing?"

He hesitated.

She stood. "I stole so many powers. At least one of them had to be traveling like Uncle Merlin, right? I've been to Wraithwood. By the rules of instant travel, I should be able to get in there."

"No, no, no." Marcus grabbed her shoulders. "That is strong magic. You're not supposed to be using *any* magic right now."

Images flashed through her mind. Nightmares of the ruins of Wraithwood. Terrors of her family, emaciated, reaching out skeletal hands in supplication. All the things she had caused.

She attempted to shake Marcus off. "I'm at least giving it a shot."

Before he could do anything else, she squeezed her eyes shut, pictured Wraithwood's kitchen, and tried to throw herself to the location.

Instead, she rammed into Marcus.

"Whoa. Brinnie—"

Her blood heated. Fate couldn't be so cruel as to give her the magic of a hundred wizards and not one of them the kind she needed. She attempted to throw her consciousness to the new location, slinging magic behind the urge.

Instead, her skin crackled, lightning sparked, and a shock jolted through both of them.

Marcus cursed. "Brinnie, calm d—"

Too late. Darkness overtook her.

"She doesn't listen to me either."

Brinnie surfaced to the sound of Marcus's voice.

Dad's baritone replied with disapproval. "You had one job, Vorath."

Her eyes opened in time to see Marcus wince at the name. He and Dad stood to her left, silhouetted by the fireplace. From the feel of sheets beneath her, someone had lifted her to the bed.

Right. She had been in the middle of something.

"You have to let me go." Brinnie propped herself on a wobbly elbow. "They need someone to get them in and out through the Maze. As the Master, I can."

"Good morning," Marcus said drily.

Dad didn't bother with sarcasm. "How are you going to get there, Brin? Through a portal?" He ran his hand through his hair. "You would likely kill yourself."

A possibility she hadn't thought available. "Do you have a portal to Wraithwood?"

"Brin."

"Alternatively, consider." She sat up all the way, ignoring how her vision tunneled at the movement, and pressed her hands together. "We drive, or fly, or whatever . . ." She trailed off. "Where are we, geographically?"

Dad raised an eyebrow. "Not sure I trust you with that information at the moment."

"Okay, so we get *most* of the way there, and then portal in. That way it's a shorter distance. Less magic. And—"

Marcus pinched the bridge of his nose. "That's not how it works."

"And *then*," she continued, shooting him a glare, "being at Wraithwood is likely to stabilize my magic. If I'm the Master, Wraithwood is my home base. If anything, I should feel the best there."

Dad and Marcus shot each other a look. For a moment, the only sound was the crackling of the fire.

"That does actually check out," Marcus admitted. "The stabilizing on her own estate part, anyway."

Brinnie did an internal fist pump. She had completely made up that theory on the spot.

Dad sighed. "If it will help you to stop burning or exploding everything you touch—"

"Not *everything*—"

"—and get you feeling better, I'm willing to sign off."

"Yes." This time she fist pumped externally. And made herself so dizzy she fell back into bed.

"Do you have portals to somewhere near Wraithwood?" Marcus directed his words toward Dad while fluffing a pillow for Brinnie. "We'll still have to walk in through the Maze . . . if that's possible."

Brinnie allowed Marcus to help her ease against the propped pillows, her brow furrowed. "Why? Can't we portal the way we did from Arizona to Wraithwood?"

"You did?" Marcus glanced between the two of them. "You can't use a portal to get into an estate—or so I've always been told. Even Mordred was only able to portal out of estates, not into them."

"You're right, that was the case, before the strongholds fell." Dad ran a hand through his hair, the nervous tic having him looking shaggier by the moment. "Now . . . it's technically possible. When the Anchors were destroyed, I retained most of my abilities as a Master, but without the protection spells, I can't control who exits and enters. Luckily, most portals were made while the strongholds stood, so they lead to locations outside the estates themselves."

"But that's different now, right?" Brinnie cocked her head. "Can't a traveler and a spellcaster work together to make as many as they want, going anywhere they want? A traveler just has to have been to the place, right?"

"Travelers are relatively rare," Marcus explained. "Mordizan has one young traveler, and as far as I know, Merlin was the only one Castelon had." He looked to Dad for confirmation, who nodded. "Mordizan's traveler probably hasn't been to Dirklon, considering it was closed for so long."

"Which is a relief. All to say, we don't have any portals that lead directly to Wraithwood, and last summer, we didn't actually portal to Wraithwood." Dad glanced at Brinnie with a sheepish expression. "Merlin let me know some top-secret information before you and he left. He would have shared it with you as well, Brinnie, but in such close contact with Mordred, if anything happened . . ."

"I get it." She pushed herself higher against the pillows. "You two were worried I would crack under interrogation."

She hadn't meant the words as a jab, but Dad winced anyway. His and Marcus's attention both flicked to her emaciated limbs.

Dad cleared his throat. "We didn't portal to Wraithwood itself. Instead, we portalled to a special hub leading to the door. Merlin set them up years ago with the help of a spellcaster specifically for his closest compatriots like Lydia and Oswald Goddensfeld—"

Goddensfeld. Her mind flashed back to blood, to screams of agony . . .

No. Don't go there.

"—close to their usual bases of operation," Dad continued. "Merlin didn't tell me the location of all three, but he did tell me the location of one, in case of emergency. When we portalled, we ended up at one of these places, and knocked on the door. The idea is that anyone at Wraithwood can let someone in through these specialized portal hubs, not just Merlin."

"Excellent." Marcus clasped his hands behind his back, all business. "So we have a portal to these hubs?"

"Not quite." Dad offered Brinnie a small smile. "Have you ever wanted to visit St. Louis?"

Less than twenty-four hours later, Brinnie huddled next to Marcus, avoiding the crowd of humans. Children brushed against her legs and she shivered, thinking of what she could do to them without meaning to.

The portal had dumped them off surprisingly close to their destination, only a couple of blocks away from The City Museum in St. Louis, Missouri. After Brinnie spent the first few minutes stumbling like a drunkard, she acclimated to the searing pain in her molecules and began counting out cash for their entrance fee.

The museum loomed several stories, a boxy building like so many others in downtown St. Louis. Unlike other buildings, random vehicles, tubes, and wire walkways jutted from the walls and roof, sticking out of the rows of rectangular windows. A metal tentacle pointed the way to the entrance.

Marcus had leaned over and whispered, "This isn't normal human architecture, is it?"

"No, it's certainly not."

Now inside, they waited in line for the ticket window, voices echoing off soaring stairs, colorful metal slides, and beautiful mosaics, the refuse of a city molded into art. Children continued to weave through the crowd, parents called to their offspring, somewhere a group broke into loud laughter–so many sights and sounds and life and . . .

Her heart pounded. Sensations pummeled her awareness. Her head spun, her blood bubbled, she was going to pass out or explode or—

"Hey." Marcus wrapped an arm around her and pulled her out of line off to the side. He rubbed her shoulders. "Breathe. In, out. We're okay. We're safe." He led her to a long bench.

She sank onto the seat with wobbling knees. She closed her eyes, took deep breaths. "I'm fine." *I'm not.* Too many things going on, overwhelming her senses. "You have eyes out for enemies?"

"I'm on alert. Don't worry about it."

As unlikely as it was that anyone would find them here, even in outdated American clothing pilfered from Dirklon's stashes, they couldn't be too careful. In fact, just in case of spies, only Dad and a few trusted advisors knew Brinnie and Marcus had left Dirklon at all.

She had forgotten how *loud* humans were. How vibrant the world could be. She sucked in another breath.

A sharp voice pierced through her thoughts. "Maybe if you ate something, you wouldn't feel this way."

Brinnie lifted her head to see a middle-aged woman scowling down her nose. The woman rolled her eyes to her companion. "Kids these days." As she turned away, the second part came just loud enough for Brinnie to hear as the woman glanced at Marcus. "Probably one of those 'anxiety attacks' for attention."

Brinnie looked down at her emaciated arms, at the jeans barely clinging to her waist with a belt. She clenched her fists, her breath shuddering. *Relax. It's just an ignorant comment.*

Words flitted through her head. *Too skinny. Too skittish. Too weird. Too strange-looking. Too broken.* She had hardly carved out a space for herself in the human world before all of this. Now, she felt like an alien. Would she ever feel comfortable in the real world again?

Marcus's eyes flashed. "If she knew the half of it . . ." he growled.

Brinnie put a hand on his arm. "It's fine." She sighed. "That's humans for you. Can't fathom the things they can't see, so they make stupid assumptions." She took a breath. "Okay. I'm ready."

They rejoined the line snaking to the ticket counter. After they paid and received their wristbands, they wandered toward the maze of bars, branches, tiles, and—was that a wall made out of bread tins?

Brinnie kept her voice low. "The hub is warded against human discovery, which makes me think we need to find places where humans are not."

"Right." He wove toward a gigantic white whale. "Something about an organ, and a shaft? Are there maps of this place?"

"Unfortunately, that's the whole point of the museum. No maps. It's an exploring adventure." Which, under any other circumstances, she would love.

Marcus turned, scanning tunnels, stairs, and ladders ascending toward the ceiling, twisting through synthetic caves and trees. "You're not climbing through all of this."

She didn't bother protesting. Sweat already beaded on her brow from the slight exertion so far. Magical overload aside, she needed to spend some serious time building back the muscle she had lost so soon after gaining it. *All that training for nothing.*

Like most thoughts lately, it made her want to cry.

They made their way to a cafe on the second floor. To avoid suspicion, Brinnie bought a sports drink at the counter and settled at a table near the railing, offering a view of a good portion of the first floor. From here, she could monitor people entering the museum.

Marcus nodded to her. "I'll check in periodically. If you're in trouble, scream. It doesn't matter if you make a scene."

"I can defend myself."

"That's what I'm afraid of." He indicated the surrounding crowd with a bob of his head. "You can defend yourself a little too well right now." His expression grew teasing. "As impressive as it would be to see you level half this building—"

"Okay, okay." She waved him off.

He chuckled. "I'll come back for you once I find the, ah, organ in the shaft. By which I am assuming—and hoping—Merlin meant a musical instrument."

With Marcus gone to crawl through the maze of tunnels with all the kids, and hopefully not get stuck in the process, Brinnie pulled her knees in and rested her feet on the seat of the chair, nursing the blue sports drink. Hopefully electrolytes and hydration would do a bit of good, though it might take months to get back into fighting shape.

Months she didn't have.

She scanned the crowd, all smiles and carefree chatter from patrons of all ages. They had no idea how very close their world was to crumbling apart. Although, if human history had shown anything, the cycle of life and work and play paused for no man or force of nature. Humanity was a race of tenacious, if foolish, little buggers.

She leaned her head against a nearby column, content to watch children run and frolic. Maybe if her blood could stop pumping like acid through her veins, she might feel peaceful.

She didn't realize she'd fallen asleep until a gentle touch on her shoulder jerked her awake, arm swinging.

Marcus caught her fist before it could crash into his face. "It's okay, it's me." He pointed his head to the right. "I found the organ."

She followed him through a network of caves and tunnels, some that she assumed were dark as Marcus bumped into the walls. She snorted. "Aren't you used to this from the passages in Mordizan?"

"Hey, I've known those passageways for years. This is new to me."

He led the way until they reached metal stairs surrounded with bars of the same dark metal. Music drifted from ahead.

To her chagrin, Marcus half-carried Brinnie up the narrow steps. They emerged to a sight that made her inhale sharply.

A massive organ's pipes soared several stories high in a room filled with twisting staircases, bars, and chutes. Panels built into the walls of the room moved with the organ's powerful chords, turning the old factory building into a living, breathing musical instrument.

As the dramatic music crescendoed around her, tears rose to Brinnie's eyes. "It makes sense he would pick here," she whispered. Strange, but beautiful. Just like Wraithwood.

Marcus placed his hand over hers where she clutched the railing. "I wish I'd had a chance to know him."

She swallowed and took a shaky breath. Now wasn't the time to lose control. "Where is this door?"

Marcus swept an arm toward the maze of stairs. "Somewhere in here. And I'm not confident if I found it alone, I would be able to lead us back to it again."

"Then let's get climbing. And look for someplace humans aren't."

Two hours later, Brinnie slumped on a small landing, breath coming in ragged gasps. They had tromped up and down the staircases, even slid down the metal slides, and come across nothing that could be construed as a hidden door.

"This is not working," Brinnie panted. She lifted a hand. "Are you sure I can't send some wolves out to scout for us? Work off some magic?"

Marcus gave her a look. "Your father will kill me if I let you start using magic before you're supposed to. Not until Wraithwood."

"We're getting nowhere." She stood and sighed, leaning back against the wall.

Or, she meant to. Instead, she fell straight through where the wall had been.

She squeaked, but only fell a few feet before she landed on her back on hard concrete with a thump—five feet away from an ornate wooden door. *Wraithwood's* front door.

Marcus followed a second later, landing gracefully on his feet. "I didn't expect an illusion, but I suppose I should have. Just in case some wizard got the urge to go exploring." He held out a hand to help her up. "Are you okay?"

"Yeah." She dusted off the back of her pants and took a few halting steps until she stood directly in front of the familiar wooden door, so out of place in this small, concrete room. On the other side—home. Home, after so many long months. Her last glimpse of Wraithwood felt half a lifetime ago. Yet, in her darkest moments, she'd imagined going back. The warmth of the kitchen fireplace. Bruno's floppy ears. Mrs. Winslow's tea. The smell of the library. Those tiny slices of joy, of hope, that even Mordizan's dank dungeon couldn't quite squash.

She lifted her fist and knocked.

At first, the door didn't move.

Great. Makes sense for this crazy museum. I'm knocking on a fancy maintenance closet or emergency exit. A replica or something.

But then, slowly, the handle turned. And on the other side, a wary furrowed brow over warm blue eyes peeked through the crack.

A gasp. "Brinnie?"

That voice. So familiar, so full of love and comfort, bringing to mind images of fresh-baked cookies and warm hugs and kind smiles.

She bit her lip, but a sob still escaped. "Mrs. Winslow."

The door flung wide open, and Brinnie fell into a motherly embrace, not caring about painful touch or dangerous powers or anything else.

A moment later, the magic of the door hit her, vibrating her cells.

But that was it. No new influx of magic. No settling or stabilization of the fire roaring through her veins. With the pain still wriggling through her neurons came realization. Another sob followed the first, this one not of joy, but of horror.

"I'm not the Master."

CHAPTER FOUR

Brinnie opened her eyes slowly, vision blurry. Something white above her, blue around her.

Her room at Wraithwood. Realization came flooding back, and she groaned.

I'm not the Master.

"Brynna." At Brinnie's stirring, Mom jumped up from a chair beside the bed. "Brynna, how are you, sweetie?" Tears formed in her eyes. "What can I do?"

"Nothing, really. Just magical overload again." Seconds after making the realization she was not, in fact, the Master of Wraithwood, she had overloaded on magic, nearly scorched the floor, and sparked so hard she knocked herself out. "How long have I been unconscious?"

"Only a few hours."

Brinnie winced, pushing herself upright. Mom's gaze flicked from Brinnie's pained expression, to her shaking limbs, to—yup, scorched bedsheets again.

Mom took her hand, a single tear rolling down her cheek. "I'm so sorry."

Before Brinnie could respond, the door opened and Quentin stuck his head in. "Hey, Mrs. Lane, Mrs. Winslow sent me up to ask if you wanted any food and . . . oh, Brinnie! You're alive!"

A smile broke through her sour mood. "Good to see you again, Quentin."

"Hey!" He went running out the door. "Hey, everyone, she's awake!"

Within moments, the Winslows, Miss Burtle, Marcie, Jerry, Maddy, and Ms. Tynsdale joined them in the room. Brinnie wriggled herself to a full sitting position. The last thing she needed was them clustering around her like an invalid.

Wait. Ms. Tynsdale? Brinnie's eyes locked on the thin blonde woman. "You're . . . you're up and walking around."

She smiled faintly, holding onto the door frame with a scarred hand. "Of course, I am. Didn't think I'd let those dark wizards win, did you? Looks like they couldn't keep you down, either."

Brinnie glanced around, then turned to Mom. "Where's Marcus?"

"The young man you came here with? He said something about scouting the perimeter." Mom braced as if delivering bad news. "We don't have a protection spell anymore. The last stronghold fell."

"I know." Brinnie's jaw tightened. "I was there." It struck her how little any of them knew. They must have only received basic information from Dad. Mom didn't even seem to know who Marcus was—a wise move on his part.

Movement drew her attention to the doorway as Marcus himself slipped into the room. They made eye contact. *"Good to see you awake again."*

She raised an eyebrow. *We really need to figure out what's going on with this whole telepathy thing.*

"We need to find a place to hide," Mom was saying, "at least until the worst of the invasions passes over."

Brinnie turned her attention to her mother. "Wait. We're not hiding. We're fighting."

Mom blinked back tears. "I'm sorry, Brinnie. If you aren't the Master, if you can't secure the Maze . . . we can't stand against Mordred. Mordizan has no quarrel with the human residents of Wraithwood, but for wizards . . . our best hope is to take cover in the human world. If nothing else, by staying alive, we keep the Enchantment alive."

"We can't just give up." Brinnie looked toward Marcus, Miss Burtle, Ms. Tynsdale, for support. "I may not be the Master, but we have to be able to find Excalibur. The answer to its location must be hiding somewhere here at Wraithwood."

Mom exchanged a glance with Mrs. Winslow. "Okay," she said finally. "We'll give it a few days at least. After that, there comes a point where this isn't our fight."

"Understood." For now.

Because even if everyone else fled, she couldn't leave behind the mess she'd made.

"Nope." *Click.* "Nope." *Click.* "Nope." *Click.*

"Quentin!" Maddy looked up from the book she was reading, shoving her short brown hair out of her face. "Honestly. Do you have to say 'nope' *every* time? Can't we just assume?"

"Maybe it will lead to the right place of these times." He opened the front door again and looked out on a sandy desert. "Nope." *Click.*

"I think what Maddy is trying to say is that you're driving her crazy." Brinnie pulled the quilt up higher and shivered, nestling deeper into the settee in the adjoining parlor. "How about you say 'nope' in your head?"

"Fine." He opened the door and yelled in surprise.

The figure outside dusted off his snow-laden hat. "Sorry." Marcus stepped in, stomping the snow off his boots. "I was just looking at the Maze with Lady Drakon . . . er, Mrs. Lane."

Brinnie sat up straighter. "And?"

"Can't tell." He shut the door, shuffling out of Quentin's way. "It might still be magical, and it might not be. No way of knowing without going in."

Brinnie slumped. *So we're still stuck.*

Her father had Mastership powers, even without a protection spell. So shouldn't she?

Perhaps Wraithwood's magic had rejected her.

She pulled her knees closer, huddling farther under the quilt.

Marcus made eye contact with Brinnie. *"How are you doing?"*

She winced. *Don't ask.*

Maddy heaved an enormous sigh. "You're doing it again."

Brinnie redirected her attention. "Doing what?"

"That weird thing where you both just stare at each other." Maddy pointed from Brinnie to Marcus. "What's that about?"

"Uh." Brinnie shifted her weight, trying to figure out how to even begin explaining.

Before she had to come up with an answer, Miss Burtle poked her head through the dining room door. "Anything yet?"

"No." Quentin swung the door shut on a jungle landscape.

Miss Burtle stepped forward, letting the dining room door swing shut behind her, and crossed her arms. "Can you affect it at all, Brynna?"

Brinnie scowled. "I've tried. I'm definitely not a traveler like Uncle Merlin. Out of all the powers I, uh, was exposed to, you'd think that would have been one of them."

They had been trying to get the door to open near Castelon, Dirklon, or any friendly and fortified estate for two days—somewhere that one of the wizards could find supplies and a portal to get them back to Merlin's special door, through which they could carry said supplies.

A week since the final stronghold fell. *A week of being completely useless.* Without Mastership powers, she couldn't even get her family to safety.

Miss Burtle gave Brinnie a second look. "Wait. Aren't you supposed to be in bed?"

"I wanted company." An understatement. Alone in her room, her thoughts had free rein to gallop in agonizing loops of memories and worries, the calming blue tones contrasting her swirling emotions. Not to mention accenting the extreme cold of upstate New York in winter.

"Better not let your mother know." Miss Burtle popped back out again.

Maddy rocked to her feet and picked a peapod off the stalk growing in a garden box in the corner of the parlor. "I can't wait for some real food."

Without anyone to guide them through the Maze, those at Wraithwood had been living off of whatever they could grow, Mrs. Winslow's canned foods and preserves, and the eggs the chickens produced. But as winter wore on, the supplies were running low.

"Well, I'll gladly take one of those," Brinnie said. Maddy tossed her a peapod, and she relished the crunch as she bit through the outer pod. "I never thought I would miss vegetables so much."

The dining room door opened and Mom stepped through, a slight dusting of snow in her hair. She must have circled to enter the house from the back door. Her eyes immediately went to Brinnie on the settee. "Brinnie. What are you doing in here?"

"I was bored."

Mom glanced at the staircase. "You made it down the stairs by yourself?"

Near the front door, Marcus finished pulling off his boots. "I helped her," he admitted.

Mom sighed. "At least you brought the quilt with you."

"Nope," Quentin said. *Click.*

"That's it." Maddy set her book down on the arm of the chair. "I'm going for a walk."

Mom rubbed the bridge of her nose. "Wear a coat." She turned to Brinnie. "You're purple. You need to come sit by the fire."

Brinnie didn't have the energy to argue. She let Mom help her through the dining room and to a comfortable seat in the kitchen near the hearth. A small pile of logs sat near the chair.

Logs. "Mom. Where are you getting the wood from?"

"Don't worry." Mom pulled the quilt up around Brinnie's shoulders. "We'll plant more apple trees after all this dies down."

Of all the reasons to cry, the thought of Wraithwood's beautiful trees chopped down to stumps brought tears to her eyes. She had made a terrible mistake. Certainly, she had learned of Mordred's bane, but in the process, she had helped to destroy the protection spells, isolated her family at Wraithwood, and led Uncle Merlin to his death. Instead of fixing any of it, here she was, stuck just as much as anyone else, frail and useless.

Uncle Merlin. She hadn't yet worked up the courage to visit where they had buried him. Not that Mom would let her go out in this cold, but Brinnie had confidence in her own stealth abilities if she truly wanted to leave.

She was a coward—and she hadn't been able to face the finality of the headstone beneath a spreading tree by the rose garden. Far away from where his parents had been buried, because they couldn't risk the Maze to lay him to rest in the cemetery.

Mom's voice brought her back. "I'm going to go find Marcie and see whether Isaac has eaten recently." She patted Brinnie on the shoulder and turned to leave.

With a scrabbling of paws on wood, Bruno stood from his place in the corner and came to stick his bony head under Brinnie's arm for pets as soon as Mom exited the room. Brinnie ran her hand down his sides, fingers catching on his protruding ribs. She hugged him closer.

"Wraithwood is dying, boy," she whispered. "It can't live without Uncle Merlin."

She hated to think what would become of the animals. They couldn't be transported by magic. She dashed her tears away.

"*Mrow.*" Ami, Morgana's old cat, jumped into Brinnie's lap and purred as Brinnie stroked the feline's silky head. *I wish Morgana were here. She would probably know what to do.* But Mordred killed her, too.

In the past two days at Wraithwood, Miss Burtle had been in contact with Castelon on the subject of Mordred's bane, but still no one there had found any information on the location of Excalibur, seeming to confirm what they already feared—only the Masters of Wraithwood had been entrusted with the knowledge. The only hope there rested in Castelon's Archives, which, they had been told, scholars were currently combing.

Wraithwood posed the most likely avenue of success. Brinnie had been banned from searching through the Wraithwood Scrolls—irreplaceable scrolls and artifacts in the hands of her unpredictable magic would be a recipe for disaster—but Miss Burtle doubted any clues would be found there either.

She had pressed her lips together, clearly perturbed. "There weren't many things Merlin didn't share with me. The hereditary secrets of the Masters, though—he stuck to tradition on that."

Nevertheless, Miss Burtle and the wizards of the household searched the scrolls every spare moment, with rotational help from Maddy or other human members of Wraithwood who took turns with the translator stone.

And when they weren't researching, everyone kept out an eye and an ear for news of Anna and David. Brinnie had begun to wonder if Lana really did free them after all. If the door didn't open near an enchantment estate soon . . .

Her fingers sparked and Ami yowled, jumping off her lap. "I'm so sorry!" Brinnie clenched her hand.

"You scaring the cat again?"

She looked up to see Ms. Tynsdale enter the kitchen.

"Yeah. Shocked her this time."

Ms. Tynsdale pulled a chair from beside the kitchen table and set it next to Brinnie, easing into the seat. She had filled out slightly and gained a bit of color since Brinnie saw her half-conscious months ago, but the scars and boniness remained. Most striking, Lydia Tynsdale remained in her true form, without the red-headed spitfire making a single appearance.

But the dry inflection of the beautiful, soft-voiced blonde was the same. "How you feeling?"

Brinnie shrugged, opting for honesty. If anyone understood, Ms. Tynsdale would. "Exhausted. Everything hurts. But I've kind of gotten used to that. Not being starving is nice."

"I know how that feels." She shot Brinnie a wry look. "And I know it's worse than just the physical."

Brinnie rubbed her arm, too uncomfortable to make direct eye contact.

Ms. Tynsdale shook her head. "I went through Ignatius's brand of 'reeducation' for three months. He got busy with something else after that and they assigned me to a different guy with a bit more . . . finesse. Psychologically." Her gaze turned vacant. "That's what did me in."

She could almost feel the guilt rolling off Ms. Tynsdale in waves. But all she had done was leak information. Brinnie had done much, much worse. "So . . . what is the last thing you remember?"

"Saying goodbye to you before I left." She rubbed her temple. "Heck, I don't even remember getting to Mordizan. Whatever he did wiped me clean. All I remember after that is . . . you know."

She did. Far too well. "You're the one who told me about the prophecy and pointed me to Mordred's bane." Brinnie offered a half-smile. "Somehow you found it."

"Well, kudos to younger me." She sat back, staring into the fire. "I don't remember any of it, though."

They sat in companionable silence for a moment. The nightmares from last night played through Brinnie's head, flashbacks to Ignatius, darkness, images of Goddensfeld's blood, then waking up shivering and gasping for breath, drenched in sweat. She coughed and barely whispered, "It was rough."

"Oh, kid." She put her arm gently around Brinnie's shoulders, and by some blessing, the contact didn't hurt, and Brinnie didn't scorch either of them. There didn't seem to be anything else Ms. Tynsdale could say.

Or perhaps she knew no one could ever say anything that would begin to cover the darkness of those months.

So Brinnie pushed it down, locked the panic in a drawer. She shrugged. "I survived."

The back door burst open. Brinnie jumped, a poof of flowers bursting forth around her this time. *That's new.* She would need to look into that ability more.

Maddy charged inside, gasping for breath and waving a cell phone with a pink case over her head. "You'll never believe this. I just *happened* to turn on my phone to check for updates today, and look at my news feed!"

Brinnie flinched away from the device thrust toward her. "If you want that to keep working, I'd keep it far away from me."

Maddy pulled the phone back, tapping the screen. "Listen to this headline. 'Couple claims to have been abducted by evil wizards.' It's David and Anna!"

CHAPTER FIVE

Brinnie leaned forward, gripping the chair. "What does the article say?"

Maddy scrolled. "'David and Anna Matthew, an ordinary Arizona couple, claim to have had an extraordinary experience. After their mysterious disappearance five months ago, the two unexpectedly appeared near Syracuse, New York claiming to have been abducted by magic-wielding wizards. The couple is now searching for their almost two-year-old son, Isaac, and Anna's extended family, also missing. Both are extremely malnourished with evidence of physical abuse.' And then there's a link for the full story."

Brinnie's face threatened to split with a grin. "No way. She really did it."

Maddy lowered the phone. "Who did what?"

"Lana, my friend in Mordizan. She freed them." She sparked and set the quilt on fire, but quickly patted it out. "We need to tell everyone."

Maddy saluted. "On it."

Within moments, everyone gathered in the kitchen as Maddy read the article again.

Mom clapped her hands over her mouth. Tears gathered in her eyes and streamed down her cheeks as Maddy finished reading. "We have to go get them. We have to tell them we're okay."

"And rescue them before they get themselves caught again." Ms. Tynsdale maintained a grim expression.

Mom nodded. "ASAP. They're obviously drawing attention to themselves." She hesitated. "But there isn't really a way for us to bring them here."

After an uncomfortable silence, Mrs. Winslow finally said, "I think we need to split up, dear." She took Mr. Winslow's hand. "Edna, Tom, and I . . . we'll stay. You wizards, and you younger humans, you all need to go."

"Not without you." Brinnie's jaw clenched.

Miss Burtle shook her head. "We can't. We're too old, and I for one have gone through the door too many times. We would likely die. But not you three and the baby." She turned to Marcie, Jerry, and Maddy. "You're young. You would survive the journey."

Marcie and Jerry looked at each other. "We're not leaving you," Marcie said firmly. "This is our home. We'll stick it out."

Maddy glanced at them. "Well, that's nice, but not for me. I'll give the door a shot."

Mrs. Winslow placed a hand on Mom's shoulder. "Go save your daughter, Eira. Don't worry about us. With fewer of us here, our supplies will last longer."

Marcus shifted uncomfortably. "I hate to be the one to say this, but what about finding Excalibur? I agree someone should find Anna and David, but Mordred is on the brink of taking over the world."

"We'll split up into even smaller groups." Brinnie tapped her fingers in thought, then stopped as sparks began to flicker from her fingertips. "Some of us will find Anna and David, some of us will stay here searching the Wraithwood Scrolls, and some of us will go to Castelon to search the Archives. Even if we can't find the exact location of Excalibur, we should be able to find clues in the Archives, right?"

Mom nodded. "Finding Anna and David will be dangerous, considering they've put targets on their backs by going public. As much as Anna will be upset not to see him, Isaac should stay here."

Marcie raised a hand. "We can take care of him." She smiled at Jerry. "We've gotten pretty attached to the little guy."

"Thank you, Marcie." Mom pointed to Brinnie, Marcus, Maddy, and Quentin. "And you four should go to Castelon. That's probably the safest place in the world right now."

"Whoa, wait a minute." Quentin held up his hands. "I'm assigned to guard the Master Key."

"I don't think that really matters anymore. The protection spells are already gone." Mom bit her lip. "You can help the three of them get into Castelon. I'm sure security is tight."

He puffed up with the responsibility. "Yes, ma'am."

Mom nodded, all business. "I don't think the door is going to work for anyone getting to Castelon. The odds are incredibly slim, and we don't have time to keep trying. We'll all exit the door to wherever it takes us and fly, walk, or drive as needed."

"Give me twenty-four hours and I'll have the papers forged," Miss Burtle said.

Maddy's mouth dropped open. "Forged? Passports, IDs, everything? I don't really want to spend the end of the world in jail."

"Not to worry, dear. Edna's been doing this for years." Mrs. Winslow smiled. "I don't know how she does it, but she's hacked just about every government system there is."

From the little solar and mechanically powered computer in the office? *To be fair, she's probably traveled around a bit with Uncle Merlin, and he probably brought her top-secret info and passwords.* Brinnie looked at the secretary with new respect. "That's impressive."

"That's incredibly illegal," Maddy pointed out.

"That's settled then." Mom brushed her hands together. "I'll leave to get Anna and David tomorrow morning if you wouldn't mind making up papers for me."

"You're not going alone." Ms. Tynsdale put a fist on her hip. "I'm coming with you. I've got my papers already."

Mom smiled. "I'm not going to argue. Thank you, Lydia."

Even in the midst of the chaos, Brinnie couldn't help a mirroring smile. The glimpses of Mom and Ms. Tynsdale's old friendship, the easy relationship Mom had with the Winslows and Miss Burtle, even the way Mom calmly made plans instead of scolding everyone involved . . . time at Wraithwood had changed her, somehow.

And not a single word blaming Brinnie or her "soldier friend from Mordizan" for any of this.

Her heart clenched. *At least, not yet.* Brinnie had disclosed that she was exposed to Mordred's magic coupled with the Case of the Master Key, endowing her with an overload of magic. But she hadn't been able to bring herself to tell the truth. That the protection spells were all down because of her, and that she had stolen all of the powers she now possessed.

It was only a matter of time before Mom and the others talked to the wrong person, someone from Dirklon or Castelon, and learned the truth. Even with no enchantment wizard survivors from the stronghold, word would get out through the grapevine, from Mordizan, to dark estates, to spies. Then everyone would know what she'd done.

And Mom's delight that Brinnie survived, her gratitude for Brinnie's "sacrifice" on behalf of Anna . . . would it evaporate, replaced by loathing?

"Well, that's that." Miss Burtle's sharp voice brought Brinnie back to the present. "I'll get to work."

That night, Brinnie lay awake shivering and staring at the ceiling. The warm brick at the foot of her bed, heated by the fire, wasn't enough. *You would think with all this magical fire raging inside me, I wouldn't still be freezing.* At this rate, they might as well dogpile in the kitchen near the hearth.

In the stillness, she could hear every creak and groan of the old house, Jerry snoring, Quentin talking in his sleep. Then a door opening. Footsteps sounded down the hall, then on the stairs. Strangely, the footsteps seemed to continue right above her. Why was someone on the third floor?

She gingerly swung her legs out of bed and stood, knees and muscles protesting. She needed to convince Marcus to start training with her again.

On the way up the stairs, her legs wobbled, and she climbed on all fours for balance, glad no one could see her embarrassing position. At the top, she scanned the sitting area, where she had once played Wizard's Chess. No one. She continued down the hall, headed for a door at the end, slightly ajar.

She peered through the crack to see a small, simple room containing little more than a bed, a nightstand, a small desk, and a bookshelf. In the middle of the bedroom stood Ms. Tynsdale, candle in hand, turned away from Brinnie, her distinctive golden hair cascading down her back. Hair that now swayed, disturbed by her shaking shoulders.

Brinnie debated interrupting. She gave a hesitant knock on the door, causing it to swing open a little more. "Ms. Tynsdale? Are you okay?"

She whirled around, candlelight glinting off her tears. "Brinnie. What are you doing here?"

Awkward. She almost wished she'd never gotten out of bed. "I couldn't sleep and heard someone up here." Understanding dawned. "This is Uncle Merlin's room, isn't it?"

Ms. Tynsdale turned her face away. "Yes." Her words came out so soft, Brinnie barely caught them. "He grew up in this room. He remodeled the rest of the floor into the testing rooms, moved them down from the fourth floor. I think he couldn't stand to walk by Eira's and his parents' old rooms. But he kept this one."

Brinnie rested her hand on the doorframe of the sparse room. "Not really one for extravagance, was he?" Her grip tightened. "Not unless it was for someone else."

"He spared no cost for others. Including his own life." She sniffed and wiped a hand under her eyes. "I never told him goodbye, almost two years ago. I just snuck out."

Brinnie moved into the room. "But he saw you before . . . before he died. You were unconscious, but he was always sitting with you. He insisted you were in there, even when the rest of us thought there was no hope." Her voice wobbled. "I'd never seen him so . . . I don't know."

Ms. Tynsdale dashed tears from her cheeks, and Brinnie caught a glimpse of something in her free hand. She seemed to notice Brinnie's attention and flicked open the small box with her thumb, revealing a diamond ring. "He kept it. Sitting on his nightstand."

Brinnie took a moment to process. An engagement ring. "Who was it for?"

"I turned him down." Ms. Tynsdale took a shuddering breath.

Brinnie's eyes widened. *Well, that's an interesting development.*

Ms. Tynsdale shot her a glance. "I know you're feeling guilty about not being the Master, but it seems that anytime any of us try to make plans around inheritances . . . Myrddin's spells spite us." She snapped the box shut.

"What do you mean?"

"I guess I'll hit you with a brief rendition of my dramatic love life." Ms. Tynsdale snorted, but the humor didn't quite reach her eyes. "He proposed years ago, long before you were born—I know, I'm old. I knew he was going to ask one day, and I fully intended to say yes. We were young and stupid, but I loved him with all my heart."

Brinnie bit her lip. She almost didn't want to hear the rest.

"Then everything happened. The attack on Wraithwood. Antony was gone, and we thought he was dead. Which meant, we thought, I was the heir of Dirklon. So when Merlin proposed, a few years later, I said no. I couldn't marry a Master. Not when I had the chance to be a Master myself, take Dirklon for our side."

"But then my dad wasn't dead."

"We figured that out eventually, when my father died, and I wasn't the Master." Ms. Tynsdale leaned against the wall and sighed. "The odds were slim I'd run across him, but if I did, I had every intention of killing him. Even if he died some other way, I was still next in line. So Merlin never asked again." She gave a dry laugh. "And here you and I are. Both of us counting on Masterships that never came." She sobered. "There's no shame in not inheriting Wraithwood, kid, whatever the strange reason is. You're not letting us down. The shame is in giving up so much more for something that was never necessary."

For thirty-plus years, they had been in love but acted like they weren't. Only for Dirklon to go to the enchantment wizards after all. "Wow. I . . . I mean, you did what you thought was right."

"Maybe, in a twisted way." She shrugged. "I followed my ambition. He thought I was making the self-sacrificial decision, but I was making the selfish one. I wanted to be a Master, be a martyr-type hero, giving up everything to gain power for the good of the cause. I realized I was wrong when I was at the Academy. By then it was too late. He told me he'd gotten over everything and he was happy to just be friends." She looked down at the ring. "Turns out he only said that because he thought it would make me happy."

Brinnie twisted her hair around her finger, trying to come up with something to say. "I'm sorry."

"It's all done now." She pushed off the wall. "I guess what I'm saying, kid . . . don't get so caught up in being the martyr that you leave behind what's important. You're worth more to people than just what you can do for a cause." She took a few steps toward the door and placed a hand on Brinnie's shoulder on her way out. "And if you ever love someone . . . don't you dare let them die without telling them."

CHAPTER SIX

The next day found Brinnie, Marcus, Maddy, and Quentin standing in front of the door, accepting their forged passports from Miss Burtle. They had propped the door open in front of a snowy landscape that revealed a highway intersection and several fast food chains—definitely somewhere in America.

Brinnie turned her passport over, running her fingers over the dark surface and flipping the booklet open to reveal her picture inside, a picture similar to but not the same as the one on her driver's license. "This looks like the real thing. I'd be fooled."

"I imagine that wouldn't take much, but thank you." Miss Burtle crossed her arms. "Remember, wherever you end up, head for the nearest major airport. Maddy can book a flight from her phone. You need a flight through to London. Don't lose your luggage—you'll look strange without it. All of your papers say that you're at least eighteen, so that's taken care of. All right." She set a hand on her hip. "Anything else?"

Brinnie hugged her. "Thanks for everything. Don't worry. Flying is easier than battling evil wizards any day."

"And you." She shook her finger at Brinnie. "You be careful. No stray magic, and don't overexert yourself. Marcus, I'm counting on you to make sure she behaves."

He nodded. "Yes, ma'am."

"Goodbye, dears." Mrs. Winslow enveloped each of them in a hug, even Marcus.

Brinnie pushed down the lump in her throat as she said goodbye to each of the Wraithwooders. Mom and Ms. Tynsdale had already left, but that was an easier parting knowing she would most likely see them soon. She couldn't be sure when—or if—she would see the human denizens of Wraithwood again.

Marcie gave her an extra squeeze. "I'll keep an eye on all of them." She pulled away. "It's the least I can do after everything this family has done for me."

Brinnie nodded, unable to form words.

Finally, the four turned to the door, standing open with a view of the snow-covered town. With a last wave, Brinnie stepped through.

The magic ripped through her in a burning current. As she landed in the snow, suitcase filled with old clothing beside her, she fell to her knees gasping. Quentin and Marcus appeared after her, seemingly unaffected. Maddy appeared last, careening forward and landing face-first in a snow drift.

As Quentin went to help Maddy up, Marcus made his way to Brinnie. "Are you okay?"

"Not bad." She stood shakily. "I probably feel like humans must feel."

Now outside the door, she spun to take in more of the landscape. They had emerged near a gas station and hotel off a highway.

Maddy pointed and snickered. "Look at that water tower. I guess we're in some place called Gas City."

"Very mature." Brinnie rolled her eyes, but her lips twitched. "Want to look up where that is, exactly?"

Maddy pulled out her phone, miraculously still working after its second trip through space and time. Her fingers flew over the screen for a few seconds before she replied. "Hmm, Indiana. Nearby airports . . . Fort Wayne is about an hour away and Indianapolis is about an hour and a half. I'll take a look at flights and flight times."

Marcus glanced at Brinnie's trembling limbs. She tried to control her shivering, but to no avail. The coat she had borrowed from Wraithwood didn't do much against the wet snow that worked its way in when she fell. He bobbed his head toward the nearby buildings. "How about looking while we wait somewhere inside?"

"Like a restaurant with real food." Quentin pulled out a wallet. "I've got the money card."

"Credit card," Maddy corrected. "I second the motion. Real food." She looked around and her gaze settled on a billboard. "Hey, apparently there's a fish and chips place around here. We can get in the British spirit."

Around humans? Brinnie steeled her spine. This could be good. She would be in close quarters with humans in the airport and on the plane. She needed to ease her way into being around crowds. She hadn't shocked anyone at Wraithwood recently. With luck, she could continue to ignore the magic simmering under her skin, pushing it all down, down into the pool deep inside her where it couldn't hurt anyone, as long as she didn't touch it.

Which is fine. I don't need to use magic for anything.

Brinnie pointed across the street at an almost barn-like building. "Over there."

They crossed the road and entered the quirky red restaurant. Brinnie sighed in relief at the warmth. A waitress sat them at a circular table with wobbly metal chairs. Brinnie scanned the room. Most of the patrons seemed to be college students, several sporting the purple of what must be the local university. None of them gave the young group a second glance.

After they had ordered a round of fish and chips for everyone, Maddy scrolled through her phone. "No good flights out of Fort Wayne for a week, but there's one out of Indianapolis tomorrow with a few seats left headed for New York with a connection to London."

"Book it." Brinnie sat back, breathing in the scent of fried food. *Both nauseating and tantalizing at the same time.*

Quentin passed Maddy the credit card.

Brinnie raised an eyebrow. "Whose is that, anyway?"

"Used to be Master Ludovic's." He bounced a little in his seat. "I always wanted a money card. Mrs. Winslow gave it to me for the trip."

Brinnie strongly questioned Mrs. Winslow's judgment in giving such power to Quentin, even if he was the oldest, but she kept her mouth shut.

"Glad I'm not paying." Maddy tapped away. "Last minute international flights are *expensive*."

When the food arrived, Brinnie decided that if there were fish and chips in heaven, they couldn't taste any better. Marcus poked his meal a few times before digging in, his eyes going wide. No one spoke for several minutes, even Maddy, until they had shoveled plenty of food in.

Fry in one hand, Maddy tapped away at her phone again. "I got us an Uber. It should be here in half an hour. We're kind of in the middle of nowhere."

"What's an Uber?" Quentin shoved three fries in his mouth at once.

"A ride-share service. Er, a taxi." Brinnie glanced at Marcus. "Like the brooms in Mordizan, but cars, driven by people."

"I know what a taxi is. Kind of." Marcus dipped his fish in tartar sauce. "Three wizards in one vehicle seems a bit risky, though. Especially when one of them is you."

"Ah. Good point." She turned to Maddy. "Can we get a second one?"

"On it."

As Maddy searched, Quentin and Marcus discussed the wonder of chips, a.k.a. French fries. Marcus held one up to the light. "They don't have these in Mordizan."

"Not in Castelon, either." Quentin dunked a fry in ketchup.

"We should introduce them." Marcus shot Brinnie a smirk. "They're made of potatoes, yes? Maybe we could have a fish fry and invite the Allied and enchantment wizards."

"Peace by the power of the French fry." Brinnie nodded. "I can see it."

"There." Maddy looked up. "Got another one. Twenty-minute wait."

"Thanks, Maddy." Brinnie picked at her food to make it last longer, unwilling to go out in the cold. "You know, it's probably about seventy degrees in Arizona right now. Sunny. Perfect weather."

Quentin leaned back. "Why aren't we going there? Arizona sounds like a paradise."

Maddy snorted. "Don't let her fool you. Most of the year, it's an oven that wants to melt your face off."

The check came and Quentin put down the card. Brinnie taught him how to figure out the tip. As the waitress took it away, Brinnie turned to the three of them. "Now remember, everyone. We're college students. We're tourists. We're traveling to London on vacation. We know how the world works. If you don't know, act like you do."

"We know." Maddy rolled her eyes.

Brinnie pressed her lips together. "You and I might be okay on the navigating-the-human-world front, but we're going to have to step up our game to look older." She waved a hand at the two wizards. "You two are fine since you actually are college-age, but Maddy, honestly, you're going to need to work the hardest in the age department."

She heaved a sigh. "Sure, rub it in, I'm the youngest. I've got makeup in my bag and Miss Burtle's old-lady clothes."

"Good." Brinnie sat back, rubbing her temple. "I'd hoped I was done with all the secrecy after I left Mordizan."

"Welcome to being a wizard," Quentin said. The waitress gave him a funny look as she handed back the check.

A few minutes later, they stood outside the nearby gas station, waiting for their rides. "So, uh, this is going to be pricey. Not like, four tickets to London pricey, but . . ." Maddy gestured around them. "We're kind of in the middle of nowhere, a long way from the airport."

"The beauty of credit cards." Brinnie shrugged. "From the size of Wraithwood, I'm thinking money is a non-issue." A slight smile emerged as she remembered two years ago, when Mr. Winslow made it sound like Uncle Merlin was a speculator. Long-lived wizards probably had plenty of time to play the stock market. "Maddy, why don't you and Quentin wander into the gas station? Marcus and I will take the first car that arrives, and you two can take the second. It's going to look weird if we're all together and don't get in the same one."

Quentin's brow wrinkled. "Shouldn't we put Brinnie and Maddy together? You know, most magic with no magic?"

Maddy grabbed his arm and tugged him toward the convenience store. "Come on, Mr. Logic. I want some beef jerky for the road." She winked over her shoulder at Brinnie.

Brinnie felt her cheeks redden. "That's not—" But Maddy was already gone. She shut her mouth and spun to face Marcus. "Anyway."

"I understand." His lips twitched. "Out of the three of us, only one is fireproof."

"Exactly." She sagged in relief. *Of course he wouldn't make it weird. It's Marcus.*

A gray sedan pulled up and the driver stepped out and lifted a hand.

Brinnie stared for a moment, wondering if her eyes deceived her. "Bert?"

The driver's head cocked, then a slow grin broke across his face. He lifted his cap. "Well, if it isn't miss Brinnie. Long time no see."

"You remember me?"

He laughed. "My most interesting shuttle experience in over a decade? You bet."

"And now you work here? In Indiana?"

"My wife and I just moved a few months ago for her masters' program. Seems we were meant to meet again." He gestured to their bags. "I can put those in the trunk. Why don't you introduce me to your friend?"

"Right." She turned to a bemused Marcus. "This is Marcus, a friend from school. And this is Bert, a, uh, friend by circumstance of broken-down shuttle and the forest around Wraithwood."

Marcus raised an eyebrow. "Sounds like quite the story." He shook hands with Bert. "Nice to meet you."

Once the bags were in, Marcus and Brinnie slid into the back seat. Bert pulled out from the gas station. "Indy, huh?"

"Yes, indeed. The airport, please." Brinnie's heart rate began to subside. A friendly face in the car made this so much easier.

"You've got it." He took a left. "I imagine you had a good summer . . . what, almost two years ago?"

They kept up a friendly conversation on and off during the hour and a half drive to the airport. Brinnie made up a story about visiting family in Indiana—Marcus suddenly became her cousin—and heading to the airport to visit their other family members in New York. She adequately supplied answers to Bert's questions about school and studies, and Bert told them about his niece's soccer team and his nephew's taekwondo. All went well until he asked, "So when does your flight leave?"

"Tomorrow morning," Brinnie answered without thinking.

"Tomorrow morning? You're not planning to stay the night in the airport, are you?"

Brinnie shrugged. "We're too young to get a hotel room."

"Well, I can't let you stay in the airport all night." He glanced into the rearview mirror. "Besides, they won't let you go through security until tomorrow anyway. Do your parents know?"

Brinnie shot a glance at Marcus. *I have made an error.* "Yeah. It's fine."

"Well, I'm not sure . . ." He trailed off, brow furrowed as he kept his eyes on his mirrors. "You're comin' up real fast there, buddy."

Brinnie turned to look out the back window. A pickup truck ate up the distance between the two vehicles, quickly swerving into the left lane. The truck veered over the line, nearly bumping into Bert's car.

"Whoa, there." Bert gave the horn a sharp tap.

Marcus grabbed Brinnie's arm, gaining her attention. She met his gaze. *"Those are wizards—at least, some of them."*

Her heart rate spiked. *What? How?*

"I don't know, but I recognize one of them from our human ops team."

Bert yanked on the wheel as the truck drifted over the line again. This time, he hammered on the horn. "Hey, buddy, look out!"

Bert eased on the brakes, presumably trying to let the truck pass, but instead it slowed as well, continuing to box them toward the shoulder.

Brinnie gripped the door, trying to keep herself calm. *Don't freak out or you'll make this car malfunction in the middle of the highway.* "I think they want you to pull over."

Bert grappled in his pocket and tossed his phone back to Brinnie and Marcus. "Call the cops. I'm going to try to pull over safely." Sweat beaded on his forehead. "Hopefully that's safer than trying to outrace them."

"I think that's a good call." Marcus held up a hand toward the window and made a few gestures. The three men in the truck seemed to understand, because they eased off edging the car into the shoulder.

Bert slowed and pulled off onto the side of the highway, no exits in sight, just empty fields. The truck pulled over a couple dozen yards ahead of them.

"How?" Brinnie hissed to Marcus. "We portaled here. They can't be tracing us."

His brow furrowed as he reached for the door handle. "Maddy's phone, the money card . . . They're technology, right? I don't understand anything about our human world operatives, but they can track things on the, uh, internet." He pushed the door open. "We have dozens of humans who work for us doing just that. Anything connected to you and me is probably number one priority."

"Hey, there, I wouldn't get out just yet." Bert held out a hand toward Marcus. "We'll see what these people want."

Brinnie reached for her door handle. "I'm so sorry, Bert. We know what they want, unfortunately. It's probably best if you just drive away."

"And you're going with him." Marcus pointed at Brinnie.

"Excuse me?"

"I'll take care of them." He stood outside the car. "You go. You're not supposed to be fighting."

"And leave you here? Alone in the human world where you don't know how anything works? I don't think so."

Bert's eyes ping-ponged between the two of them. "Did you kids call the police?"

"No." Their reply came in unison. Brinnie sighed, glancing at the three men striding toward them. "They're not usually this bold, Marcus, are they?"

"Nope." His jaw set. "It appears Mordizan has decided they don't care too much what the humans think anymore, with victory at hand."

"It's not." Brinnie stepped out of the car. She waved to Bert. "Get out of here. Thanks for getting us this far—we'll figure it out from here."

He set his cap on his head and climbed out of the vehicle as well. "I don't think so, miss. I'm not letting a couple of kids face thugs alone. Not on my watch."

The three approached before Brinnie could argue, one all in black leading the way. "Using a human shield, Vorath?" the lead man called, coming to a stop about five yards away. His cronies flanked him on either side, one wielding a semi-automatic rifle—presumably a human, and the driver—and the other clad in what looked like dusty burlap. "Seems a bit beneath you."

Marcus strode in front of Bert. "I don't need one, Jepp. Get out of here. You're outmatched."

"Remembered my name and everything." The man grinned, revealing a crooked smile. "We have backup on the way. You and your lady friend might as well come along easy."

Brinnie took two steps forward, blood boiling—from agitated magic as much as anger. "You should be ashamed of yourselves, causing problems in broad daylight, going after an innocent human—nearly two millennia of secrecy and you do something like this?" She crossed her arms. She wished she could quickly summon a pack of shadow wolves to put an end to this. "You're an embarrassment."

Bert shuffled toward her protectively, mumbling under his breath, "Careful now, you don't want to antagonize them."

"Please, Marcus?" She sighed. "A few wolves."

"Both of your parents would kill me." He lifted his hands and his voice. "Last chance, Jepp. Get out of here. It wasn't fair of them to send such a small team after us and we all know it."

Jepp gritted his teeth. "There are teams searching the world for you, Vorath. If not us, someone else will get the glory. Help a man out and maybe they'll go easy on you."

Marcus flicked his wrist, sending a fireball cascading toward the human holding a rifle. The flames hit the ground inches in front of the man, sending him yelling and jumping back. "Don't bring a gun to a magical fight."

The human turned tail and ran.

Marcus faced the two wizards. "Your move."

The man in burlap raised his arms and clapped his palms together. The earth on the side of the road cracked, chunks lifting into the air.

Great. Brinnie grabbed Bert's arm and pulled him in the other direction. "You don't want to be in the middle of this."

Brinnie dragged the wide-eyed driver back up the highway the way they came. "It's okay, Marcus can handle just two of them easily."

"Is your . . . your family part of the mob?" Bert put his hands up. "I'm not judging. Or telling. I'll take it to my grave."

An excellent excuse. "Uh, kind of. I really didn't think this would happen, though. I wouldn't have intentionally put you in harm's way."

"Oh, no worries." He started to glance back as an explosion boomed behind them, but Brinnie tugged him forward. "Are you sure your cousin is all right?"

"He's fine." She glanced back. Good, the explosion seemed to be some sort of earth/fire mashup, *not* the vehicle. "If they blow up your car, we'll get you another one."

He gave a shaky laugh. "That's not really what I was most worried about at the moment, miss."

Now a safe few dozen yards away, Brinnie turned to watch in time to see Marcus shove Jepp to the ground and stand over both him and the terra wizard with—where did he get a sword? Brinnie couldn't help but chuckle. She imagined Marcus would be loath to give that up after this kerfuffle was over.

The sound of an engine and crunching wheels caused her to turn as another car slowed, cruising to a stop next to her and Bert. Maddy rolled down the window. "Are you guys okay?"

"We were tracked," Brinnie called back. "Marcus has these guys handled, but they mentioned backup."

Their driver, a young man with rectangular glasses and box braids, leaned forward. "You guys need me to call the cops or something?"

"Nope, we're good." Brinnie waved them on. "We'll see you at the airport."

As the other car pulled away, Brinnie strode back toward Marcus and the captured wizards, and Bert followed with shaky steps. He wiped his forehead. "I . . . I can't help feeling like the authorities should be involved somehow."

Brinnie grimaced. "That would make things very complicated." They arrived at Bert's vehicle, and she stopped. "If you want to leave, please do. We'll still pay in full—and I'll tell my friend to give you five stars." She hooked her thumb toward the truck. "We can always take that."

Bert blanched. "I don't think you should steal a vehicle."

Marcus nodded to Brinnie. "Do you want to watch them while I search their uh, car for something to tie them up?"

"Sure." He passed over the sword, and she pointed it at the scowling wizards. She glared back at them. "I don't need to use this sword to end you, so I would suggest you don't move."

She glanced up and briefly made eye contact with Marcus. He suppressed a smile.

What, you don't think I'm scary?

"I do. And I'm appreciating the bravado."

You think it's too much?

"Nah."

You're mocking me. Go look for rope.

He gave a salute. *"Yes, ma'am."*

Fifteen minutes later, Brinnie and Marcus rode in the back seat of Bert's vehicle once more, Bert wiping his forehead occasionally as they sped down the highway in silence, two men tied up and left next to their truck behind them.

As they pulled into the "Departures" area of the Indianapolis airport, Brinnie pressed her hand to her chest. "Thank you so, so much, Bert. I'm so sorry about what happened back there."

Bert gave a shaky laugh. "Well, it wouldn't be a normal drive with you if something crazy didn't happen, would it? Stay safe, young lady."

"Will do, and you too."

Luggage in hand, they watched the car pull away. Brinnie turned toward the airport and took a deep breath. Crowds that could be concealing enemies, security investigating their forged identification, even the magic pulsing in her fingertips, antsy from remaining dormant during the long car ride . . .

"Here we go. Adventure time."

CHAPTER SEVEN

That night, Maddy snored so loudly that Brinnie whacked her with a bag five times. An airport security officer gave them a strange look, but he didn't say anything.

Brinnie wriggled in her seat, trying to get comfortable with a blanket from their luggage wrapped around her. Maybe they should have tried to book a hotel rather than wait out the night outside security in the airport. Not that she would likely sleep anyway. The nightmares . . . images of the dead, the screams . . . Bleary-eyed, she jolted as she found herself nodding off.

While Maddy snored on one side of Brinnie and Quentin drooled, bent in half, to Maddy's right, Marcus sat in a deceptively relaxed position, eyes sweeping the wide atrium. At night, only a few stragglers passed through.

Brinnie stared at him until he made eye contact. *You can go to sleep if you want.*

"Someone needs to keep watch."

I can. Not like I'm sleeping anyway.

He broke contact, gaze sweeping the area once more. "You know," he said, just loud enough for her to hear, "we really need to figure out what's going on with this mind-speak situation. I haven't had a chance to talk to you alone since it started."

She giggled. "You can literally talk to me alone anytime you're near me."

He shot her a longsuffering look, but his lips twitched. "All right, but not without staring at you awkwardly. I assume you've noticed it only works if we're making eye contact."

"Yes. Any idea how we can do telepathy all of a sudden? My magical education is sadly lacking. Have you heard of an incident like this before?"

"Never. I didn't know—telepathy, did you call it?—was even possible."

Brinnie stretched out her aching legs. "Well, it doesn't seem to be possible with anyone else, just you, so it's not one of my crazy new powers."

He remained silent for a moment, gaze wandering as his fingers tapped on the armrest. "Well, this might be a crazy thought, but I felt like something weird happened when we went through the portal to get to Dirklon."

"Weird how?"

He shifted slightly in his seat, using the motion to surreptitiously check the movements of a security guard patrolling behind them. "Portals aren't supposed to feel like they're ripping you apart. But when we went through . . . I felt like I was pulled into pieces for a moment."

"I definitely felt that from magical overload. Like my molecules all flew apart." She pulled her legs back in.

Maddy stirred in her sleep, and both of them went quiet. As the snoring recommenced, Marcus continued.

"Right. So what if in the process, while you were still so volatile . . ."

"Our molecules got mixed." Her eyes widened. "Is that possible?"

"Maybe. It's just a thought."

She leaned back. "I'll accept that. It's not the craziest thing I've had to believe in the past two years."

She traced the lines of the high ceiling with her eyes, following the airy curves. There was something calm, peaceful, about the quiet of a metro hub at night.

"Marcus?"

"Yeah?"

"I was wondering." She looked back down. "Do you think we actually have a chance of winning this war?"

He sighed and ran a hand through his hair. "How do you define winning?"

"Finding Mordred's bane. Stopping the attack. Securing the estates. Bringing things back to how they were."

"Then, honestly, no." He rested his elbows on his knees. "From a practical standpoint, I don't know if that's possible." As she bit her lip, he put a hand on her arm. "But I do think we can keep Mordred from winning completely. Maybe if a few enchantment wizards like Quentin go into hiding, they can keep Mordred from destroying the human world . . . even if our world doesn't withstand."

Brinnie hugged her arms around her legs, staring at the floor. "We're not going to find anything on Excalibur at Castelon. It was pretty clear. Only the Masters of Wraithwood knew where it was hidden. That information died with Uncle Merlin." She hesitated. "So what are we supposed to do? There are people looking for us—both of us—everywhere. Mordred will find us eventually. Are we just supposed to wait to die?"

He sat up and faced her squarely. "No. It might be a lost cause, but we'll go down fighting. Remember what you told me when I said we were playing a low hand with the cards on fire?"

Her lips twitched. "Something about setting the whole card table on fire and Mordred burning with us."

"Something like that." He smiled. "Besides, except for Mordred, we have the most powerful wizard in the world on our side."

"Who?"

"You."

She bit the inside of her cheek. "A power I gained at the expense of the estates. Uncle Merlin warned me. So did Quentin, for that matter. They said it was easy to do terrible things if you thought you were doing them for the right reason." Her fists clenched, trembling. She stared down at her white knuckles. "Well, I killed people. Every one of those deaths could have been avoided and we would be in exactly the same situation we are now, and probably a better one—without Mordred's bane, either way." Her breath shuddered. "I don't think I can do it. I don't think I can kill anyone else." She tried to hold back the tears. "You're the only one who knows what I've done. I'm afraid if I tell my family . . ." She trailed off.

"Hey." He folded her into an awkward side hug. "We didn't know. You made the best decisions you could at the time. They seemed right. You're not the only one with a guilty conscience." He looked down, pulled his arm away. "While you were in the dungeon and I was away at the strongholds, I ordered the attacks, made the battle strategies. I . . . led some of those charges myself." Taut lines ran across his jaw.

She shook her head. "You don't have to tell me this."

"I was raised to be a war leader. Taught how to rationalize the deaths of thousands. But I couldn't keep playing every side of the game." He let out a shaky sigh. "I thought I could care about humans, and you, *and* Mordizan and freedom for wizards. In the end I had to choose."

"You chose humanity," Brinnie whispered.

"No. That would be more noble, but no." Hesitantly, he placed his hand over hers and met her gaze. His voice echoed in her mind. *"I chose you."*

Her heart gave a strange flutter.

Before she could respond, Maddy heaved a gigantic yawn.

Quentin bolted upright, eyes wide and hair askew. "DI, stand down!"

"Shut up." Maddy shushed him. "Were you having some sort of grandiose cop dream?"

Brinnie and Marcus exchanged a look, and she giggled, a nervous catch in her throat. He removed his hand, and Brinnie glanced at Maddy's lit up phone screen displaying the time. "It looks like we can probably try to go through security soon. Join me in the restrooms, Maddy?"

"Heck, yeah." She whipped out a toiletry case. "Time for our transformations. Let's get old."

"Flight two eighty-five for Philadelphia now boarding."

Brinnie sat with her overpriced water bottle clenched firmly in her hands, trying not to shift uncomfortably in Miss Burtle's clothes.

Marcus perched on the edge of an airport seat next to her, turning his fake ID over in his hands. "Humans are so strange. To think I'm considered a real person because I have this little card."

"Don't let them hear you say that."

He tucked the ID away. "They didn't question us. We should be fine."

She frowned at him. "This is the simple part. Just wait until we have to make an international flight. I'm not sure our passports are going to hold up."

"If not, we'll get there some other way."

"Or get thrown in jail." She resisted the urge to rub her eye, stinging from mascara.

He didn't speak for a moment, observing the people sitting around them waiting for their flight. "How do those, ah, paintings keep changing?" He nodded to the screens. "Are they like Maddy's phone?"

Oh, brother. "Those are TVs. A similar concept."

"Oh. I've heard of those." He almost looked embarrassed. "There are a lot of things I only know about in theory."

"Hey." Maddy waved at them and hurried over from across the gate. "Check out what I've got." She held up an enormous coffee. "Double shot espresso."

"Terrible idea, Maddy." Brinnie rubbed her temples, not at all ready to deal with an over-caffeinated Maddy. "Please tell me you didn't lose Quentin."

She glanced back toward the moving walkways and shops. "I don't know. Last I saw he was shopping. He still can't get over how humans use 'money cards' to pay for things."

Brinnie shook her head. "No. Not acceptable. Please go rescue the credit card."

Maddy shrugged. "Fine. Watch my coffee."

Brinnie took a deep breath and tried to calm herself. *It's going to be fine.* They made it through security with no major problems, though her heart pounded the entire time. Miss Burtle knew what she was doing. They arrived at their gate with an hour to spare. And thus, Marcus discreetly gawked at the busy airport while Quentin not-so-discreetly shopped and Maddy chugged a venti.

Brinnie bounced her knee while waiting for Maddy to retrieve Quentin, glancing at the clock. Only twenty minutes until boarding. *I don't like us being separated.* If they could get past security, so could Mordred's men. And with so many more people than last night, they might be able to blend in.

She nudged Marcus. "Do you think that man is looking at us suspiciously?" She nodded toward a tattooed man a few rows over.

Marcus watched him out of the corner of his eye. "I don't think so."

"He keeps looking at me."

Marcus shifted. "I don't think it's . . . malicious. You look very nice."

Brinnie's eyebrows shot up. "He's checking me out? Oh, yuck." By force of habit, she tugged at her right sleeve, making sure her scar was covered. "He's got to be at least twenty-five."

"You look older in your 'disguise.'" He shot her a smirk. "You could turn invisible. Then he couldn't see you."

"Not funny." She gripped her water bottle tighter. "Do you know how hard it's been not to break anything or accidentally combust with all this stress?"

"At least you weren't the one to break the scanner."

She snorted as she thought of the strange malfunctions that occurred when Marcus went through airport security. Secretly, she suspected she'd messed up the machine by going through before him, but blaming Marcus was far more entertaining. "Well done. Those things must be expensive."

Maddy wove her way through the crowd toward them, Quentin in tow. Brinnie raised a brow. The wizard sported an Indiana hat, carried an Indianapolis mug, and had four neck pillows precariously stacked around his head. "Quentin, why?" Brinnie sighed.

"I got one for each of us." Quentin struggled to shuck the stack of pillows off his neck. "They're so you can sleep comfortably sitting up." He handed one neck pillow to each of them. "The woman at the counter was so friendly, she convinced me to buy the hat and mug, too."

"Wonderful. Mind if I hold onto that for a bit?" Before Quentin could say anything, Marcus snagged the credit card and stuck it in his pocket.

Maddy slurped her coffee. "Mission accomplished. Can we board already?"

"Soon." Brinnie glanced around, still on the lookout for anyone suspicious. She made eye contact with Marcus. *What about that lady in blue?*

Marcus looked over and chuckled under his breath. *"I think she was just interested in Quentin's attire."*

"Now boarding flight three eighty-two for New York JFK. All first-class passengers are welcome to board."

Brinnie took a deep breath. Almost there. Another group called.

Then another. In just a few minutes, they would be in their seats and she could stop worrying until it was time for their next flight.

"All passengers in group three are welcome to board."

"That's us." Brinnie stood. The other three trailed her like a brood of ducklings as they joined the line to scan their boarding passes. Brinnie glanced back one last time and gasped. For just a moment, she thought she saw a familiar face. Dread overtook her so quickly her vision tunneled.

Then the figure was gone again, lost in the crowd.

Marcus slid past Maddy to stand beside her. "What's the matter?"

She shook her head and took a shaky breath. "Nothing. I thought I saw Ignatius for a minute." She held out her boarding pass to be scanned, then waited for Marcus to follow suit and join her on the jet bridge. "But they wouldn't send *him* after us."

"Who's Ignatius?" Maddy wedged her way in between them.

"One of Mordizan's . . . re-educators." Marcus's jaw tightened.

Quentin made a face. "I hope you're wrong about seeing him."

"Me too." The skin between her shoulder blades prickled. Brinnie glanced back, but she couldn't see anything past the people crowded behind them.

On the plane, they were forced to split up, since Maddy couldn't find seats together. Quentin and Maddy ended up toward the front of the plane, while Marcus and Brinnie sat near the back, Marcus three rows up from Brinnie. Brinnie squeezed into her assigned middle seat next to an old man who was already wearing headphones with his eyes closed. No one in the aisle seat so far. Good. She didn't know if she could handle being boxed in, not with her heart still racing from an encounter that didn't even happen. She hoped the seat would remain empty.

It didn't. A young man in a black hoodie pulled low plopped into the seat next to her.

She shot to her feet, but he grabbed her arm and pulled her back down. The hood shifted enough to reveal a flash of a smarmy smile. "Relax, Brinnie. The flight hasn't even left yet."

"Ignatius." Her heart pounded. Not her imagination. Real. Here. A thousand images, sensations, flashed through her memory. Phantom manacles chafed her wrists. "What are you doing here?"

He grinned. "I saw a lovely young lady walking through the airport and thought I'd go where she was going."

"How?" Her voice came out too loud. She glanced at the old man on her right. Eyes still closed. "You can't just hop on a plane."

"I had a ticket, of course." He crossed one leg over the other, balancing his ankle on his other knee, his foot in her seat space. "Poor man. I imagine they'll find him soon. I didn't kill him. Couldn't, you know." He winked. "But he won't be feeling well."

"You're disgusting." She craned her neck forward, hands trembling in her lap. How could she get Marcus's attention without causing a scene? "You can't do anything here, you know. Not in front of all these people."

"Oh, maybe not." He put his hands behind his head, elbow in her face. "But we'll deplane together. You can't stay with a crowd forever."

She resisted the urge to shove him into the aisle, even as the other half of her mind screamed at her to run at all costs, anger and fear at war. "You think you can take on three wizards at once and win?"

"No. But I can kill one." His cheeky expression sobered. He reached toward her. Before she could flinch away, he cupped her chin, staring into her eyes. "You're going to die, Brynna Ludovic. You're going to die for what you did to me."

The voice of a flight attendant came over the intercom, beginning the safety tutorial, as if several rows away, one passenger wasn't promising to kill another.

Her stomach turned, threatening to mutiny at his clammy fingers on her skin. "Excuse me? What I did to you? From what I recall, you tortured me."

"Hush now." He bopped her nose with his index finger and sat back. "You're missing the safety instructions. Wouldn't want anything to happen to you before your untimely death."

The rumbling of the plane increased, and the scenery outside the porthole window began to move. Brinnie tracked the progress of the flight attendant as she wrapped up the safety presentation. *Breathe in. Breathe out. Think.*

She could report Ignatius for harassment, but involving humans could be dangerous. *He can't kill you on the plane. Wait until you get off. Marcus will know what to do.*

She sat rigid through taxi and takeoff. A few minutes after the plane leveled out in the sky, Ignatius turned to her once again. "Did you know I got kicked out of Mordizan? You'll never guess why."

She focused on the glowing "fasten seatbelt" light, ignoring him.

He continued undeterred. "It was because I was supposed to break a certain prisoner. Well, the little brat didn't want to be broken. I did everything I could to her, but she embarrassed Mordred in front of the troops, and someone had to be blamed." His long fingers gripped her knee in a vise. "Mordred blamed me."

She kept her eyes ahead, counting the glowing orange seatbelt icons, tuning out the sensation of his fingertips. *Don't touch me, don't touch me, don't touch me.*

"But it wasn't my fault. No, it was that little brat's fault." He leaned forward enough that she could see his grin out of the corner of her eye. "So you can't escape me. I don't have anything better to do, anything else to live for except getting my revenge and dragging your corpse into the council chamber of Mordizan."

"Ignatius, you're crazy." She gritted her teeth. "You're blaming me for what Mordred did to you? I had no control over that."

"Sure, you didn't." He crossed his arms and leaned back. "I'm going to enjoy killing you."

Her back ached from her rigid posture the rest of the flight, one eye on Ignatius. Fatigue and adrenaline took turns pumping through her. Once they touched down, the pilot came on over the intercom. "We've arrived at New York John F. Kennedy Airport, local time five thirty-six. Please remain in your seats while flight attendants make a routine identification check. Nothing to worry about, just a safety precaution."

Ignatius glared at Brinnie. "You told them somehow."

"You watched me the whole time." Her voice wobbled, and she cleared her throat. "More likely that poor man came to and told the airport what happened to him. They're on the lookout for you."

His jaw twitched and a wild glint sparked in his eye. "Then I'll kill you now."

Before she could react, one of his hands shot around her neck while the other ripped off her seatbelt. She wriggled, attempting to drive an elbow into his side, but he dragged her out of her seat into the aisle, shoving downward. The back of her head hit the aisle floor with a crack as he pinned her, both hands squeezing. Shrieks rang out around them, the clacking sound of flight attendants' heels running toward them, and the thudding footsteps of—

Ignatius's hold on her neck ripped away as Marcus slammed into him. Brinnie gasped for breath. She looked up to see Marcus punch Ignatius in the nose, sending blood spraying over the surrounding seats. Ignatius reached for Brinnie again, but Marcus landed a kick in his gut, sending him tumbling over backward. Something small and round rolled out of Ignatius's pocket, and Brinnie snatched it.

Some passengers dove over seats out of the way, while others reached for the three of them, arms grabbing Brinnie to pull her away. Her magic sparked, setting off shouts of pain, but they let go. "Marcus! Let's get out of here. Off the plane."

He grabbed her arm and pulled her up. Pushing people out of their way, they ran for the exit. As they approached, Quentin and Maddy climbed out of their seats. Quentin started to reach for the overhead compartment, but Brinnie yanked him onward by the wrist. "Forget the luggage, come on."

The pilot blocked the open exit, but Marcus shoved him out of the way. "Sorry, sir."

Their four sets of feet pounded up the flight bridge until they burst into the busy airport, two uniformed officers heading straight for them.

Brinnie held up the opaque, off-white orb that had fallen out of Ignatius's pocket. "Where does it go?"

Marcus's eyes widened. "An anywhere portal. Ignatius has been working on improving them for years. They're unstable and easy to make incorrectly, but they're supposed to be able to take you anywhere, if you've been there and can envision it clearly enough."

"Perfect." She shoved the marble-like object into Quentin's hands. "You heard that. Get us to Castelon."

His eyes went wide. "I don't know if—"

"Hurry up and do it."

He muttered a string of protests, but he scrunched his eyes closed and then threw the portal against the ground, stomping it for good measure. "Castelon," he breathed.

The officers shouted. Brinnie grabbed Marcus and Maddy. "Hold on."

The mist exploded around them, whipping like a dust devil and obscuring everything but swirling white. Brinnie's veins burned, and something in her temple popped. Marcus threw an arm around her and another around Quentin, pulling them closer as the wind shrieked.

Then it dissipated, revealing an enormous silver gate soaring high in front of them.

"We actually survived the illegal magic." Quentin's voice cracked and squeaked. "Welcome to the gates of Castelon."

CHAPTER EIGHT

Maddy fell flat on her face.

"Oh." Brinnie winced. She clutched her own spinning head while kneeling next to Maddy. "What's the limit on portal journeys for humans before . . ." She trailed off.

Marcus and Quentin looked at each other. Quentin shrugged. "This sounds like a question for a Mordizan wizard. We don't do that to humans, since, you know, they're not supposed to go through portals at all."

Marcus sighed. "Usually a few times is fine. Then they start losing limbs, losing their mind, that sort of thing."

Maddy groaned and rolled over. "I like my limbs. And my mind. This is my last time portal-traveling."

Brinnie breathed a sigh of relief. "You got it."

Brinnie couldn't identify the metal of the gate, but it shone luminous in the moonlight. A smaller door had been set into the wall beside the gate, where Quentin lifted a knocker and let it fall. A sliding window opened, and an old man peered out. He seemed to ask a question in what sounded like the ancient language.

Quentin answered, presumably in the same tongue. The two carried on a conversation in which Quentin gestured to his three companions. The old man nodded and stepped away, closing the slider. After several clicks, the smaller door swung open.

Quentin turned to the rest of their party. "Come on through."

They entered through a stone passageway about five feet thick. On the other side, four guards toting spears stood at the ready. One of the guards said something in the ancient language. Quentin answered in kind, and the guard waved for him to follow.

Brinnie made eye contact with Marcus. *Translation? What's with the lack of English? We're in Britain.*

"Mordizan adopted English as the lingua franca as the human world did. Castelon . . . well, we crack jokes about how, uh, snobbish and hypocritical they are clinging to old ways and old language while protecting humans. Basically, we're going to be questioned."

She raised a brow. *We're prisoners?*

"Not yet."

They followed the guards through a wide courtyard paved with light gray flagstone, empty at this time of night, and passed through a pillared walkway into a small room off to the side.

One of the guards closed the heavy door after them. A single light orb hung over a metal desk where a man with a shaved head sat, papers and ledgers stacked in front of him. He addressed the group. "*Enwau*?"

Quentin stepped forward. "Quentin Morain. And pardon me, sir, but not all of us understand the ancient language."

"Is English acceptable, then?" the man asked with a slight British accent. Quentin nodded. "Good." He shuffled his papers. "Quentin Morain. In good standing." He gestured to a door on the opposite wall. "Please pass through to the magical binding room."

"Yes, sir." Quentin stepped past the man and through a door leading out the back.

Brinnie's eyes darted from Quentin to the man at the desk. "Is he . . . good?"

"Not to worry." The man adjusted his wire-rimmed glasses. *Do wizards even need glasses?* "Each of you must simply pass through a room that strips magic to assure you are who you say you are." He looked at Maddy. "Now you, miss, what is your name?"

"Maddison Matthew. I don't think I'll be in your records. I'm not a wizard."

He nodded. "All right. Human. Joel will escort you to the testing room. We have to be sure you're really a human and not a wizard."

One of the guards stepped forward and led Maddy off.

Brinnie glanced at Marcus. *I don't like this. We shouldn't be separated.*

His jaw tightened. *"I agree. You make the call and we'll fight our way out of here."*

"And you, miss?"

Brinnie turned back to the man. "Brynna . . . well, it's Drakon, but I've always thought it was Lane, and some people call me Ludovic. I'm not sure I'll be in your records either."

His eyebrows went up. "Brynna Drakon, you say?" He marked something down. "I think this is a case for the Council."

"Is there a problem?"

"Not necessarily." He tapped his pen. "Your loyalties must be determined after your stay at Mordizan and your lifetime non-report status."

Figures. "I was a spy there. And I didn't know I was a wizard, so I couldn't report."

"Those are good things to tell the Council." He pointed his pen at Marcus. "And you are?"

"Marcus, sir."

"Marcus what?"

He looked at Brinnie. *"Thoughts?"*

I don't think you can lie and get away with it. This is Castelon, after all.

He took a deep breath. "All right, before I say this, I want you to know that it's not what it seems. Brynna convinced me to switch sides."

"Your name, please."

"Marcus Vorath."

The three remaining guards lowered their spears.

The man stood. "Get the Council. Call an emergency council session."

One of the guards hurried for the exit.

"We'll have to restrain you." The man folded his hands. "A safety precaution."

Marcus shot Brinnie a questioning look, but she shook her head. *Best to play along and assure them we're friendly.* She clenched her teeth. From Quentin and Uncle Merlin's tales of Castelon, she had expected red tape and bureaucracy, but she hadn't quite expected this.

They submitted to handcuffs and blindfolds. Brinnie closed her eyes and took a few deep breaths, trying to remain calm. The cool metal around her wrists pricked memories and raised emotions she couldn't deal with right now. Her heart pounded as a guard's hand on her back near the base of her neck propelled her forward.

They walked a long way in the darkness created by the blindfold. She struggled to keep her breathing regular. *Darkness. Darkness. Darkness.* She stumbled on a few flights of stairs, fumbled turns, until finally the blindfolds were removed.

She blinked, allowing her eyes to adjust. They stood in the center of a circular room, benches ringing the chamber in concentric rising circles like a small, official-looking coliseum. At one end of the floor stood a wide door, opposite a row of fancy chairs rather than benches, presumably for the more important representatives. A broad-shouldered, frowning man presided from the central chair, regal with impeccably kept gray hair and a flowing black robe.

Brinnie made eye contact with Marcus, standing beside her.

"Should I be worried?"

I have no idea. I don't know how Castelon works, but I don't think beheading is quite their style.

"Good. I prefer the firing squad over the guillotine."

She rolled her eyes. *I was thinking more along the lines of imprisonment, but I appreciate the optimism.*

Soon five out of the seven main chairs had been occupied, while a few black-robed wizards trickled in to sit on the benches.

The gray-haired man in the central seat glanced at a note handed to him and frowned ominously down at Brinnie and Marcus. He cleared his throat, then his booming voice filled the chamber. "Brynna Ludovic-Drakon, here today to be tried for high treason against the Council, and Marcus Vorath, here tried as a dark wizard." He gave the note a disdainful look. "Hearing requested in English."

Murmuring trickled from above them. Brinnie craned her neck to see spectators sitting high in the gallery, despite the hour.

She squared her shoulders and faced the man. "Excuse me, sir, I believe there may have been a misunderstanding. If we work together, we can—"

"Silence."

Her mouth snapped shut at the authoritative tone. She forced herself not to flinch away. *He's not a teacher, and you're not some misbehaving student.*

His eyes narrowed, glaring down at her like a hawk honing in on a rabbit. "Is it true that you have not reported to Castelon for more than sixteen years?"

"Yes, but that was because—"

He bulldozed on. "And is it true that you have recently spent a matter of months at the enemy estate of Mordizan?"

"Yes, for the purposes of—"

"And"—his voice rose—"did you not open the gates of the seventh stronghold to the attack of the enemy, thus enabling a complete massacre of the forces stationed there?"

The accusation hit her like a punch in the gut. Of course they would know. But the words spoken aloud . . . "I did," she whispered.

Marcus's brow furrowed with concern. He tried to step closer, but one of the guards poked him with the butt of his spear.

The man's lips twitched, as if hiding a self-satisfied smirk. "And finally, did you not steal the magic of the garrison at the last stronghold, thus opening it to attack and allowing the protection spells to fall?"

She clenched her fists. *Brave, Brinnie. Be brave.* "That is true, but in the situation . . ."

He cut her off. "Are you not currently in *possession* of these great and illegally gained powers?"

How did he even know that? She glanced at Marcus, whose expression of confusion mirrored her own. "If I was, I could hardly help—"

"Then can you but plead guilty to the charge of high treason?" He scoffed a short laugh. "Just *one* of these offenses is enough to convict you, *Drakon.*"

She flinched at the way he sneered the name.

"No." Marcus sidestepped the guard, taking up a protective position to the front right of Brinnie. "Those things might be true, but you must understand the circumstances. Everything she did was to save the enchantment wizards. If you would give her a chance to speak, she would explain." He surveyed the Council, a brow raised. "Even in Mordizan, we allow the accused a chance to defend themselves."

"Ah, yes, you would know the ways of Mordizan well, wouldn't you, Marcus *Vorath*? What was the name they gave you? 'Scourge of the Strongholds'?" The lead councilman stood and glared down at him. "Are we truly to believe that after defeating stronghold after stronghold, you've changed your mind and come running to us as a friend? All because of this *girl*, guilty of high treason?"

The four other men seated in the chairs exchanged knowing looks.

"What happened to innocent until proven guilty?" Brinnie blurted. Her nails dug into her palms. "He's right. Everything I did was for the enchantment wizards, and Marcus has joined me in opposing Mordred. Together we can—"

"So you not only admit to all these things, but also presume to defend the heir of Mordizan?"

Brinnie resisted the urge to stomp her foot. "If you would please *listen.*" She threw up her hands toward the Council in what she intended as supplication.

Instead, a bolt of lightning shot from her fingers. The bolt slammed into a cornice behind the Council members, shattering stone.

Chaos erupted as two of the guards jumped on top of her, pinning her to the ground. Her bones slammed into stone. Shouts resounded in the echoing chamber, feet thundering as more guards pounded into the center.

"I'm so sorry! It was an accident, I promise, I didn't mean to." *Calm. Calm thoughts.* She noticed a buzzing sensation—prickles of static electricity running along her fingertips. *No, stop, go away.*

A knee dug into her back, while a hand grabbed her hair, holding her head still. The magic inside of her boiled. *No. No, no, no. Stop that. It's okay.* She closed her eyes, mentally counting to ten several times.

"You've seen what she's done." She opened her eyes at the sound of the lead councilman's voice ringing over the subsiding din. He offered a somber grimace to his fellow Council members. "She attacks us in our own Council Chamber. I vote her guilty. Does anyone second the motion?"

Every black-robed man Brinnie could see from her cramped, limited vision raised his hand.

He nodded. "It's settled. Guards, take them to the holding chambers. We will discuss the method of execution without the endangering presence of the condemned."

"That's absurd!"

Out of the corner of her eye, Brinnie could make out Marcus surrounded by several guards. He dodged one of their spears and shoulder-slammed the man out of the way, barreling toward Brinnie. More guards grabbed him, but he swung his bound hands into the nose of one and drove his elbow into the gut of another. As she lost sight of him in a mass of soldiers, she saw a flash of fire, followed by yells of pain.

Brinnie didn't dare fight with magic. She doubted the lethal force roiling inside of her could be controlled once unleashed. Instead, she attempted to wriggle her head high enough to properly shout. "We're both here to help destroy Mordred!" She winced as a guard planted the butt of his spear in Marcus's skull, and he crumpled. "You need Wraithwood to get Excali—"

Someone shoved a rough sack over her head, stifling her words. Something about the fabric smelled . . . strange. Sickly sweet. Her head spun.

Oh great. I've been drugged. Classy.

All sensations faded.

Brinnie awoke with her aching cheek pressed against damp stone. She groaned, rolling onto her back.

Her wrists chafed in cuffs. She stared up at the stone ceiling, then at the walls pressing in on her in the tight square cell, broken only by what appeared to be an iron door with a small barred window.

Stone dug into her shoulder blades, the cold seeping through the material of Miss Burtle's blouse. They hadn't needed to go through customs after all.

She closed her eyes again. Everything hurt. Her head spun with exhaustion and the aftereffects of whatever they had used to knock her out. Probably something magically enhanced. But instead of panic, only resignation weighed in her chest, her heart leaden.

What's the point?

For months, she fought to survive Mordizan's dungeons. She withstood every torturous day, every freezing night, everything Ignatius inflicted. Because she had to bring news of Mordred's bane.

Turned out it didn't matter. Excalibur was lost to time. She wasn't the Master of Wraithwood. She was just the girl who murdered wizards and stripped their powers.

At least Anna and David are free. Not that she had even done that.

She let her muscles go limp. Why fight this prison? Why fight this execution? She was useless as a wizard, useless in a fight, useless as a Master or a spy. After everything she had screwed up, the world might be a better place without her in it.

I give up. I'm ready to die.

"Brinnie?" Marcus's voice echoed from beyond the door.

She couldn't force her eyes to open. *It's done, Marcus. It's done.*

"Brinnie? Are you in here somewhere?" A scraping sound. "I'm looking for something to use to escape. This hall looks clear—no guards." A huffed laugh. "Either I'm talking to myself or hopefully you'll hear me."

A tear slipped from beneath her eyelid, tracking a warm trail down her cheek. Where did the endless optimism come from? The relentless drive to survive?

"Looks like they threw us in a warded dungeon. Magic won't work here. Incidentally, I can't see a thing, so if you're here, please try to make some noise."

She stared up at the ceiling and bit her lip. It wasn't fair for her to give up without telling him. She couldn't let him wonder. She opened her mouth, then paused.

Wait. The ceiling. The walls. She pushed herself up on one elbow. She could see—everything. No darkness, nothing obscured.

"I—I'm here." Her voice croaked, and she cleared her throat before trying again. "I'm here and I still have magic."

"Thank goodness." The words floated from beyond the barred window. "I'm not just a crazy person talking to myself in the dark."

She reluctantly forced her way to her feet and stumbled to the door, peering out. Across a narrow hall and a bit to the right, Marcus squinted through the tiny window of an identical door. "I see you. I'm across the hall."

"Good." His head turned toward her voice. "You still have magic?"

"I guess. Not sure how." *Nor is it particularly useful at the moment.*

"Maybe the force of so much magic is too much for the wards to stop." Marcus went still, and his voice lowered. "Footsteps."

Brinnie waited. She heard them too as they drew closer. Light footsteps, like regular shoes instead of a soldier's boots. A flickering lantern preceded a familiar blonde woman Brinnie hadn't encountered since that first summer at Wraithwood.

She blinked, not quite sure if she was seeing correctly. "Anika?"

"Brinnie." The healer drew near to the cell, voice low. "I managed to get in during a guard change." Anika's eyes searched her face. "How are you?"

Embarrassment swept through her. *Fine, just thinking about wanting to die instead of focusing on breaking my friend out of prison.* "I'm okay, but we need to get out of here. Or at least Marcus does. He switched sides. He can be super helpful against Mordizan. Even if they can't trust me, they should allow him to—"

Anika held up a hand. "I believe you. And I agree. But there's something you really need to know." She glanced up and down the hall, then made eye contact with Marcus, then Brinnie. Her voice lowered even more. "Merlin isn't dead."

CHAPTER NINE

The words didn't register for a moment. Brinnie stared at Anika. "He . . . he was buried at Wraithwood."

Anika shifted her feet, looking uncomfortable for the first time Brinnie had ever seen. "Yes, he was. But . . . he, uh, wasn't dead."

Brinnie's eyebrows shot up. Her voice squeaked. "Uncle Merlin was *buried alive?*"

"No. Well, not quite." Anika took a deep breath, glancing between Brinnie and Marcus. "After he was wounded several months ago, he came to me first. Just showed up in the middle of my lecture while I was instructing students, lying on the floor of my offices covered in blood with a large abdominal wound."

Brinnie tried to contain a wince.

Apparently not well enough. "Right." Anika gave her a sympathetic look. "I ran to help him immediately, but he was run through by an enchanted blade. My magic can't do anything against that. I could only try to staunch the bleeding manually. We had just long enough for me to tell him I couldn't save him, and he told me he wanted to die at Wraithwood, not in—well, he said some derogatory things about Castelon I can't help but agree with."

Brinnie bounced on her toes, resisting the urge to scream, *Get to the point!* "But he didn't die."

"Right. Well. Kind of." She shook her head. "I'm sorry. I'm getting off track. I think he meant only to transport himself to Wraithwood, but I was touching him, and we both ended up there." She took a deep breath. "I've known Merlin most of my life. We've been through a lot together. As I was watching the life seep out of him . . . I couldn't do it. I couldn't let him die." Her last words blurted out almost as one. "I cast the sleeper's curse."

Marcus sucked in a breath.

Anika looked at Brinnie as if that explained everything. Brinnie cleared her throat. "I'm sorry, but I don't know what that is."

She took a shaky breath. "It's against the healer's code. I could be imprisoned for it. But I couldn't help myself. I couldn't just let him die."

Brinnie glanced at Marcus for more explanation. Anika didn't seem to be in an emotional state to properly explain.

"Healers are capable of performing one last act for the dying when they can't be saved." Marcus nodded to Anika. "It's the sleeper's curse. That's what Mordred cast on his wife Nimue before the Great Battle. It sends the dying into a millennium long sleep. When they wake up, they're healed."

"But we're not supposed to do it." Anika fiddled with the lantern. "It's a fate worse than death, waking up a thousand years later to find the world you know completely gone. It's especially forbidden to perform on Masters, considering it renders the estate virtually Masterless, since the original Master isn't actually dead."

Everything snapped into place. She wasn't the Master . . . because Uncle Merlin *was still alive.*

Anger stirred in her gut. "So when he wakes up, we'll all be gone, and Wraithwood will wait a thousand years for a Master, if anything survives this war."

"No!" The word burst out loud, and Anika lowered her voice. "That's what I had to tell you. It's like what Marcus said about Mordred and Nimue. It was possible to break the curse in pre-Myrddin times. That was Mordred's plan for his wife, until he too was cursed. But somehow, Mordred's eternal sleeper's curse was broken. You, Brinnie, are practically a pre-Myrddin wizard now." Anika gripped the lantern tighter. "I believe you can resurrect Merlin."

Brinnie's mouth opened and closed. "I . . . yes. Of course." Her heart clenched. *If I can get any of this magic to work for me instead of exploding everywhere.* "We'll have to do research. Figure out how it's done."

"But first we need to get out of here," Marcus put in.

"Right." Anika pulled out a strange-looking tool. "Don't ask where I got this. It's for picking locks, but I don't know how. Do either of you?"

Marcus raised a hand. "I do. If you can get mine undone, I can get

Brinnie out too." He nodded to the doors. "Looks like Brinnie has an extra lock."

While Marcus coached Anika through using the tool to open the door to his cell, Brinnie examined the locks on her own. She had power down here, though diluted. The pain didn't burn quite so strongly in her veins. Maybe this would be a safe place to test the waters.

She wiggled her fingers through the bars of the window and reached for the lock. Not enough space. Instead, she gripped the bars and closed her eyes. *Channel Marcus. Use his power.*

Heat sizzled. The bars began to bend in her grasp. She pulled the hot, softened metal apart, opening her eyes as she created a space wide enough for her full arm.

She released the bars and shook out her hands, the skin red and slightly blistered—but not melted, as they should be after heating metal to what had to be over a thousand degrees. Her heat resistance wasn't as good as Marcus's, but she could work around that.

"Brinnie, what are you doing over there?" Marcus peered through his window.

Anika looked up as well, then swore under her breath. "Lost the pin." She readjusted the lockpick.

"Using my power, without frying myself." Brinnie reached for the first padlock holding the heavy metal bolt shut.

Marcus's eyebrows shot up. "Impressive. Can you manipulate metal?"

"That would be easier than melting through iron, wouldn't it?" She bit her lip, wedging her shoulder at an awkward angle and grasping the padlock. "I'm not sure if I gained any metallurgical powers. We'll stick with old faithful—destroying things."

She melted through the loop until the padlock fell off, then did the same for the second lock. She pushed open the door and joined Anika. "May I?"

Anika stepped back, and Brinnie pinched the loop of the padlock until the metal melted away.

Marcus exited the cell and immediately looked at Brinnie's hands. "You burned yourself."

"Only a little." She hid the blistered flesh behind her back, turning to Anika. "Where to?"

"We'll need a portal. They're kept in the portal archive, but it's well guarded."

Brinnie gingerly flexed her fingers. *Mistakes may have been made.* She couldn't bring herself to care. Uncle Merlin was alive. She hadn't killed him. He knew the location of Excalibur. If she could find a way to wake him . . . "Cool. We just need to get Maddy and Quentin."

Anika shook her head. "You mean Morain and the human? They made it past inspection. Morain has quite a reputation around here after the Battle of the Master Key. They're safer if you leave them behind."

Marcus and Brinnie looked at each other. *Thoughts?*

"I hate to say it, but I doubt Maddy will make it through another portal. I think Anika is right. Quentin is in good standing, and they can look out for each other."

Hopefully they'll understand and not be too mad at us. She nodded to Anika. "All right. Let's get to the portals. I'm sure we can come up with something on the way."

That "something" turned out to be blunt force trauma.

As they slunk down the halls of the near-empty nighttime castle, Brinnie darted ahead invisibly, magic sparking in her veins. The fiery sensation hadn't grown too terrible yet. The shadows sang to her, welcoming her back as she invisibly bonked the guards she encountered over the head with Anika's lantern before returning to Anika for instructions on which way to go next. Anika and Marcus followed, Anika with her cowl raised against recognition.

The twists and turns of Castelon reminded Brinnie of a lighter-stone version of Mordizan. Through careful maneuvering, she only ended up having to incapacitate four guards by the time they made it through the castle to an inner courtyard that contained a door monitored by two sentries sitting at a nearby booth.

The three of them hid around the corner. *Great. How am I supposed to bonk one without the other raising the alarm?*

Apparently, she'd been looking at Marcus when she thought it. *"Really? 'Bonk'?"*

Shut up. She held in a snort.

The voices of the guards distracted her, and she tuned in.

"Heard Riverdell is being hit hard," one of the sentries was saying. "Artema doesn't have any more fighters to send."

"Heard that too." The other sniffed, coughed. "They almost went down with the Master Key situation last year. And that was with Ludovic bringing in fighters. Probably don't stand a chance."

Brinnie and Marcus locked eyes. He gave his head a sharp shake. *"We already have a task."*

If I try to resurrect Uncle Merlin power blazing, I'm likely to hurt someone. I need practice with using my magic.

"You have an interesting definition of practice." He sighed and gave a slight, wry smile. *"But I'm with you, as usual."*

Brinnie leaned close and whispered, "Anika, we'll need your help."

After hashing out the plan, Marcus lit the wick in the lantern and handed it over to Anika. The healer straightened her hood, then strode forward and struck up a conversation with the guards, something about recent research pointing to the health benefits of late-night walks.

While they chatted, Brinnie invisibly slipped behind the two guards and tried the door. Unlocked. *Great security, guys.* She slipped inside.

Rows of shelves like a library greeted her. Rather than books, carefully labeled boxes, each the size of a ring box, lined the shelves.

She wandered closer. Each shelf had a primary label at the top, presumably a designated region of the world. To her chagrin, the writing appeared to be in the ancient language. Which, though it made sense for a global hub, proved inconvenient for a mostly illiterate wizard like herself.

She could recognize enough of the letters that she found the shelf for North America. She squinted at the labels. *Come on, Brinnie. You had like, a couple weeks of studies on this in Mordizan.*

A few minutes later, she exited the archive, three portals in her pockets. She slid beside Marcus and returned to visibility. "Got them. Let's get out of here."

Marcus poked his hand around the corner and motioned to Anika. The healer wrapped up her conversation and wandered back over.

The three of them slipped into an alcove. Out of sight of the guards, Anika returned to a no-nonsense posture. "Let's get going."

Brinnie held up the three orbs. "I found St. Lou—er, Wraithwood—Castelon, and Riverdell."

Anika frowned. "Why Riverdell?"

"Because we're making a detour first." Her eyes darted to Marcus, who nodded. "Got to help out Riverdell before we get Uncle Merlin."

Anika looked between Brinnie and Marcus. "What? When was this decided?"

"I was skeptical, but I think Brinnie's right." Marcus gave her a slight smile. "Merlin isn't going anywhere, and Riverdell is suffering now. If we can help, then we should."

Brinnie's heart warmed. She was starting to like this telepathy thing.

"I am, too."

Brinnie looked at him sharply. *We weren't making eye contact.*

His eyes widened. *"Is it getting stronger?"*

"All right." Anika adjusted her cowl. "Let's go fight."

Brinnie cocked her head. "You're coming too?"

Anika grimaced. "I can't stand being here at Castelon doing nothing." She sighed. "When your uncle was around, his networks kept me busy. I still had my front of teaching here, but I also traveled, serving as a healer to his operatives all over the world. Now, I'm stuck in an estate full of people who pretend like this war isn't happening."

"Then we're glad to have you."

Brinnie smashed the Riverdell portal and the three of them stepped in. As the mist swirled and began to recede, she firmed her jaw. *This isn't over, Uncle Merlin. I* will *save you.*

Then an arrow whizzed past her ear.

CHAPTER TEN

"Duck!" Brinnie hit the ground, knees crashing into stone. *A bridge.* The sound of water rushed below, presumably the river for which Riverdell was named.

She whipped her head in the direction the arrow had come from. On one bank of the river, sentries posted in front of a mass of tents gestured toward them. One of the sentries drew his arm back, nocking another arrow.

"This way." Anika waved Brinnie and Marcus toward the opposite bank.

Brinnie scrambled to her feet. Marcus grabbed her arm, pulling her up faster. As they ran, she heard a whiz. A projectile soared toward them from the bank opposite the original archer. A meaty thunk accompanied a grunt and stumble from Marcus, who quickly recovered and kept running. She turned to see where he'd been hit, but he urged her forward, the shaft of an arrow protruding from his shoulder. "I'm fine. Keep going."

"Stop! We're friends." Anika waved her arms over her head, still running toward the tree-lined bank.

An archer stepped out from behind the trees, bow ready. "Anika. Is that you?"

"Yes." She panted as Marcus and Brinnie caught up to her.

The archer lowered his bow. "Come this way, quickly."

Stone gave way to dirt under Miss Burtle's clompy loafers as Brinnie darted from the bridge with Marcus and Anika into the cover of the trees.

Once inside the tree line, Anika stopped, hands on her knees. Brinnie pressed her back against a trunk, panting for breath and cursing her pathetic body.

The sandy-haired archer scratched the back of his neck sheepishly. "I'm sorry. I couldn't tell who you were in the dark." His accent sounded familiar, similar to the one that occasionally tinged Anika's words, but more pronounced. "Did I shoot anyone?"

"Not too badly," Marcus said through clenched teeth.

"Ooo." The archer winced. "Sorry about that."

Another man dropped from a nearby tree, a bow slung over his shoulder. "Did you shoot allies, you dunce?" The larger man gestured to Marcus. "Take them to the house and someone can fix that for you."

"No need. I can do it here." Anika straightened and looked at Marcus's shoulder. "Good. All the way through. Makes it easy." She broke off the arrow shaft and drew out the ends from either side.

Marcus went pale but didn't flinch.

"Dawson, what did I tell you about shooting randomly?" Anika shook her head at the archer. "Brinnie, Marcus, meet my little brother, Dawson."

"Pleasure to meet you." He grinned. "Especially a pleasure since I'm assuming you're here to fight. Except you, of course, Ani." He winked at Brinnie. "Useless in a fight, you know."

"Keep insulting me and I won't heal you next time you get yourself in trouble." Anika made a face at her brother. She passed her hand over Marcus's wound. "There. Should be good enough until we get somewhere safer."

He rolled his shoulder and grimaced. "Thanks."

The man who had called Dawson a dunce grabbed a branch and swung up into the trees with the ease of a monkey. "I can hold down the fort here until you return. Go take care of your sister and friends."

"You got it." Dawson gave a three-finger salute, then turned and began to lead the way through the trees. "I'll show you guys to headquarters. We haven't gotten any new fighters, so Master Irvin will be glad to see you. We're just about defeated."

Brinnie raised an eyebrow. *Awfully cheery for someone in a near-defeated army.*

"What are you doing way out here?" Anika asked him.

"Sentry duty during the nightly truce."

Brinnie glanced at Marcus. *Nightly truce? That's chivalrous of Mordred.*

"Not chivalrous as much as tactical. Fighting in the dark often leads to friendly

fire. It happens with magic flying everywhere. Mordred's forces don't have much to lose by taking a break, considering they're the besieging army."

Gotcha.

A shiver ran down her spine at his casual tone. He *led* armies once. Yet now, here he was, following her along with whatever half-baked plan she thought up. *Too bad Marcus and I hadn't switched places. I would have botched everything in his position, and if he was in mine, he probably would have defeated Mordred already.*

Luckily, he didn't seem to hear that thought.

Dawson led them to a mansion built of river stones and rich wood, like a forest resort or ski lodge Brinnie had seen in pictures. They entered through a massive arched doorway into a high-ceilinged foyer cluttered with soldiers. Some wizards lay snoring in the midst of piles of weapons and battle gear, while others tended to their wounds and sharpened their weapons. Brinnie's chest tightened. The disorganization reminded her of the summer at Wraithwood when they had hosted fighters from Riverdell, ill-equipped to handle an army of any size. Such a contrast to the regimented armies of Mordizan or the fortress of Dirklon. Like Wraithwood, this estate hadn't been built for war.

Dawson led them around the chaos to a back room. He knocked on the open door, looking in on a group of about ten people surrounding battle plans drawn out on the table. "Master Irvin. New recruits!"

A man with a close-shaven gray beard raised his head from leaning over a map. He turned and said something to the woman beside him, then circled the table to greet them. Brinnie attempted to straighten her shoulders, aware how little she looked like a capable recruit.

As Master Irvin grew closer, she could make out the laugh lines accenting his rich brown eyes, but he wasn't laughing now—instead, dark circles hung beneath them. "Young Dawson." His voice was deep, but gentle. Brinnie could see why he and Uncle Merlin were friends. "Who have you brought us?"

"You've met Anika." He gestured to his sister.

"Anika." The Master smiled. "A pleasure to see you again. Celon is our only healer. He'll be happy for your help."

Dawson bounced on his toes and pointed. "And these are Marcus and Brinnie. They're fighters."

"Wonderful." He shook their hands, and Brinnie focused on not electrocuting him. He hesitated. "Do you come from Artema?"

Brinnie held back a snicker at his hesitation. If her own physique hadn't been bad enough, they certainly didn't look like fighters with her old lady clothes and Marcus's jeans.

"No." Marcus released his hand. "Unfortunately, we heard they have no more fighters to send. We came on our own to help."

He sighed. "I suspected as much." But instead of mocking, his eyes sparked with gratitude. "I greatly appreciate your assistance. I'll tell you truthfully, it isn't looking good. But the longer we hold them, the longer they aren't attacking Castelon."

Brinnie bit her lip. *Maybe that wouldn't be so bad. Castelon could use a wakeup call.* "What can we do, sir?"

"Rest, for now. Tomorrow morning, they attack again. Dawson can show you to the armory. There are many weapons that have lost their owners, if you need them, and some extra clothes and gear." He rubbed his face. "We've lost many good wizards. We hardly have enough to form a line around the premises. Tomorrow morning, your only orders are to fill in a gap somewhere and hold the line."

Brinnie could tell from Marcus's stiff spine that the lack of actual strategy was almost physically painful, but he nodded. "Yes, my lord."

As they left Master Irvin, Dawson turned to Anika. "I have to get back to my post. You know where the armory is, right?"

"I grew up here too, idiot." She bumped him with her shoulder, smiling.

He shot his strange little salute to Brinnie and Marcus. "I'll see you two tomorrow." Then he grinned at Anika. "And hopefully I won't be seeing you, sis."

"You better not. Stay safe."

A bittersweet smile played on Brinnie's lips. She and Anna had never been the teasing type to each other, but she missed her sister. *Please let Mom and Ms. Tynsdale find them.*

As Dawson loped away, Anika turned to Brinnie and Marcus. "I'll show you the arsenal, then we can find someplace to sleep."

In the armory, Brinnie picked out a couple of eight-inch daggers and some leather bracers, while Marcus examined the options and waffled between two blades before picking a hand-and-a-halfer over the greatsword and opting for a leather breastplate, helmet, and metal bracers.

He held a shortsword out to her. "This one is well-balanced, if you'd like."

She shook her head. "You know me. I'm better off sticking to magic." Especially with her muscle mass gone.

"Take this, at least." He pushed a helmet into her arms. When she wrinkled her nose, he rolled his eyes. "This one doesn't even have a face guard. You'll see fine. Battle is too chaotic not to wear proper gear."

She grumbled but accepted. She knew in *theory* head protection was important, but she preferred fighting unhindered, and her instructors at Mordizan often hadn't cared one way or another. A difference between the contained combat she'd grown used to and the large-scale conflict she had only experienced secondhand at the strongholds. *This is a whole new world of fighting.* She would do well to remember that.

As a bonus, Brinnie found some clothes and combat boots in her size. She didn't think they came from fallen soldiers—she hoped—considering they were contained in what looked like a collection of various human and wizard wardrobe pieces she assumed were for espionage.

After a bit of searching, they found an unoccupied corner in an upstairs room with some spare blankets. Anika fell asleep almost instantly, her deep breathing mixing with that of a few other wizards in the room, but Brinnie sat against the wall and initiated conversation with Marcus with her eyes while he arranged their new gear.

My magic is still a little iffy. What do I do tomorrow? Just scare them, or actually try to wound them? I don't want to go too far and seriously hurt anyone.

He blinked, hesitated for a minute. *"Brinnie. You can't do either of those things. You have to fight to kill."*

She shook her head so vigorously a pain twinged through her skull. *I can't. It's bad enough causing death. I can't be the one to do it . . . to actually . . .* She curled her knees in, hugging her arms.

He sighed. He picked up a blanket and sat beside her, draping it over both of them. His warmth instantly heated the chill she hadn't even noticed had penetrated to her bones. *"I understand. But in war . . . you don't have a choice. They're not going to stop. If you only wound them, they'll go back to their healer and return to fight us tomorrow."*

Then we'll fight them again tomorrow. She hugged herself tighter. *I can't just kill people.*

"They're fighting to the death. They won't give us that courtesy."

What he said made sense. If she didn't destroy her enemy, they would keep fighting and killing the enchantment wizards. They would take over the world, massacring billions of humans.

But she couldn't accept it. She shook her head. *There has to be another way.*

"This is how war works." She flinched, and he winced. *"Sorry."* He ran a hand through his hair. *"I'm not the right person for this. I know war and killing. Peacemaking . . . isn't my forte."*

But you do know strategy. She grabbed his hand and squeezed. His eyes widened for a moment, and she realized she wasn't usually the one to initiate any sort of contact. She felt her face heat but ignored it. *You may not know peacemaking, but you do know battle strategy better than anyone I know. Together, we can think of something.*

His jaw set, and he nodded. *"I'm willing to give it a try."*

For the next few hours, they bounced ideas back and forth. Brinnie lay on her side, on her stomach, kicked her feet in the air. Finally, while upside down with her feet against the wall where her head should be, the idea hit her.

Gideon.

Marcus cocked his head, eyes bleary. *"What?"*

She awkwardly wriggled into a sitting position. *I've got it.* A smile grew. *I'll need your help with the details, but I just thought of a plan of biblical proportions.*

Once she finished explaining, he nodded. *"I think we can work with that."*

After they spent several minutes throwing refinements to the plan back and forth, Marcus stood. *"I think it's worth a shot. Let's go talk to Master Irvin."*

Exhaustion dragged Brinnie's limbs. With the changing time zones, night seemed to stretch on and on. Here, only a couple hours remained until dawn.

She tramped up a hill, down a hill, passed within ten feet of an enemy sentry. *Oops. Didn't see you there, buddy.* Not that it mattered. She continued on her invisible way, making for the regimented lines of tents.

Between the rows, she took a deep breath. She had attempted to practice the next part back at Riverdell with Marcus's feedback on her level of success. She had failed terribly—until she used a random soldier for reference.

She wandered the still camp until she found six men gathered around a campfire, polishing armor, occasionally talking. She hid behind a tent and squeezed her eyes shut. *Here's hoping this works.*

She imagined the soldier she had studied, an average-looking man of average size with brown eyes, brown hair, and a medium voice. She let the magic flow and felt herself morphing, becoming taller. *But not stronger.* Her limbs felt just as weak as before—worse, perhaps, with the aggressive buzz of magic humming through her veins, begging to be freed, complaining that such a small transformation only teased the depth of power waiting to be unleashed. She looked down at her hands, thick man hands now, and thanked the heavens one of the powers she'd stolen had been shapeshifting.

Then she stepped out into the light of the campfire.

She shuffled toward the fire, the appearance of a tired soldier coming easily with her own exhaustion. "Room for one more?" Her voice felt strange coming out of her mouth.

One of the men shrugged and nodded to an empty spot.

She sat and heaved a manly sigh—she hoped. "Did you hear?"

"Hear what?" One of them spat on his armor, then continued polishing.

"The troops of Artema are on their way here."

"Says who?" Another man scratched his back with a stick, then threw the twig in the fire. "Last I heard, they're busy with our forces at Habrin."

"Not anymore." She pulled one of her knives from her belt and polished it on the edge of her tunic. Her skills at transforming clothing along with her body had been lacking, so she'd just worn clothes way too big for her normal size that had, in fact, been taken off a fallen enemy soldier.

She suppressed a shudder. *Don't think about that.* "The enemy deserted the estate. Apparently, they're taking the loss because they think they can defeat us here."

A few of the men exchanged glances. Brinnie could see fear begin to glint in their eyes.

"We're a small force." The man polishing armor cleared his throat. "They're sending reinforcements, I assume?"

She tucked the knife away and rested her arms on her knees. "Not from what I hear. We're all tied up everywhere else. Our forces are spread too thin."

"I said that was a bad move." A bearded man snapped a stick in his meaty fist. "I said it was too aggressive."

"Quiet," another growled. "Don't let someone catch you questioning Lord Mordred."

The man feeding the fire gave a suspicious scowl. "Why haven't we heard about this earlier?"

She shrugged. "A buddy heard the lieutenant and the commander talking. The commander told him not to say anything—thinks it might weaken morale."

She could only cross her fingers they wouldn't ask for any more information. She knew enough of rank from her time at Mordizan to get by, but names . . .

The men looked at each other. "It must be bad if they don't want us to know," the bearded man said.

Brinnie spread her large palms over the fire, then rubbed them together before standing with a grunt. "I should get going. I appreciate the warmth."

She continued to the next campfire she found, and then the next, telling her tale. Though most of the camp lay asleep, those awake whispered, some dispersing to other fires, to tents, presumably to discuss the gossip. Everywhere she went, she left unease in her wake. After visiting a couple more groups and chatting with a few sentries, she looked back on her handiwork to see wizards wandering amongst the tents, whispering to each other about the news. Her work here was done.

She turned invisible and slunk back out past the sentries.

She let the shapeshifting magic fall away, hiking up the baggy pants and tightening her belt as she climbed a hill to the north, across from a fording point in the river.

Behind the rise, a couple dozen wizards waited in the darkness. She dropped her shadows and approached Master Irvin, near the front of the group. "It's done. They're scared." She glanced over her shoulder, as if she could see the chaos of the camp from here.

"Excellent." He gave a sharp nod to the wizard beside him.

The woman pointed her finger up in the air and a spark blazed out, soaring into the night sky. At the same time, the wizards ignited torches, multiple per person. Some carried pitchfork-like creations, branching to hold two, three, four torches.

From the east and south, voices rang out. "For Artema!"

From the west came the cry, "For Riverdell!"

Around her, wizards banged swords and spears against shields and yelled with magically amplified voices, "For Artema!"

The small force spread out and surged over the hill, multitudinous torches blazing, heading for the camp, some with weapons at ready while others raised their hands, summoning magic.

Brinnie crested the hill, making use of her night vision by scanning the area. More torches emerged from the surrounding hills, giving the appearance of three times as many wizards as there actually were.

Master Irvin stood with her. "All where they should be," she reported.

Within the camp, soldiers yelled, rolling from their tents and scrambling for weapons.

Brinnie closed her eyes, focusing on the camp below. Tentatively, she reached out for the shadows around her.

They flew to her, eager, dancing over her fingers, almost as if she had been neglecting them, only choosing one or two to cover her invisible escapades. A smile twitched across her lips. Here, in the shadows, her magic felt right.

Go. She sent them flowing, forward toward the camp. Not since her training with Keilrie had she attempted to manipulate shadows from such a distance. She opened her eyes, watching the shadows take form, mirroring the surrounding warriors, plunging past them into the enemy encampment.

Magic blazed as wizards shrieked and yelled, swiping at the shadowy soldiers. She could make out a cry of, "They're among us!"

But weapons passed through the nebulous warriors springing out of the shadows of tents or materializing from the darkness. In a panic, the wizards lashed out at one another, magic erupting, swords clashing. Commanding officers ran among them, shouting for order.

"Incredible," Master Irvin breathed. Then he spoke with a magically amplified voice, "Stand down—you are surrounded. Surrender peacefully and live!"

As the enemy wizards stumbled from the camp, fleeing unkillable soldiers, enchantment wizards intercepted them. Through some magic of Master Irvin, apparently a sonic wizard by birth, the noise of the army amplified, as if each torch truly was carried by a warrior.

Many of the enemy wizards threw down their weapons, putting their hands in the air, while others fought one another or slashed at shadows. The enchantment wizards pressed inward, taking down any soldiers standing in the way.

Beside her, Master Irvin's mouth moved as he spoke, casting his voice to one segment of the troops or another, giving instructions. Learning of his power had made her and Marcus's plan even better.

As the sun began to rise, Brinnie released her hold on the shadows as morning dawned on a body-strewn camp and scores of disarmed and surrounded dark wizards being herded to the dungeons of Riverdell.

We did it.

With that realization, feeling returned to her body. Her limbs trembled. Spots appeared before her eyes, and she dropped to her knees in the grass, letting the cool blades keep her awake.

"It worked." Master Irvin bent down and placed a hand on her shoulder, a mist in his eyes. "Thank you."

She nodded, unable to form words.

The Master descended the hill to oversee the process more directly, and Brinnie rolled onto her back, not caring about the wet grass soaking through her clothes.

The magic within her buzzed. *More. More. Not just the shadows. The fire and earth and air and water and . . .*

She cut off that train of thought, her shivering limbs and chattering teeth attesting to precisely why she should *not* channel any more magic through her right now.

After a few moments, she closed her eyes, took a deep breath, and opened them again before forcing herself to her feet, descending the hill into the camp.

An efficient force worked around her, retrieving weapons and supplies from enemy stores, funneling the last of the prisoners toward the bridge.

She knelt beside the first body she encountered, a patch of a crest she recognized from a dark estate on his shirt, and checked for signs of breathing. Nothing. Her stomach clenched, threatening to rebel, but she stood and continued to the next fallen soldier.

She soon found a man gasping for breath, blood flowing from his side. She knelt, and he flinched away from her, pressing his hand tighter to the wound. "Please. Don't kill me."

Her chest squeezed. "I don't want to kill you." She nudged his hand aside and placed her fingers over his bleeding side, blood oozing warm and sticky. She allowed herself to dip a toe into the magic within, testing the waters, searching for the correct kind.

There. She let the magic flow down her arms, warming her palms. Beneath her fingers, the flesh grew together, first deeper inside, then subcutaneously. She focused, intent on her limited knowledge from anatomy and physiology studies, as the wound sealed into a rough, red scar.

She removed her hands and let out a shuddering breath. "That's the best I can do."

He reached for the wound, tracing the scar with a trembling hand. Then he sat up, eyes wide. "I know who you are." He scooted back, fear glinting in his eyes. "The shadowmaster. The magic thief."

She stared down at her bloody hands. "I didn't mean for any of this to happen. I hoped it would be a peaceful surrender." Her gaze passed glassy over the surrounding bodies. "Do you know of anyone else I could help?"

He shook his head, scooting farther away. "I don't think anyone wants your help. What side are you on, shadowmaster? Or do you just want to kill us all?"

His words punched into her gut like a knife. Then he scrambled to his feet and ran.

Maybe she should stop him. She wanted to say so much. *I don't want anyone to die. I'm trying so hard, but it just keeps going wrong. I don't know what I'm doing, why I'm always the one making these decisions. It seems like the wrong decision no matter what I decide.* Instead, she stood wordlessly, continuing on her way to search for the next casualty.

Marcus found her crouched over a body hours later, as the sun was reaching its zenith. "Brinnie." His voice was soft. "What are you doing?"

"Searching for survivors." She felt for a pulse. Ridiculous, considering the woman's state with a stake driven through her, eyes staring straight at the sky, sightless. But maybe. Maybe.

He knelt beside her, putting a hand on her shoulder. "They're all dead."

"No." She shook her head, not making eye contact. "I found three. Three were alive. They're imprisoned now." She turned, ready to examine the next body. She'd made it through most of the camp and surrounding area.

"Brinnie." He stepped in front of her, forcing her to look at him. He opened his mouth, sighed, closed it again. Finally he asked, "Is any of that blood yours?"

She looked down at her stained hands, arms, and clothes. "No."

He gave a slight nod. "I'll help you."

Tears threatened, but she only blinked them away and nodded.

Together, they checked the last of the bodies. No survivors. As they crouched beside two soldiers piled nearly on top of each other, Brinnie whispered, "They weren't supposed to die. This was supposed to be a peaceful surrender."

"In many ways, it was." He hesitated. "People at Riverdell are celebrating. We lost only two warriors. And the prisoners that were taken would otherwise likely be dead in the case of a traditional victory. That so many surrendered rather than fight was a military miracle."

"But people are still dead." She stood. "It's not right."

He stood as well. "It's not."

He looked back over the camp for a long moment. She followed his gaze, toward the dead whom others had begun to collect to bury, the still-burning tents, the blood on the ground.

She didn't think he would say anything else, but he added softly, "I don't think in war it's so much about right as it is about the lesser of two evils."

She rubbed her fingers together, drying blood flaking from her fingertips. "Every one of them, when I look at their face . . . I see Lana. I see Nimue. And mostly . . ." She bit her lip, holding back tears. "I see you. What if they were just like you? What if they didn't know any alternative? What if . . . ?" She trailed off with a shuddering breath.

He wrapped his arms around her, and she leaned into him, holding him tight, leaning her head on his chest to hear his heart still beating. Still alive.

"I know." His voice sounded choked. "I know."

CHAPTER ELEVEN

Savory smells drifted from within the stone and mortar residence, washing over Brinnie as she sat next to Marcus on the front step outside the open door of the home. Across the street in the town square, people danced, children spun, and musicians played a rollicking tune. Here in the double space, the stone houses and shops of the citizens resembled smaller versions of the Riverdell mansion, safe, for now, from any warriors outside the magical dimension accessible only by Riverdell's Gate.

Within the home, a sweet middle-aged woman bustled around a pot of stew. Said woman had shooed Brinnie out of the kitchen earlier. "Go, celebrate your victory."

On the step beside her, Marcus fiddled with a small dagger, flipping the knife over and over and catching it by the handle.

She didn't even need to make eye contact. *Don't cut yourself.*

"I won't." But he still sheathed the dagger in his belt.

In case the woman inside could hear them, Brinnie continued to speak to Marcus with her mind. *What are you worrying about?*

"Nothing."

She turned from aimlessly gazing across the street and gave him a look.

He sighed and pointed his chin toward the crowd. *"This celebration. They're unprepared. Mordizan will send another division in a few days. This wave might be won, but it's far from over, and the same trick isn't going to work twice."*

It might. And hopefully better this time.

She could sense him struggling not to argue, not to tell her that war didn't work that way, that the low number of casualties was good.

Because she refused to call death good.

Instead, he said, *"Maybe, but no matter what, Mordred will send out a detail once no word comes back from the troops here. The people need to be ready."*

Brinnie watched a circle of little girls in the square link hands and spin, laughing and tugging until they tumbled over one another into a giggling heap. Parents and neighbors chuckled. *They're not warriors. They're just people. They need this.*

She didn't realize her thoughts had transmitted until Marcus replied. *"I agree. That's why I worry. Mordizan has hordes of well-trained warriors. The enchantment wizards have quiet families who have never picked up a sword."*

That should tell you something. Though her chest still ached from the aftermath of the battle, the lilting music flowed over her heart like a balm, and she smiled slightly. *That's the difference. These wizards are content to live their lives. They aren't focused on conquest. And it works. It's beautiful.* She took a deep breath and spoke aloud. "There's something about the society the estates create, at least how they can be. I saw it first as a glimpse at Wraithwood—a slower-paced life, focused on enjoying the little things." Flashes of the Winslows, Marcie, Miss Burtle flitted across her mind's eye. "They don't need the world. They don't need power. They just live."

Marcus nodded. "I wish everyone at Mordizan could see that." He gave a wry smile. "But Castelon doesn't appear to be much better. Something about power breeds cruelty, corruption."

"Or maybe power attracts the cruel and corrupt." She sighed. "Either way, it doesn't end well."

"I didn't mean to drag the conversation down." He stood. "We can't do anything about any of that right now. But we can fight against this spirit of war another way." He held out his hand, and a spark lit his deep brown eyes. "Want to dance?"

A slow grin grew across her face and warmth spread to her heart. "To make up for those balls at Mordizan where we had to focus on espionage and sieges?"

"Exactly." His expression grew serious. "I want to dance with you for real."

She took his hand, and it engulfed hers as she stood. For a moment, she only stood looking up at him, one hand in his, and gratefulness flowed through her. Gratefulness that in her darkest moments, her shame and weakness and failings, he knew all of it, yet remained beside her. Understood the pain of Mordizan, of war. And looked at her as a person—not as a burden, or a weapon, or a curse, or a child to be protected, or a monster.

But she didn't voice those thoughts. They crossed the street to the green at the center of the square and joined the lively dance, Marcus spinning her around and around. She laughed, and for a moment the heaviness left her heart, the heaviness of war and death and a world on the brink of destruction. Here, a battle was being won. A battle for joy instead of pain, for goodness instead of darkness, for love instead of hate. As she spun, she thought she saw darkness spinning away from her, destroyed by the light of joy.

And so she danced away the darkness.

Another dark night—or so Brinnie assumed. She marched boldly past the sentry. *Time to cause more trouble.*

The last two days had passed in a slow, golden haze. The people of Riverdell returned to their ordinary lives, other than recovering from battle. Brinnie and Marcus helped clear the debris from the abandoned camp, assess which supplies could be requisitioned, and dig graves for the enemy warriors, though Brinnie's depleted physical stamina meant she could only assist with manual labor in bursts. Marcus had helped to bury the bodies, but Brinnie remained in town, unable to face the dead.

The morning after the battle, Brinnie and Marcus had joined Master Irvin and a few of his leaders in his council room when someone brought him a phone. "Castelon, my lord."

Brinnie shot Marcus an anxious glance, but they had no time to come up with a plan. Master Irvin's eyebrows slowly rose as he listened to the caller. Finally, he looked at Brinnie, winked, then replied on the phone, "No, I haven't seen them."

Once he hung up, Brinnie cleared her throat. The other wizards appeared to be distracted by battle maps, not paying attention, offering a brief opportunity for questioning. "Won't you get in trouble for covering for us?"

Master Irvin shook his head. "What trouble can Castelon give me that comes close to that of Mordizan? We need you two—and your brilliant plans—here."

The people of Riverdell seemed to be of a similar opinion. Everywhere Brinnie went, smiles and gratitude greeted her. Little girls shyly offered her flower crowns while mothers invited her to meals. At one point she found herself wearing five floral circlets and eating a second dinner while Marcus laughed at her struggle.

Marcus. In the present, as she slipped past another sentry, she smiled to herself. For the first time, she got to see him in an environment where life and death weren't hanging in the balance. He taught little boys to shoot bows and arrows, made the matrons blush as he complimented their cooking, and led the young men in lessons of swordplay, not to mention making all the young ladies swoon. He didn't seem to notice that last one, though. She kept her amusement to herself, watching how ridiculously flustered they became, and how completely oblivious Marcus was. She supposed he had learned to tune out the attention at Mordizan.

Most of all, she loved when the moon came out. It started the first night, after the dancing had given way to a hearty meal, which she tucked into, trying to gain any weight she could. When the celebration wound down and they were finally alone, Marcus suggested a walk within the safety of the double space.

With a chill in the air and silver moonlight dusting the leaves, Brinnie felt as if they had wandered into a fairy world.

"We'll do it one more time," she had said. "After we fight off this next wave, we can go awaken Uncle Merlin, find Excalibur, and end Mordred."

One thing led to another, and soon they began discussing what would happen after they won the war.

"I'll return to Mordizan." Marcus ducked under a branch. "Hopefully, I can convince my father to quit this war, if he survives Mordred's demise. If he doesn't listen . . ."

He didn't have to finish the sentence. Marcus would put aside any familial ties to keep Mordizan out of war.

"Mordizan could learn from other estates. You have a thriving economy. It could be even better if you put the resources used to maintain an army into infrastructure."

Marcus's brows rose. "I agree."

She laughed. "Don't look so impressed. I've spent most of my life doing pretty much nothing but reading." She nudged him with her elbow. "You're not the only one who's studied government and economics."

He held up his hands. "Trust me, I don't think anyone I know can hold a candle to your voracious book consumption. I saw the way you went through texts at the University. It was unsettling." He wrinkled his nose, peering at her.

"What are you doing, weirdo?"

"Trying to see if you're a bookworm hiding in human skin."

She snorted and hopped over a large rock. "Very funny."

He sobered as they crossed a small field, circling the town. "I'd like you to join me there. In Mordizan."

She slowed. In Mordizan?

She hadn't given much thought to where she would end up after . . . all this. Maybe because she hadn't wanted to hope too hard for an "after."

But she could never go back to the human world at this point. Her friends, her family, were all entangled with magic. Dad presided over Dirklon, and Uncle Merlin would return to Wraithwood. Maybe she'd thought she would stay at Wraithwood forever—and someday, perhaps, it would pass to her, though she hoped that wouldn't be for another hundred years—but in the meantime . . .

"It's more of an offer, an invitation, if you wanted." Marcus rubbed the back of his neck. "I know Mordizan doesn't exactly hold good memories for you, and you have family at Dirklon and Wraithwood. But I think you would have a lot to offer when it comes to leading Mordizan into a new era."

A new era. Her skin prickled. Morgana had said something like that before she died.

Helping Mordizan transition . . . the nightmares might grow stronger in those dark walls. But . . . She looked sidelong at Marcus. She wouldn't have to deal with them alone.

"One condition." The corner of her mouth twitched upward. "Keilrie gets exiled."

He laughed. "Deal."

They spoke of plans and possibilities. Expanding the University. Revamping the council. Liberating those wrongfully imprisoned from the dungeons.

They took another moonlit walk the next evening, the same subjects at hand.

Brinnie smiled. Everything seemed possible. "We'll teach them how to influence the world for good with their powers. Make alliances." She wrinkled her nose. "But not too close of an alliance with Castelon."

He laughed. "Agreed."

They outlined their plans with more detail, basking in dreams and expectations, and some of the pain began to fade. Hope blossomed that maybe, in the end, all this would be worth it.

Now, as Brinnie passed a final sentry, stepped into the enemy camp, and morphed once again into a man, she anticipated victory once more —hopefully this time with even fewer casualties.

"Did you hear?" she asked, stepping into the light of a campfire.

A woman looked up, leaning one arm on her knee. "Hear what?"

"I heard people talking. The troops of Artema are coming."

The four wizards around the fire immediately stood. The one closest to her drew his sword and pointed it at her chest. "Liar."

She put her hands in the air, trying not to let her panic show on her face. "Whoa. What are you doing?"

Two wizards circled behind her, while the other two remained in front, swords and spears at ready. "We're catching an infiltrator," the first woman said. She removed a small horn from her belt, lifted it to her lips, and blew.

Oh, no.

Wizards emerged from the surrounding tents, weapons ready. The woman tucked the horn away and stood in front of Brinnie, offering Brinnie a view of the insignia on her breastplate and . . . *oh. That's bad.*

The woman was an officer. No chance of lying about higher-ups.

"Where are they?" The officer jerked her chin toward the surrounding hills. "Where is the tiny force of Riverdell hiding this time?"

Brinnie's mind spun. *They know. Somehow, they found out and were ready.*

Memories hit her. The man she'd healed. A sick feeling grew in her stomach as she saw him running away in her mind's eye. Had he made it back somehow and told them?

Instead of replying, she turned invisible. Among yells of confusion, she panicked and did the first thing she could think of, yanking masses of shadows toward herself.

The shadows morphed into plumage, talons, and a razor-sharp beak. She hadn't made any creatures in so long—not an eagle since the night she caused a massacre at the stronghold—but she didn't stop to think about whether it would hold. She leaped on its back and whispered, "Fly."

With a screech, the bird of prey took off into the night sky.

She directed the creature to a nearby hill where she leaped off, hitting the top at a run and stumbling down the incline, sliding to a stop in front of Master Irvin. She yanked off the shadows, turning visible. "They saw through our ruse." Her breath came in short gasps. "They already knew about our plan when I got there."

Wizards murmured behind him. Master Irvin's eyes widened. "If they know about our tactic . . . then they also know we've left the house almost unattended."

"The double space gate," Brinnie breathed.

"Retreat," Master Irvin shouted. "Back to the house!"

Brinnie scrambled back to the eagle. "I'll tell the other divisions."

As the raptor took off and wheeled, Brinnie clung to its feathers, leaning out to watch Master Irvin's division beat a hasty retreat around the enemy camp. Turning her gaze to the camp, she sucked in a breath. Enemy warriors poured toward the bridge. Riverdell's forces had taken the long way around to get into position. They would never get there in time. Someone needed to block the bridge, now.

She changed course. Speeding downward, she tumbled off the eagle in the middle of the bridge, rolling across the stone as the bird of prey evaporated. *This is a stupid, stupid plan.*

But it was all she had.

Magic vibrated in her bones. A panicked voice within warned against using more, but a louder force drowned it out, buzzing to be let free, awakening, protesting at so much power contained in such a small vessel.

If she tore herself to pieces with magic, at least it would be for a good cause.

The first enemy soldiers reached the edge of the bridge. Arrows flew toward her, and she threw out an arm, sweeping them away with a gust of wind. As the yelling horde approached, she summoned a shadow sword and a shield of shadow. Then she reached deeper. Fire exploded along the length of shadowy metal, her dark sword blazing. She set her stance, blocking the bridge. She searched her magic, sorting through water, fire, wind, levitation—aha! She amplified her voice as loud as she could make it. "To the bridge! Riverdell, to the bridge!"

She knew her call was in vain. By the time the army of Riverdell forded the river upstream, she would doubtless have lost her position. This bridge afforded the only way across the river, especially with heavy armor and weaponry, the waters too swift and deep for aqua wizards to part, and Brinnie knew Riverdell's small force lacked any levitation wizards or spellcasters to assist. Even if a few aqua wizards could cross its swift-flowing waters with their magic, it would take a while to skirt the camp and reach a crossing point without being picked off by archers. At best, her allies could attack Mordizan's masses from the back. She was alone, standing between the armies of Mordizan and the unsuspecting innocents of Riverdell.

The horde descended. She swung, her blazing blade scything through the enemy with far greater ease than a natural sword. Screams, thuds, as bodies fell. Bile rose in her throat, but she forced it down. *I killed them. I just killed them.* But she couldn't stop. She had to protect Riverdell.

She turned invisible, making herself a more difficult target. All the skills she had learned in Mordizan's own school kicked in. She slashed, thrust, and blocked. Some tried to slip past on the sides, but she raised a pack of wolves to guard her flanks. Someone threw a fireball directly in her face, but she emerged unharmed. She was a fire wizard, now. Another tried to blast her with water, but she threw up her shield and the water sloshed off her, listening to her command. Ivy grew up to entangle her, but she whispered to the vines and they turned and pulled down her enemies instead. A few brave—or stupid—warriors tried to jump off the bridge and swim, but she turned the water to churning whirlpools, sucking them down.

As she fought, a strange sensation rose in her chest, a euphoria of invincibility. Magic sang through her, rejoicing to be unleashed.

She could really do it. She could keep them from getting to Riverdell.

She fought almost blindly, her body and instincts taking over. Warrior after warrior fell to her blade until suddenly, she realized she was swinging at nothing. She wiped blood and sweat from her eyes with a dirty sleeve and looked up to see her enemies falling back.

Did I . . . did I win? She lowered her sword, gasping for breath. Her wolves surrounded her, tongues lolling.

Then her arm glowed with a familiar coolness. *No.*

A dark-robed figure emerged from the troops, stalking forward with glowing blade at the ready.

Mordred.

Exhaustion hit like a train. Brinnie dropped her cover of invisibility, allowing her arm to glow. Mordred knew exactly where she was anyway.

The two stood, staring at one another from fifteen feet apart. His steely eyes matched the color of the bridge under their feet, as unyielding as the stone.

Mordred spoke first. "Brynna Drakon. Look at you. Look what you have become."

Slowly, she lowered her eyes, her gaze sweeping the body-strewn bridge, her splattered leather armor, her blood-covered blade. Her stomach turned, but she spat out, "A defender of the innocent."

"No." His lips curled upward. "The most powerful wizard ever to live since the time of Myrddin."

Her breath came ragged. How had she kept going so long? Had the magic alone propelled her? *Too much magic.*

"So much talent to waste on the losing side." Mordred held out a hand, the one not gripping the blade. "Why don't you join us? We will put the past behind us."

She glared at him. "Never."

"Why not? Because of your sensitivity to causing death?" He gave a slow smirk. "It looks like you're doing plenty of that anyway."

The words scythed through her, threatening to buckle her knees—but she would never give in to Mordred. She gritted her teeth. "Fight me." If nothing else, she could delay him, buy more time.

Where were the soldiers of Riverdell? Why weren't they here yet?

Mordred chuckled. "Bold words. You might change your mind once you see this." He sheathed the blade, and the shining scar on her arm subsided to a dull glow. He held out his hand, and a soldier beside him bowed and handed him a box. No, a leather chest.

When she didn't react, he raised an eyebrow. "Nothing? Surely you recognize the Case of the Master Key."

A sense of foreboding crept up her spine. "Sure. What does that have to do with anything?"

"Everything." He balanced the chest in both hands. "This Case gave you your power. And though it cannot take away that power permanently, it seems that once in the presence of your power source, you temporarily lose your abilities." He flipped the latch. "The Case begins treating *you* like the Master Key. It becomes your . . . well, your bane, you might say."

With a wicked grin, he opened the box.

The world spun, shifted, as her muscles turned to liquid. She fell to her knees, sword, shield, and wolves evaporating. She felt as if she had run twenty marathons. She pitched forward, holding herself up with trembling arms on hands and knees, feeling as if her cells would implode from sudden loss of pressure. She gasped for breath.

He laughed and strode closer, robe brushing against stone. "You understand, if you don't join me, you do have to die."

Her arms shook. *Stand up. Run.* She couldn't manage to lift her head as she heard the blade whisper out of its sheath and felt cold pierce her scar.

Then a crackling noise, a burst of heat.

She looked up in time to see a fireball come sailing from behind her and slam into Mordred's sword hand. He hissed and dropped the blade.

Another fireball whizzed toward his other hand, knocking the Case to the ground. It thudded and fell sideways, knocking the lid shut. Brinnie gasped for air and scrambled away, turning toward the source of the flames.

Marcus stood ten yards behind her, sword in one hand, fire at the ready in the other. "Brinnie, go!"

"Advance!" Mordred called.

The forces behind him streamed forward. Weaponless and without magic, Brinnie stumbled to her feet and ran. She took up position next to Marcus. "Have an extra blade?"

"No. Get out of here." He gave her a push behind him.

"Not without you." She reached for magic to fight with. Only the shadows responded to her call. *Fair enough.* She formed a sword.

"Brinnie." Marcus gritted his teeth, shooting flames at the oncoming warriors. "Go! Mordred has the Case. You'll be killed."

"Then we'll go down swinging." She set her feet.

"Listen to me." A front-running soldier reached them and he swung, locking blades. "This army on the bridge is just a diversion. The rest of the army forded upstream to attack Riverdell itself. This is a lesser cohort."

Her heart stopped. *No.*

Her head spun with panic. She summoned her giant eagle once again, clashing swords with a few warriors, shoving them away to give her enough space to vault onto the creature's back. "Come on." She reached for Marcus, and he launched onto the eagle behind her, blasting fire at the wizards trying to grab them.

The bird took off, soaring back toward Riverdell in time for Brinnie to see Mordred at the head of the troops, blade and Case at ready, only seconds from debilitating her again.

She leaned low over the eagle's neck. "Where are they? Where are we needed?"

"It's too late. The larger army took Riverdell."

Can't come in from the air. They'll see us. Land in the woods. Sneak attack. She directed the eagle toward the trees.

"Brinnie, are you listening to me? Riverdell fell."

The eagle landed and Brinnie jumped off, the words still not computing. The bird disappeared, depositing Marcus unceremoniously on the ground. He popped to his feet, and she noticed his armor caked in blood and dirt, small wounds weeping on his arms, a cut above his eye. Her brain grasped for sense. "Not the Gate. Not the double space."

He nodded, slowly. "Yes. The village. It's . . . all of it is gone."

No. *No, no, no.* She took off running toward Riverdell, plowing through branches.

"Stop." Marcus darted after her and caught her. She tried to shake him off, and they both ended up crashing to the ground. He didn't let go. "No more! It fell. It's gone. Mordred has the Case. He'll kill you."

"I have to try! I have to help our armies." She shoved him away, scrambling to her feet.

"Listen!" He grabbed her by the shoulders, gaze boring into hers, forcing her to look at him. "There *is* no army. The army on the bridge was a diversion specifically for you, to keep you away from the main fighting. Only a few of us escaped. I don't know how many. I fought through and came to find you."

"No." Tears formed in her eyes. "No! I wasn't fighting that long. There wasn't enough time."

"Brinnie." His hands tentatively relaxed their grip on her shoulders, as if he worried she still might run off. "You were fighting for almost three hours."

She didn't know what to say. She had thought she was defending them. Instead, she'd been distracted with a pointless battle. "I should have been there. I should have done something." Tears trickled down her cheeks.

"No." He pushed a lock of wild, tangled hair out of her eyes. "There or at the bridge, it didn't matter. The army was huge, far larger than Riverdell warranted. It was a trap. Mordred was waiting for you with the Case. He must have found out you were at the bridge and came for you there."

She couldn't control the sobs shaking her body, catching in her lungs like hooks. "The children . . . the little flower girls . . ."

"Stop." His eyes glistened. "We need to leave before Mordred comes for you."

She nodded slowly and tried to gain control of herself, sucking in ragged breaths. *Live to fight another battle.*

She formed the eagle once again. Her legs ached as she climbed on its back, Marcus behind her. As the raptor took off, she hoped it knew the way better than she did, her vision too blurred with tears to see anything but rough shapes.

She didn't know for sure how Mordred had learned of their trick, but she would bet he was told by the man she had healed. Even the act of saving lives took them. She had trusted that mercy would cause change.

She was wrong.

She glanced over her shoulder at Marcus. “It’s not going to work.”

He looked up from broodingly contemplating one shadowy wing. “What isn’t?”

“What we keep talking about. Changing Mordizan.”

He heaved a weary sigh. “Why do you say that?”

“We’ve been assuming that people will make logical choices. That they’ll naturally do the right thing if they can.” She shook her head. “We were wrong. People can’t handle power.”

“So what do we do?” His voice was raw, almost angry, though she could tell the anger wasn’t directed at her. “How do we stop this?”

She closed her eyes. “You said it when we were at the airport. It’s a lost cause. We forgot that for a moment at Riverdell. We had too much hope. Foolish hope.”

“We can still go down fighting.” He rubbed a hand across his face. “We can still set the cards on fire.”

She slumped against him, all energy leaving her body. The eagle wobbled for a moment, then straightened out. “I think the cards may already be turned to ash.”

He didn’t have a response for that.

CHAPTER TWELVE

The eagle touched down in a small clearing in the middle of a forest, just wide enough to accommodate its wingspan. Brinnie slid off on wobbly legs. Marcus steadied her, leaning his other hand against a nearby tree trunk. He had to be exhausted as well.

She reached into her pocket and retrieved a small pouch. She pulled out the ring-sized box inside and dumped a portal into her palm, remarkably unharmed. "Let's get back to Wraithwood."

"Wait." He straightened away from the tree, tripping a little on his own feet. "Sorry, leg fell asleep." Rubbing the side of his thigh, he continued, "We can't go traipsing into a human city covered in blood. Not to mention you just used a lot of magic. A portal might not be a good idea right now."

She sighed. He was right. She didn't know exactly where in St. Louis or the surrounding area this portal would dump them, and the museum would be unlikely to let them in looking like this anyway.

"I saw a stream in that direction from the air." He gestured to the right. "We can at least rinse off most of the grime."

They trudged through frost-dusted underbrush. The temperatures thankfully didn't drop as low at Riverdell as they did at Dirklon or Mordizan, nor were they as cold wherever they had landed, about an hour's flight away.

The creek luckily hadn't frozen over. The sight of water made her realize just how long it had been since she'd had a drink. She lowered herself to her knees and submerged her bloody hands in the water, cold biting her skin. She scooped a handful of dirt as an abrasive and scrubbed. Once the water no longer flowed red, she cupped her hands to her mouth and drank.

Marcus unbuckled pieces of scraped and dented armor, laying them on the bank. He pushed up sleeves caked in blood and grime and plunged his arms into the water, then his whole face and head, washing away blood both his own and that of others.

That must be freezing. Then she blinked and laughed at herself internally. Fire wizards didn't get cold. And neither should she. She pushed heat into her hands, warming the water that she splashed on her face and neck. Then she sighed. "Forget it." She shucked off her armor and boots, set the portals aside, and dunked her entire self into the water.

She gasped as the cold hit her with an icy shock, but as she summoned heat, her body adjusted. Too tired to do much else but sit on an underwater boulder and let the current wash away the grime, she sighed and closed her eyes. She heard a splash as Marcus joined her, then sloshing as he sat beside her.

She cracked one eye open, her gaze going to the gash above his eye. "Let me." She gently pressed her fingers to the wound, and it sealed beneath her touch.

Her fingers trailed down to his cheek, and she rested her hand there, reaffirming that he was still beside her, alive. She felt a subtle shift as he leaned into her touch, almost as if he didn't realize he had done so. Then he nodded to shore. "Magic or not, we shouldn't freeze ourselves in this stream."

They scarcely spoke as they collected their things in a hollow between two roots. Marcus gathered a pile of sticks and branches and set them alight. The slight tremble in his fingers told what he wouldn't say aloud—even his magic was exhausted after the fight.

They hung outer garments on branches near the fire to dry and curled together in the hollow without speaking. She scooted near, laying her head on his chest, and he wrapped his arms around her. His warmth prevented the chill from reaching her bones as an almost blissful sense of emptiness filled her, the boiling of magic through her veins quieted to a low hum.

"I'm sorry." His voice came out gravelly. "I didn't stay with the troops and go down fighting like a warrior." He sighed, his breath ruffling the hair on top of her head. "When I knew we couldn't win . . . I ran. I ran to find you."

She looked up. "Are you really apologizing for not dying?"

"I'm apologizing for deserting." He didn't make eye contact. "I've never abandoned my troops."

"Stop it." She gripped his shirt in her fist, sudden anger flashing through her. "If you had stayed there and died some stupid martyr's death, we'd both be dead. I would have had no idea what was going on, and Mordred would have killed me."

"I'm not sure he actually would have done it." He glanced at the fire, which had begun to subside, and the flames leaped higher again. "You're valuable."

"If he killed me or took me prisoner or I somehow escaped, it doesn't matter." Her voice cracked. "I need you to be there with me. You can't die and leave me alone in this." She trailed off to a whisper. "You're the only person who makes me feel okay."

She could have been more poetic. She could have told him how afraid she was that her family, her friends, would hate her when they knew what she'd done. She could have said how few people ever took the time to get to know her, to sit with her, to interpret all the things she never voiced aloud. She could have told him losing the way they moved and plotted in synch would be like losing an arm, that she'd never had a real friend near her own age, someone she could be honest with, someone who could match her wits.

She could have told him how she'd admired so many things about him from the beginning, that the list grew by the day as he turned every expectation for Mordizan on its head, gave up his home and his title to join her on this mad goose chase.

But all of those things flew from her head as a horrible, startling realization slammed into her like a sack of bricks.

I love him.

What a terrible, dangerous thing to feel in the middle of a war.

She realized she was staring at him with wide, shocked eyes. His brow wrinkled. "Brinnie? What's wrong?"

"Nothing." She flipped over to her other side, away from him. She didn't need him reading her face. "Just tired. Don't you even think about dying or I'll murder you, got it?"

He chuckled. "Not sure that makes sense, but I appreciate the sentiment." Leaves rustled as he sat up. "Rest for an hour or two. I'll keep watch. Then we can head to St. Louis and get back to Wraithwood."

She shivered with his heat gone, but she didn't protest. *I'm going to lock that treacherous thought far, far away.*

To defeat Mordred, she couldn't allow any distractions.

Brinnie lifted her fist and knocked on the door, bracing herself for another encounter with magic.

The portal had dumped them in the park near the Gateway Arch, right in front of a runner who screamed and tripped over his own feet.

Brinnie was too busy feeling ill from the portal to say anything, but Marcus gave the man a strange look and offered him a hand. "Are you okay, there?"

The runner hesitantly took his hand and stood. "You . . . appeared out of nowhere."

Marcus glanced at Brinnie, who had the presence of mind to shrug.

"We were just walking across the grass." Marcus hooked a thumb over his shoulder. "Sorry to startle you."

The man's mouth opened, closed. "Right. Um. Thanks." He jogged away, but Brinnie saw him look back over his shoulder several times. The poor man would probably be questioning his sanity for the rest of the day.

After a half-hour walk that felt like five with Brinnie's aching muscles, they arrived at the museum. With no money, Brinnie entered invisibly and Marcus managed to slip in with a large group.

Now standing in front of the door, Brinnie waited for someone to answer her knock. "They'll be surprised to see us."

Marcus took up position behind her. "They'll be even more surprised when they hear about Merlin."

A few seconds later, the door opened a crack and a familiar honey-haired, brown-eyed woman peered through.

Brinnie froze for a moment, then shrieked, "Anna!"

"Brinnie!"

She launched herself across the threshold, ignoring the shock of magic ripping through her as she embraced her sister. "Are you okay? What happened? How did you get here?"

"Whoa, slow down." Anna laughed, squeezing Brinnie back. "Come inside first. We have a lot to talk about."

Marcus joined them in the great hall, and Anna led them through the dining room toward the kitchen. Brinnie looked her sister up and down. Thinner, with prominent collarbones. She couldn't see much else beneath Anna's winter garments, but she didn't show any signs of injuries. Brinnie held back a shuddering breath. *Okay. She's okay.*

In the kitchen, several denizens sat at the table sipping mugs of tea—Mom, Ms. Tynsdale, Miss Burtle, and David, holding a babbling Isaac in his lap.

"I heard a knock on the front door and look who I found." Anna put an arm around Brinnie's shoulders and pulled her into the room.

Now that she'd recovered from the shock of seeing her sister, Brinnie tried not to wince at the unexpected contact. Her skin still stung as if magical wasps had attacked them in the portal, injecting their destabilizing venom to complement the already raw, wobbly feeling in her bones after the battle. But she leaned into Anna anyway, delighted that after all this time, she was *here*.

Mom sat forward. "Brinnie! What are you doing here?"

"Hi, Mom." She turned her attention to her brother-in-law. "Hey, David. It's good to see you alive."

He returned her tired smile and set Isaac down. He reached for something leaning against the table—a crutch—and stood, limping toward her. "Same goes for you."

Her gaze shot to his leg—or rather, where his leg had been. Her hand flew to her mouth. "David, I'm . . . I'm so sorry."

He glanced down at the stump. "Eh, two seemed excessive anyway, you know? Why do I need more than one?" He folded her into a one-armed hug.

She blinked back tears. The infection hadn't killed him, but it had left permanent damage. A constant reminder of pain and loss to both him and Anna.

Another tragedy she'd caused and could never fix.

When he released her, Brinnie looked from him, to Anna, to Mom and Ms. Tynsdale. "How did you get here? The Maze . . ."

"Merlin made more than one secret door." Ms. Tynsdale took a sip of her tea. "Long story, but we followed the tabloids to Anna and David, broke 'em out of a hospital, and booked it to some connections of mine. We were able to pick up several portals as well, in case we need to hop around again."

"And you guys." Brinnie turned to Anna and David. "You escaped Mordizan. How?"

"We had help." Anna smiled as she picked up her son. "A girl there freed us. Unfortunately, she was caught, but we managed to escape."

Brinnie's chest tightened. "Did she tell you her name?"

"Yes." David placed a tender hand on Anna's shoulder. "And we'll never forget it after what she did for us. Her name was Lana."

I knew it. A bittersweet smile tugged at the corners of her lips.

"A bigger question." Mom pointed between Brinnie and Marcus. "What are you two doing here?"

Brinnie pushed down her annoyance. Did Mom not *want* them there? *Trick question. She never wants to see me.* "There was a bit of drama at Castelon. Maddy and Quentin are fine, but they wanted to execute the two of us. So we had to escape."

"Execute you?" Ms. Tynsdale snorted. "Harsh, but not surprising." She raised her cup in Brinnie's direction. "You I understand, Brinnie—no offense—but what did you do, Marcus? Normal policy is to accept low-profile converts."

Marcus shifted slightly, just enough for Brinnie to note his discomfort. "Might have been because of my family—but we have some more important news." He looked at Brinnie.

"Right." She took a deep breath. "Uncle Merlin isn't really dead."

Silence.

Miss Burtle cleared her throat. "We buried him months ago. If he wasn't dead then, he certainly is now."

A sweet voice responded from behind them. "Well, that's a bit of a gruesome thing to say."

Brinnie turned toward Mrs. Winslow, wiping her hands on a rag.

The motherly woman smiled and wrapped Brinnie in a hug. "I thought I heard a commotion down here. Good to see you, dear."

"You too." Brinnie faced the room. "I understand what you're saying, Miss Burtle, and that would be true, but Uncle Merlin is under a sleeper's curse. We met Anika at Castelon, and she told us the truth. She cast it on him."

Ms. Tynsdale's countenance darkened, and she gripped her mug. "So he'll face a fate worse than death a thousand years from now." She rubbed her temple. "Great. That's comforting."

Mom leaned an elbow on the table, hand to her head. "It all makes sense. Why no one became the Master." She took a deep breath. "Because he still is."

Isaac began to whimper. "We'll be back." Anna stepped out of the room, baby-talking to her son.

"No, this is good news." Brinnie took a few steps forward to lean against the back of an empty chair, the series of portals beginning to catch up to her even faster now. *Do not faint.* "It takes a powerful wizard to break the spell, a wizard with pre-Myrddin powers."

At the blank looks, Marcus nodded to her. "A wizard like Brinnie."

Ms. Tynsdale jumped up first, heading straight for the back door. "Let's go."

"Hold your horses." Mom stood. "We need supplies, and it's almost dark outside. Is it wise to dig up my brother at night?" She grimaced. "Digging up a body incorrectly . . ."

"I can see just fine." Brinnie glanced around. "Marcus has fire." She saw him open his mouth, probably to tell her she needed rest, and pointedly rushed on before he could speak. "With a couple torches, we should be okay. Where are Mr. Winslow and Jerry and Marcie, by the way?"

"Tom went out to chop more wood." Mrs. Winslow worried the rag in her hands. "Jerry and Marcie . . . once Anna and David arrived needing a place to hide, we all decided we should have fewer mouths to feed if possible. Since no one is looking for them, they headed out the Door to make their way back to Lyle until things blow over. We got a call yesterday that they're staying with Marcie's parents."

Until things blow over. Which could be never. She didn't want to think about how tearful that parting must have been. "That makes sense."

"But with Merlin back, we won't have to worry about who stays and goes anymore." Ms. Tynsdale brushed her hands together. "Let's get to it."

Brinnie's heart buoyed with hope she couldn't quite suppress. "Where are the shovels?"

Brinnie pulled her hands into the sleeves of a borrowed jacket and shivered as they tramped through the snow. Everyone had joined the expedition except David, who stayed behind with Isaac, since the snow made for difficult terrain with a crutch.

Brinnie's chest squeezed, thinking of her brother-in-law. He'd put on a casual demeanor, but after being thrown into a warring world of wizards . . . what deeper damage had that caused them both that Brinnie couldn't see, just as permanent as the loss of David's leg?

The cold dragged her away from her dark thoughts. Distracted, she tried to pull a Marcus trick of heating herself up using her fire powers, as she'd heated the water yesterday. She focused on her skin getting warm.

Instead, her clothes caught on fire.

She squeaked and rolled in the snow to put out the flames. Not that it hurt—fire couldn't hurt her anymore–but she didn't want her clothes burned off.

"Brinnie!" She looked up to see Mom standing over her, mouth open. "What on *earth*?"

Her cheeks burned as she stood and dusted off snow. "Sorry. Failed experiment."

Anna gave her a horrified look. Marcus tried to cover up his laughter with a few coughs.

Mom raised an eyebrow. "Okay, then."

They made their way through the rose garden to a bare tree standing guard over a simple headstone. As the group came to a stop, Anna stood beside Brinnie and shuddered. "It doesn't feel right to go digging up a body."

"It's perfectly right if he's not dead." Ms. Tynsdale stepped between them, shovel in hand.

Brinnie couldn't help a small chuckle at her enthusiasm. Then it dawned on her.

She can finally tell him she loves him.

"She does?"

Brinnie physically jumped. Luckily, Anna had moved away. Brinnie swung her attention to Marcus, standing near the grave with a ball of flame in his hands. *Why are you in my head?*

"Didn't mean to be. Just overheard." He spread the flames across the ground in front of the headstone, melting away snow and hopefully softening frozen turf.

Better be careful what I think.

"Why?" She could see a smirk teasing the corner of his lips. *"Are you thinking things you shouldn't be?"*

Marcus! You weren't supposed to hear that either.

With two large shovels and a few trowels, they made slow work chopping through half-frozen dirt, heated as much as possible by Marcus and Brinnie without setting anything—or anyone—on fire. Marcus lit secondary fires to illuminate the work as evening faded to night, which also served to keep them warm as temperatures dropped.

Brinnie's muscles ached, protesting after the battle less than forty-eight hours before. Marcus put a hand on her shoulder. "Hey. Take a breather for a minute."

She wiped sweat from her brow with a trembling hand and could feel the streak of dirt she left in its wake. "I'm fine."

He gently removed the trowel from her grip and held it up, revealing char marks in the shape of fingers. "You scorched the handle."

"Oh."

He gave her a hand, and she hauled herself out of the growing hole. He hopped back in while she sat on a root of the tree, catching her breath. But with time to think, her heart started to beat faster.

How was she going to essentially raise the dead? What if it didn't work?

Finally, the shovels hit something hard. They dug around until they had created enough room for Mr. Winslow, Mom, Brinnie, and Marcus to set their feet and lift the coffin to the other four at the top of the wide hole, who hauled it up and dragged the box to flatter ground.

Ms. Tynsdale quickly set to work with a hammer prying the lid off.

"You did a little too good of a job nailing this down," she grunted to Mr. Winslow.

He shrugged with a slight chuckle. "Didn't expect to have to take it off again."

Marcus pitched in using a trowel as a crowbar, and soon enough, they lifted the lid.

Brinnie's heart caught in her throat when she saw him. His face shone deathly pale beneath that familiar mustache. The shirt he wore appeared to have been replaced post mortem, only stained with a bit of dark, dried blood. She reached in to touch his hand, but pulled back at its cold stiffness, a shiver running down her spine. "Any ideas?" she whispered.

"I thought you knew how." Mom hovered several steps away. Brinnie wondered if she couldn't bring herself to look on the cold body of her brother.

"Not how." Brinnie cringed. "Just that I can."

Miss Burtle tapped her chin. "According to old manuscripts . . . I think I remember something about pre-Myrddin wizards breaking sleeper's curses by transferring life magic."

Brinnie looked down at her uncle. "Life magic? What division is that?"

"Magic wasn't divided so strictly then." Miss Burtle raised one shoulder. "I would need to do more research."

Marcus stepped in closer, peering into the casket. "Nimue raised Mordred from his sleep. Maybe you could do what she did."

"Nimue raised Mordred?" Brinnie's brow furrowed. "The rhetoric I heard at Mordizan was that he 'woke up when the time was right for revolution' or something like that."

"Obviously propaganda." Ms. Tynsdale crossed her arms. "But I didn't know my *sister* did it. Figures."

"Master Vorath didn't think it would be a good idea to divulge too much to the general public," Marcus explained. "After Nimue's father died, all she could think about was raising Mordred." He continued to Brinnie, *"I remember because she would always talk to my mother about it. My mom didn't think it was a good idea."*

Ms. Tynsdale raised a brow.

Danger alert. Brinnie spoke before Ms. Tynsdale could ask any questions. "So how did she do it?"

"I don't know. Years ago, Nimue said the same thing, that the victim must receive life magic. I know she said a healer alone couldn't do it, but at that point she hadn't figured out how the magic *could* be done."

Ms. Tynsdale opened her mouth to speak, but Brinnie barreled onward. "Well, I'm a healer plus a lot of other things. I guess I'll just give it a shot." *You know too much,* she thought to Marcus. *Ms. Tynsdale is getting suspicious about who you are.*

"Saw that. I'll keep my mouth shut for a while."

Brinnie placed a hand on Uncle Merlin's head, forcing herself not to snatch her fingers away from his icy skin. She hated the stiff, waxy stillness, so different from the warm, smiling Uncle Merlin she had known. She tried to think warming thoughts, quickening thoughts.

Her hand heated, but Uncle Merlin didn't move, didn't change. She reached out with the healer part of her, probing for something to heal, but the magic returned empty, as if she were trying to touch a void.

She scrunched her eyes shut. *Warm thoughts. Life thoughts. Healing thoughts.* She searched through her magic, pawing through the pile of random odds and ends, but still nothing happened.

A cold breeze blew through her hair and nipped her nose. She opened her eyes with a sigh. "It's not working."

Mom rubbed her arms. "Nimue is a flora wizard. Maybe her plant life magic worked on Mordred."

I doubt it. Brinnie searched for plant magic anyway. She tried to send some of that energy to Uncle Merlin, but instead his coffin erupted with grass.

She rubbed her forehead. "I'm open to ideas."

Everyone suggested different things—fire to warm, water to get the blood flowing, maybe something to do with animals, but all failed. At last, Brinnie mixed them all together and tried to infuse them as one.

Nothing happened. Or rather, nothing useful. The coffin filled with water, fire erupted on the lid, and field mice went scurrying across their feet.

Brinnie shook her fingers. "Nothing." She glanced around at her shivering friends and family. "It's cold out here. Why don't we take him back to the house and warm up while we think?"

Marcus, Mr. Winslow, Ms. Tynsdale, Mom, Anna, and Brinnie hoisted the coffin. As they tromped through the snow, Brinnie wracked her mind. Anika had said pre-Myrddin wizards could do it. *But I'm not technically a pre-Myrddin wizard.* Yet Nimue had somehow awoken Mordred without pre-Myrddin powers. What was she missing?

Back at the house, they left the coffin at the door and settled Uncle Merlin in an upstairs bed. In the library, Miss Burtle brought down armfuls of the Wraithwood Scrolls, while Brinnie pulled every book in English she could think of from the shelves, piling them on the conference table. Marcus followed, selecting potentially relevant tomes in the ancient language, and Mom and Ms. Tynsdale unrolled scrolls, muttering to each other occasionally.

Anna entered with bowls of stew on a tray. "Mrs. Winslow warmed some up for the library night owls."

Brinnie accepted a bowl. "Thank you." On her own, she would forget to eat, but after the dungeons, she jumped at every chance to put meat on her bones. "Maybe we'll find something quickly."

Miss Burtle laid another armful of scrolls on the table. "I've read just about all of these at one point or another. I've never read anything about how the sleeper's curse is broken. It may take longer than you think."

Marcus turned a page. "I've never read anything about it in my studies at Mordizan, either. Trust me, if someone had figured it out, we would have broken into Arthrys and awoken Mordred long before now."

Brinnie sighed. "All right, then. I take that back."

They spent the next few hours poring over scrolls and books. Mom left to check on Uncle Merlin, and Miss Burtle squinted until she sighed and admitted, "My eyes aren't what they used to be. I may need to turn in for the night and resume in the morning."

Marcus remained beside Brinnie, while at the other end of the table, Ms. Tynsdale scowled at scrolls. Brinnie rubbed her eyes, her vision blurring in and out. *Come on, Brinnie. You're better than this. How many near all-nighters have you pulled finishing a good book?*

Her head bobbed, and Marcus nudged her. *"Hey. We can keep looking tomorrow. If you don't rest, you might end up setting books on fire or something."*

A valid point. *You may have gotten me with that argument.*

A slight smile. *"I've learned appealing to your sense of self-preservation and the necessity of taking care of yourself is useless."*

Not wrong, but I didn't need to be called out like that. She stood and looked over at Ms. Tynsdale. "I'm heading to bed."

Ms. Tynsdale nodded. "I will, too. Soon."

Brinnie left the library and passed through the great hall and the dining room into the kitchen. At the table, Anna sat alone staring down into a mug of tea cupped between her hands.

"Hey." Brinnie took a tentative step forward. "What are you still doing up?"

Her sister blinked and looked up. "I couldn't sleep."

"Is something wrong?" Brinnie drifted closer.

"Is anything not wrong?" She bit her lip. "Do you realize how crazy this is? I worked in some rough parts of the world in field hospitals. I didn't think anything would faze me at this point. But this . . . wizards don't exist. Magic isn't even real."

She knew the gravity of the situation, but Brinnie couldn't help biting back a smile. "Well, from personal experience, I'd say we do exist, and so does magic."

Anna snorted. "Goose." Then her smile faded. "I mean that I thought I had this world figured out. Then all of this happened. How could we be living our lives all this time, completely unaware? How did we have such a limited view of reality? Not even realizing the danger we're all in?"

"I'm so sorry you got dragged into this." Brinnie leaned against the back of the chair next to Anna and looked down at her hands. "I would have done anything to keep you from being captured. And unfortunately, Mordred knew that."

"It's not your fault. At all." She sighed. "I just wish Mom and Dad would have told me *something*." She gestured to Brinnie. "If they hadn't been so set on keeping secrets from us and each other, maybe we could have protected you, kept all of this from happening."

"They were doing what they thought was best." Brinnie shrugged, still not quite making eye contact.

"Best for who?" Anna placed her hand over Brinnie's. "Not you. Has anyone been looking out for *you*? You're only sixteen."

"I caused this." She managed to keep her voice even. "So I should be the one to fix it."

"Excuse me? *How* could you possibly have caused any of this?"

She finally looked up and met her sister's eyes. "By being born." Her voice cracked. "You and Mom and Dad would never have been dragged into this war if it weren't for me. I ruined all of your lives, and I wish I could reverse time and just—"

"Don't you dare finish that sentence." Anna stood and put her hands on Brinnie's shoulders, her gaze watery. "I wasn't there when you were a kid. I went off to college, med school, residency, then across the world with David . . . I should have said something about how Mom treated you differently, but I didn't. I noticed. I know Dad noticed, and I don't know why he didn't do anything either."

Brinnie shifted uncomfortably. "I don't think—"

"You don't have to make excuses for them." Anna's jaw clenched. "You're not the one who ran away from the fight. You're not the one who chose to lie and not tell your kids anything."

Brinnie blinked, trying to force back tears, a thousand protests rattling through her mind. *If not for me, it would have worked. If not for me, Mordred would have no interest in our family. If not for me, David wouldn't be hurt, Uncle Merlin wouldn't be cursed, the last stronghold might still stand.*

Anna squeezed her shoulders. "This entire time, you've been running *toward* the fight. You've been giving it everything you've got and more. No complaints that it shouldn't be your job to fix a war you had no say in. That you're too young. That it's too hard so you're going to hide and let other people deal with it." She met Brinnie's eyes. "You don't have to earn your right to be alive, you know. You deserve to be here and be loved just as much as anyone else."

Brinnie folded her sister into a hug, trying to hide her tears, though her trembling breaths probably gave them away. "I missed you."

Anna's voice came muffled through Brinnie's hair. "I missed you too. My little sister, all grown up."

Brinnie pulled away, setting her jaw. "I'm going to figure this out. We're all going to be okay."

"That's a lot of pressure on yourself." Anna bobbed her head in the direction of the rest of the house. "You have a lot of people in your corner. Let them help you."

"Okay." Brinnie glanced at the cup of tea on the table, now cold and untouched. "And the same goes for you."

As Brinnie crawled under the covers a few moments later, her mind mulled the issue of Uncle Merlin. Despite what Anna said, she rolled over, her chest squeezing. The defenders at the strongholds. Oswald Goddensfeld. Riverdell. She had failed them all. She couldn't stand the thought that she would fail Uncle Merlin, too.

A thought began to form, based on Anna's words. There was someone. Not necessarily someone in her corner, but someone who could help.

Nimue Drakon.

CHAPTER THIRTEEN

"So you want to go *back* to Mordizan?" Mom thumped her book shut.

Brinnie nodded, glancing around at the crowd gathered at the conference table in the library, missing only David and Isaac. "Nimue is the only one who knows how to break a sleeper's curse. We need to talk to her."

Brinnie had telepathically informed Marcus of her plan first thing in the morning, despite her urge to share right when she'd thought of it last night. No need to wake the entire household. As soon as the time hit a reasonable hour, she called for a meeting in the library, where she, Marcus, and Miss Burtle had already begun sifting through books and scrolls.

"Wouldn't she be out fighting anyway?" Ms. Tynsdale set one scroll aside and picked up another. "Who's to say she's at Mordizan?"

"Nimue serves mostly in a political and government capacity," Marcus explained. "Sometimes she trains fighters, usually spies and assassins, but she doesn't often go out in the field herself. She made an exception when Mordred was weak and needed her help navigating the Maze, but she usually stays at Mordizan."

Ms. Tynsdale's eyes narrowed slightly, as though contemplating Marcus. *Oh, well.* They would find out about him soon anyway.

That morning, after their telepathic conversation, Brinnie and Marcus had met on the portico outside the library. Though cold, Brinnie thought she felt a slight turn in the air toward warmer weather. *Spring.*

She shivered, and he opened his arms. Brinnie snuggled in with her head against his chest, basking in his usual warmth.

"It's still dark out." He kept his voice low.

After half a night spent tossing and turning, the warm rumble of his voice lulled her eyes closed. "Couldn't sleep. How about we sleep here instead?"

He chuckled. "I don't think sleeping standing up would be very comfortable." She felt him sober and looked up to meet his eyes. "Nightmares?"

She gave a half-shrug. "As usual." She raised a brow. "You were awake too when I asked you about Nimue, though."

His lips twitched. "Caught me."

He didn't need to say more. She knew the nightmares plagued him as well.

Wordlessly, they brushed snow from the porch swing and sat, huddled together.

"You're probably going to have to tell them who you are." She hugged her knees to her chest. "Is that okay?"

"Is that okay with *you*?" He glanced at her. "I don't know anyone here well enough that their hatred will affect me. But it may make things a bit awkward for you."

"We'll leave right after anyway." She snuggled closer. "If they're being unreasonable, that should give them time to adjust and cool down."

"I'm a tactically wise ally. I imagine they won't disagree with that."

She looked up at him and the serious set to his jaw. "You're more than that. I want them to think of you as more than that."

A teasing smirk flitted across his lips. "Oh, yes? Also as a masterful ballet dancer, I assume?"

She elbowed him. "Do you know anything about ballet?"

"I've heard about tutus. I think I would look dashing."

She snorted, shaking her head. "You're ridiculous. I mean as my best friend."

Their eyes met, and something fluttered in her stomach. Why did it feel like she'd said too much? He knew that, of course. An innocuous statement.

"I'll continue to be on my best behavior for your family." He offered a wry smile. "They can't dislike me any more than your father does."

She groaned. "He's a little overprotective."

"I understand the impulse, though I've learned to curb it." He nudged her. "Someone doesn't take kindly to being told what to do."

At that moment, the door to the library swung open and Miss Burtle stuck her head out, frowning. "If you're going to canoodle, at least do it inside where you won't catch your death of cold."

"We're not *canoodling*," Brinnie protested, ears burning with embarrassment.

At nearly the same time, Marcus said, "Apologies. Fire wizards tend to be impervious to cold."

Miss Burtle looked upward. "Good for you, but she isn't. Bring the girl inside." With that, she turned around and shut the door.

"I'm one too, now," Brinnie said to the closed door. Then she glanced back at Marcus and giggled. "Well, you're already on a bad track with Miss Burtle."

"Is anyone not?"

"You raise a fair point."

In the present, Mom crossed her arms, jolting Brinnie out of the memory. "So what are you proposing? Capturing Nimue? I would think she's more likely to turn anyone over to Mordred than share her secrets."

"I don't think capturing is on the table." Marcus glanced at Brinnie, then back at the group. "Nimue would die for what she thinks is right. Even lengthy torture might not be effective."

"Good heavens, dear, we don't torture people here." Mrs. Winslow clutched a hand to her chest.

"I'm not suggesting we do. I only mean to say I don't think capture is wise."

Ms. Tynsdale hooked a thumb at Mom. "So the two of us go in there and . . . ask her politely?"

Brinnie raised an eyebrow. "Why you two?"

"There are four wizards here." Mom gave her a stern look. "You're not going back there, Brinnie, and I want someone I know well like Lydia at my side." She nodded to Marcus. "No offense to you."

"None taken." He leaned against the table. "However, I do think Nimue may be more inclined to talk to her protege niece than her estranged sister and a Ludovic. As for me, I've known Nimue my entire life, and she's like another cousin to me. I think she would be willing to at least hear me out."

Ms. Tynsdale's eyes narrowed further. "How do you know Nimue so well?"

Mom ignored both of them, frowning at Brinnie. "I'm not letting you go back there."

"Mom, I have more magic than all of you combined. I'll be safer than anyone."

"She does have a point," Miss Burtle said.

Mom sighed. "After everything went wrong last time—"

"You haven't answered me, Marcus." Ms. Tynsdale's voice increased in volume. She fixed him with a pointed stare. "I think we should *all* be asking questions. How do you know so much? About everything? Who *are* you?"

"You'll forgive the two of us," he said, nodding to Brinnie, "but we didn't think it wise to tell you before." He paused. "I'm Marcus Vorath, heir of Mordizan."

Mom gasped. Her expression of shock was mirrored around the table, except for Mrs. Winslow, who seemed strangely calm.

And except for Ms. Tynsdale.

Her face had gone white, and she clutched the edge of the table. "I . . . I remember you."

"Pardon?" His tone remained calm, but Brinnie noticed a slight twitch in his fingers. "I thought you forgot everything about your time at Mordizan."

"Almost." She stared at him as if he'd transformed into some horrifying creature. "But you. I remember your face . . ." Her tone hardened, and she slowly stood. "I remember you forcing me to tell you Brynna's location."

Brinnie's brain stuttered to a stop. She glanced at him. *Is that true?*

He didn't respond.

Marcus. I know you can hear me.

His jaw set. "I'm fully committed to the enchantment wizards now."

"Oh, that makes me feel so much better. I completely buy everything a *torturer* says." Ms. Tynsdale clenched her fists. "How dare you come here?"

"Marcus." Brinnie's voice came out faint. "Please explain."

He finally looked at her, jaw tight. "I didn't know you then. At the time, Ignatius and I were assigned to a prisoner in order to extract the location of an enemy shadowmaster."

"And you didn't think to tell me this?"

He looked away. "It never came up."

Brinnie's jaw dropped. "It never came up? Seriously?" She stood, her chair screeching behind her. "You're saying you planned this all along? That's how you knew where Anna and David were. That's how you knew how to get me on your side. You were the one who got us all there."

He flinched, eyes glinting with pain. "None of this was planned."

Something in her chest cracked, while her mind still refused to believe it. Hoped there was some other explanation, someone else who nearly destroyed Ms. Tynsdale, who pointed Mordred to her, dragged her family into war. "Then you better start explaining. Or are you still just putting on an act to try to get rid of Mordred and take back your throne?"

"That . . ." His mouth opened and closed. "That's not the case."

Mom raised her hands, palms out, with her eyes narrowed. "Step away from him, Brynna. I'll kill him if he moves."

Ms. Tynsdale pulled a knife from a concealed sheath. "I have your flank."

Even Miss Burtle's hand inched toward a heavy tome. Mr. Winslow started to rise, but Mrs. Winslow shook her head at him.

Brinnie waved them all off. "I don't need to be protected." She kept eye contact with Marcus. "We've dueled. We know who would win."

Slowly, he put both hands behind his head in a gesture of surrender. "I would never fight you, Brinnie."

Despite anything else, she did believe that.

No matter how many times they had lied to each other, how many secrets they had kept, that shred of truth had always shone through, and after the dungeons of Mordizan, she had never doubted it again.

He could never hurt her. Any more than she could actually follow through on her threat to hurt him.

"Explain." She fought the wobble in her voice. "To all of us."

His words came out stumbling. "I have done horrible things. I don't expect you to forgive them, but I do want you to know that none of this was planned, and I regret every part of it." He took a deep breath, looking up at her, and his voice steadied, though the expression in his eyes remained pained, as if speaking twisted a knife of regret in his gut. "When you originally arrived at Mordizan, I was spying on you to report to my father, like I said. Then I saw you as a potential ally against Mordred. Finally, I came to my senses and realized the truth that Mordizan's regime itself needs to be ended."

She wouldn't be distracted. "You told me before that you wanted a way to stop the fighting. We became allies because of it. Was that a lie too?"

"No. That was true." His spine remained stiff as he maintained a calm, neutral tone. She knew from experience that demeanor hid the turmoil of emotions within, overcorrecting to avoid losing his poise.

If she knew him so well, how had he gotten away with lying so thoroughly?

"Before I met you," he continued, "I had never met anyone from the other side, and—"

"Enough of that." Mom glared at him. "What did you do to Lydia, and why?"

A crack in the stiff demeanor, a flash of what looked like shame. "My father believed sending me to assist Ignatius would strengthen me to do what is necessary to rule Mordizan. I had only ever been assigned to our own deserters." He turned to Ms. Tynsdale. "Then I was assigned to you. I assure you that I hated myself, hated every moment of it."

"Rightly," she muttered.

"I did what I believed was necessary. I broke a spy. That's war, right?" He gave a short, mirthless laugh. "Then innocent humans were suffering in our dungeons, and Brinnie was captured. I understood why my mother used to help prisoners escape." He sighed. "I always wanted to stop the fighting. I'd hoped the way to do it was to win the war quickly and have it over with, so I resolved to be the best warrior possible. But once I encountered you . . . Anna and David . . . Brinnie." He glanced at her, a sheen in his eyes. "What I thought I knew fell apart."

"Pretty speech." Ms. Tynsdale looked at Mom. "I still say we cut off his head and send it to Mordizan as a lesson."

"What, as a gift to Mordred?" Mom scowled. "I'm sure he'd appreciate it."

While the two bickered, Brinnie made eye contact with Marcus. *Why didn't you tell me?*

"I meant to. Wanted to. But every time . . . I didn't. I still planned to tell you." He bobbed his head toward Mom and Ms. Tynsdale. *"I just didn't expect it to happen like this."*

So instead you lied. Excellent.

"I know." He stared at the ground. *"I'm a coward. I . . . worried you wouldn't forgive me. Mrs. Winslow said I should tell you as soon as possible, and I should have listened—"*

"Mrs. Winslow knew?" Brinnie blurted aloud. Her gaze shot to the motherly housekeeper.

She twisted her apron in her hands and nodded. "Yes, dear. We've had some conversations." She bit her lip. "I wouldn't give him too hard of a time." She looked at Marcus, as if urging him to say something.

He didn't. Brinnie reached out for his mind. It was fuzzy, but she caught a name. *Ignatius.*

What about Ignatius?

For the first time, a wall seemed to slam down between them, blocking her from his thoughts.

Ms. Tynsdale eyed Marcus. "I would rather send him on a long trip to the moon without a spacesuit, but if he wants Mordred dead, our enemy's enemies are almost as good as friends at this point." Her nose crinkled in disgust. "And if he is Marcus Vorath, they're right. My degenerate half-sister is more likely to listen to him."

"Well, I don't want my daughter around him." Mom crossed her arms. "He can go by himself."

"What we have planned requires both of us . . ." Brinnie began.

Mom cut her off. "I don't want to hear it. You *knew* who he is, and still brought him here?"

As much as Brinnie wanted to shake Marcus at the moment, she needed him. "Dad didn't like the Vorath connection much either, but he didn't have any problem with me working with Marcus."

"Don't bring your father into this." Mom rolled her eyes. "I have enough problems with that man."

Maybe not the best argument she could have come up with.

"Please allow us to explain the plan." Marcus bobbed his head to Mom. "I won't let anything happen to her, Lady Drakon."

"Don't call me that." Mom shuddered. "I have zero confidence in your promises, young man."

He winced.

"Anyway." Brinnie pressed her lips into a thin line, looking around the table. "Let me outline our plan. Then we can all get back to yelling at each other."

No one protested, so she took a deep breath. "Okay. Here's what we're thinking . . ."

Brinnie balanced Isaac on one hip while stirring a pot with her free hand, trying not to scowl as thoughts swirled through her head.

Not much earlier, after Brinnie and Marcus had finished outlining their plan, Mom leaned back. "Fine. But you." She pointed her finger at Marcus. "If something happens to her, there are several people here and at least one more at Dirklon who will make sure you die a painful death."

"Yes, ma'am."

"All right." Ms. Tynsdale pushed away from the table. "That's settled. I call first dibs on killing him if needed. Now I'm going to go look for more scrolls to see if there's anything we can find to help. You never know."

Miss Burtle sighed and brushed off her hands. "I'll get some more books."

"I can help." Anna glanced between them. "Though I'm not exactly sure what I'm looking for."

"I'll give you a list," Miss Burtle said.

As everyone dispersed to their various tasks, many to keep searching the library, Brinnie had joined Mrs. Winslow in the kitchen after the housekeeper insisted they at least have some lunch before heading out.

Brinnie set down the ladle, watching Mrs. Winslow toast grilled cheese sandwiches. "Where did you get bread?"

"Your mother and the others brought supplies with them when they came back. They can get more with the portals if we need it." She looked sideways at Brinnie. "How are you and Marcus?"

Their parting from the library had been . . . chilly. After Mrs. Winslow insisted on lunch, Marcus had asked after disguises, to be reluctantly led away by Miss Burtle.

"Do you want to—" he began.

"No." Brinnie had cut him off. "I'll help Mrs. Winslow."

Brinnie picked up the ladle again. "I trust him well enough to complete the mission." She hesitated. "You two talked?"

Mrs. Winslow flipped a sandwich to toast the other side. "Yes, dear. The young man needed someone to talk to."

Not surprising that Mrs. Winslow would be Marcus's first choice. If Brinnie had anything weighing on her mind she didn't want to share with him, she would probably talk to Mrs. Winslow as well. Isaac squirmed, and Brinnie handed him a block to play with. "I just wonder how many other lies he's told."

"That I can't tell you, dear." Mrs. Winslow set a new piece of buttered bread in the pan. "I think you should talk to him about it. There may be . . . more to the story."

It seemed Mrs. Winslow didn't feel right being the one to tell it.

"I'll definitely talk to him." The bitter words spilled out. "Though who knows if he'll answer truthfully."

"I get the impression that he will, though I don't know him well enough to be certain." The pan sizzled. "There is one thing I'm sure of, dear. He cares about you more than anything else in the world."

Brinnie shrugged uncomfortably, setting Isaac down to play with the rest of the rough blocks in the corner of the kitchen. "I'm sure that's an exaggeration."

Mrs. Winslow chuckled. "You should have seen him when you fainted after first arriving here. Hovering like a mother hen."

She felt her cheeks heat and was grateful for the distraction of keeping Isaac from climbing on one of the chairs. "We have a special connection."

"I can see that."

"That's not what I mean." She returned to the pot. "After we went through the portal when I first ended up with all this magic, something happened. We can mind-speak to each other."

Mrs. Winslow stopped with a spatula in mid-air. "You can what?"

"It's like telepathy. We have conversations in our minds. At first, we had to be making eye contact, but now we sometimes hear each other's thoughts from the other room."

She shook her head, wrinkles creasing her brow. "I've never heard of something like that."

"We thought maybe I was so volatile when we went through the portal that some of us got mixed up together on the way over here." Brinnie lifted a shoulder. "So, we're kind of stuck with each other."

"Hmm." She pulled a stack of plates from the cupboard. "A gift like that comes for a reason."

"Right now, that reason seems to be sneaking back into Mordizan." Brinnie retrieved bowls for the tomato soup. "The mission is more important than any interpersonal drama."

Mrs. Winslow pressed her lips together. "All right, dear." She sighed. "Maybe it's the silly old woman in me, but I'd like to sit your whole family down to talk. The group of you could use some time to sort things out."

Brinnie set the bowls on the counter. "After all this calms down, after the war, I'll help you do just that." She giggled. "I'd like to see you tell everyone to speak kindly. Maybe you could use a talking stick."

Mrs. Winslow's grim expression eased only slightly with a tight smile. "Right. After the war."

But the way she said it . . . Brinnie began to suspect Mrs. Winslow didn't anticipate an end in sight.

CHAPTER FOURTEEN

The door dumped them in an unknown location, grasslands swaying around them. Brinnie stumbled, magic shocking her system once more. Marcus held out a hand to steady her, but she sidestepped.

"Portal." She nodded to the orb in his hand.

To his credit, only his eyes gave away his hurt. "Do you want a moment to recover in between?"

"Let's just get it over with."

He smashed the portal, and they emerged into a much colder landscape, surrounded by pine. This portal had been the one leading the closest to Mordizan of the ones Mom and Ms. Tynsdale had acquired, though not as near as Brinnie would have hoped.

Her stomach turned with nausea. Door then portal in quick succession hadn't been the wisest choice. She rested her hands on her knees, taking deep breaths while waiting for the world to stop spinning.

"Brinnie . . ."

"I'm fine." She straightened and began gathering shadows.

He adjusted the pack on his shoulder, hesitating. "I owe you an explanation. I shouldn't have shut you out."

She didn't speak as the shadows coalesced into an enormous eagle, large enough for two.

The fact that he had been the one to torture Ms. Tynsdale—she wasn't so much mad at him for that. Things were different then. They'd both done things they regretted. Her throat tightened. But why did he feel the need to lie to her?

Really, Marcus. You're my best friend. We've both done terrible things. We understand each other. Why didn't you think I could handle that?

"Because last time I tortured someone's family, it drove them mad."

She jumped, turning away from the eagle. "I didn't mean to send that thought to you."

"Sorry." He looked away. "I heard my name. I didn't mean to pry."

She vaulted onto the eagle's back. "Since you did, care to explain what you mean by that?"

He climbed on behind her. The eagle didn't provide enough room for them not to touch, and she cursed herself for it. *Should have made a dragon or something.* Although sustaining an entire dragon for that long of a flight . . . close proximity it was.

"I'd been trying to make myself tell you. Trying to make up for it, not that I ever could, but at least a little." As the eagle took off and the sound of beating wings and rushing air muffled his voice, the conversation switched to her mind. *"I told you before that I'm a coward. I hate myself for everything that happened, and I, selfishly, kept avoiding the topic so that you wouldn't hate me just as much."*

Let's suspend the whole hate thing. She directed the eagle northward. *Just tell me.*

"It starts with Ignatius."

Brinnie wrinkled her nose.

"We were good friends growing up, as you might expect from two heirs close to the same age. He had a younger sister that he doted on, though I never interacted with her much. One day, she was caught helping the enemy."

A sinking feeling grew in her chest.

"My father had only recently assigned me to extracting information. Ignatius hated it. He didn't understand how I could do that sort of thing to people."

"Ignatius?" she blurted aloud. *Sorry, I can't imagine him having any qualms.*

"That's my fault." She felt his chest rise and fall in a sigh against her back. *"I didn't like it any more than he did, but I did as my father told me, and I made myself stomach it because they were traitors and deserters. But. Then I got assigned to his sister."*

"Oh, Marcus," she whispered.

"My father told me that she knew the identities of several enemy spies. That she was a traitor of the highest degree. Someone who had betrayed us all. Any feelings of sympathy I might have for her would be because of her deceptive ways, her using the innocent girl image. And . . ." He swallowed. *"If I successfully extracted the*

information, he would consider me fit to graduate from my training and join him as his right-hand man."

So you did.

"I did."

They rode in silence for a few moments. She didn't push him for more. Maybe she should be more disgusted or angry, but she only felt a deep sadness. Sadness that like so many others, he hadn't seen any alternative.

"To be honest, she wasn't difficult to break," he continued finally. *"She was so young, after all. The spies she gave up were executed. She survived the torture, but her mind was gone. Ignatius, of course, wouldn't speak to me. They took his sister home, and he took care of her for two months, but she didn't make it. I never thought Ignatius would speak to me again."*

The complicated dynamic she'd observed between the two at Mordizan had been so much deeper than she could have guessed.

"Instead, he came to me right after she died. He looked . . . different. Nothing behind his eyes. He asked me to teach him how to do what I did. He said he wanted the sort of power that I had, to break people completely to my will. Despite my protests, he kept insisting. So . . . I taught him. I guess I thought he might learn to despise it as much as I did. Instead, he fell in love with it, with this sick, sadistic joy. I watched my friend turn into something I didn't recognize."

He wanted to cause pain the way he had felt pain. The nausea from earlier twisted in her gut again.

He took a deep breath. *"So, there it is. I tortured Lydia Tynsdale. I brought you to Mordizan. I made Ignatius what he is."* How was it possible for a mind-voice to sound choked? *"The things he did to you . . . he knew how much you meant to me. He went above and beyond, just to spite me. So I would feel what he felt."* His breath shuddered. *"Everything that happened to you was my fault."*

She closed her eyes, taking a moment before she responded. *Well, I'm not going to go off the deep end and take up a hobby of torture because you did horrible things to Ms. Tynsdale.*

Maybe she should feel angry. Heartbroken. Betrayed. Instead, she only felt sick. Marcus grew up in a world where even teenagers were forced to murder one another. Would she have done anything different with his background and situation?

Or was the greater miracle that he was here with her now, not leading the charges of victorious armies?

She didn't want to think about Marcus in that position. She could remember the sadistic gleam in Ignatius's eye, the glint reflecting from the fire he used to heat his tools . . .

She shuddered, dragging herself back and slamming the door closed on those memories. If she allowed them to surface, she might not be able to pull herself back to sanity.

No wonder Marcus had been so willing to join her, to go behind his father's back. He had obviously thought the world of his father, but after being coerced into doing such terrible things . . . Part of her heart broke for him and the weight of guilt he carried.

She struggled for words. *I understand the guilt you must feel, to some extent. I feel that guilt too.* She remembered how quick he was to comfort her every time she felt guilty for lives lost. Maybe he had been reassuring himself in the process. *But you can't lie to me. We're too deep into all of this for there to be any secrets.*

"No more secrets. I promise."

She looked over her shoulder at his rigid posture. He met her eyes, his expression grim. *"I'm trying to be a better person. With varying degrees of success."*

"And that's why I admire you." The wind ripped her words away, but she knew he could hear them in her thoughts as well. "I forgive you. We're still a team."

His expression softened, his eyes filled with something she had seen before, but perhaps not quite so strongly. Something that frightened her, made her want to tell him not to do that.

She turned back around. *Can you tell how close we are to Mordizan?*

"We'll want to touch down soon."

She directed the eagle to a clearing that Marcus pointed out. They dismounted, and she waved the bird away. "Okay." She took a deep breath. "Showtime."

Brinnie knew little of inter-estate politics, but luckily, Marcus did. When they had plotted that morning, he pointed out a way they could sneak in.

"A lot of refugees have been trickling into Mordizan from Dirklon after your father took over," Marcus had explained. "He gave them all a choice to join him or leave, and many left. What if we pretended to be refugees who lost our way and just now made it to Mordizan?"

From there, the plan had grown. They would need disguises, of course. Luckily, Brinnie had gained powers of both shapeshifting and spellcasting.

She closed her eyes and imagined her hair turning a lighter shade, becoming a chestnut brown. Her stature didn't need to change much, but she gave herself a more childish shape, her clothes shrinking to fit. Her eyes melted from striking blue to brown, and she darkened her skin and added a dash of freckles across her cheeks and nose.

She opened her eyes and twirled, showing off the form of a twelve-year-old girl. "What do you think?"

"Very cute and non-threatening." He slung their light pack off his shoulder and set the bag on the ground. "Well done."

"Now you." She scrutinized him, hand out as if wielding an invisible paint brush, pooling together the spellcasting and shapeshifting magic. First, she shrank his height and slimmed down his muscled physique to that of a normal pre-teen. She lightened his hair a shade and grew it longer, left his eyes the same, and added a matching dash of freckles. She nodded. "Good. So nice to meet you, twin brother Mark."

Twelve had seemed a good age to fly under the radar as just a couple of kids, while old enough to feasibly have made it to Mordizan on their own. The twin idea had been Brinnie's. "They say twins can practically read each other's minds," she'd pointed out. "That has tactical advantages if we're suspiciously good at communicating." She had also suggested they keep their aliases similar to their real names, in case one of them slipped up.

Marcus held out his newly-scrawnified arms one at a time, looking them over while using the other hand to hold up too-big pants. Unfortunately, Brinnie hadn't quite figured out changing clothes on someone else, only herself. "Nice to meet you as well, twin sister Brianna." He offered a slightly crooked smile.

Brinnie giggled. "Whoops. I definitely need to change your voice."

"What's wrong with my voice?" His brow crinkled.

She guffawed. "It doesn't match your body at all." She gave a few stomping steps, imitating him. "It's still all big-burly-I'm-tough-Marcus."

He raised an eyebrow. "Excuse me? Since when do I walk around like this?" He swung his arms like a gangly ape, taking awkward steps with his newly shorter legs.

"Since right now, apparently. I watched you do it." She laughed at his expression. "Okay, voice makeover. Just talk for a few minutes while I play with it."

"And say what?"

"I don't care. Describe that tree."

As Brinnie worked, Marcus said, "Okay, that's a tree. It's brown. Its leaves are all gone. Oh, very nice. Thank you for the falsetto."

She snickered. "Keep talking."

"Yes, ma'am. Oh good, I sound like Miss Burtle. Why?"

As he kept up the monologue, she tweaked his voice until his tone matched his tween form.

"Gotta say, there are some fun parts to these powers," Brinnie admitted.

"Speaking of your powers." His voice cracked, and he wrinkled his nose. "Don't miss this age. Anyway, you're going to have to pick one when we go in there. People can't see you using all different kinds."

She shrugged. "I'll be a shapeshifter, then. In case something slips or someone catches me asleep in my true form."

"Good." He picked up the bag. "Wardrobe change, and I'll be ready."

He exchanged his current garments for smaller garb they had brought, then stashed the bag under some roots. They tramped through the trees for a while until they emerged into the fields around Mordizan, lying fallow and dusted with snow. In the distance, the fortress loomed, a black blight against the blanket of white.

Brinnie shuddered, memories flooding back—dark dungeon, Ignatius's leer, searing pain, blood, the mangled body of Oswald Goddensfeld, flashes of fire . . .

She registered hands on her upper arms, her entire body trembling. A boy's voice. No, Marcus's new voice. His face swimming into focus. "Brinnie. Come back. You're here, in this field, with me, in the cold. Not there."

Why was her face wet? She lifted her hand to feel tears on her cheeks. She dashed them away, anger at herself surging through her. "Sorry. I'm fine. That was dumb."

The old, world-weary look in his eyes didn't match his youthful countenance. "It's not dumb. You should be allowed to grieve and recover. The fact that you're still going is a miracle."

"I don't have a choice, do I?" She offered a watery smile.

His lips formed a thin line. "I wish you did." He held out a hand. "Together?"

She took a deep breath. "Together."

They plodded, hand in hand, toward the dark fortress.

A makeshift guard post had sprung up beside the main road leading to the gates of the fortress. As Brinnie and Marcus approached, a guard in Mordizan colors stepped out to greet them. "State your business here."

"My sister and I are refugees from Dirklon, sir." Marcus gestured to Brinnie. "We were told to seek shelter at Mordizan."

Another guard leaned in the doorway of the squat building. "Took you a while to get here."

"We got lost." Brinnie widened her eyes, playing into her character. "Please, sir. We've been traveling for so long. We were in the human world, and there were things called cars . . ."

"Laying it on thick?"

I'm adorable and you know it.

The first guard waved to the one in the doorway. "They're here now. You can take them to refugee processing to be screened."

Brinnie forced herself not to fidget. What would screening consist of?

"Fine." The second guard pushed off the doorframe. "Come on."

The two of them followed along the road toward the fortress. *Hopefully screening is just a few questions. We have our story straight?*

"We only repeated it ten times."

Cool. But if this turns out to be Castelon all over again, all holds are off. I'm going after Nimue full-power.

"I'll be right behind you."

The soldier glanced down at them. "You two twins?"

They nodded in unison.

"My sister has twins. Younger than you, though." He looked them over. "Do your parents know where you are?"

Marcus shook his head. "They died resisting Drakon." He added a lip quiver, halted by a forward jut of his chin, like a boy trying to be strong.

Now who's laying it on thick?

"That's a shame." The soldier turned his attention back toward the fortress, as if bored now. "I've heard a couple of those stories."

Brinnie's stomach clenched. She wanted to think the people who had resisted her father's takeover were evil wizards dedicated to Mordizan's terrible cause.

But experience had taught her better.

The fortress grew closer, towering into the sky, dark stone blotting out the clouds as figures came into view on the walls. Brinnie's heart galloped, and she tried to keep her breathing even. *This isn't like before. You're so much more powerful than you were then.*

At the gates, their escort led them through and handed them off to another guard. "Refugees."

"I'll take them to the guards of the gate." The new soldier said nothing to the two of them, only turned and gave them a sharp gesture to follow.

Brinnie shot Marcus a wide-eyed glance. The specially trained guards who could detect any lie. *I didn't think they would be using them for this.*

"I didn't either." He scanned their surroundings, the guards and people occupying the courtyard. Behind them, the gate now led to the city of Mordizan, no farmlands in sight. Above, archers patrolled the walls. *"If things go south, we'll take to the skies and pray we can dodge those arrows and any magic they throw at us. Maybe hide in the city with new forms?"*

Agreed. Though the odds they could successfully escape the heavily fortified castle, even from the air . . .

The guard led them right to the guardhouse beside the gate. He stepped inside, Brinnie and Marcus trailing. "Betram, Stephan. Refugees to be questioned."

Brinnie perked up at the names. Inside, the familiar rotund form of Betram and stick-thin Stephan sat at the card table. *We might actually be able to make this work.*

The original guard wandered away to stand outside while Betram set down a hand of cards and gave them a jolly smile. "Well, welcome to Mordizan."

"You too. I mean, thank you." *Off to a great start, Brinnie.*

Betram laughed heartily. "No need to be nervous. Just have to ask you a couple of questions. Where did you come from?"

"Dirklon," Marcus responded.

Technically not untrue, though Dirklon had been several stops ago.

Betram's brow wrinkled, and he frowned. Apparently not close enough to the truth.

As Betram opened his mouth to say something, Brinnie glanced toward the door. The guard didn't seem to be looking.

For one second, she flashed to her true form, put a finger to her lips, and then settled back into the character of refugee Brianna.

His eyes widened. Stephan's mouth dropped open.

Betram cleared his throat, glancing between Brinnie and Marcus. "I see. And why are you here?"

Brinnie took over. "We're seeking refuge. We were hoping to see Lady Nimue Drakon."

He nodded slowly, processing her truth and lie. "Well, that won't be necessary. We can handle your needs right here without bothering the lady. One last question. Are your intentions here peaceful?"

The most important question. She straightened her shoulders and looked straight into his eyes. "We don't want to hurt anyone."

His expression relaxed. "They're fine," he called to the guard. "Send them along."

Stephan's wide eyes ping-ponged between Brinnie and Betram, but he said nothing.

The original guard gave another sharp gesture. "All right. You two, follow me."

As they exited, Marcus shot her a shocked glance. *"How did you do that?"*

Old friends. They've helped me out before.

"Traitors among the guards?"

She almost laughed aloud at his indignant tone.

"I mean." His chuckle, in his usual voice, floated into her mind. *"That's a good thing. Sometimes I forget they're not my guards anymore."*

The guard led them to the gate and pointed. "Go down this main street, then take a right at the broom shop. Keep going to the end of the street, then turn right again. You'll find the refugee encampment. They'll help you there."

"Thank you, sir." Marcus bobbed his head. Then he and Brinnie stepped through the gate and into the city.

The vibrant crowds that once filled the streets had diminished. Wizards still entered shops, still led floating items or exotic pets, but the atmosphere felt different. Subdued.

"I can't believe that worked." Marcus wove through the wizards on Mordizan's main street.

Brinnie followed his lead. *Praise the Lord for good old Betram.*

"I understand you made friends with him, but why would he risk himself to help you?"

Not shockingly, humans like the guards aren't a fan of Mordred and his kill-the-humans ideas. She ducked a floating basket. *I made it known that I'm anti-Mordred and anti-human-killing, and we got along.*

They turned right at the broom shop and continued onto a smaller road. *"You make friends everywhere you go."*

I try. She rubbed her arm. *Speaking of, while we're here, I'm keeping an eye out for Lana.*

He pressed his lips together but nodded. *"She may no longer be at Mordizan."*

I know. But if we get any chance to get into the fortress itself, I'm going in.

After the second right, shops grew smaller and gave way to dilapidated houses. "I'm assuming this isn't the nice part of Mordizan."

"The worst part, actually." Marcus moved closer to her protectively. "And it's getting dark. Stay close."

She chuckled. "We were on the battlefield a couple days ago. I think I can take care of myself in a rough neighborhood."

They passed through without incident and emerged into a square littered with ramshackle tents. A few people shuffled about, pulling laundry from where it hung on ropes, dipping water from a well in the center of the square before plodding inside their tents with listless expressions. None took notice of Marcus and Brinnie standing awkwardly in the street.

"I thought we did a better job taking care of the refugees." Marcus scanned their surroundings with his mouth in a grim line. *"I was told they were given shelter and provisions. This doesn't count."*

Brinnie decided not to comment on the wisdom of trusting Mordizan's promises. *Honestly surprised they offered shelter at all. Look. It's only women and kids. All the men must have been taken for war.*

Marcus nodded. *"They were beginning to talk about the draft when I left. If they followed through, men and unmarried women ages eighteen to seventy are required to fight. Plus, they encouraged men older than that to join."*

Seventy? They're making old people fight?

His lips twitched. *"Seventy isn't that old for a wizard when you live a couple hundred years."*

A fact she didn't like to think about much. Sure, the wizards in her family hadn't seemed to age a day past thirty-five, but she'd chalked that up to good genetics before she learned better. The thought that the wizards in her family were still comparatively quite young, the fact that she might have another two hundred years to watch history grow and change . . .

Maybe part of the reason wizards struggled to empathize with humans had to do with how fleeting their lives seemed in comparison. Especially to the thousand years someone like Mordred or Morgana might live.

"Well." She squared her shoulders. "Let's find a place to establish base." *We can figure out a way to get Nimue's attention tomorrow.*

As they wandered into camp, a matronly woman carrying a dented bucket caught sight of them. "You two." Her accent seemed something akin to Scottish. "Are you new here?"

Time to turn on the charm. Brinnie nodded, all fearful wide-eyed innocence.

The woman set the bucket on the ground with a clank. "Where are you from?"

"Dirklon," Marcus answered.

"Didn't know Dirklon refugees were still coming in." She put a hand on her hip. "Where are your parents?"

Brinnie scrunched up her face. "They . . . they're . . ."

"They died trying to defend Dirklon." Marcus looked down as if heartbroken.

"You poor things. You can stay in my tent with me." She hefted her pail. "There's not much food, but I'll make sure you get some."

"Thank you, ma'am." Marcus added a convincing waver to his voice.

"You can call me Miss Trish." She set off across the square. "Now what are your names?"

"I'm Mark, and this is Brianna." Marcus cleared his throat. "Miss Trish, we heard that Lady Nimue is helping people find their families. Is that true?"

"Well, yes, son, but only if you have family to find."

"Our aunt. We think she's somewhere in the city." Brinnie bounced on her small feet. She had perhaps been a bit proud of that little not-quite lie. *We're looking for my aunt and Nimue. They just happen to be the same person.*

"Yes, yes, you are very clever and hilarious."

If you don't want to enjoy irony with me, you don't have to listen to my thoughts. She stuck her tongue out at him behind the woman's back, and he rolled his eyes, lips twitching in a suppressed smile.

"It would be great if you could find your aunt." Miss Trish switched the bucket to her other hand. "But Lady Nimue is so busy organizing the draft, I don't think you'll be able to see her. You're lucky you aren't a few years older, or you'd both be drafted, too."

"We can make that happen if it means getting to Nimue."

Agreed. "Do they come here looking for people?"

"About once a week. They came last a few days ago." Miss Trish stopped outside a tent that looked more like a blanket stuck on poles. "Here we are."

Brinnie glanced at Marcus. *Can we wait a few days to try? Or should we take more drastic measures?*

"If we want to get both of us into the fortress, I think this is our best bet."

Miss Trish pulled aside the curtain, revealing another couple of blankets on the ground and the charred remnants of a small fire. "Make yourselves cozy."

They thanked her, then huddled together and wrapped one of the blankets around the both of them. The woman took the other, and soon began snoring.

We still might not see Nimue even if we get ourselves taken in by the draft.

Marcus's brow crinkled—quite adorably. She'd done a good job on these characters. *"True. Maybe we'll just have to cause such a problem at the draft that she gets called in."*

Brinnie smirked. *Lucky for us, I am very good at causing problems.*

CHAPTER
FIFTEEN

The next two days passed at a snail's pace. In the morning, Marcus and Brinnie accompanied Miss Trish to a food cart that rolled up every morning to receive the day's meager rations of bread, potatoes, maybe some dried meat, and a bit of firewood. Miss Trish sent them off for most of the day to "look for their aunt," which they took as an opportunity to walk around the walls of the fortress and the main roads of the city, scoping out where guards had been stationed.

"The same basic patterns they've always kept, with the added security the forces were taught for times of active war or danger." Marcus gave a half-laugh. "You would think my father would know better. I guess he didn't expect anyone who escaped Mordizan to be crazy enough to come back."

"Crazy is our specialty."

They wandered back toward the camp as the afternoon turned to evening. Brinnie's feet ached. Being in a different body didn't seem to allay the aches and pains of her true form, something Ms. Tynsdale had warned her about. She remembered the woman's serious tone. *"Now you remember, just because you can jump into a different appearance doesn't mean you can burn through bodies. You get hurt in one, you're hurt in all of them, even if it isn't visible to the outside eye. You only* look *different."*

She found herself wishing, again, that her education hadn't been neglected. She had all of this magic, but little knowledge of the hows and whys. *Maybe someday, I'll spend like five years solely studying magic.*

Marcus held out an arm, stopping her and jolting her out of her thoughts. "Look."

A familiar form stood with his back to them, facing a refugee woman and gesturing as he talked.

Ignatius.

"What on earth is he doing here?" Marcus muttered.

Brinnie's heart pounded, her palms clammy. "I don't know. There's no possible way he could've found out where we were going."

"I'll get closer and see if I can find out." Marcus started forward.

"Wait." Brinnie put a shaky hand on his arm and took a deep breath. "I can do it."

They stepped into an alley, and Brinnie turned invisible. Striding toward Ignatius, she attempted to calm her raging heart. *This is stupid. He has zero power over you here. This isn't the dungeons.*

His voice reached her. "My own father tried to have me killed. Some harebrained idea that I wanted to kill him."

"My," the woman breathed, eyes wide. "Such terrible luck."

As Brinnie rounded the two of them, she saw the hard set to Ignatius's jaw. "Not luck," he said. "It was all the shadowmaster's doing. And it's her fault Mordred cast me, his finest extractor, aside. I've vowed to take my revenge, if it's the last thing I do."

The woman shuddered. "I've heard her powers rival Mordred's."

Ignatius snorted. "She's nothing but a young girl who doesn't know how to use her magic. She'll die easily."

Wow. Rude, and untrue.

"You could kill him now. Dramatic irony."

Shh, I'm listening.

"Certainly, you won't find her in Mordizan itself." The woman's brow crinkled.

"No, I may not find her here, but I might find followers who will join me in the hunt. Forget this ridiculous war. If we kill her, we have the victory assured. Who else can stand against Mordred? Whoever kills her will have their name sung for a thousand years."

The woman nodded, entranced by his words. "I would join you, with stakes like that."

"There's more." Brinnie scooted closer as he leaned forward and lowered his voice. "I know what will kill her. The Case of the Master Key. Get it, and she's as good as dead."

"Where is it?"

"Mordred has the Case locked up here in the fortress. He's too busy with his dreams of conquest to use it properly." He clenched a fist. "If I can get into the fortress and take it, I'll kill her for sure.

That's where you come in. I'm a spellcaster. With the help of a shapeshifter like you, I can disguise myself to get into the fortress. Will you help me?"

The woman gasped. "Well, I don't know. To go against Mordred . . ."

Brinnie caught movement out of the corner of her eye. Marcus poked around the corner of the building and made a stabbing motion.

I can't just kill him in the middle of Mordizan.

"He's trying to kill you. *If he manages to get the Case . . . You can beat him to the punch."*

And have a body on our hands? We'll blow our cover.

"Fine." He melted around the corner, out of sight. His voice rang gruff. *"After what he's already done to you . . . I hate to see him still walking this earth."*

Let's get an answer from Nimue, then you can murder your friend to your heart's content.

He's not my friend. He hesitated. *That Ignatius died with his sister.*

Her heart clenched. *Marcus, I'm sorry.*

A mental sigh. *"No. I'm sorry. For what I made him become."*

Ignatius stalked away scowling, apparently unable to convince the woman to help him. Brinnie shrank out of his path, and her chest loosened. He wasn't getting into the fortress yet.

She rejoined Marcus, and the two of them resumed their retreat to Miss Trish's tent.

Right before they entered the square, Brinnie stopped. "Hold on. How did you know what Ignatius was saying back there?"

"I . . ." He paused, brow furrowed. "I'm not sure."

Her hands rose to her ears. "Are we sharing ears now too? Not just brains?"

"Still brains, I think." He scratched his head. "I didn't even think about it. It was like when your voice pops up in my head, but I could hear the conversation as you heard it. Maybe when your mind processed what you heard, I heard it too?"

"That's freaky." She started walking again. "I don't necessarily want to hear everything you hear. Or have you listening in on my every interaction."

"We'll have to work on controlling the mind-melding and making sure we have permission first." He rubbed the back of his neck. "I'm sorry for all the times I've just popped in. I'm working on being more intentional and paying attention to my own thoughts."

She shrugged. "I've popped into your head too. We're both learning." She shot him a smile. "I do appreciate the concern though. We'll both work on it."

Miss Trish squatted in front of her tent, holding a small, dented pot over a pitiful flame. Without speaking, Marcus stuck his hand underneath and held out a ball of fire.

"Thanks, lad." She swirled the contents, what appeared to be beans in a soupy liquid. "Didn't find your aunt today?"

"No." Brinnie sat down opposite from her with what she hoped was an endearing smile. "Any word from your son?"

She had only been able to catch bits and pieces, but from what she understood, Miss Trish's only son had left at age nineteen to join the army. Her husband had died when the son was a young boy, so she'd been living alone ever since.

"None. Little stinker probably doesn't even know I'm here."

"I'm sorry, Miss Trish." Brinnie clasped her hands in her lap, feeling awkward.

"Ach, at least I have you two to keep me company, poor as it is." Her chuckle belied her gruff words.

Marcus stiffened, looking past Brinnie. She raised an eyebrow at him.

"Ignatius."

She forced herself to turn her head slowly, glancing over her shoulder. Sure enough, Ignatius made his way toward them. She tensed. *Do you think he knows?*

"He can't. What reason would he have to even suspect?"

Brinnie curled into herself and scooted toward Miss Trish as Ignatius stopped in front of their fire. "Hello." He scanned the three of them. "Is anyone a shapeshifter here?"

"She is." Miss Trish jerked her head toward Brinnie. "Why do you ask?"

Ignatius offered Brinnie a smile that he probably meant to be kindly, but it only oozed smarm. "I'm looking for a shapeshifter to help me." He returned his attention to Miss Trish. "Could I borrow your daughter for a minute?"

"She's not mine." Miss Trish shrugged. "I'd ask her."

Ignatius turned to Brinnie. "What do you say? Would you help me out?"

The image of a shy girl shrinking back wasn't completely an act. "No, thank you."

He cocked his head. "No?"

"Don't want to." She fiddled with her shirt hem.

"Brianna." Marcus adopted a scolding tone. "Why won't you help the nice man?"

She shot him a glare. *What are you doing?*

"If we help him get the Case, we can steal it from him. Then no one will have power over you—including Mordred."

She rolled the idea around in her mind. A heist within a heist. They were here in Mordizan anyway . . . "Okay." She kept her voice timid. "What do you want me to do?"

"Nothing much. When the soldiers come down here for the draft, I just want you to make me look like someone else." He put his hands on his knees, bending down to her level. "Do you think you could do that? I'm a spellcaster, so I'll help you."

Miss Trish's nose scrunched as if she smelled something foul. "Trying to escape the draft?"

"Something like that." He didn't take his attention from Brinnie. "What do you say?"

She shrugged. "Okay."

Ignatius held out his hand, and she forced herself to shake it. Forced herself not to think about other times he had touched her, the pain that had followed . . .

His voice came from a distance. "A pleasure doing business with you, Brianna. I'll find you on draft day."

As he walked away, Miss Trish sighed. "I guess I'd ask the same if I were a spellcaster, but it's still a shame."

Brinnie rubbed her hand on her pants. *Okay, what's the plan? How do we get the Case from him?*

While Miss Trish passed around the bowl of beans, Marcus kept up the mental conversation. *"We'll let him do the dirty work of stealing it, since we don't know where the Case is, and hopefully he does. He'll go into the fortress on the same day that we do. Then on his way out, we'll catch him and take it."*

Brinnie swallowed some bland, watery beans, and burned her

tongue. She passed them to Miss Trish, suppressing a wince, and subtly attempted to heal her scorched mouth, but nothing happened. Apparently, the magic didn't work on herself. Good to know. *Back to the subject at hand. I think we need a bit more than that. How are we going to catch him?*

"Our plan will have to change a little. I'll cause the scene and get to Nimue. You can turn invisible and follow Ignatius."

Brinnie nodded slowly, then realized what she was doing and stopped. *Once I take it from him, I'll head to the dungeons for Lana. Then I'll find you in the fortress and we can convince Nimue together.*

"Brinnie . . ."

She gave him a hard look. *If we make it into the fortress and she's in the dungeons, I can't leave without her. She saved my sister. And even more important, she's my friend.*

"You can try. But if you don't find her, get out. We can keep in contact with our minds."

She would search the entire fortress if she needed to. She owed it to Lana. The last she'd seen, guards had been dragging her friend deeper into the dungeons. *Will the mind-speaking work that far away?*

"Worth a shot. We already know that we don't have to be in the same room, and as we saw today, it's only getting stronger."

Miss Trish slurped a mouthful of beans. "You two are awfully quiet."

Brinnie smiled sweetly. "Just enjoying sitting here. Thank you for dinner." She glanced at Marcus. *Let's hope this crazy plan works.*

The day of the draft, the two of them slipped out of the tent before dawn. Brinnie glanced back at Miss Trish, fast asleep. *I feel bad leaving her without saying goodbye.*

"There's no way to swap appearances in front of her." Marcus ushered Brinnie away with a gentle hand on her back. *"She'll assume we've gone with Ignatius."*

And wonder why we never came back. She sighed. *Maybe someday we'll be able to tell her the truth.*

The moon still hung in the sky over the dirty, ramshackle camp as they made their way through the maze of tents to a hidden alleyway.

Brinnie turned to Marcus and held out her hands, then closed her eyes. *Here we go.* She imagined the character she had created aging, growing to about twenty years old. She opened her eyes to admire her work.

An older but still adorably be-freckled Marcus rolled his neck and stretched. His clothes were too short by several inches, but in wartime and in a refugee camp, Brinnie doubted anyone would think ill-fitting attire unusual. "This is much better. I felt cramped in that little body."

She took a deep breath. "I'll wait for Ignatius at the edge of the square. I'll change his form, then follow him invisibly. You'll get yourself drafted, I'll follow him until he gets the Case, then I'll mug him, take it, and meet you . . . wherever you are."

It was probably the worst plan—or lack thereof—they'd ever concocted.

He nodded. "I'll cause a scene and get Nimue to come in and arbitrate. Somehow, I'll get her alone and try to convince her to come with us."

"Well." She sighed. "That's what we've got. Good luck."

With a sarcastic salute, she turned invisible and made her way back to the square.

Soon, she spotted Ignatius's approaching form. She ducked around a corner, returned to visibility, and took a deep breath, trying to calm her racing heart. Then she stepped out in front of him. "I'm here, Mr. Ignatius."

"Good." He paused, and his eyes narrowed. "How do you know my name?"

Stupid, stupid, stupid. She tried to remain calm. "Didn't you say?"

"No. I specifically didn't." He grabbed her shoulders, pushing her back into the alley and slamming her against a wall. "Who are you, girl? How do you know my name?"

Rough wood dug into her back from the building behind her. Panic threatened to freeze her mind, but she fought against it. *Absolutely not. You're better than this. Think.*

An idea occurred.

She morphed into the older version of Brianna, around twenty, like the new version of Mark, and pushed herself away from the wall, wresting from his grasp. "I know who you are because I overheard you talking with that woman yesterday." She straightened and brushed off her sleeves. "You didn't think I was really a child, did you?"

He stepped back. "Why were you in disguise?"

"I have my brother to care for." She shrugged. "Couldn't let myself be taken by the draft."

He nodded slowly, expression still wary. "So you know what I really want?"

"And I want to help." She crossed her arms.

"Why?"

Good question, think fast. "I want my name known when the shadowmaster dies."

He raised an eyebrow and laughed. "Hungry for fame?"

"No." She rolled her eyes. "I want my family to hear about me and be able to find me."

"Ah." He nodded, a smirk growing. "Deal. Change my form, and I'll be sure your name is known."

She gave a sharp laugh. "Nice try. I don't trust you. You'll forget in your hunt for the shadowmaster. I want to come with you."

"You are *not* coming with me." His nose wrinkled in disdain.

"Fine, then." She turned away. "Find yourself another shapeshifter."

"Wait." His arm shot out, and he grabbed her shoulder.

Before she could even register what she was doing, she smacked his arm down with one hand, twisted, and shoved him with the other.

He stumbled back with a yelp and hit the same wall he'd pinned her against, then straightened and stared at her, mouth slightly open.

She set her jaw. "Don't. Touch me."

"Fine, crazy woman." He blew out a dramatic breath. "You can come with me. Besides, I'll need someone to change my form back at the end so Brynna knows who it is that kills her."

"Deal. Ready?"

He rolled his eyes. "Yes, I suppose. Let's get out of sight."

The transformation took longer and worked in a more clunky, roundabout way using Ignatius's spellcasting rather than her own, but by the end, he stood before her as a shorter, thicker man with dark hair and a short beard. "There." She smirked. "I think I'll call you Iggy."

"No," he growled. "Come on."

They returned to the front of the camp as the sun rose. Soon, a squad of guards came tromping down the street. "Ho, there!" one of them called. "You two. State your age."

Ignatius stepped forward. "Thirty-two." He tripped on the words a bit, as if he'd forgotten to think of what age this character appeared.

"Twenty," Brinnie offered.

The soldier planted his spear butt on the ground. "By order of Master Vorath, both of you are drafted into the army."

Ignatius straightened his shoulders. "We just got here for that purpose."

The man gave him a longsuffering look, as if he'd heard the lie a thousand times. "Fall in."

Brinnie and Ignatius stayed behind with one of the guards as the others made a sweep of the camp. Brinnie kept her eyes peeled. About ten men and women were dragged out of their tents and driven from alleyways to be herded into line with Ignatius and Brinnie. Finally, Brinnie saw one of the guards prodding Marcus along, and she breathed a sigh of relief. *Good. We're both here.*

Then she stiffened. Marcus's new form was an older version of the previous one . . . just as hers was an older version of the female twin. Though Ignatius might not have noticed the similarities between her as a young girl and Marcus as an adult twin, he certainly would now, as soon as Marcus was herded into their small huddle. Her lies would be exposed.

We have a situation. Changes incoming, Marcus.

"Got it."

While the guard's back was turned, Brinnie jerked her chin toward Marcus. His hair darkened, and his form filled out from gangly to a bit more sturdy. Not huge changes, but enough that he and Brinnie weren't clearly two sides of the same coin.

The guard glanced back at Marcus, looked forward, then did a double take, brow furrowed. "Where's the kid from before?"

Luckily, Ignatius seemed to be looking elsewhere. Brinnie could hear Marcus clear his throat. "Uh, it's still me, sir."

The guard's eyes narrowed. "I thought you said you were a fire wizard."

Oh, no. She hadn't counted on an observant guard—or one that might have asked Marcus his power already.

"It was a joke." Marcus shrugged with a goofy grin. "I meant that I'm a shapeshifter."

The guard held up a hand and blasted him with fire.

"Everyone and their dog is a fire wizard these days," Marcus griped.

I've made a huge mistake.

"The game isn't up yet."

Once the fire died away, Marcus stood in front of the guard, completely unharmed. He chuckled and shrugged. "Just kidding again, haha."

The guard stepped back with wide eyes. "Here! To me!" he cried. "I think I've found the shadowmaster!"

Still think the game isn't up?

"Fair, this is pretty bad."

Guards came rushing forward, leaping on Marcus and pinning him to the ground as he protested his innocence.

"What?" Ignatius's face turned red. "She's here?"

Brinnie jumped in front of him before he could rush headlong into the fray. "Wait. You can't kill her now, in front of everyone. She won't know it was you. Think of your perfect revenge."

Ignatius's fist shook as if he was physically restraining himself as two guards dragged an unconscious Marcus upright between them.

Oh, great. So much for the plan, pathetic as it was. Now she needed to launch a rescue.

"I'll kill her," Ignatius muttered. "I'll kill her slowly. She'll die in agony."

"Yes, she will. Just think." Brinnie turned her attention back to Ignatius. "She'll be locked up in the fortress. You can kill her without her resistance."

"Move out." The guards prodded them forward.

As the soldiers herded the group through the streets of Mordizan, early risers gave them quick, pitying glances before hurrying on their way. Brinnie glanced at Marcus's flopping head as he was dragged along by his arms and surrounded by guards. *I'm so sorry, Marcus. I didn't mean for that to happen.*

"Don't worry about it. This works too."

Marcus! Her eyes widened. He remained lifeless as ever. *You're okay?*

"I'm fine. They gave me a good knock upside the head, but I've got a thick skull. If they think I'm you, hopefully Nimue will get called in, since she's in charge of all this."

So, we just . . . caused a scene a bit early.

"I suppose I should thank you for saving me the trouble."

The tension in her shoulders eased. *Okay. Still on track. We can make this work.*

As they approached the gates, two guards jogged ahead. The remaining soldiers ushered the group into the courtyard in a single file line between guards who scanned them with calculating eyes. Brinnie forced her shoulders to relax. These fortress guards, trained to know everything about everyone, would recognize her or Ignatius in their normal forms, but like this, they were safe—as long as the guards asked no questions.

Luckily, they didn't. Once within the walls, Brinnie saw the two guards that had gone ahead returning, a familiar figure on their heels.

Nimue strode toward them, knives strapped to her hips and a short black cloak flapping in her wake. She scanned the group. "You have the shadowmaster?"

The guards carried Marcus forward. "We think so," said one. "He—er, she—displayed an ability to shapeshift *and* repel fire."

Nimue bent, squinting at Marcus's face. "Probably some sort of spellwork." She straightened. "Use caution anyway. Bring the prisoner to the dungeons for questioning." She waved them off, already striding away in a different direction. "I'll meet you there shortly."

As a contingent of guards carried Marcus off in one direction, the others directed the rest of the group to the right, toward the military side of the fortress. They passed near the inner wall, and Ignatius whispered, "Now."

Before Brinnie knew what he was doing, Ignatius drew the sword of the guard next to him and slew the man where he stood. As the guards shouted and turned on Ignatius, Brinnie started running for the inner gate, only feet away, Ignatius right behind her.

As he caught up, he took the lead. "This way!"

Where else? She rolled her eyes, sliding under the crossed spears of guards manning the inner gate. Ignatius smashed through them, sword swinging, and darted right.

Brinnie followed. He took a quick turn, rounded a column, and slipped behind a pennant hanging on the wall.

She slid in behind him into a small, hidden alcove as shouts and clangs echoed in the corridor behind them. Ignatius pushed in a stone, and the back wall opened a crack. Without a word, they both shimmied through.

He shoved the wall back into place and leaned against it, panting. "You could have given me a body in a little better shape."

She smirked but forced herself *not* to inform him that a body's strength, stamina, and most other capabilities remained the same regardless of shifts in appearance. "Would you like to return to your true form?"

"Please."

She held out her hand. As she felt him release the spell holding her magic in place, she transformed him back. "Where to now?"

"Now I don't need you anymore." He lifted the sword, ready to strike.

CHAPTER SIXTEEN

"Wait!" She backed away, but her shoulders hit the wall behind her. "How are you going to get out of the fortress without a disguise?"

"I don't need to get out." His knuckles whitened on the sword hilt. "Once I kill Brynna, my revenge will be complete."

With that, he swung.

She ducked, hitting the ground. The sword clanged against stone, swiping more than a foot over her head. *He can't see.* His aim was off in the dark passageway.

"And you don't want to live after your revenge?" She inched along the wall, eyes on his blade.

He swung again, a wild miss. "There's nothing for me to live for."

"No one you care about?"

"No one." The sword swiped closer, but she dodged by several inches. "They're all dead . . . or they betrayed me."

Great. Arguing with Ignatius about his will to live. Not what she thought she'd be doing today. "What about Marcus Vorath?"

"Don't say that name to me," he snarled. His eyes darted, trying to pick her out in the dark. "He betrayed me twice over. He killed my sister *and* sided with the shadowmaster."

Brinnie ducked out of the way of another clumsy swing. "I don't mean *befriend* him." She adopted a smirking, sinister tone. "I mean, don't you want to see the look on his face when you personally tell him that you murdered her?"

He hesitated, sword lowering. "You're a sadistic wench, aren't you?"

"I want to live. You want revenge. Don't kill me, and we'll get along splendidly."

His mouth opened and he seemed about to protest, but instead he gave a sharp nod. "Fine." He dropped his sword arm to his side. "But don't get in my way." He whipped around, heading down the passage. "We've wasted enough time."

Brinnie stood motionless for a moment, thrown off by his impetuous change of mind. *He's unhinged. Even more than before.*

She followed him through the twists and turns of the passageways. He didn't seem to know them as well as Marcus did. He hesitated at forks and felt along the walls, stopping frequently and backtracking more than once.

This could take a while.

Something tickled at the corners of Brinnie's mind. Curious, she invited the sensation in.

She stifled a gasp at the sudden shift. She stood in a dungeon cell, facing Nimue. Yet her feet kept moving, following Ignatius in the passageway. She wasn't just hearing double—she was looking through Marcus's eyes.

In the cell, Nimue stared at her through the bars. "Marcus? You expect me to believe that?"

"It's true." A male's voice, coming out of her mouth. She glanced at Ignatius to see if he noticed, but apparently the encounter only took place inside her own head. "Give the wards in this dungeon a few moments to work, and I'm sure the disguise will wear off." Her shoulders—his shoulders—shrugged. "Ask me something only Marcus would know."

Brinnie's legs wobbled a bit, and nausea grew in the pit of her stomach, like motion sickness. Seeing double apparently threw off her proprioception.

Nimue crossed her arms. "What was the name of that pathetic rag you carried everywhere when you were little?"

"Don't laugh at me." Marcus sighed. "Mr. Snuggles was not a pathetic rag, he was a handsome rabbit."

Her eyes widened. "What on earth are you doing here?"

"I'm here to talk to you."

Nimue glanced back at two guards Brinnie could make out in the hall behind her. "You may leave."

"But, my lady . . ."

"That's an order."

She turned back to Marcus as the guards retreated. Once they had passed out of sight, Nimue gripped the bars and hissed, "What were you thinking? Have you gone mad?"

Marcus gestured to his appearance. "This was the only way to get in to talk with you. Without revealing myself to everyone else, of course. I'll admit the dungeon bit wasn't part of the original plan."

"Not that." She waved his explanation away. "I meant what you did for Brinnie." Her voice rose. "What sort of idiotic impulse led you to *attack Mordred* and jump off a cliff?"

Brinnie tripped on an uneven stone, then tuned back into the conversation.

"You were the one who warned me that Mordred might have my father and me killed. But I don't think that's the end of this. Mordred isn't our salvation. He's our destruction."

"Sure, Mordred isn't the perfect solution, but we've talked about this before. At length." Nimue shoved a hand through her hair. "If some juvenile crush on a pretty girl has made you lose all your senses—"

"I think you know me *and* her better than that."

She blew out a breath. "Do you know how long I worked to bring him back? He's finally doing what we could never do. The enchantment wizards are all but destroyed."

"And then? What happens once they're gone?" His words cracked, and when he spoke again, his normal Marcus voice had returned. The magic was fading. "What happens once Mordred takes his revenge, wipes the world of humans, and it's just us? Suddenly Mordizan morphs from a militant dictatorship to a place of harmony? Mordred and my father retire as benevolent leaders?"

"At least it's better than this." She threw out an arm. "No more hiding, no more curse, no more war . . ."

"Until the Masters start warring against each other for control of the new world order."

Ignatius's voice startled Brinnie out of her eavesdropping. "We're here."

They faced an iron door with no handle. The same room Mordred had taken her to when he first showed her the Case.

Mordred must not have expected Brinnie to be stupid enough to sneak *back* into Mordizan.

Ignatius pushed at the door, but it didn't budge. He ran his hands along the surface and around the edges. "Do you see a keyhole or anything?"

"I've seen doors like this before. Let me try." Brinnie pressed her hand against the door, remembering the word Mordred had used. One she had committed to memory, just in case. "*Agoraf.*"

The door clicked and swung open.

They stepped into the room, and Brinnie blinked as her eyes adjusted to the brightness of the light orbs offering illumination. There, on the dais in the center of the room, sat the Case.

"Finally." Ignatius strode forward.

"Wait!" Brinnie held out a hand too late.

Enchanted crossbows nestled near the ceiling twanged. One of the shafts buried itself in Ignatius's chest near his collarbone, another in his side, sending him stumbling with a yell. His sword clanged on stone as it fell from his grasp. His knees hit the ground and he clutched at the wounds, blood trickling over his hands. "Curse Mordred." Air hissed between his teeth.

Brinnie stood on the threshold, watching the stain of blood spread along Ignatius's abdomen. The shaft had plunged deep, likely hitting important organs.

She could grab the Case and run. He would have no hope of stopping her. She didn't even have to wait to steal it from him later. The perfect opportunity.

But her legs didn't move. Ignatius fell to his side, gasping. This time, he lay at *her* feet, broken and bleeding. At her mercy.

She had the power to save him.

Anger crashed through her at the thought. When had he even once shown her mercy? His one driving motivation remained to kill her.

A scene arose in her mind, in which she stepped forward and revealed her true form. Where she retrieved the Case and stood over Ignatius as he gasped his last breaths. Where she whispered, *"You lost."*

He deserved it. After everything he had done. Maybe if she watched him die, even delivered the final blow, the nightmares of powerlessness would ease. She wouldn't wake up in a cold sweat, convinced she had been dragged into his sadistic chamber once again. She could prove to herself that he held no power over her.

But if she deserved to kill him, how many people deserved to kill Marcus? Dad?

Even her?

To how many people did she owe a blood debt?

She dropped to her knees beside him with a guttural growl of frustration. "Hold on. I can fix this."

"How?" His eyes had begun to glaze. "It would take a healer." He clenched his teeth, breath rattling. "May Brynna be cursed and die a long and painful death."

Brinnie's jaw set. "Just hold still." Taking less care than she should, she yanked the first shaft from his side.

He screamed as blood spewed from the wound. Brinnie pressed her hands to the ragged puncture and concentrated on flesh melding back together, muscle weaving, skin joining. Before he had a chance to react, she yanked out the second shaft and set to work on the wound to his chest. She glanced over her shoulder at the crossbows, and just to be safe, uttered Mordred's deactivation phrase. "*Sefyll i lawr.*"

She turned back to Ignatius and removed her bloody hands.

His jaw hung slack as he touched his side, his shoulder. His wide eyes traveled up to her face. "No. You can't . . . that's not . . ."

She stood and dropped her disguise, returning to her true form. Ready to defend herself if necessary, she allowed shadows to gather around her, flame to dance along her fingertips. "Hello, Ignatius."

"Brynna." He scrambled backward, pulling himself up along the wall. "You changed that man in the camp. You were here with me all along! I . . . I could have killed you." His legs wobbled. "I should have killed you, back there, when I had a chance."

"You could have tried." She took a step back and dropped her arms to her sides. "And I could have left you here to die." She inhaled a shaky breath. "Please, Ignatius. Haven't we all hurt each other enough? Don't you see that our common enemy is Mordred?"

He growled and lunged toward her, but she stepped out of the way. "You robbed me of everything."

"And you were innocent?" She barked an incredulous laugh. "You tortured me for months on end. What do you think killing me is going to do to hurt me that you haven't already done?"

He clenched his hands, breath ragged. "Not just you. Marcus." He swung a fist.

She ducked easily out of his way. "He hurt your sister. You hurt me. You're both traumatized wrecks. This is only going to make it worse." He swung again, and she shoved his arm away. "You can keep going with this system of hurting people back and forth, or you can realize that Marcus was a scared kid, you were a scared kid, your sister was a scared kid." She ducked another blow. "We inherited a messed-up system where no one wins." He lashed out with a weak right hook, and she caught his wrist, staring into his eyes. "The only way any of us will win is to tear the whole thing down. We're not enemies." Her tone softened. "We're victims."

His chest heaved with shaking breaths as he stared back at her. He could easily rip his arm away, but he didn't. Instead, he slowly lowered it. Stepped back. His words came out barely above a whisper. "You should have let me die." His voice rose. "I have nothing. Nothing left to live for. No position, cast out of my home, only my senile father turning our once-respected estate into a laughingstock because he's too mad with grief to do anything but talk to plants."

She had no argument. She had wanted, so much, to let him die. Part of her wanted to offer to do just that. To leave him to rot in this underground chamber. They could both get what they wanted.

We don't just let people die.

She took a deep breath. "Why did your sister do it?"

"Excuse me?"

"Why was your sister willing to risk her life?" She stepped forward. "Was it because she had nothing to live for? Or was it because she thought there was something worth dying for?" Goosebumps rose on her arms. "Was it to lay the foundation for you to carry the torch farther than she could?"

She didn't know if she was right. Maybe they had been diametrically opposed. Maybe the siblings had never spoken on the subject. She could be completely off base.

His expression cracked. He looked away, a hand over his face. "I was never the man she thought I was." His breath shuddered. "She was too good for any of us." He turned back to Brinnie, expression hard once more. "That goodness, that weakness, is why she died."

"Or maybe." Her voice came out softly, barely over a whisper. "Maybe it was because goodness isn't weak. It's strong. It's brave, and risky, and revolutionary." Flames sparked on her fingers. "And once given life, one spark can spread like wildfire." The flames grew. "Your sister showed Marcus something was wrong. Then he saved me. Together, we're trying to save all of us. She was the spark, and we're the flame." She stared him down. "Are you part of the flame, or are you going to be the kindling? Because I would like nothing better than to burn you down where you stand."

Orange and red reflected in his wet eyes, transfixed on her flickering fingers. Then he lifted his gaze to hers. "Mordizan killed my sister," he whispered under his breath, like a prayer, like a revelation. His eyes focused, and his tone hardened. "Master Vorath killed my sister. Mordred destroyed my life. I want to watch this fortress burn."

She stepped forward and held out an extinguished hand. He clasped it. For once, the contact didn't make her skin crawl and her heart race.

"Welcome to the fire."

CHAPTER SEVENTEEN

Brinnie released Ignatius's handshake and strode toward the Case. "Come with us. We can use another spellcaster."

His fingers twitched as she picked up the Case, as if he barely held himself back from snatching it away. She took a deep breath. *This is either a good idea or an incredibly stupid one.* She held the Case out to him. "Here. You can carry it."

He accepted the chest, eyes flicking from the box in his hands to her and back again. "You're letting me hold this?"

"A show of faith."

His suspicious expression hardened. "We're not friends. I would still rather kill you."

"Likewise. But we have a common enemy, so we'll hold off for now."

A voice resonated in her mind. *"Brinnie, Nimue has answers."*

"Marcus needs me." *And Lana, too.* She headed for the door. "How well do you know these passages?"

"Marcus?" Ignatius glanced over his shoulder as if his former friend might be hiding in the shadows. "He's here too?"

"Not right here with me, but yes. He was the guy they thought was me." She stopped in the doorway. "He's waiting in the dungeon."

Ignatius hesitated, then took the lead. "Okay." They exited, and the door slid shut behind them. "He's the one who taught me to navigate the passageways, years ago. I don't know them as well as he does, but I can get us to the dungeons."

Brinnie followed Ignatius's bumbling process for a couple of minutes before she sighed and held up a hand encased in fire, sending light flickering ahead of them. "Better?"

He gave a curt nod.

She reached out for Marcus. *I'm on my way, with Ignatius and the Case.*

"Ignatius? I thought the plan was to grab the Case and run."

Long story, but he knows who I am and we're . . . allies of a sort. We're on our way to the dungeons.

"I trust your judgment, but not him. Watch your back."

Noted. Tell Nimue I say hi.

"Yeah, shockingly I think I'm not *going to tell her the voice in my head says hi."*

Brinnie snorted. Ignatius gave her a questioning look, and she sobered. "So when we get to Marcus, you're not going to attack him, got it?"

He glowered. "For now."

"I'll take that." As they navigated the next turn, she considered her words. "He's torn apart by what he did, you know. He blames himself for what you became."

Ignatius's eyes flashed. "What I 'became'?"

"A torturer," she said bluntly. "And by extension, he blames himself for what you did to me." She bit her lip. "You wrought a more powerful revenge on him than you realize."

He didn't say anything else, keeping his eyes forward. She didn't push the subject.

They rounded a wall and squeezed through a slit of a passage, emerging into a crevice behind a dip in a wider hall, no longer in the maze of secret passageways.

This hallway . . . she recognized it.

"No secret passageways going into the dungeon itself," Ignatius whispered, creeping forward. "Trust me, I've searched."

As Ignatius led the way, the stone seemed to press in toward her. She could almost hear blood dripping with a soft *splat, splat* onto the floor, the grating of chains on stone, as guards dragged her down this very hall to the never-ending darkness of a cell with no magic.

"Well."

Ignatius's voice brought her back to the present, making her aware of her trembling fingers, her hesitant feet frozen to the ground.

He scanned her head to toe, an eyebrow rising. "Maybe it *was* a powerful revenge."

She clenched her fists. "Let's keep going."

She stomped past him. She could probably find her own way from here. As she strode down the passage, she scanned for signs of life.

Something flashed in her peripheral vision in a branching hall. She stopped and backtracked.

Ignatius nearly bumped into her. "What are you doing?"

Her heart skipped a beat. Could it be this easy?

She darted into the new hallway, pushing past an unlocked gate in a set of bars across the passage. From a rippling feeling, she could tell anti-magic wards began here. Three cells led off the small chamber beyond, and in the middle cell, a figure slumped, huddled against the far wall in chains. A figure with long blonde hair still visible despite caked-on dried blood.

Brinnie's voice almost didn't work. "Lana."

The girl's head rose slowly.

Brinnie darted forward, grasping the bars. Blood and dirt streaked the wizard's cheeks, offsetting glassy eyes. *No, no, no.*

"Brinnie?" she rasped. "Is that really you?" Lana scooted forward, chains rattling. "What are you doing here?"

"I'm breaking you out." Her blood boiled, and she channeled that energy into her hands, clasping them around the lock on the door and melting the metal before kicking it in.

"That shouldn't be possible," Ignatius whispered.

She knelt next to her friend, reaching for the cuffs. Carefully, she melted the manacles until they clattered to the ground. Some of the hot metal touched Lana's skin, and she winced. Brinnie cupped her hands around Lana's wrists, healing the burned skin and the raw abrasions from the cuffs.

She held the healed skin, magic buzzing in her fingers, and turned eyes blurred with tears to Lana's gaze. "I'm so, so sorry this happened to you."

She blinked slowly, eyes roving over Brinnie. "They said they killed you." A tear trickled down her cheek.

"They lied. All lies." Brinnie gently lifted a hand to Lana's head. "May I?"

Lana nodded, and Brinnie felt for wounds, closing scrapes, knitting together gashes.

"I escaped—and now you will too." Brinnie glanced back at Ignatius.

"Why aren't there any guards around here? I had at least two twenty-four seven."

He shrugged. "You were a high-profile prisoner." He gestured at Lana. "I don't even know who she is, but we should get going before a guard does come by during rounds."

Brinnie's stomach clenched. She had been held prisoner for a reason, to be interrogated and later used. But Lana . . . this was a punishment. They had left her here to die, slowly melting into oblivion.

She scanned her friend. With the wounds sealed, she didn't appear to be in too bad of shape underneath the blood and grime. Perhaps a bit skinnier, but the starvation look Brinnie had acquired after months of imprisonment hadn't set in yet over the course of a couple weeks Lana had been here. Thank goodness. Brinnie couldn't do anything about that.

Lana squinted at her. "How are you doing this?" She held out her arms, turning them over. "You're . . . a healer?"

"We have a lot to catch up on." Brinnie stood and offered a hand. "Do you think you're strong enough to walk?"

Lana's brow furrowed, but she placed a hesitant hand in Brinnie's. "If this is a hallucination, I'm going to be very disappointed."

"It isn't." Brinnie draped Lana's arm over her shoulders as the light wizard's legs wobbled. Surefooted warrior Lana, the perpetual grin missing from both her lips and her eyes. *She did this for me. For Anna.* "One step at a time."

Ignatius shook his head and clutched the Case. "We won't get out of here with her slowing us down."

Brinnie glared. "Remember whose life I just saved. We're taking her." When he appeared ready to say something else, she added, "If you have a problem with it, hand over the Case and you get out of here yourself."

He clenched his jaw but didn't argue.

They made their way back out of the pod of cells and down the hall. *We're on our way, Marcus. Picked up Lana.*

"You found her?"

I told you I would.

They turned the corner and Brinnie stopped short, face to face with four guards.

"Whoops!" She shrugged Lana's arm off her shoulders, leaning her toward a wall. "Sorry about this."

The first guard didn't have time to react before Brinnie conked him in the head with a club made of shadows. The others rushed at her, but she sent shadow wolves to attack them and pin them to the ground until she had whacked them all upside the head. She dissipated the club and wolves, slipping under Lana's arm again. "Okay. Let's go."

Lana stared at the guards, eyes wide. "Those classes at the University sure did something for your fighting."

"And Keilrie, as much as I hate to admit it."

Ignatius sighed, stepping over the slumped forms of the guards. "Yes, yes, we know Brinnie's wonderful."

Finally, they arrived at the cell. The door stood open, and Marcus and Nimue lingered in the doorway, conversing.

Brinnie formed a shadow sword in one hand, scanning for the guards she had seen earlier through Marcus's eyes.

"They're gone." Nimue flicked her chin toward Brinnie in acknowledgement. "I appreciate the paranoia though."

Marcus strode forward, scanning Brinnie. Seeming satisfied, he looked at Ignatius and his expression hardened. "You can turn that over now." He held out a hand for the Case.

Ignatius pulled the Case back like a basketball in a game of keep away. "You're the last person I'm handing this over to, Vorath."

Brinnie stepped between them, still supporting Lana. "I gave it to him, Marcus." She looked from one to the other, giving each a stern look. "We're a team now."

Nimue wrinkled her nose at Ignatius, raised an eyebrow at Lana. "You're just collecting heirs, aren't you, kid?"

Brinnie shrugged one shoulder. "Not intentionally. Marcus said you have answers for us."

"With conditions." Nimue glanced between Marcus and Brinnie and sighed. "I'm going to regret this. You two bring out the worst in me."

Brinnie's lips twitched in a smile. "Or the best. So, how do we raise the dead?"

Lana rested with her back against the wall outside the cell. Ignatius stood not far from her, still holding the Case with a carefully portrayed casual demeanor, as if Brinnie hadn't told him that she would murder him the second he stepped out of line.

Marcus and Brinnie huddled with Nimue out of earshot. "You made it harder for yourselves bringing those two." Nimue inclined her head toward Lana and Ignatius. "You're lucky we're short staffed down here with the war. You won't find the upper levels this empty."

"We have that part under control." Marcus nodded to Brinnie. "Tell her what needs to be done to wake Merlin."

"Caveats first." Nimue ticked points off on her fingers. "First of all, as soon as this conversation is over, I'm not offering any more help whatsoever. This is blatant treason, and if we face one another on the battlefield, I won't treat you two differently than any other warrior."

"Got it." Brinnie resisted the urge to bounce on her toes and demand answers faster.

"Second, I am *only* telling you this because I agree with Marcus—Mordred needs checks to his power. Once this is over, we need some sort of failsafe to stop him from becoming a supreme, immortal dictator." She blew out a breath. "I know we can't come to any sort of agreement to keep Excalibur in reserve to use only if necessary."

"It's already necessary." Brinnie did bounce a bit this time.

"We'll cross that bridge when we get to it." Nimue pinched the bridge of her nose. "I also can't convince you to leave the Case here, can I?"

Marcus raised a brow. "Mordred's weapon that makes Brinnie completely vulnerable? Leaving it here won't exactly help us keep his power in check."

She sighed. "Well, here's how to resurrect Merlin Ludovic, may he rot. The curse is a more powerful magic than healers have any right to wield, which means it can't be easily undone. One must take the curse in order for another to be healed. The sleeper's curse can't just go away before the thousand years are up. If a wizard is to be woken, the curse must be transferred to a different recipient."

Brinnie's eyes widened. She shot a glance at Marcus, and he nodded in confirmation. "So for Uncle Merlin to wake up . . ."

"Someone else has to take the curse." Nimue crossed her arms.

"Either of you could perform the spell—it's simple enough for any wizard. You only need to act as a conduit. You lay one hand on the cursed and one hand on the one to be cursed and let the magic flow through you. Mordred's was a little different, since it was an eternal curse rather than a millennium one, but even that worked the same way." The corner of her lips turned up slightly. "Once I managed to unearth the secret, I burned every reference that might lead anyone to find out, broke into Arthrys, and transferred Mordred's curse to one of the unconscious guards before dropping him in the sea."

Brinnie shuddered. *Dad's side of the family definitely has a brutal streak.* "So Anika was wrong about the reversal requiring special power. Really, it only takes special knowledge."

Movement in her peripheral turned her head toward Ignatius, who had shifted to lean against the wall. She shot him a warning look, and he put up a hand in wide-eyed innocence before shooting back a wink.

She rolled her eyes and returned to the conversation, latching onto a new, pressing question. "What happens to the new cursed person?"

"The curse can't die until its time is up," Marcus said quietly. "They inherit the curse's remaining time, and it can't be transferred again."

Her blood ran cold. To save one person meant to doom another. "How terrible." She cleared her throat and squared her shoulders. "Thank you, Nimue."

"Don't make me regret it more than I already do, kid." She uncrossed her arms. "I see you broke out one of our prisoners." Her expression softened. "That one won't last long in a dungeon. Consider her a gift. I'll get you out of here, then I don't want to see any of you in this fortress again."

"I have no intention of entering my father's fortress ever again." Marcus's jaw set.

No intention of entering his father's fortress. Brinnie could sense the implication.

The next time the two of them saw Mordizan, one way or another, Marcus would be claiming the Mastership for himself.

Brinnie's small feet padded on the cold stone of the fortress. She was twelve again, accompanied by younger versions of Marcus, Ignatius, and Lana, each with features altered just enough to render them unfamiliar. Their clothes didn't fit quite right, but in wartime, that wouldn't be unusual. Ignatius toted the Case in a worn sack Nimue had procured. Hopefully it wouldn't look like anything other than the meager possessions of a refugee.

Nimue led the four children through the halls of Mordizan, more empty than Brinnie remembered. The scholars with their scrolls, the finely-dressed advisors, the easy groups that formed in atriums conversing and laughing, all noticeably absent. Only a few wizards passed them, each with a quick nod, intent on their business.

Mordizan might be winning, but even the capital felt the effects of war.

"Nimue Drakon."

The salutation from a familiar voice sent a chill down Brinnie's spine. She turned to see none other than Master Vorath making his way down the hall, with what appeared to be a couple of advisors at his side.

He chuckled and gestured to the four supposed children. "What do you have now?"

Nimue turned with an easy smile. "Young refugees, my lord. Some idiots brought them in with the draft." She gestured to the four. "Behold, fine warriors for our illustrious army."

He and his advisors laughed. Vorath shook his head. "Some of the recruiters aren't too bright." He nodded to the four children. "Go home to your mothers." He turned down a branching walkway, his two men with him.

The fist around Brinnie's lungs relaxed, allowing her to breathe again.

Marcus's expression hardened. "Your war took away our homes and mothers."

Vorath stopped, turned slowly. "What was that?"

Marcus. Brinnie elbowed him hard.

He didn't look at her. "You heard what I said. Your hunger for power killed my mother. If we want to dig deeper, it killed your own wife and drove your son away."

One of the two advisors stepped forward and cuffed Marcus upside the head. His neck whipped around, and he stumbled. "Let that teach you a lesson, boy," the man sneered. He turned to Vorath. "Should we have his tongue cut out, my lord?"

Instead of rage, Vorath stood almost frozen, expressionless. "No," he said finally. He nodded to Nimue. "Send these rats out of the fortress." He gave Marcus a cold stare. "I am not unwilling to dispose of vermin that make themselves a nuisance."

"Yes, my lord." She grabbed Marcus's arm and yanked him along behind her. "Come on, all of you."

Brinnie scurried to keep up. As soon as they were out of sight, Nimue whirled on Marcus. "What were you thinking? You want to get us all killed?"

He remained impassive, despite the bruise already forming at his temple. "He needed to hear it from someone, at least once."

"You really have lost your mind." She spun on her heel, stalking forward once more. "No more idiotic tricks. Keep your mouth shut."

Brinnie supported Lana as she tripped attempting to keep up. She sent her thoughts to Marcus. *I say this not in a judging way—what were you hoping to accomplish?*

His mouth remained in a grim line. *"The old fool is still my father. It didn't feel right not to at least give him a chance to think about his actions."*

She couldn't argue with that. If Dad were the one intent on world domination . . .

She had forgiven her own father for horrible things, but Vorath had given no indication he had any intention of changing. Her heart ached for Marcus.

They reached the courtyard with no further incidents. Nimue ambled past the guards of the gate, only giving them a passing nod. They didn't question her. Once the group reached the street outside, Nimue turned to the four of them. "All right, you're on your own. If you get caught, it's your own fault."

"Thank you, Nimue." Brinnie hesitated. "Come with us. You don't have to stay here. My dad would be ecstatic if you joined him at Dirklon."

"Sorry, kid." She gave a rueful smile. "Your dad made his choice. I can't help that, but I promise, once this new world is created, I'll put in a good word for both of you." She nodded to Marcus. "All three of you. And if you come to your senses, I'll be here."

Brinnie bit down her protests. Why, when the way seemed so clear, did intelligent people like Nimue still choose the opposite? Why did people she cared about align themselves with foul causes and leaders?

But then, Castelon's actions had little to recommend them.

"Goodbye, Aunt Nimue. And thank you."

"Hey, now. None of this 'aunt' business. Makes me sound old." She winked and slapped Brinnie's shoulder, propelling her down the road. "Get out of here, and good luck."

CHAPTER EIGHTEEN

If Brinnie had to pay the entry fee for The City Museum one more time, she would look into buying a membership. Especially with four people.

They blindfolded Ignatius once they reached the organ chamber. He might know the general location of the door, but at least he wouldn't know the exact spot. The group split, and Marcus steered him in a few rounds of the place to further disorient him before joining Brinnie and Lana.

"I don't like this." Marcus kept one hand on Ignatius's shoulder. *"We're showing him too much. How do we know he won't betray us to get back into Mordred's good graces?"*

We don't. Brinnie helped Lana to her feet from where they had sat near the door, waiting for Marcus and Ignatius to arrive. *But it's this, let him loose to cause trouble, or kill him.*

Lana hardly responded as she stood next to Brinnie, expression distant. Brinnie's chest squeezed, longing to do something, anything, to bring a spark back to Lana's eyes, replace the glassy gaze with a twinkle of mischief once more.

If we kill him, then we're admitting we all deserve to die.

She didn't mean to send that thought to Marcus, but he set his jaw and nodded. The understanding that passed between them didn't need to be voiced.

Let the one without sin cast the first stone.

Marcus removed the blindfold. Brinnie stepped to the door, picked up the knocker, and let it fall.

Within seconds, Mrs. Winslow opened the door, as if she had been waiting. "You're back!" She wrapped Brinnie into a hug, pulling her inside. "Praise the Lord."

"Safe and sound." Brinnie squeezed her back, then extricated herself. She gestured to Lana and Ignatius as Marcus directed them inside. "We also did a little dungeon-rescuing while we were there. This is Lana and Ignatius."

"Poor dears." Mrs. Winslow herded them forward. "Come, come, let's get you warmed up by the fire."

Marcus shut the door behind them, his eyes not leaving Ignatius. For his part, the spellcaster only scanned the great hall with an assessing gaze. Brinnie shot him a warning look that she hoped conveyed, *Behave yourself, we're both watching.*

As they passed from the dining room into the kitchen, Mom rounded the corner from the stairs, breathless. "I thought I heard something." She dashed forward and enveloped Brinnie in a giant hug. "Are you okay? Did everything go well?"

"We're fine." She lingered in the embrace for a moment. It felt . . . real. "And we got answers from Nimue."

The kitchen filled with denizens of Wraithwood—Miss Burtle, Mr. Winslow, then Anna and David.

Upon entering and seeing Lana, Anna ran to her and hugged the girl, dungeon grime and all. "Lana. I'm so glad you're here! We can never thank you enough for what you did."

For a brief moment, light returned to her eyes. She offered a half-smile. "You're safe. It worked."

David joined, leaning on his crutch and grinning. "We owe you a debt."

Lana's eyes darted to his leg, then back to his face. "I only wish I'd done it sooner."

"Here, dear." Mrs. Winslow guided her to a chair. "You look like you've had a rough time of it lately. I'll get you some tea and soup." She looked to the other three. "All of you, in fact."

Lana sat, the blank expression returning. At least there had been a moment of light, an indication of hope.

Brinnie plopped into a chair, exhaustion hitting her like a shovel to the head. They'd had a long day of crawling through secret passageways, fighting, wielding various kinds of magic . . . Her stomach rumbled.

"What's he doing here?"

Brinnie turned at the sharp voice. Ms. Tynsdale stood in the doorway to the dining room, glaring at Ignatius. The woman's arms tensed, as if ready to rip him to shreds.

"All good!" Brinnie shot to her feet, stepping between them. "It may be hard to believe, but he's on our side now."

Ms. Tynsdale's eyebrows rose. "Bringing home *another* torturer?"

Ignatius casually tucked his hands in his pockets. "Any enemy of Mordred is an ally of mine."

Brinnie doubted anyone would be making friends, so she sighed and tilted her head toward Marcus. "We're keeping an eye on him."

"So?" Miss Burtle crossed her arms, apparently too impatient to wait for interpersonal drama to play out. "Did you find the answers you were looking for?"

"Yes. We know how to wake Uncle Merlin." Brinnie hesitated.

"And?" Mom prompted.

Several pairs of hopeful eyes seemed to burn her skin. "In order for a wizard to awaken from the curse, another wizard has to take the curse in their stead."

A beat of silence.

Then everyone began speaking at once.

"Reckon I'll take it," Mr. Winslow said. "I've lived a good, long life."

"You can't, dear. You're human," Mrs. Winslow reminded him.

"It seems obvious." Ms. Tynsdale put her hands on her hips. "I'll have to be the one."

"Lydia, I can't let you do that." Mom pressed her lips together. "It should be me. He's my brother."

Marcus spoke just loud enough to be heard through the arguing. "This whole situation is my fault. I should be the one."

Brinnie's heart skipped a beat at the thought. "I would rather take it myself."

"That's clearly out of the question." Miss Burtle rolled her eyes. "You're our biggest asset."

From behind her, a quiet voice said, "I'll do it."

The room silenced.

Brinnie turned slowly to face Ignatius. "What did you say?"

He shrugged and stepped forward. "I said I'll do it." His gaze traveled the room. "All of you are warriors with powers you can use in a fight. I've never been much of a fighter, and spellcasting isn't really a battlefield skill." He gestured to her. "Besides, you have Brinnie to do the spellcasting around here. I'm not necessary. I'll take the curse."

Ms. Tynsdale's eyes narrowed. "What's in it for you?"

He hooked his thumbs in his pockets. "I don't have anything else going for me. If I can be a part of getting Excalibur and taking down Mordred after all he's done to me . . . that's good enough for me."

No smirking, no guile. His expression seemed almost . . . hopeless. Brinnie wasn't about to argue and trample upon what might be the one shining good deed he'd ever committed, as revenge-motivated as it might be. "In that case, let's do this."

A thought shot to her. *"The anywhere portals."*

Her eyes snapped to Marcus. *What?*

"You figured out the anywhere portals," he said aloud. He focused on Ignatius. "We used one, and it worked. Could you make more?"

He shrugged one shoulder. "With a traveler, yes."

Marcus turned to the rest of the room. "The tactical advantage we would have with portals that could take us literally anywhere we can imagine . . ."

"Anywhere portals are purely theoretical." Miss Burtle raised an eyebrow. "Wizards have been studying the potential mechanics for centuries but have never successfully created one."

"Ignatius is brilliant." Marcus didn't look at Ignatius as he said it, but Brinnie saw surprise, then a brief moment of pride flash across the spellcaster's countenance. "He's been fascinated with the concept since we were children, and he's finally figured it out."

"The one we used was pretty cool," Brinnie admitted.

Ms. Tynsdale heaved a sigh. "Theoretical magic aside, we're heavily lacking spellcasters. We need portals for armies, enchanted weapons, things only spellcasters can provide. Brinnie can do a lot, but she can't be everywhere. As long as he doesn't get himself stabbed for double-crossing, the torturer could be a major asset."

His shoulders slumped, tension releasing. *A part of him still doesn't want to die.* "Then who will do it?"

"Me." Ms. Tynsdale held up a hand to stop the arguments from Mom. "I'm still weak physically. I can hardly get my magic to work, definitely not long enough to keep up an espionage mission, and shapeshifting isn't a whole lot of use in combat." She placed a hand on

Mom's shoulder. "Eira, your daughters need their mother." Her teeth clenched, then relaxed as she begrudgingly turned to Marcus. "Vorath, you're our only hope of bringing dark wizards to our side. It has to be me."

The heavy silence pressed down on Brinnie like a smothering smog.

This is wrong. All wrong.

"I'll be the one to perform the transfer," Brinnie said. "Ms. Tynsdale, we should confer beforehand."

Without waiting for a response, she turned and pushed through the door to the dining room, heading she didn't know where. Away.

Chess and pawns. Sacrificing one for another. Choosing which pieces were worth more.

What a loathsome game.

She waited in the great hall for Ms. Tynsdale. When her aunt stepped through the doors, Brinnie spoke immediately. "If you do this, you'll never be able to tell him you love him."

"No. This is how I tell him." Close up, Brinnie could see the dark circles hanging under her eyes. "If I don't do this, then what? I sabotage our way to recruit dark wizards to our side. I take away your mother, his sister, my brother's wife. Take away you? The best hope any of us have?"

The words struck her. *She* was their hope? A battered, traumatized girl who had messed everything up countless times? She shouldn't be entrusted with anything, especially not something as fragile as hope.

"The words 'I love you' mean so much less than the actions that show them to be true." She gave a half-smile and clapped Brinnie on the shoulder. "I think he'll figure it out."

Brinnie's breath shuddered. "But I'll miss you."

"Oh, kid." She folded Brinnie into her arms. "You know I don't do goodbyes."

She swallowed, forcing her voice not to waver. "I'll see you again. If not in this life . . ."

"Then the next," she finished. "I'll be waiting for you, if you aren't already waiting for me."

The old promise weighed heavy on her heart.

She feared this wouldn't be the last parting in which the war would force her to utter the phrase with a sense of finality.

And next time, she might not have the luxury of saying goodbye at all.

Brinnie stood at the foot—head?—of the bed. Uncle Merlin's lifeless form lay on one side, and Ms. Tynsdale lowered herself onto the other, her head near Uncle Merlin's so that Brinnie could place a hand on each of their foreheads.

The Wraithwood crew crowded the room, and Brinnie tried to ignore the tense anxiety in the air, trying not to think about the tears, the hugs, the goodbyes.

Tried not to feel like the executioner.

She placed one hand on Uncle Merlin's cold brow. She reached toward Ms. Tynsdale with the other, and the woman closed her eyes—

"Wait." Marcus stepped forward, then dropped to one knee and bowed his head. "Before you do this, Lydia Tynsdale, I have something to say. I am so, so sorry for what I did. There is no excuse for it, and I can do nothing to change or make up for my actions, as much as I would give anything to go back and fix them." He raised his eyes and placed a hand over his heart. "I don't ask for your forgiveness—I in no way deserve it—but I pledge to you that I will do everything in my power from now on to protect your family, and I can only hope to one day be as courageous as you."

"Another pretty speech." Ms. Tynsdale offered a slight, rueful smile. "But . . . I can tell you mean it. And I suppose I don't want unfinished business on my hands. I forgive you."

His mouth opened slightly, a baffled look of surprise. "I . . . thank you."

She looked back at Brinnie. "Do it."

Brinnie rested her palm on her aunt's forehead. "You're a brave woman."

Her voice came out so quietly that Brinnie wasn't sure if anyone else heard it. "Sometimes you have to do crazy things for the people you love."

Brinnie took a deep breath and closed her eyes. With her hands on each of them, she finally felt something, the magic that she'd tried to find in Uncle Merlin before. It hummed, as if waiting to jump from one to the other, like a magnet faced with an opposite charge.

Slowly, gently, she allowed the force to flow through her.

Beneath her fingers, she felt Ms. Tynsdale sink into limpness. She squeezed her eyes shut tighter, trying to keep in moisture that threatened to escape.

When had she become the chess master, sacrificing pieces? Why was she forced to play the game she most hated?

The flow of magic ceased, coiling dormant in Ms. Tynsdale's still form.

"It's done." Brinnie opened her eyes, and at almost exactly the same moment, so did Uncle Merlin.

CHAPTER NINETEEN

"Uncle Merlin." Brinnie removed her hands and stepped back. "Can you hear me?"

He sat up slowly. One hand went to his abdomen, and he drew it away, looking at his fingers in confusion. His gaze drifted to Brinnie, and his brow furrowed. "I didn't expect you to greet me here."

He looked around the room, at Mom with her hands clasped over her mouth and tears in her eyes, at the Winslows hugging each other in relief, wide-eyed Anna and David, Miss Burtle and Marcus and Lana and Ignatius. "Or . . . any of you. How did you all die?"

A laugh bubbled out of her as Brinnie threw her arms around him. "You're not dead. None of us are." Tears came to her eyes as she released him. "We all thought you were dead, but Anika saved you. She put you under a sleeper's curse."

He swung his legs off the side of the bed, then froze, looking down at Ms. Tynsdale. "Wait." His eyes didn't leave her face. "What's wrong with Lydia?"

Mom stepped forward hesitantly, her voice unusually gentle. "So, that's the thing about a sleeper's curse. In order to wake one person, the curse must be transferred to another."

"No." He shot to his feet, only to stumble and nearly fall. "No! You can't let her do that."

"Careful." Mom steadied him. "You just woke up. Take things slow."

He sank back onto the bed and took Ms. Tynsdale's hand as if he could will her back to consciousness. "I should be dead, not her. We need to change it back."

Brinnie bit her lip, chest tight. *I hate this. I hate everything about this.*

"It's not your fault. None of this is right."

She glanced at Marcus, and he gave her a reassuring nod. What would she be feeling if the roles were switched, if she were in the same position, Marcus motionless after bringing her back to life? Her heart ached, but she forced herself to speak. "I'm sorry. Once the sleeper's curse is transferred, it's irreversible. She insisted she be the one to take it."

"She can't. That's . . . I . . ." He ran a hand through his hair, scanning the room. "I've missed a lot, haven't I? What happened? I don't know some of you. Brynna, you're not at Mordizan. You look so much older. How long was I gone?"

"Several months." Mom rested a hand on his shoulder. "It's nearly spring."

"There's quite a bit to fill you in on," Brinnie added.

"But we don't need to do that right away." Mrs. Winslow wrung her hands. "We can get some food in you first and get you back on your feet."

"I think I'd prefer answers for now, though I appreciate it." He turned toward Miss Burtle. As they all did, when they wanted the plain truth.

"Long story short," she began, "the strongholds were all overtaken, the protection spells are gone, the Mastership powers are no longer limited, and direct warfare is now being waged at the estates."

A heavy silence hung over the room.

Anna cleared her throat. "*But*, on the bright side, David and I were rescued and Brinnie gained the power of hundreds of wizards." She stepped forward. "Nice to meet you. I'm your niece, Anna."

"Anna." He smiled, some of the lines of tension easing from his brow. "I saw a shapeshifter in your form before I . . . well, before whatever happened to me. So, Brinnie, it seems you succeeded?"

"Um, kind of." She shifted on her feet. "I did get found out, and I ended up taking down the last stronghold for Mordred."

He raised an eyebrow. "I see there's a lot to discuss."

For ease of conversation, they descended and relocated to the dining room, where enough chairs were present for all—but not before Uncle Merlin gently tucked Ms. Tynsdale into the bed.

Brinnie looked away, a guilt she knew was irrational squeezing her heart. They'd taken the best course of action out of many bad options.

Bringing Uncle Merlin up to date lasted hours. Brinnie tried to gloss over some of the more harrowing Mordizan experiences, telling only as much as necessary to move the story along. By the time they had finished, they had taken multiple snack breaks and Lana had fallen asleep leaning on Brinnie's shoulder, unwilling to leave her side.

Uncle Merlin rubbed his temple. "So things are as bad as our worst fears anticipated back when all this started." He turned tired eyes to Brinnie. "I am incredibly sorry you had to go through that. If I had a chance to do it over again, I wouldn't let you go."

She shrugged one shoulder and offered a wry half-smile. "You probably couldn't have stopped me from doing it on my own anyway. Besides, we did get Anna and David back—just not in the way we anticipated."

He raised one eyebrow, and she knew he didn't buy a bit of her flippant attitude, but thankfully, he moved on. "Antony has Dirklon under control. What about the other estates?"

"Six have fallen, as far as I know." Miss Burtle pushed a map toward him. "Riverdell, Habrin, Carator, Iriselie, Brookdam, and Ledovin."

"They're picking off the smaller estates first," Uncle Merlin observed. "Though they haven't struck here, strangely enough."

Mom toyed with the mug in her hands. "I would think because of the Maze. As far as anyone knows, it's still magical."

"Good. That should buy us time." He squinted. "It's a bit disorienting, but I'm not sure about the Maze either. I can't sense anyone on the estate—beyond being unable to enforce protection spell rules, that Master's power seems to be gone as well." He turned to Marcus. "Other than hitting the easy targets, any inkling of the battle plan?"

He shook his head, leaning over the map. "If my father were in charge, they would have hit Castelon first, as soon as the last stronghold fell. His battle strategy tends to be to strike at the head, no nonsense."

Brinnie shifted in her chair, trying not to disturb Lana napping on her shoulder. The lack of hostility between Uncle Merlin and Marcus was refreshing after the usual animosity of her family.

"This slow and steady has Mordred written all over it," Marcus continued. He tapped his finger on the widespread, seemingly random points. "I can't predict what he'll do, which is probably the goal. If no one knows where Mordred will attack next, they can't be prepared."

"Castelon wasn't prepared in the first place, of course," Uncle Merlin muttered. "I imagine they finally believe there's a threat now and are taking at least some action. Even if that action happens to be that fuzzy-eyed fool Castelius deciding you two were enemies." He gestured to Brinnie and Marcus.

Miss Burtle chuckled. "I forgot how much I missed his insulting the Head of the Council."

Uncle Merlin scowled. "I'll talk to him—and have allies talk to him as well if he continues to be difficult." He leaned on his elbows. "Brinnie, you have the Case of the Master Key, yes? We'll need to take both it and the Key back to Castelon before Mordred hits Wraithwood. We don't have enough fighters here to withstand an attack, and we can't risk them falling into Mordred's hands."

"Hold on." Brinnie held up a hand. "We're abandoning Wraithwood?"

"Not necessarily. He may not strike here at all—but we should have such powerful magical items better protected, just in case."

She forced herself not to argue. Precautions were good, but she couldn't even think about abandoning Wraithwood to the enemy.

"What about Excalibur?"

Brinnie's head swiveled toward Ignatius. She'd nearly forgotten him. He kept uncharacteristically quiet near the end of the table, but with one foot on the chair with his leg bent and his elbow resting on his knee, he still exuded a cool arrogance she tried not to let irk her.

"If we have the sword, we can defeat Mordred and get this whole thing done and over with." He shrugged. "No need for involving Castelon at all."

"That's true." Mom leaned forward. "Merlin, where *is* Excalibur?"

He sighed. "Therein lies the problem. The legendary sword was destroyed in the battle at Camlan, where Arthur died. As far as we know, not even shards remain."

Brinnie's mind struggled to process for a moment. She saw her shocked expression mirrored on the faces of those around the table. "So the grand secret of Excalibur . . . is that it doesn't exist?"

The sound of crying floated from the other room. Anna stood. "Sounds like Isaac is awake. I'll go get him."

Silence reigned with only the sound of the door swishing shut breaking the quiet. Brinnie tried to calm her racing thoughts. What now? What hope remained without Excalibur?

Marcus placed his hand over hers under the table. She hadn't realized how tightly her fist was clenched. *"It will be okay. We'll figure something out."*

Uncle Merlin ran a hand through his hair. "I believe I will regret telling all of you this, considering the self-sacrificial tendencies of the room, but . . . even though Excalibur no longer exists, it once did. In the past."

"What enlightening information." Mom barked a short laugh. "Thank you, Merlin, very helpful."

He didn't react to the condescending tone. "The secret the Masters of Wraithwood have passed down is this. If someone remains inside a portal after it closes, they will be lost in space and time forever. But . . ." He let out a long breath. "If that person holds the Master Key, the magic in the Key, linked to that of Excalibur, will draw that person to the time and space where Excalibur exists."

The knowledge sank in.

Brinnie's mouth dropped open. "Time travel?"

"In theory. It has never been tested."

Exclamations and questions erupted. Miss Burtle's voice rose above the rest. "How does a person return once they find Excalibur?"

"That's the problem, and why I don't think anyone should be diving into any portals." Uncle Merlin gave Brinnie a stern look as if she were the most likely offender. She would have been insulted, if he wasn't right. "No one knows. Without an anchor point on the other side, you would have no guarantee of being drawn to your own time."

We can work with that.

"Brinnie . . ."

"What about the Case?" She ignored Marcus's look and instead focused on leaning Lana back in her chair and massaging the sore shoulder on which her friend had been resting. Lana, for her part, hardly stirred. "Would that be enough to pull the Master Key back to the present?"

"You can't send the Master Key through a portal on its own." Miss Burtle sniffed, as if that should be obvious. "The Key's draining magic will destroy the portal."

"Correct." Uncle Merlin's expression remained grim. "Previous Masters of Wraithwood dedicated an absurd amount of time to studying the possibilities, and they postulated that with the Case, the Key could be contained from destroying the portal. It has to go as well, so it can't be used as an anchor point."

"So we need to try." Brinnie stood. "I volunteer."

"Sit down, Brynna." Mom scowled at her. "You're the last person we're sending, for reasons that have been discussed before."

"Besides dear, no matter who we send, if it doesn't work, we'll lose a powerful weapon—the Key," Mrs. Winslow reminded her. "Is it worth the risk?"

"I don't think you have much choice." Ignatius twirled a tea spoon between his fingers. "Your forces don't stand a chance against Mordred regardless. Might as well die in an interesting way."

Marcus raised a brow. "Helpful, Ignatius."

He offered back a mocking salute.

Don't antagonize each other.

"I'm not." Marcus gave him a warning look. *"He's being disrespectful."*

"I think you're probably right," Uncle Merlin admitted, "but I can't let any of you go. If anyone is going to suffer for a harebrained scheme, it will be me this time." His attention turned to Brinnie, his expression softening, eyes tight with pain. "You were right, Eira. Everything that happened to Brynna is my fault."

Brinnie put a hand on her hip. "That's not true at all."

"Honestly . . ." Mom sighed. "This might have happened no matter what. Mordred would still rise. The strongholds would still fall." She glanced at Brinnie, and for a moment, a hint of affection glinted in her eyes. "But at least this way Brynna can fight. The truth is out about Antony, and with both of them, we all might have more of a chance of surviving this war."

Brinnie's eyebrows rose. This might be the closest she'd ever heard to an apology from Mom.

Uncle Merlin gave a slow half-smile. "I missed you, Eira."

Miss Burtle cleared her throat. "On the topic of who should go, I don't think you're the wise choice, Merlin. Wraithwood has been a mess without a Master, and we need you as a traveler as well as before the Council. They may not listen to you well, but at least they listen at all."

"Plus, we need your connections." Brinnie glanced at Marcus and smiled. "I was so proud when I heard that you were number two on Mordizan's hit list. After I got done being devastated that you were dead, that is."

"Then it's settled." Ignatius set down the spoon he'd been playing with. "I'm off to find Excalibur."

Marcus barked a laugh. "You? I don't trust you out of my sight, let alone with the Master Key *and* Excalibur."

Brinnie nudged him. *This isn't playing nice.*

Ignatius leaned back in his chair with a taunting smirk. "It only makes sense to send a spellcaster to deal with portals—but I'm sure you can make your own portals too, fire boy?"

"This is painful," Miss Burtle muttered.

Marcus glared down the table. "If there was some way I could go back and trade my life for your sister's, I would do it. Since I can't, and since you became *this*"—he gestured to Ignatius—"we're going to have to tolerate each other. So I'm coming too."

"That's not what I meant either," Brinnie broke in.

"I don't trust *either* of you two." Mom crossed her arms.

Miss Burtle shrugged. "It's better than Merlin."

Uncle Merlin stroked his mustache. "The spellcaster raises a good point about the portals. Especially if he truly can create anywhere portals. However, I agree with Vorath. I don't trust him alone." He looked between Ignatius and Marcus. "Between the two of them, I don't think they'll let each other get away with anything. I like the pairing."

Brinnie's heart beat a panicked staccato. *You can't go without me.*

"You're needed here." He placed a comforting hand on her knee. *"I'll be back soon."*

What if you're not? If he was going on a suicide mission, she wanted to be there too.

"Hey." He met her eyes, gave her a reassuring smile. *"I will come back to you. I wouldn't leave you here alone if the world depended on it."*

She took a shaky breath. She couldn't act like this, not in wartime. *Okay. I'm holding you to that.*

"Well, if we're in agreement." Uncle Merlin paused, but no one argued. "First things first, where is the Case?" He glanced between Brinnie, Marcus, and Ignatius.

They looked at each other. Brinnie bit her lip. "Don't laugh at us." She rubbed her shoulder. "We, uh, buried it."

"You did *what?*" Miss Burtle raised a hand to her heart, scandalized.

"We couldn't carry the Case into the museum," Marcus explained. "So we buried it in a sack outside St. Louis."

Uncle Merlin stared at them for a moment. "You buried the Case. One of the most powerful magical items ever to exist."

Lana stirred beside Brinnie. Her voice came out sleepy and slightly slurred. "Brinnie planted flowers on top of it though."

An incredulous silence reigned.

Then the tension in the room snapped as Uncle Merlin burst into laughter. Brinnie snorted, and soon half of the room was chuckling.

"Very well." Uncle Merlin wiped a tear from his eye. "Let's go dig up a flowerbed."

CHAPTER TWENTY

Keilrie hunched behind her low table, the thick smoke from sickly sweet incense wafting in front of her so that her face seemed to flicker in and out of the visible plane. Shadows lurked around them, just out of sight, their malevolent aura seeping into Brinnie's bones until she felt ill. Not her shadows. Not her friends.

Keilrie smiled, her blackened teeth on display. "Brynna Drakon. So opposed to us, yet willing to sacrifice everyone she loves for power."

Brinnie's limbs trembled. The darkness. The smell. The walls of the underground fortress pressing in on her. The phantom sensation of manacles chafed around her wrists. Trapped. Alone. Surrounded.

"So you decide who lives and dies?" Keilrie chuckled. "You decide whose life is worth a weapon?" She pointed a crooked finger. "You sneer at dark magic, yet you're willing to send the one you love to his death for the chance to defeat your enemy." Her chuckle became a cackle. "A blood sacrifice, like the Mistress of Darkness you are."

Brinnie clenched her fists. "I know this isn't real. Marcus and Ignatius are *coming back. And they're coming back with Excalibur."*

Keilrie's grating, screeching cackle continued, bouncing off the stone walls. "Power corrupts, child. So much power. So much corruption. You feel it, don't you? Your mortal form breaking apart?" She stood, moved so quickly Brinnie couldn't flinch away before Keilrie gripped her chin in one iron claw. "How much longer do you think you have, girl? How much longer does he *have?"*

Brinnie yanked her face away. "I'm not selling out to dark magic. Not even if it kills me."

Keilrie raised a brow. "We'll see. We'll see how many die before you come to your senses." She grinned. "And every death will be on your head."

Brinnie sucked in a ragged breath, shooting upright in bed. She clutched her racing heart. Another dream. Another warning.

She grasped the bedsheets with sweaty palms, staring down at her hands. Nightmares had become part of her reality ever since Mordizan—vivid replays of the massacre at the stronghold, Ignatius's chamber of horrors, Oswald Goddensfeld. But these dreams, of encounters that never really happened, almost like warnings for the future . . . she hadn't had them since before the dungeon.

Now this was the third time she'd dreamed of Keilrie's warning this week.

She sighed and swung her legs off the side of the bed. Marcus and Ignatius had been gone a week and a half. After Uncle Merlin took them to retrieve the Case, they had stepped into a portal with the Key and hadn't been heard from since.

Could it really take over a week to retrieve a sword?

Thankfully, she had work to distract her. Those remaining at Wraithwood had been building defenses while waiting for Marcus and Ignatius to return. Earthworks around the grounds, traps in the Maze. They didn't dare risk sending anyone in without Uncle Merlin to check if the Maze remained magical or not, but if it served only as a simple hedge maze now, they needed to be prepared in case of invaders.

Not that they could stave off a full army. But at least they could buy Marcus and Ignatius time, fight off any smaller parties that might approach.

A burning smell tickled her nose. She looked down at the covers and blew out a frustrated breath. She'd singed the sheets again in her sleep.

She stood, stepped away from the bed, and let fire consume her.

The flames crackled around her, an outlet for the magic, but she kept them from burning her clothing or the floor. It took the edge off, just slightly. Too much magic.

At first, using the magic had hurt. The power felt foreign, burning, uncontrollable.

However, as she'd used it at Riverdell, at Mordizan, here, the power seemed to become a part of her. The internal fire didn't ebb, but it changed. Almost as if instead of warring against her body . . .

The magic had begun to replace it.

Something I definitely will not be sharing with anyone. She didn't know what it meant that she felt completely fine while Lana still healed. What it meant that she could perform almost any magic with a wave of her hand and barely a thought. But it didn't feel right.

It didn't feel real, and Marcus wasn't here to ground her.

A quiet knock sounded at the door, and Lana tentatively poked her head in. "Brinnie?" Her eyes widened at the flames. "Are you okay?"

"I'm fine." She let them dissipate and glanced toward her window. Too far to see the sky. "What time is it?"

"Very early morning. I saw the light under your door." Her hands fidgeted. "I was wandering. Couldn't sleep."

Dark circles outlined her haunted eyes. Not that Lana ever spoke of the memories that darkened them. By day, she remained quiet, helpful, polite, if a bit distant. But the spark had left her eyes and had yet to return.

Brinnie crossed to the bed and sat. "Nightmares?"

"Yes."

"Same." She bobbed her head toward the space beside her.

Lana stepped all the way in and closed the door. She crossed the room, and Brinnie lifted the blankets. They both slid under the covers of the queen-sized bed, a silent ritual.

Brinnie rested her head on her arm. "We should just start out the night this way. Maybe we wouldn't have as many nightmares."

Lana pulled the covers up around her ears, eyes already closing. "I guess I don't know how to live without a roommate anymore."

Brinnie felt her own eyes begin to close. The first night she'd encountered Lana—also wandering the halls of Wraithwood at night—they had returned to Brinnie's room to sit together in silence. The comforting presence of someone else soon lulled them to sleep, the best rest Brinnie had gotten since Marcus left. After the first couple of times, she stopped worrying she would torch Lana while they slept.

"We can't have a sleepover every night, I guess," Brinnie mumbled, sinking into the pillow.

"It's nice until I go home."

Brinnie's eyes snapped open, focusing on Lana curled in a dozy ball. "Home?"

"Yeah, when I go back to Ariondam." Lana opened one eye. "My parents and my brother must be worried sick about me."

Brinnie propped herself up on one elbow. "But you're a fugitive. If you go back to enemy territory, Mordizan will come knocking and throw you in the dungeon again."

Lana winced, and Brinnie immediately regretted her words. "I'm sorry. Not enemy territory. Ariondam is your home, and you should get to go back to your family."

She fiddled with a loose thread on the quilt, both eyes open now. "Maybe you're right. I don't know what side I'm on anymore." She looked up at Brinnie. "I helped you because, well, you're you, and I thought it was wrong for your sister and her husband to be locked up. But I also can't fight my family. How am I supposed to pick a side?"

Brinnie rolled onto her back, staring upward. Black and white, good and evil, two opponents . . . "Maybe you don't have to pick a side. Follow what seems right. Whichever side lines up best with that, align with them, as far as that can carry you." She sighed. "I don't think either side of this war deserves anyone's blind allegiance."

"I don't think I can get behind Castelon." Lana rubbed the bridge of her nose. "But I can't fight for Mordizan anymore either." She offered a small, sleepy smile. "Maybe I'll just fight for Wraithwood."

Brinnie's heart squeezed. "Yeah. I think I'll do that too."

Brinnie spun, bringing her sword down against Lana's shield with a crash. Lana shoved with the shield, pushing Brinnie's sword away, and thrust forward with her own. The tip rested against Brinnie's abdomen.

Lana's lips twitched in a smile as she stepped back. "You know better than that, Brinnie."

"Oh yeah, of course, definitely, but our audience might not." Brinnie assumed a serious air. "Just demonstrating for training purposes, you know."

Lana snorted, and Brinnie broke down into giggles. The blonde warrior cracked a full grin. "Uh-huh. You've gotten rusty."

The sun warmed Brinnie's back, ushering in spring. Melted slush turned the grass to mud, so she and Lana faced off in the gravel drive, observed by Mom, Miss Burtle, David, and Anna—although at the moment Anna was chasing a runaway toddler down the steps.

She scooped up a shrieking and giggling Isaac and swung him around. "I appreciate the demonstration, but I don't think I'm the sword-wielding type." Anna set down her son, who headed for David. "We're not planning on joining any battles."

Brinnie released the shadow sword she had been using. "We don't want you to. Going into battle against wizards would be . . ."

"Ridiculous," Mom supplied.

"Er, yeah, I think I was going for dangerous." She rotated the shoulder of her sword arm. "But I would rather you have some rudimentary knowledge in case you need to protect yourself."

Miss Burtle sniffed. "Most places don't exactly have handguns just lying around, but wizards leave medieval weaponry everywhere."

Anna sank onto the steps beside David. "I appreciate it, Brinnie, I really do, but I've taken self-defense classes." She put a hand on David's knee. "We're doctors, not fighters. I don't think I have it in me to hurt someone."

The words twisted a knife in Brinnie's gut. *Right. They don't have it in them to hurt people. Unlike me, who's apparently a violent murderer void of morality.*

She knew Anna didn't intend the words as a jab, so she held her tongue. She didn't voice the response bubbling inside her. *I didn't think I had it in me to hurt someone either. Unfortunately, I don't have the luxury of sitting out of this fight.*

"That's fine." Mom stood. "We'll keep you as far from the conflict as possible, and you'll always be surrounded by wizards." She glanced at Lana's weapon. "A sword won't do much good against battle magic anyway."

Brinnie held her tongue again. Wizards like Lana, Mom, and herself might have useful magic for battle—powerful wizards from Masters families—but many possessed only niche talents or magic ill-suited for conflict, which meant armed combat was the battle strategy of choice.

As she had learned time and again in her classes at Mordizan, magic was waning. Just because magic scared Mom didn't mean she shouldn't be aware of the sociopolitical environment.

Without being able to offer Marcus snide commentary in her mind, each day she grew closer to saying things she might regret. *I need you back, Marcus—and not just because I'm going to murder you if you got yourself killed.*

"I guess we can go in." Brinnie took a step toward the door.

Just then, a form snapped into existence in front of her. She stumbled back as she almost slammed straight into Uncle Merlin.

He stepped back as well. "Oh dear, my apologies. I'm used to knowing where people are before traveling. Are you all right, Brynna?"

"I'm fine." She took in his harried expression. "What's wrong?"

"Enemies in the Maze." His jaw hardened. "From the way they're moving, either they've cracked the code, or it doesn't look like the Maze is magical anymore."

CHAPTER
TWENTY-ONE

Brinnie climbed over the earthen fortification and slid down the other side, avoiding the spikes protruding from the mound. Lana slid down after her, one hand on her sword hilt, and they entered the Maze side by side.

"Right, left, right," Brinnie repeated.

"Second left, first right," Lana added. "Then work our way back."

Soon they came to their first installment, a tripwire lying along the ground, not yet activated. They stepped over, taking the twists and turns until they reached the farthest defense. Lana adjusted the blanket they had covered with dirt and grass and stretched across the pit. Within, wooden stakes pointed upward, toward any hapless foot soldier who tromped forward across the flimsy blanket, falling into the hole below.

A gruesome, but not necessarily fatal, trap.

They worked their way backward. Brinnie pulled back a log on a vine and set the thin tripwire, made of fishing line. Next came the nooses, made of vines she had grown, nestled under fallen leaves, and nets set to spring. The traps wouldn't stop the advancing army, but they could certainly delay them, and hopefully take out a few soldiers. All made from plants Brinnie had grown and random supplies found around the house and garage.

Mr. Winslow had first proposed the idea, based on his and Jerry's ill-fated inventions. "At least half of them were liable to take an eye out," he mused. "Might as well use that to our advantage."

Brinnie didn't want to think about the damage the automatic corn husker they had set up along another path might do.

"Last chance." Brinnie glanced at Lana. "I talked to Uncle Merlin. He's willing to take you to Ariondam."

She tightened her bracers around her forearms. "I'm not leaving Wraithwood. Not until Excalibur returns."

Brinnie placed a hand on Lana's shoulder, her throat tight. "Thank you."

Ironically, Brinnie's Mordizan roommate was doing more to help than all of Castelon. Uncle Merlin had sent a request for backup to Castelon as soon as enemies were spotted in the Maze, but he was denied on the grounds that forces were spread thin, and Wraithwood didn't rank high on the list of estates to defend. Even Uncle Merlin's usual connections failed. After his "death," his networks had fallen into disrepair, and friends and allies had been displaced or dispatched by war.

They were alone.

They had risked transporting humans by portal to send Anna, David, and Isaac to Castelon, where Uncle Merlin had been able to secure their refugee status, at least.

"I didn't disclose any relation," he had explained to them. "It's better that they don't know you're Eira's daughter. Not with the way Castelon feels about our family. Unfortunately, it's probably best that you don't attempt to make contact with your sister either, David, as she arrived with Brynna. You'll be housed with other human refugees displaced from conquered estates."

David gripped his crutch, expression grim. "Anna, you take Isaac and go with Merlin. I'll stay here to help."

"Absolutely not." Anna grabbed his hand. "These people have magic. We can't do anything but get in the way." She gestured to Brinnie, standing nearby. "Even our field hospital experience isn't really relevant with Brinnie able to magically heal anyone."

"She's right," Brinnie said quietly. "When this place becomes a battleground, anyone who isn't ready to fight is a liability. No offense, but it's no place for humans."

He shook his head. "And it's no place for a kid either." He gave her a serious look, something deeply sympathetic sparking in his eyes. "Yet here you are. It isn't right."

"Nothing has been right for a long time." She nodded to Uncle Merlin. "Let's make this portal."

Anna clutched Isaac close. "Is it safe for him?"

"For him, certainly." Uncle Merlin gestured to the couple. "You two have traveled before, so if I took you through the Door, you might not survive, but with a portal, there should be minimal complications since it's only your second time."

And there hadn't been any complications, Uncle Merlin reported.

Brinnie glanced at Lana as they headed back to the house. The Winslows remained, and Miss Burtle. Four wizards, with herself, Mom, Uncle Merlin, and Lana. Ms. Tynsdale, unconscious forever, laid to rest in one of the rooms beneath Wraithwood. A room that had become a tomb Uncle Merlin visited often, when he didn't think anyone was paying attention. But Brinnie had seen him sit beside the fresh wooden coffin, tears rolling silently down his cheeks. Heard him whisper, "You shouldn't have done it, Lydia. Not for me."

She never went to check on him again.

Three humans, four wizards. Seven people against an army.

As they entered the kitchen, Bruno came loping toward them, tail wagging. He butted his head against Brinnie's hand, begging for pets.

Of all the things that had happened, that broke her.

She dropped to her knees and wrapped her arms around his neck. He licked away the tears on her cheeks, leaning in as she rubbed his ears, scratched that favorite spot on his back.

She tried to keep her breathing quiet, contain the sobs heaving her chest.

"Brinnie?" Lana knelt beside her and placed a hand on her shoulder. "Are you okay?"

She could barely force the words out through shuddering breaths. "Animals can't go through portals. They have to be left behind."

Lost. Left behind. So much innocent loss. Towns wiped out, defenders massacred. So many she loved ripped away, gone, snatched from her grasping attempts to keep them all safe. Ms. Tynsdale, Marcus, who knew who else.

Bruno nudged her a few times, reminding her to continue petting him. She sank into a crossed legged position, the big hound in her lap as if he were a little Pomeranian.

"Brinnie, sweet dear." Mrs. Winslow's voice.

She looked up, and the housekeeper brushed back hair from Brinnie's face. "If we have to leave Wraithwood, I'm sure Bruno and Ami will be fine. Everyone loves pets, not just us. Even a dark wizard couldn't resist a face like Bruno's."

Brinnie bit her lip, swiping away tears. "We'll have to make sure no one makes it through. Just to be sure."

"Of course, dear. We won't leave Wraithwood unless we have to." She turned and retrieved a kettle from the stove. "I've brewed your favorite blueberry tea. Why don't you girls take a rest and warm up?"

"The others are still fortifying the earthworks." Brinnie took a deep breath, trying to pull herself together. Thank goodness no one was around but Lana and Mrs. Winslow to see her break down like this. "We should help."

"In a moment." Lana rubbed her arms. "She's right, it's chilly out there, and we could use something warm."

You would make a terrible spy, Lana. Brinnie decided not to call Lana out on her fake-coldness. Instead, she nodded and stood. "We can take a minute."

Mrs. Winslow prepared food while the two of them sat sipping from mugs. Teacups were too small for the feelings Brinnie hoped to drown.

With the warmth of the crackling fire, Mrs. Winslow's soft humming as she cooked, hot tea . . . nothing seemed quite so bad. Mrs. Winslow's calming presence soothed Brinnie's ragged thoughts.

As Brinnie set aside her mug to head outside once more, she hugged the motherly woman. "Thank you."

"Of course, dear." She folded her into a soft embrace. "Everything will be okay." Then she released her. "Tell all of them out there dinner will be ready in about half an hour."

"Will do." Was it time for dinner already? They had started the day with morning sword fighting, moved on to sending away Anna and her family, and had spent the rest of the day on defenses. Dusk must be approaching.

Outside, they found Uncle Merlin, Mom, Mr. Winslow, and Miss Burtle hammering spikes into the ditch surrounding the front of the fortifications. Mr. Winslow leaned on a shovel. "Right side is falling apart a little."

"I'm on it." Brinnie grabbed a spare shovel. "I'll add some roots or something." She turned to Uncle Merlin. "How long do we have?"

He screwed another spike into the ground and brushed his hands on his pants. "Depending how skilled their scouts are at solving mazes, I'd give us anywhere from two hours until daybreak."

"Did you get a read on how many?" Lana asked.

He shook his head. "They're coming in waves. Scouts, front runners. I imagine they didn't want to get the entire force lost if something went wrong. I could tell there was a camp outside the Maze, but I can only make a guess on the numbers."

A non-answer. Brinnie's eyes narrowed. "So what *is* your guess?"

He hesitated. "A smaller force, all things considered. Maybe two, two and a half score, mostly low-level magic wielders."

"*Fifty* soldiers?" Mom drove her shovel into the ground, leaving it standing straight up. "You said 'a not unreasonable number.'"

"I have Masters powers. Brinnie has nearly every power imaginable. That's worth quite a bit." He reached for another stake lying along the ground. "And we have the advantage of fortifications, a defensible position, and a bottleneck at the entrance to the Maze." As Mom continued glaring, he sighed. "I'm not saying it will be an easy win, Eira, but I'm saying we can at least hold them off for the time being."

Brinnie tried to will Mom not to say it. Not to voice what they were all thinking.

But she did. "How long do we hold them off before it isn't worth fighting any longer?" She glanced at Brinnie. "When do we accept they're not coming back?"

Uncle Merlin's jaw tightened.

Before he could form words, Miss Burtle spoke up. "We'll hold out as long as we can." She crossed her arms. "We aren't just holding down the fort until those two return with Excalibur. We're fighting for the estate and its capabilities—the Door, the defenses, the Wraithwood Scrolls and all the magical items we don't want the enemy to get their hands on. This place itself is a weapon." She dropped her arms, and her tone softened slightly. "And we're fighting for our home, Eira. At least, the rest of us are, even if it isn't home to you anymore." She hefted a shovel. "I may not live through a portal anyway, so I'll take my chances in battle here. I have too many friends buried in the soil of Wraithwood to leave without a fight."

Silence. Mom held Uncle Merlin's gaze for a moment, then looked away. "Let's make these walls a little higher then."

After dinner, they gathered in the great hall in front of the door, armed with weapons and dressed in an assortment of protective gear, from Uncle Merlin opting for chain mail, to Lana's heavier metal armor and shield, to Brinnie's light leather armor—she hated being restricted. Lana appeared natural, but the rest of them . . . they looked ready to attend a Renaissance Festival, not fight for their lives.

Uncle Merlin turned to the assembled group. "There are seven of us and who knows how many of them. This won't be easy. If anyone wants to leave, I will happily escort you wherever you want to go." He looked to Lana. "Especially you. I know this isn't your home. I'm happy to take you to Ariondam before things get interesting."

She placed a hand on her sword pommel, shoulders square. "Mordred in power is bad news for all of us. We need to protect this place until Marcus and Ignatius get back with Excalibur to defeat him. I'm in."

"In that case, a recap of the plan." He nodded to the three humans. "We have three firearms. Edna and Tom will be our sharpshooters from behind the fortifications while Mrs. Winslow loads, and jumps in if necessary. Brinnie, Eira, Lana, and I will remain closer to the entrance and use long-range magic for as long as we can and try to hold them at the gate, getting into hand-to-hand combat only if we need to. Once we fall back to the fortifications, we'll all be firing with magic and munitions. If they take the fortifications, we'll fall back to the great hall. We can fire at them from the balcony as they enter the house and give us enough time to get through a portal." He gave them all a hard look. "No heroics. If you're in trouble, fall back. If you're injured, get to Brinnie for healing. We live to fight another day."

Mr. Winslow shouldered his rifle. "Reckon we better get into position."

As they made their way to the earthworks, Uncle Merlin disappeared, off to check on the progress of the enemy. Brinnie's heart thundered in her chest. Battle always brought on its own bout of nerves, but she didn't usually have to worry about the safety of her family as well.

She found solid footing directly in front of the gate leading into the Maze, head and shoulders above the fortifications, Mom and Lana on either side of her. Mr. Winslow and Miss Burtle carved out positions for their firearms, nothing but the barrels and the top of their heads peeking above the dirt wall.

Uncle Merlin appeared on the other side of Mom. “I’d give us fifteen minutes before they’re on us.”

Lana loosened her sword in its sheath. “When they get closer, I’ll throw a light orb over the gate so we can see what we’re shooting at.”

Right. Dusk had fallen. An issue for everyone but Brinnie.

The seconds ticked by slowly. Every breeze, every sound was the approaching army. Brinnie’s heart beat faster and faster. Uncle Merlin may have said no heroics, but knowing everyone here . . . This wasn’t just any battle. This was a battle for their home, for the people they loved . . . for Excalibur. Abandon Wraithwood, and they would lose their only way to defeat Mordred. *Come on, Marcus. Get back before we have to give in.*

And then the first twig snapped.

CHAPTER TWENTY-TWO

The man poked his head around the corner, hesitant.

"Hold," Uncle Merlin whispered.

The soldier advanced, sword ready, four others behind him. The gate provided enough room for four or five to enter abreast. One held out a hand, a light orb beginning to form.

"Now."

Lana shot a blinding light toward them, and they all covered their eyes. In the confusion, Mom swiped out a hand. Icicles shot toward the soldiers like projectiles, eliciting cries. Uncle Merlin's fingers twitched, and the ground itself rose up to swallow them, dragging them down.

A beat of silence.

Then the forces charged forward with a roar.

Gunshots rang out behind her and two warriors fell to the ground, but the army kept coming right over top of them.

Brinnie sent wolves racing toward the oncoming forces. At the same time, Lana blasted light toward them. The stream of light scythed through Brinnie's wolves, evaporating them, but the oncoming warriors stumbled, covering their eyes.

"Oh shoot, sorry, Brinnie." Lana pulled her hand back.

"It's fine, change of tactics." Brinnie formed new wolves. "Can you send targeted beams straight at individuals? That should keep from hitting my shadows."

"You got it." Lana shot beams of light like lasers straight into the eyes of oncoming soldiers. With her other hand, she formed a light orb larger than her head, then launched it above the gate, illuminating the oncoming horde.

Gunshots, icicles, beams of light, wolves, fists of earth punching up to batter and hit the enemy, and yet they kept coming. Mom gestured, and a layer of ice shot across the ground, sending soldiers slipping and sliding. A few slid right off the edge, crashing into the spikes driven into the trench in front of the earthworks. Brinnie averted her eyes from them, forming shadowy birds of prey that dive-bombed the oncomers, raking faces with their talons.

To the left of the gate, a row of soldiers dropped to one knee, holding up body-length shields. Another row darted behind them, protected. Before Brinnie could discern their plan, arrows shot over the row of shields, heading for the defenders.

"Duck!" She dropped below the earthworks. Dirt tumbled around her as arrows hit the top of the mound.

"Be careful." Uncle Merlin drew his shortsword. "I'll take care of this." He disappeared.

Brinnie peered over the earthworks. She didn't see anything for a moment, but then the shields began to waver. Behind them, she caught flashes of Uncle Merlin, appearing and reappearing, slashing down the archers and popping out of existence before anyone could retaliate.

He appeared next to the three of them again, holding a bow and quiver of arrows. "If anyone wants it." He dropped the weapons on the ground and turned to shoot projectiles over the barrier once more.

"That's pretty cool." Lana shot out several more beams of light, then snatched up the bow and quiver, nocking an arrow. "We should have Masters join battles more often." She let fly, and the arrow struck an oncoming warrior directly through the throat.

"Is there any weapon you *aren't* good at?" Just to add some variety, Brinnie threw a fireball at an attacker.

"My power isn't very useful as battle magic against anyone but you." She shot another arrow, another man down. "I had to get pretty good at other things to make up for it."

It occurred to Brinnie that during the time she had been in the dungeon, Lana must have been on the battlefield—at least until she was imprisoned for freeing Anna and David.

Brinnie wasn't the only killer here.

Just then, a ferocious wind slammed into them, sending them flying back. Brinnie hit the ground with a thud, the breath knocked out of her.

"Apparently they do have some useful magic." Uncle Merlin alone of the four remained standing. He held out both hands, and from what

Brinnie could see, a whirlwind of his own slammed into the wind pressing them down. "Brinnie, your wolves are fading. I see the aerial wizard behind those shields."

"Got it." She scrambled to her feet and poked her head back over the barrier. She spotted the wizard, hands lifted above two shield bearers in front of her. Brinnie directed a wolf behind them, charging for the wizard.

It passed through.

Mordred must have warned the aerial wizard of Brinnie's vulnerability. "She's immune."

Uncle Merlin gave a sharp nod. He kept one hand up, fighting off the wind, and with the other, he made a fist. A matching fist of earth rose up and grabbed the wizard's leg, yanking her to the ground. With her distracted, Uncle Merlin blasted the shield bearers with a tempest of his own, sending them stumbling. With the wizard exposed, Mom shot a flurry of knifelike icicles toward her.

Brinnie looked away from the result.

Hope rose within her as they continued to hold off the assault. Bodies piled up, and limping and injured warriors were dragged back inside the Maze.

But eventually, something felt wrong.

"Uncle Merlin." Her shadow wolf passed through a soldier, so she blasted him with fire instead. "Am I counting wrong, or does this feel like more than fifty?"

He frowned, deflecting a javelin thrown toward him with a gust of wind. "I was beginning to think the same thing."

A bead of sweat shone on Mom's temple. She grabbed a bottle of water they had stashed behind the fortifications and took a swig. "Are you sure there weren't more in that camp?"

"Wait." Lana stood on her tiptoes. "I think they're falling back."

Indeed, the warriors began trickling back through the gate, some dragging the dead and wounded with them. Brinnie called off her wolves and raptors.

Within a few moments, they were all gone.

"Looks like we at least have a break."

Brinnie turned to see Miss Burtle making her way toward them, a bit of dirt streaked across her cheek.

Uncle Merlin nodded, stepping back from the barricade. "We should rest while we can. One or two at a time can go back to the house for supplies, more food, whatever you need. Return with a blanket or two, and if they offer us enough time, we can sleep here in shifts. No one should be too far away in case they regroup."

"Do we have any extra long-range weapons?" Miss Burtle tilted her head back toward where she'd come from. "We're almost out of ammunition, and I'm letting Tom take the lead on sharpshooting."

Out of ammo already? Brinnie turned to Lana and whispered, "How long have we been at this?"

"At least a few hours." She raised an eyebrow at Brinnie's surprised expression. "You're not even winded, are you?"

Brinnie glanced at Mom's trembling fingers, the sheen of sweat on Lana's brow. This much magic—and in Lana's case, an hour or two of archery on top of that—took it out of them.

But if anything, these few hours had only taken the edge off the burning depth of power within her. As long as her body lasted, the magic could keep going and going.

Her body. The moment she thought about her physical form, her knees wobbled. She sank into a sitting position, her limbs like noodles.

"Oh, I'm definitely winded." She gave a slight smile. *But if I could get a chair, maybe prop my feet up, I think I could do this all day.* Evidently a few hours of standing was more taxing than summoning hordes of shadowy creatures and throwing balls of magic.

"Here." Lana held the bow out to Miss Burtle. "Can you shoot? I only have two arrows left, but we can gather more from the field."

Miss Burtle accepted the weapon. "Not with excellence, but well enough that I should be able to hit something."

While her friends and family began to disperse, preparing for the next wave of battle, Brinnie stared at her limbs. Pasty white, as usual. Still too thin. The dark circles she saw under her eyes in the mirror could just as well be from nights spent awake from nightmares as from some sort of toll from magic.

Now that it had settled within her, she didn't know what magic was doing to her body anymore. And at this point, she would almost rather not find out.

Time passed. Brinnie started a campfire to keep everyone warm and wrapped herself in a blanket, using a springy patch of moss she grew as a pillow.

She had fallen into a fitful sleep when Uncle Merlin's strained voice awoke her. "We have a problem."

She forced her eyes open, sitting up. He had a cut slashed across one cheek, his sword out. She scrambled to her feet. "What happened?"

"I just got back from reconnaissance. The camp I saw earlier was a diversion, a smaller force they sent to trick us." His grip tightened on his sword. "They're digging under the Maze. They plan to attack from multiple sides."

CHAPTER

TWENTY-THREE

At the same moment, a shout echoed from the gate. Brinnie scrambled to the top of the fortifications to see soldiers pouring in.

"Where's the other force coming through?" Lana grabbed her sword. "I'm of little use long-range, but I can defend a breach."

Before Uncle Merlin could respond, an explosion echoed from somewhere behind the house.

"That answers that." Lana strapped on her sword belt, smashed a helmet on her head, and took off running.

"I'll go with her." Brinnie kept speaking before Mom could argue. "We're trained to fight together and I have as many swords as I can summon."

"Signal for backup if you need it." Uncle Merlin threw a gust of wind over the fortification. "Two blasts to the sky."

She nodded once and turned to run.

Two wizards per entry point, one each with multiple powers. *We can make this work.* The Winslows and Miss Burtle would stay at the semicircular fortifications, where they could shoot from a protected, safe distance.

And hopefully not get hurt without Brinnie there to heal them.

Maybe Uncle Merlin should have gone with Lana instead, but it was too late now. Brinnie's breath came in ragged gasps, unused to this level of exertion, especially with the added weight of even the sparse armor she wore. Armor. *Shoot.* She'd taken her breastplate off while sleeping and hadn't grabbed it before running. *Just don't get stabbed, I guess.* She sent wolves running ahead of her, far faster than she was with her short, out-of-shape legs.

Not quite exactly opposite from the gate, a ragged opening had been hacked and blasted through the hedge, half hole in the ground, half breach in the foliage. Soldiers muscled their way through, pouring toward the house.

Lana slashed two down while still running toward the breach. Brinnie's wolves took two more. Brinnie formed a shadow sword in her hand and slid into position near Lana, blocking a swing from an attacker.

"You take left, I'll take right," Lana shouted.

"Got it."

She turned invisible and summoned a shield to match the sword. She slammed into another attacker, shoving with her shield and stabbing beneath his guard. These wizards weren't as strong as the ones at the bridge at Riverdell. She pushed her way through them to the entrance hole and blasted the opening with a fiery inferno. Warriors screamed, and flames licked the hedge. She quenched the blazing branches with blasts of water but left the wizards to burn.

As she whirled toward the wizards remaining on their side of the hedge, separated from the others by the blaze, she met Lana's gaze. A wide-eyed, almost horrified gaze. One that said burning multiple soldiers alive had crossed some sort of line.

They can burn now or be stabbed later.

Anger clenched her heart as she blasted one attacker with fire and sent a wolf after another. *I don't* want *to be killing anyone.* Riverdell flashed before her mind. *But last time I showed mercy in battle, it ended in even more bloodshed.*

As the sun rose high in the sky, sweat began to drip from her temples, even in the cold. No matter how many she and Lana cut down, more appeared. The hole in the hedge widened. Brinnie's arms shook as she swung again and again, her movements beginning to feel sloppy. Her fingers had gone numb, and her mouth felt as dry as the Arizona desert. A nick across her forehead bled, stinging her eye, and she wiped the blood away, accidentally smearing more blood on her face from a slash across her arm.

She glanced toward Lana. Her friend appeared to be favoring one leg, and the amount of blood on her arm hinted at a wound, not just blood splatter from enemies. Brinnie fought her way to Lana and threw out a wall of fire around them, holding back the fray momentarily. Lana cut down the one warrior trapped in the circle with them and spun, sword out, almost taking off Brinnie's head.

"Sorry, it's me." She turned visible and grabbed Lana's arm.

"Oh." She relaxed slightly. "What's up?"

"You're injured." Brinnie laid a hand on her friend's forehead, letting healing magic flow through her. Then she let the firewall drop and spun away to continue fighting before Lana even finished saying thank you.

Before she could return to invisibility, Uncle Merlin appeared next to her. "We need you."

The statement sent fear through her heart. Space warped and twirled so quickly her head spun. They appeared behind the fortifications, where Miss Burtle leaned against the earthworks, teeth clenched, holding her hands around a knife embedded in her side.

"On it." Brinnie pressed her hands around the wound and removed the knife with one swift movement. Blood flowed over her fingers for a few seconds before the skin knit together.

Brinnie felt as if her heart could beat again. *Nothing terrible. Easy healing.*

Miss Burtle nodded. "Thanks." Hands trembling with exhaustion, she reached for a bow and an almost empty quiver.

Brinnie took a second to assess the situation. Mr. and Mrs. Winslow appeared to be throwing rocks at the enemy. Mom had dropped to her knees on top of the earthworks, now beginning to crumble, face so pale it was almost blue as she shot icicles with shaking arms.

"Stars above," she heard Uncle Merlin breathe. "They've managed another breach."

Brinnie turned. About a hundred yards down the hedge, warriors poured through a third opening in the Maze, headed straight toward them.

"Fall back!" Uncle Merlin shouted. He pointed at Brinnie. "Get everyone here back to the house. I'll get Lana." He disappeared.

Brinnie amplified her voice. "Retreat! To the house!"

Miss Burtle raised her bow, an arrow nocked. "I have our back."

Mom slid down the earthworks, stumbling like a newborn foal. The Winslows turned toward Brinnie. Mrs. Winslow took a step.

And then time slowed as a large man rose above the fortification, a spear raised. Up, then down. Plunging. Plunging toward Mrs. Winslow's exposed back.

"Look out!" The scream tore from Brinnie's throat at the same time her arms shot out, a fireball and an eagle both soaring toward the man.

Too late. Too slow. The spear plunged. Mrs. Winslow stiffened, slumped.

Then the ball of fire hit the man, and the eagle raked its talons across his face. As the attacker tumbled backward, Brinnie sprinted toward Mrs. Winslow.

Mr. Winslow dropped to his knees, catching his wife right before she hit the ground. The spear had stabbed all the way through. "Break the shaft!" Brinnie called, coming in so hard she slid on her knee like she was sliding into home plate.

Mr. Winslow grabbed a short sword and sawed through the shaft. As soon as it broke, he flipped Mrs. Winslow over onto her back, the point of the spear protruding from her chest, coated in blood.

Brinnie placed her hands around the wound. "I got you, Mrs. Winslow. I'll heal you."

No response. Her eyes stared upward, glassy.

"That's okay. That's okay." Brinnie sent healing magic down her arms, pushing toward the wound. Nothing. She grasped the spear, accidentally slicing her hand in the process. "We'll get this out. Then it will work." Her hands kept slipping on the bloody weapon.

"Brinnie."

She didn't look up, didn't meet Mr. Winslow's gaze. She couldn't see his face, not when she could hear the tears in his voice. "I've got this." From her peripheral, she saw more soldiers climbing up the wall, and she sent wolves to deal with them.

She finally managed to yank out the spear. No blood gushed forth. A bad sign she refused to acknowledge. She pressed both hands to the wound, squeezed her eyes shut. "Come on, come on."

She tried again, and again. Mr. Winslow reached for her hands, but she shook him off. She pressed red fingers to Mrs. Winslow's neck, feeling for a pulse. Nothing. Wrist? No. Somewhere. Maybe she just couldn't feel it right. She felt for a pulse again, but her shaking fingers couldn't find one.

Mrs. Winslow was dead.

Brinnie stood, slowly. She didn't look at Mr. Winslow as she spoke. "Get back to the house. Get everyone back to the house."

"I don't reckon—"

"Leave." Her breath burned in her lungs. "Run. Before I accidentally kill you all too."

She stalked forward, down the earthworks, past the spikes. Any attackers who drew near, her wolves ripped out their throats. She kept walking. Toward the gate. Toward the middle of the horde.

Not Mrs. Winslow. Too far. They had gone too far.

She screamed, and the battlefield exploded into flames.

Bodies dropped all around her. Through the flickering fire, she could see her friends and family running for the house. Good. Out of range.

Wolves sprinted away from her, headed for the third opening in the hedge and the attackers pouring in there. At the gate, she continued to burn. A few warriors pushed forward through the inferno, presumably fire wizards. For them, she let the wolves do her work. To shadow or flame, all would fall.

Water splashed toward her fire from new wizards standing just outside the gate. A giggle rose within her at the futility. They thought they could smother her flame?

She shot columns of fire through the entrance, blasting them away.

"It doesn't matter how many warriors you send." She held out her hands, power welling. "You will not take Wraithwood."

No more. No more loss. No more losing. She would avenge Mrs. Winslow. Get Marcus back. Destroy Mordred.

As if summoned by her thoughts, a robed figure stepped through the gateway, unharmed by the flames. He unsheathed a glowing blade, and Brinnie's arm burned cold.

She picked up a sword from a fallen soldier and pointed it at him. She amplified her voice, the blade in her hand an arrow to Mordred. "I vow to you, Mordred. Your death is mine."

He strode forward. "No matter how many tools you steal, Brynna Ludovic, you are still powerless against me."

She didn't release the flames—let them burn, keep anyone from interfering with this fight. She raised her hand, sending a pack of shadow wolves in his direction.

The wolves leaped straight through him. He smirked, not breaking stride. "You can't hurt me with your imaginary dogs."

"I didn't expect to." While his eyes were on the wolves, ropelike vines rose from the ground, grasping for his legs. Brinnie struggled to maintain them as they caught fire, but she managed to hold on and turn invisible at the same time.

"Diverting." He plowed through the vines, turning them to ash. "Your tricks won't work on me."

He lifted his hand and blasted her with a flash of light. She felt the shadows hiding her rip away. She stumbled backward, trying to recover. The flames dropped along with her concentration as she threw up a shield of shadows to block the light, but his onslaught kept coming, one pulse of blinding light after another. Disoriented, she barely managed to hold up her own sword to deflect as he swung down at her. But wait, that wasn't the enchanted blade. Where—

Sharp pain in her side gave her the answer. He had swung with a sword and slashed with the enchanted blade in his other hand, luckily only making what felt like superficial contact. She managed to shove him back, stumbling away. His burning eyes were the only thing she saw before he blasted her with light again in the face. She tripped over something, fell over backward seeing stars.

She managed not to drop her sword, and with limited eyesight, she parried his swinging blade out of the way, rolling to the side. His sword twisted, wresting hers from her grasp—leaving her on her back, weaponless, staring up at him. She grappled for a weapon, reaching for anything, eyes burning, trying to shove to her feet.

Too slow. His blade plunged downward. She tried to roll out of the way, but she wasn't fast enough. Searing pain. She felt the blade pass through her, felt the tip pierce the earth beneath her, then yank back out again. Her throat burned, and she realized it was from her own scream. He lifted his blade again, swinging down.

Then something blocked her view, and the weapon hit a shield raised above her with a clang. "We have to go." One arm holding the shield above them, Uncle Merlin wrapped his other around Brinnie.

Space warped. A brief glimpse of the Door. They appeared on the landing above the great hall, Mom, Mr. Winslow, Miss Burtle, and Lana standing waiting for them, Ms. Tynsdale supported among them.

"Now," Uncle Merlin said.

Mom threw down a portal, mist rising around them.

No. We can't leave yet. We can win. Let me go back. Why couldn't she make the words come out? Why couldn't she feel . . . anything?

With that, consciousness slipped from her grasp.

CHAPTER TWENTY-FOUR

She was dying, and she couldn't bring herself to particularly care.

Don't let Mordred win, Lana had whispered to her.

You can survive this. Mom's voice had floated from somewhere far away. *Come on, Brinnie. Live.*

Yesterday—longer? She couldn't keep track of time. She had almost had hope. The first voice she'd heard after swimming up from the darkness of unconsciousness had been unfamiliar.

"I can't heal her." The voice sounded warped. "We've done our best to seal the wound, but with an enchanted blade . . . I have to be honest with you. It will likely only be a matter of time."

Don't speak for me. Brinnie had opened her eyes slowly to see the unfamiliar man standing at her bedside. The stone ceiling and walls around her hinted at a castle—was she at Castelon? Mom and Uncle Merlin hovered nearby. She could hardly feel her limbs, but she forced words out of her mouth in a rasping voice that shot pain through her torso. "We need to go back. With reinforcements from Castelon."

The healer startled. "She's awake."

Her vision faded in and out. "The Maze isn't magical anymore. We can march on Wraithwood. Take it back."

"Brinnie, hush." Mom stepped forward, smoothed hair away from her brow.

Stay conscious, stay conscious. The pain shooting through her threatened to boot her back into darkness. "Marcus. Excalibur. Wraithwood."

"Wraithwood is occupied." Uncle Merlin's voice, not that she could see him. "We would need a force larger than we could muster to fight them, even if we pulled defenders from other estates."

"I can fight. If Mordred isn't there, I can take them. I can." Her breath heaved, and she felt at least one stitch rip. "We can't let Excalibur fall into enemy hands."

"Brinnie." Mom took a deep breath. "We've done research. As far as wizards before us have calculated, you can't survive in a time not your own. Your matter doesn't belong there, so you can't intake and process other matter."

Her thoughts were too fuzzy to interpret what that meant. "What?"

"It means you can't eat or drink anything there," Uncle Merlin explained. "A person can survive perhaps a week without water." His tone was gentle—too gentle. "It's been far longer than that."

The words finally clicked.

They're gone. They're dead. They're not coming back.

"We have to accept that Excalibur is lost," Mom confirmed.

Lost. Marcus. Mrs. Winslow. Wraithwood. *Hope.* Their only hope against Mordizan's might, lost.

"My lady." The healer edged around Mom. "Excuse me, she's bleeding again."

Let the blood drain away. At least she wouldn't have to watch the rest of her friends and family die, powerless to stop it.

Perhaps that would be better for everyone. Everything she'd tried, all of her time fighting, had gone horribly wrong. Perhaps they had a better chance without her.

Consciousness fled, leaving her in blessed darkness.

And so the whispers floated around her. She tried to open her eyes at times, but nothing happened. She felt as if she floated in a void, disembodied, connected only to her corporeal form by a telephone with poor service through which words occasionally traveled, tinny and far away.

"I don't think she's going to make it, Merlin."

Mom's voice seemed . . . teary. Was she crying?

"She was severely wounded, Eira." Uncle Merlin. "Give her time to heal. It's only been a couple days. It's a miracle she survived at all. If she made it this far, we have to believe she'll pull through."

"I thought she would, when she woke up toward the beginning. We should have lied to her. When we told her the truth . . . I saw the light leave her eyes." Mom took a shuddering breath. "She's so stubborn. She wouldn't have slipped away again like that. Not unless . . . unless her will to live is gone."

Come on, Uncle Merlin. Say something encouraging.

Instead, he sighed. "Can you blame her? It seems all any of us can do at this point is delay the inevitable." A pause. "In a sad, strange way, it's been good to see her actually resting, not wandering the halls at night or waking up screaming."

The words shot an arrow through her. They had noticed. Of course, they had.

"You can't say that, Merlin. I know it's been hard—it's been hard on everyone. But she has to keep going, just like we did after what happened to Mom and Dad."

"Keep going?" He gave a dry half-laugh. "You ran away, Eira. You left everything."

"I'm here now, aren't I?" The indignation in her tone faded to quiet contemplation. "And you stayed. You took care of Wraithwood. You were always the stronger one, and all I ever did was mock you for it."

"We've all done things we regret." His voice sounded tight. "Allowing Brinnie to go to Mordizan is one of those for me. She's endured things we can barely begin to imagine, Eira. She's fought through so many impossible odds. If she doesn't have it in her to keep fighting anymore . . . if she decides this is the end of the line . . . I don't think any of us can begrudge her that."

Mom might be arguing with him. Might be telling him he shouldn't say something like that. But Brinnie wasn't listening anymore.

I'm allowed to rest.

In Uncle Merlin's mind, she had fought long and hard. If she didn't want to fight anymore . . . that was okay.

It wasn't her duty as a sixteen-year-old to save the world, and it was cruel to expect that of her. If she couldn't do it, she wasn't a failure, a disappointment, a monster. At least not to him. She was just a normal kid.

A weight lifted from her chest. *I'm allowed to give up.*

She sank back into comforting blackness.

But as she drifted in and out, she realized, maybe she didn't want to give up yet. Maybe she could give life one more Hail Mary and see where that led. She couldn't exactly make things worse at this point.

Okay, Uncle Merlin. Maybe for spite. Maybe just to see the look on Mordred's face, or to annoy Castelius with my continued existence. I don't think I can do a single thing about this situation, but screw it, I'm going to try anyway.

When she inevitably did go down in flames and joined Mrs. Winslow and Marcus in the afterlife, she would have a wild tale worthy of telling.

Deciding to live proved more difficult than anticipated.

As it turned out, the decision didn't flip a switch that made her body start functioning. She was able to open her eyes after a while, remain cognizant of her surroundings for longer. In time, she could accept water, broth. The searing pain of . . . *everything* . . . threatened to send her back to darkness, but the healers did have some remedies, even if they couldn't magically heal the wound. She heard the healers muttering to each other, to Mom, Uncle Merlin, Miss Burtle. *She shouldn't be alive. Master Castelius was waiting to pronounce her death. No one expected a recovery.*

She allowed a small smirk to herself. No one expected her to live. So live she would. *And Marcus, Mrs. Winslow, I will do so as spectacularly as I can.*

Two days later, she stared up at the ceiling, mustering her strength. *Big day today.* She shouldn't be moving out of bed other than to a chair or the bathroom, but what was the worst that could happen? Death? *Ha.*

The door opened slowly. Mom stepped in wearing a flowing green velvet gown. "Good morning, honey."

Brinnie eased herself into a sitting position. Agonizing. She should be septic. Her organs should be ruptured, done for. Too much magic in her to allow that to happen, probably. "Was anyone able to find anything for me to wear?"

"Brinnie." Mom sat on the foot of the bed. "We can petition the Council to put off the meeting a few more days. If you do go, you only have to be there. Let us take care of the talking."

"But I have so much to say." She gave a dry smile. "I can't beat Mordred, but I have plenty of words for Scott Castelius." A snorting snicker forced its way through her nose.

Mom raised an eyebrow. "What's so funny?"

"His name. Scott." At Mom's continued blank expression, Brinnie explained, "Not Septimus or Ignatius or Merlin or Antony or you know, all those other wizardy-sounding names everyone else has. Just *Scott.* Like he works in accounting and his best pals are Bob and Jim." Another snort. "Do you think it makes him self-conscious?"

Mom rubbed a hand over her face. "You sound like Merlin." Her expression sobered, and she placed a hand on Brinnie's leg. "You don't have to face any of this alone. We're all here, too."

She decided to keep her thoughts on how well that had worked in the past to herself. "I'm looking forward to talking to Scott myself."

"Heaven help us." Mom stood. "Miss Burtle is bringing some dresses for you to choose from. Would you like to eat anything?"

"I had some broth earlier. That's about all I can handle right now."

Mom pursed her lips, brow furrowed as she assessed Brinnie. "I can't express how happy I am to see you awake and stubborn again, but you may be taking this a little far."

A knock on the door interrupted before Brinnie could say anything. Miss Burtle entered, carrying what appeared to be three dresses over her arm. "These were all I could find." She crossed to the small wardrobe in the corner and hung them on the door. "People are unusually prickly around here." She shot them a look. "And yes, I know that means a lot coming from me."

Mom's lips twitched. Brinnie noticed the dark circles under her eyes. None of this had been easy on her either. "Thank you, Edna."

She nodded and left.

Mom turned to the dresses. "Hmm. This blue one looks nice."

Ever so carefully, Brinnie swung one leg and then the other off the side of the bed. She tilted her head, squinting at the dresses.

The blue one was out for sure. Demure, simple, and not at all her color. The green one could work, but—

Mom moved it aside, revealing the third dress.

"That one."

"Brinnie . . ."

"What?" She batted her eyelashes innocently. "Black is only appropriate. I'm in mourning."

Her chest panged at her own words. *They deserve someone to properly mourn them.* In her own way, she hoped to honor their memory.

Mom helped her into the dress, maneuvering the fabric around the many bandages as well as they could. The neckline rested right below her shoulders, intricate black lace in the bodice continuing into tight long sleeves of lace like spiderwebs and flaring into a dramatic full skirt. Absolutely over the top, evil queen energy.

Mom moved to put her hair up, but Brinnie stopped her. "I'd rather leave it down and long." She turned to the mirror inside the door of the wardrobe. They didn't have any beauty products, but she used shapeshifter magic to add a slight wave to her hair and red lips as if she was wearing lipstick. "There."

Mom sighed. "You certainly look beautiful."

Beautiful . . . and dangerous. Brinnie turned to her. "Shall we?"

The two of them made their way slowly through the halls of Castelon. Brinnie tried not to wince with each step. She'd asked for extra bandaging today, to prevent blood from seeping onto her outfit, but she was beginning to think that was a lost cause.

She attempted to remove her mind from the situation, simply putting one foot in front of the other, Mom beside her. Mom's shoes clacked against the stone floors in a steady cadence.

By the time they reached the staircase at the end of the hall, sweat beaded on Brinnie's brow. She stared at the stairs. *There's no way.*

She pressed her lips together and summoned several shadows. With a mixture of shadow magic and levitation, she formed a floating, shadowy seat for herself and sat upon it. Then she nodded to Mom. "Ready."

She floated down the stairs on her homemade magical stairlift. Her lips twitched. "Didn't think I would need one of these for at least several more decades."

Mom's expression didn't register humor. "We can still go back."

"I'm fine. This is perfect, actually."

Passersby shot Brinnie strange looks as they made their way through the castle. "Reminds me of Mordizan," Brinnie remarked.

"Brynna."

Soon enough, they approached wide doors manned by two guards. *Nice to be joining the meeting without a blindfold this time.* Brinnie dismissed her shadow chair and brushed out her skirts.

Mom turned to her. "This is it." Worry lined her brow. "I can't join you on the floor. Are you really sure about this?"

Was she? Not really. But she couldn't bring herself to care anymore.

So she smiled. "I am. I'm ready. It will be okay, Mom."

Mom hesitated, then pressed a quick kiss to Brinnie's forehead before striding away, headed for the smaller entry lesser members of Masters families and other prominent figures used.

Brinnie waited a moment to allow Mom time to head to her seat, then straightened her shoulders and stepped up to the doors. She flashed a smile at the guards.

They didn't react, other than to open the doors for her, revealing a view of the council room floor.

Master Castelius scowled from his place in the center chair, the elected Council to either side of him filling all seven seats. Five more black-robed wizards occupied the coliseum seating to the side, each in a clearly designated box, Uncle Merlin among them, with a host of wizards like Mom in formal attire sitting farther back. A crowd Brinnie could hardly see lined the gallery.

"The accused, Lady Brynna Ludovic-Drakon," a herald near the door announced. He gestured to a stand to the right—one they hadn't had the courtesy to offer for her trial with Marcus.

Brinnie nodded to him and strode to the small platform, which supported a few seats—presumably for the accused and the wizard equivalent of lawyers—and steps leading to a podium. She felt the eyes of all the wizards upon her, Masters, heirs, prominent figures. Most importantly, all of the people who had refused to come to Wraithwood's aid.

She took her place at the stand and surveyed the room, chin tilted back, daring anyone to look her in the eye.

Uncle Merlin did—and offered a slight, mischievous smile.

"We gather here today for the trial of Brynna Ludovic-Drakon, retried for high treason." Master Castelius's voice boomed throughout the arena. "As many of you will recall, a previous trial was held in which she was deemed guilty."

"Objection." Uncle Merlin stood, expression all business now. "The results of that trial were cast out due to improper procedure. They have no bearing on this trial."

"As I was about to state." Master Castelius glared at him as he sat down, then turned back to the room at large, holding up a paper in front of him to read. "The accused is facing the following charges—unregistered status, fraternizing with the enemy, attacking and conquering the fifth stronghold, and stealing the magic of those in the final stronghold, thereby opening the estates to attack." He looked up from the page. "Drakon, how do you plead to these charges?"

She stood in front of the empty seats on the stand, making sure the entire room could see her as she looked directly at the Master of Castelon.

"Thanks for asking, Scott." They made eye contact, and she offered him a slow, small smirk as his eyes narrowed and his face reddened. "Guilty. I plead guilty to all charges."

CHAPTER TWENTY-FIVE

A flurry of muttering rustled in the gallery, murmurs running through the crowd within the stadium.

Master Castelius's expression registered a range of emotions from surprise, to satisfaction, to annoyance.

Didn't think I would plead guilty, did you, Scott?

He tapped a gavel and nodded to Brinnie. "You may sit. Your representative will speak for you now."

"I will be representing myself." She took the two steps up to the podium and placed her hands on either side of it in a calculated show of ease. As a bonus, no one would be able to tell she was supporting herself against the stand, abdomen screaming at her to stop. "I would like to make my opening statements."

She didn't know how wizard trials worked, and even her knowledge of human courts came mostly from fiction, but hopefully confidence would get her where knowledge couldn't.

Master Castelius's lips pressed in a thin line. "Proceed. You may have one minute before questioning. Any show of contempt for the Council, and you will be asked to cease."

From Uncle Merlin's disgruntled expression, Brinnie gathered that the time limit wasn't usual. Oh well. The quicker the trial, the sooner she could rest.

Don't even think about that. Just the thought of giving in to the pain made her knees weak—and she couldn't be weak.

"I wouldn't dream of *showing* the depth of my contempt for the Council." Brinnie flashed a sweet smile. "I try to be polite. I also try to drive straight to the point. So here's my thesis—you may not like me, but you need me."

From the corner of her eye, she saw Mom rub her temple and Uncle Merlin hide a smile.

"Oh, really?" One of the Council members beside Master Castelius raised an eyebrow. "We need a traitorous child?"

"I believe calling me a traitor isn't proper protocol during a trial to figure out what I am, but we'll let that one slide." She leaned one arm against the podium, other hand on her hip. "Let's get one thing straight. You don't like me, I don't like you. Nothing I did had anything to do with any loyalty to Castelon. However, I think you'll find our goals more or less align."

She caught sight of several pairs of wide eyes in both the gallery and the Council. Evidently not many people dared stand up to the useless old men.

"Let's start with Mordizan. When I went to the stronghold of the dark wizards, I was on a reconnaissance mission to find Mordred's bane. Naturally, I had to 'fraternize' with the enemy, convincing them that I had turned to their side." She cocked her head at Master Castelius. "I assume you're aware of the concept of espionage, Scott? Or shall I explain it?"

Someone snorted in the gallery, though the laugh was quickly muffled.

"You're inching dangerously close to contempt," he growled.

"Only checking in." She turned her attention to the rest of the Council once more. "Unfortunately, they did eventually discover me and threw me in the dungeon for a long period of torturing, but not before I managed to break into Mordred's room and discover his bane, the one thing prophesied to be able to destroy him." She lifted an eyebrow at Castelius. "If we can play nice, maybe I'll tell you what it is."

This time the Masters' benches erupted with talk. Brinnie caught snippets. "Is it true? Could there be a way to defeat him?"

"Order!" Master Castelius thumped the gavel and scowled at Brinnie. "This is a trial, not a negotiation. You are an unregistered wizard, operating in secret. Why should we trust anything you say?"

"Fair enough, let's continue this trial." She gestured to him. "You bring up a fair point about being an unregistered wizard, but it's easily explained. I was hiding from Mordred, who was on the hunt for me, and

I couldn't risk spies within Castelon's ranks leaking my location." Master Castelius began to open his mouth, but she kept talking. "Don't even try to tell me you don't have plenty of infiltrators. I *did* spend a significant time at Mordizan, after all." The corner of her lips twitched upward. "Losing the Master Key alone . . . I don't think it would be contempt of the Council to call that an embarrassment, right? It's simply a fact."

Some of the Council members had the decency to look ashamed. Luckily, none had the presence of mind to shoot back that the Wraithwooders had technically lost the Master Key as well—as far as anyone here knew, they had left it behind at Wraithwood during the escape.

"I can call up any number of people to verify these reasons for my unregistered status, if you'd like."

"That won't be necessary." Master Castelius shuffled to a new sheet of paper. "You claim you were on an unauthorized espionage mission at Mordizan. If that is the case, why did you break into the fifth stronghold and open the gates for the enemy? Not to mention steal the magic of the last stronghold?" He turned a self-satisfied smirk upon her. "As you did, indeed, confess to being guilty of doing."

Brinnie sighed, as if these questions were quite tedious and boring. Her vision flickered. *Don't black out now.* She perched on the bar across the front of the platform, swinging one foot. "To be honest, I didn't intend for the massacre at the fifth stronghold to occur. It was supposed to be a peaceful surrender after I opened the gates, but I didn't anticipate the brutality of the dark wizards."

"Peaceful surrender or not, you defeated a stronghold."

"*I* defeated it?" She leaned back on her hands with a slight laugh. "I appreciate the confidence, Scott, but before I gained these powers, even I couldn't do that by myself." She inspected the lace on her sleeve. "I had to play a role in the takedown to convince Mordred of my loyalty to him. Incidentally, it worked, and he unveiled his plan to defeat the strongholds using the Case of the Master Key."

"Which *you* then proceeded to do." A white-haired Council member wrinkled his nose at her.

"A good point." Master Castelius didn't take his eyes off her. "If you destroyed one stronghold in a grand plan to save the others—as unlikely as that sounds—that does not explain your theft of the magic at the last stronghold using said Case."

She could feel her strength fading, and with it, her arrogant persona. But Brinnie the Mistress of Shadows didn't care about anyone questioning her decisions, her morals. *Keep up the charade. Keep going.*

"As part of the torture, Mordred dismembered and murdered an enchantment wizard in front of me. He intended to kill children one by one until I did as he wanted—steal the magic of the stronghold and give it to him. With the assistance of his lie-detecting guards, he secured my agreement."

Master Castelius's voice dripped with disdain. "And you made all the estates vulnerable for the sakes of a few dark wizard children?"

"I'm not a monster, Scott." She tilted her head. "I wasn't aware that Castelon condoned killing children."

While various members of the Council spluttered angrily, Brinnie's gaze wandered the room, gauging the reactions of the five other Masters and the nobility. A few seemed to regard her with outright hatred, others with curiosity, but most seemed to hold a mix of disdain and fascination. In their eyes, she was a despicable creature—but perhaps one who was right.

She raised her voice slightly to be heard over the ruckus. "The stronghold would have fallen anyway. I simply sped up the process. I thought it better to do that than to let innocent children die."

While the Council members continued to splutter, those in the seats leaned toward one another, murmuring, presumably discussing the validity of her decision.

"But Mordred did not receive the magic. You did." Master Castelius gestured toward her with the gavel. "How do you explain this?"

"I couldn't just let Mordred have all that magic. With the help of Marcus Vorath, I saw my chance and took it. I also took the magic of the dark wizards before the two of us escaped."

Sure, taking the magic for herself had been more of an accident than anything, but they didn't need to know that. *We can let them think our mad scramble was a calculated move.*

Her heart gave such a sharp pang that she nearly doubled over. Without thinking, she'd sent that thought to Marcus . . . who wasn't there.

She forced herself to tune back into the trial, Master Castelius's voice assaulting her ears.

"Regardless of your reasoning and excuses, you have pled guilty to the charges. These amount to high treason, which requires the death penalty." He looked around at the assembly. "After all who have died by Brynna Drakon's hand, and all the estates left open to attack, why shouldn't she die?"

"It's very simple." Brinnie hopped down from the railing, ignoring the feeling of more stitches tearing in her side, blood seeping through her dress. For extra power, she added a slight magical amplification to the volume of her voice, just enough so any wizard would note the sound's magical nature. "You need me."

She strode into the middle of the room, hints of shadows trailing behind her, tiny sparks of fire flickering in her skirts, an unseen breeze lifting her hair. She allowed herself to grow taller, magic and shadows dancing on her fingertips.

She met Castelius's gaze, head held high. "I know of Mordred's bane. Other than Mordred, I am the most powerful wizard on earth. In battle, I'm worth at least twenty wizards. In knowledge of Mordred, I have no equal. Without me, you *will* lose this war. Your estates *will* fall. And you will all die." She scanned the room, making eye contact with as many wizards as possible. "But with me, you might have a chance."

Scattered applause echoed from the gallery. Brinnie looked up and could barely make out what appeared to be Lana, Miss Burtle, and . . . she swallowed hard. Mr. Winslow.

As perhaps a blessing in disguise, the portal travel had hit Mr. Winslow the hardest, leaving him barely conscious for a couple of days. Brinnie hadn't yet seen him since the events of Wraithwood, as they had both been bedbound.

Yet he was still here to support her. Even if she couldn't save Mrs. Winslow. Couldn't save anyone. Not even the people she had just promised she might be giving a chance.

But wait . . . the applause came from more than three people. She continued scanning.

There. Quentin and Maddy. She couldn't be sure, but it looked like Maddy put her fingers to her mouth and whistled. *They're safe too.* And somehow, even as a human, Maddy had weaseled her way into the trial.

"Order in the gallery," Master Castelius growled. "Let us take a vote. Those in favor of letting Brynna Ludovic-*Drakon*," he paused, emphasizing the name, "roam free and unsupervised, raise your hand."

Wow, nothing like leading language.

Four hands went up around the room, Uncle Merlin's among them, and one from a member of the Council.

"And those in favor of her punishment."

Brinnie nodded grimly as eight hands rose for her execution. She had put on a good show. Not that it mattered. They were doomed with or without her. But she didn't intend to let them take her to the dungeons alive. Not when Mordred remained at large. Not when she still could oppose him. She prepared to turn invisible.

"Objection." Uncle Merlin stood.

Brinnie paused.

Master Castelius failed to fully bite back a sigh. "What is it, Ludovic?"

He clasped his hands behind his back. "A death penalty for one of Masters descent cannot be given without the consent of a two-thirds majority of all Masters."

"Your point, Ludovic?" He gestured to the gathering. "As you can see, we have a two-thirds majority."

"We are missing representatives from eleven estates."

The white-haired Council member who had spoken before harrumphed. "Six of them are dead, and five are occupied defending their estates and unable to attend."

What are you doing, Uncle Merlin? She had played all of her cards. Did he have something else up his sleeve?

"Yes, but those who have passed on have heirs, as do those who are alive. Our laws state that if a Master is unable to attend, he may send as proxy his heir in his stead." He gestured toward the upper rings of seats, where Mom sat. "I've taken the liberty of inviting these heirs here today."

Upon his motion, eleven wizards stood.

"Lady Ariana Iris, heir of Iriselie."

A woman in a shimmering blue dress descended the stairs, taking her place in one of the boxes.

"Lord Artor Ronan, heir of Habrin."

A stocky, bearded man grinned at the Council, bowed, and headed for the benches.

"Lord Baylor Ichabod, heir of Brookdam."

As each sounded off, heir after heir, descendants of estates both fallen and fighting, Brinnie's chest swelled. While she had drifted in and out of consciousness, Uncle Merlin had been fighting for her—fighting for all of them.

Master Castelius glowered. "Recount granted. Those in favor of the release of Brynna Drakon?"

Four of the newcomers raised their hands along with the smattering that had before.

"And those in favor of her execution."

The same number of hands rose . . . plus seven of the newcomers. Brinnie's heart sank once more. *I guess his plan didn't work out so well after all.* She bit her lip. It almost added insult to injury to come all this way just to condemn her.

A smile teased Castelius's lips. "It seems we have fifteen votes against her, the minimum required for a two-thirds majority. Lady Brynna Ludovic-Drakon, the Council hereby sentences you to—"

"Objection." Uncle Merlin smiled. "Pardon the interruption, but we are still missing a vote. There are not twenty-three estates aligned with Castelon anymore, but rather twenty-four." He nodded to Brinnie. "I present Lady Brynna Drakon, heir and representative of Dirklon."

Gasps rose from the onlookers. Master Castelius's mouth opened and closed.

Brinnie grinned. "I think we need a recount."

As they counted once again, Brinnie raised her hand in her own favor—nine votes for her, fifteen against her.

She had won.

She wasn't condemned to die, but her sentence remained to be decided.

The Council took a recess. Rather than make the trek all the way back to her previous room, Brinnie, Mom, and Uncle Merlin met in a nearby chamber furnished with a desk and a few chairs, as if meant for meetings in between sessions.

Brinnie pressed a hand to her abdomen and drew it away bloody. Even the all-black dress was beginning to show the seeping liquid. Her head spun. "Think I could get a quick refresh with a healer?"

Uncle Merlin disappeared.

Mom shut the door, and away from prying eyes, Brinnie sank into one of the chairs, biting back a yelp of pain. She clenched her eyes shut, forcing herself not to retch, or faint, or both.

"I think you're done for the day." She could feel Mom hovering over her. "You said your piece. Let your uncle and me negotiate the rest."

"I can't." Her breath hissed between her teeth. "I can't look weak."

"You should be *dead.* No one should survive a wound like that from an enchanted blade. No one thinks you're weak."

Brinnie opened her eyes, the corner of her mouth twitching up. "I don't need them to think I'm strong. I need them to think I'm superhuman. Or I guess, super-wizard." She slumped and leaned her head against the back of the chair, eyes closed once more, hoping that would help the room to stop spinning. "These idiots clearly don't care about saving people, or they would have done more for this war. But they respect power."

"Brynna, listen to me." Mom put a hand on her shoulder, and she flinched even from the slight contact. Mom removed her hand. "Some of these wizards you're arguing with are centuries old. I don't think you should be trying to *get* them to do anything. We're here to make sure you don't end up in a dungeon, and your attitude isn't helping."

Brinnie's eyes shot open, and she released a breathy laugh. "They couldn't put me in the dungeon if they wanted to. I'm here to enlist help against Mordred, but if they won't agree, I'll face him myself."

"Brynna." That stern voice—she knew it well. The Mom voice. The I'm-the-parent voice. "If this was a football game, you'd be on the bench. You're done. It's time to let the adults take care of things."

Something inside her had come undone. For some reason, the tone that used to make her fall in line had no effect—no effect other than to stoke the burning coals of resentment into a full-blown anger.

"*Now* it's time for me to step down?" Brinnie stood, ignoring the black spots dancing in front of her vision. "It's too late, Mom. Anna and

Dad, your 'real' family, are already embroiled in this. Everything you feared was true—I got us all here. I can't do anything to fix that or the fact that I was born, but I *will* go down swinging and buy everyone as much time as possible."

Mom's mouth opened.

Brinnie wasn't done. "I know I turned out to be everything you feared and worse, so don't try to worry about me now." She gave a sardonic smile. "Villains can be redeemed by dying, right? So let me."

"Don't be dramatic, Brynna." Mom's eyes narrowed. "I know it was hard, losing Wraithwood, Mrs. Winslow, Marcus, and the hope of Excalibur, all at the same time, but there's no need to make a martyr of yourself. The war is far from over."

"You don't really believe that, do you?" Brinnie looked her straight in the eyes. "You don't believe anyone stands a lasting chance against Mordred?"

Mom set her jaw. "I'm trying to—and maybe you should, too."

The door swung open then, and Uncle Merlin entered, followed by a woman with a large black bag whom Brinnie assumed was a healer, cutting off their conversation.

Brinnie sent both Mom and Uncle Merlin out of the room, carefully sliding out of the dress to allow the healer access to the wound. She tried to keep her mind off the physical sensations, but that just led her to spiral into Mrs. Winslow's words. *"I'd like to sit your whole family down to talk with each other."*

If this interaction with Mom is any indication, it wouldn't go well.

Tears welled in her eyes. Hopefully the healer would think they were due to the stitching, a few of which she'd ripped, again. She would do anything to have Mrs. Winslow here with her, the woman who had offered more motherly love than her own mother ever had.

I should have been faster.

She couldn't think about that right now. Not without collapsing into a useless puddle on the floor. But thinking about Mom didn't help either.

Mom hadn't denied any of it—that she didn't consider Brinnie her real family. That Brinnie had become everything she feared. That her birth was a problem.

For some reason, it stung less now. Mom had been right, and Brinnie was done trying to prove her wrong, to be a good daughter. Who cared what anyone thought anymore? If she was good or bad? She hadn't been able to save anyone.

If I can't be a good hero, then I'll be the villain you all think I am. And nothing and no one can stand between me and my vengeance.

Keilrie had been right all along.

Sorry, Marcus. But if dark magic can help me defeat Mordred, dark magic it is.

If I lose my life and soul in the process, good riddance.

A knock sounded at the door. "The Council is preparing to resume," Mom said.

"I'll be right there."

The healer checked the bandages through the dress, then gave her a thumbs up.

Brinnie stalked toward the door. Time to antagonize some stuffy old wizards.

CHAPTER TWENTY-SIX

An escort of guards at all times whenever she left her room. No leaving Castelon without permission. No weapons allowed.

The rules were laughable. As if guards could stop her. As if she needed weapons.

Surely everyone on the Council knew it too. The stipulations were only posturing, a show of power in an attempt to pretend they had any control over her whatsoever.

But Brinnie acquiesced, then dropped the truth bomb of Excalibur, reciting the prophecy for them all—and leaving out the part about the sword being lost to time.

She left the Council Chamber buzzing with discussion as she made her exit. "Do with that information what you will," she'd told them. "Now if we're finished here, I'll be taking my leave."

Then she'd promptly gone back to her room, changed into loose pants and a baggy shirt, and slept for several hours, only waking for the broth Mom insisted she drink.

Now, almost twenty-four hours after her foray into the shark tank, Brinnie lay on her bed, staring up at the ceiling and trying to work up the energy to get up. She should visit Quentin and Maddy, talk with Miss Burtle and Mr. Winslow. She couldn't reach out overtly to Anna without revealing their relation, but if she was careful, she might be able to find information on how they were doing. And of course, she needed to meet with some Masters, ransack a few libraries, and work on her plan.

Sleeping or working. If she didn't retreat into slumber or stay moving while conscious, the grief would overtake her, and she wasn't sure she could rise from it again.

Okay, probably the Archives first. I'm not sure how much energy I have for socializing.

She heaved herself out of bed and changed into a fresh tunic and low, loose pants, the wizard equivalent of a baggy t-shirt and sweats, throwing her hair in a ponytail. She didn't need to impress anyone today, and anything even brushing the bandages around her wound hurt. *The blade had to go all the way through. Couldn't leave me with one side of my body that didn't hurt.*

A knock sounded on the door. She summoned a dagger of shadows and flipped it into her hand, just to be safe. "Come in."

The door opened and an unfamiliar young man stepped inside, probably somewhere between sixteen and eighteen, with blond, curly hair and a pearly-white grin. "Brynna Ludovic-Drakon, I presume." His voice held a slight British accent. Coupled with his finely made blue jacket with shiny buttons, he gave off a princely vibe. Some sort of Castelon elite, then.

"Correct. And who are you?"

"Nathan. Nathan Castelius." He gave a bow. "A pleasure to meet you."

What do you want? His wide smile grated on her nerves. So did the fact that his last name was Castelius. "A relation to Scott?"

"Master Castelius? He's my grandfather." The young man strode forward, a spring in his step. "I saw you at the trial. He really doesn't like you."

"I'm aware." She released the shadow dagger and it dissipated. He didn't seem like a threat.

"I thought you were brilliant. I hear you don't speak the ancient language. That was the first trial I've seen conducted in English. Luckily all the Masters learn it or we'd have a terrible time. You know not all estates are from English-speaking countries. My favorite is Chateau Vert in France. Do you have a favorite estate?"

She blinked at his rapid speech. "Um, Wraithwood."

He nodded, still in motion, running a hand over the room's small table, looking out the window, tapping his fingers against the wall. "Heard it's pretty, in its own way. Never been there myself. Have you been to Castelon before?"

"A few weeks ago. When I was sentenced to execution."

"Right, and you escaped from the dungeons. Impressive, really." He spun back toward her. "I meant before that. I imagine you've hardly seen it then. Would you like a tour?"

Not with you. His chatter made her head spin. "Maybe when I'm feeling better."

"Right. You were injured. Deadly wounded." He made himself at home at the foot of her bed, one leg crossed over the other. "So you have a lot of powers. Do you like them? Which one do you like best?"

Her posture remained rigid. "What are you doing here?"

"Trying to make you feel better." He gestured to the room. "I know it can't be fun being in here when you've been out fighting and adventuring all this time."

"Fighting and adventuring is not fun."

"Okay." He smiled. "So what is fun?"

She just looked at him. He obviously wasn't moving. Well, maybe she could turn this to her advantage. "Reading, probably."

"Got it." He snapped his fingers. "We'll include the Archives on the tour."

She raised an eyebrow. Apparently, this tour was now a thing. She should learn the layout of the castle, after all, especially for the plans she intended. Maybe she could get him to leave her at the library. "You know, I am feeling better today. I would be interested in a tour. Especially of the Archives."

"Excellent." He sprang to his feet. "To the library it is!"

She started to follow when she heard a clacking, clattering sound behind her. She squinted for a moment, trying to make sense of the absurd sight. Someone in all black was crawling in the window.

"What are you . . ." she started to ask, but then the person landed, pulled out a knife, and charged toward her.

With a flick of her wrist, she sent a pair of shadow wolves after him. They leaped, one pinning him to the ground, teeth at his throat, and one snapping for the knife.

She took two steps to stand over him. "Um, what do you think you're doing?"

"Killing you," he hissed. Then he yanked his knife hand free and plunged it into his own heart.

Brinnie cursed and dove forward to heal him, but too late. He was dead.

"An assassin!" Nathan ran for the door. "I'll tell the guards!"

As he threw open the door, Brinnie stood, staring down at the dead man. If he'd remained alive, she could have questioned who sent him. A cold finger of doubt trailed down her spine. A couple hours earlier, and she would have been fast asleep. Would she have awoken in time to fight him off?

Ten minutes later, Nathan Castelius had disappeared, and Mom, Uncle Merlin, and several guards crowded into the room. The guards investigated the man.

"We don't recognize him," one said, standing. "No identifying items on his person, but his blade was enchanted. Maybe we can trace it to one of the forges around here."

"If it's from a local forge." Uncle Merlin frowned. "We can hope, considering he did reach the double space. Thank you for your assistance."

As the guards took the body away, Mom hugged Brinnie awkwardly around the shoulders. "I'm glad you're okay."

So they still weren't addressing their argument. Good. "My wolves had him pinned as soon as he got in the window." She glanced at the opening. "It should have bars."

"This part of the castle looks out on an interior courtyard. It shouldn't have been a problem." She bit her lip. "Maybe we should ask for a guard to stay in the room with you."

The thought of a stranger staring at her while she slept made her cringe. "I don't trust Castelon's guards."

Uncle Merlin rubbed his chin. "The odds of Mordred sending more than one assassin are fairly high, considering there's no protection spell. Mordred or others, to be honest. You have a lot of enemies, especially after the trial." He didn't seem annoyed with her about it—if anything, the slight twitch of his mustache indicated pride—but Mom scowled. "You already have guards posted outside, order of Castelius, but what about Lana as a personal guard? She was successfully cleared at her trial. Especially now that I won't be here, I want to know that you'll be safe."

If Lana followed her everywhere, she might try to stop Brinnie's plans. But something else caught her attention for now. "Wait. Where are you going?"

"To the remaining estates. They need all the help they can get. Especially now that Castelon is pulling the troops of Artema back to Artema itself."

"Hold on." Brinnie held up a hand. "They're pulling back the career warriors and leaving the estates to defend themselves?"

"That is correct." A muscle worked in his jaw. "They're making a strategic move to fortify the most *important* estates. Otherwise known as those closest in physical proximity to Castelon, like Chateau Vert, Constancia, and Eringaard."

Brinnie narrowed her eyes. "Those are all estates with Council members, aren't they?"

"It's not fair, but there's nothing to be done now." Mom sighed. "Those remaining at other estates have to decide whether to try to defend their homes or escape while they still can. Especially since portals are few and far between."

"I'll be helping make dozens of them," said Uncle Merlin, "but many prefer to stay and fight." His eyes darkened. "Our home may be lost, but I can help defend others, even if Castelon won't. If nothing else, it may buy us time to evacuate civilians and come up with better strategies against Mordred." Brinnie opened her mouth, but before she could say anything, he held up a hand. "And no, you can't come with me. You're injured and a liability."

Her mouth snapped shut and she nodded. It might be for the best—she had research to do anyway. She turned to Mom. "And you? Are you going to join Dad at Dirklon?"

She shook her head. "Right now my place is with you."

"I don't want to hold you back. I'll be fine, Mom. Really."

"Will you?" She gestured to the window. "You're being targeted by assassins. I'm staying here for now." She lowered her voice. "And we need someone representing Wraithwood and Dirklon's interests here. Someone not quite as controversial as you are."

Brinnie raised a brow. After so much running and hiding, it seemed Mom had committed to the fight—and not just because she had to, in the face of attacking enemies. She was wading into the political cesspool of Castelon of her own free will. "All right then. I guess we're both staying here." She turned to Uncle Merlin. "When do you leave?"

"Today, actually. I was on my way to wish you farewell when we received word of the assassin." Sure enough, he was in travel garb, wearing boots and a cloak, a short sword strapped to his side.

"Then I love you. Please be careful." She gingerly went in for a hug, favoring her injuries. As she pulled back, she fixed him with a hard look. "I mean it. Be careful." Her voice cracked. "I don't think any of us can stand to lose anyone else."

He nodded, then reached for Mom's arm and squeezed it. "Look out for Lydia for me?"

Mom hesitated for a moment, expression sympathetic, as if weighing the words Brinnie was also thinking. *She doesn't need to be looked after. She can't be hurt under a sleeper's curse.* But Mom must have seen the sadness in his eyes. She only said, "Of course."

With that, he stepped back and disappeared.

Brinnie sighed. "All right, where did Nathan go? He's supposed to show me the library."

Brinnie leaned over to Lana, voice low. "Is it rude to say Mordizan's is better?"

"Brinnie!" Lana started to elbow her but stopped short before she made contact.

She snickered under her breath as they followed Nathan Castelius into the Archives, a three-story library densely packed with tomes crowding sturdy shelves set a bit too close together, as if the collection had grown beyond the appropriate size for the library.

Nathan turned toward them, eyes alight. "This is the Archives! Scrolls on the third floor, study rooms on the second floor, and everything else is books. Are you sure you don't want a full castle tour?"

"I'm sure, thank you." Brinnie put a hand to her abdomen. "That might be a bit much for me today."

"All right, I'll leave you to it." His voice bounced off the shelves.

Luckily, the stuffy surroundings muffled the noise. "I'm not much of a reader." He nearly skipped away.

Brinnie glanced behind her. She wished the two Castelon guards in their blue livery would skip away as well. Two guards. What was the point?

"So." Lana cocked her head. "Are we pleasure reading, or researching?"

"Who says they aren't the same thing?" Brinnie headed for the stairs. "You don't have to read the same things as me, though. Feel free to wander."

"Nope, I'm sticking to your side like glue." Lana patted the sword at her hip. "Bodyguard and all that. Not that I hold a candle to your own ability to protect yourself, but I don't need your mom or uncle to murder me for slacking off."

So much for that. She would begin her more innocuous research first, then. "Okay. I need resources on the estates whose Masters serve on the Council. Genealogies, of course, and histories of alliances and which estates get along best with each other. Also, if we can find some recent news and read up on the current power dynamics . . ."

"When you do research, you don't mess around." Lana grinned. "I'm right behind you. By the end of this, we'll both be experts."

Her heart warmed. Especially seeing a genuine smile on Lana's face . . . "I'm glad your trial went well."

She shrugged. "I helped random humans—as far as they know—escape Mordizan, was imprisoned by Mordred, fought for Wraithwood . . . I guess they considered me a pretty safe bet. Especially when I said I would try to talk to my family about switching sides."

Brinnie's eyes widened, and she stopped at the bottom of the stairs. "You would do that?"

She shrugged, not quite making eye contact. "I could try. I don't know that it would do any good. We've been fiercely loyal to Mordizan for centuries." She bit her lip. "Honestly . . . I don't know what they think of me right now. If they know I'm alive, they probably think I'm a disappointment." She shook her head, making her ponytail sway, and gave a half-hearted laugh. "Anyway. There are way more important things going on right now than my family drama. Let's get to researching."

Brinnie let Lana sweep past her without pressing the issue. Part of her twinged with guilt at how little she knew about Lana's background. She and Marcus had been so focused on taking down Mordred, Brinnie hadn't spent as much time learning about her friend as she should have.

As they ascended the stairs, though, Brinnie frowned in sympathy. Lana was the oldest of two, but the second in line for the Mastership after her younger brother. She'd done everything in her power to make her parents proud, to be Mordizan's best warrior.

Then she'd thrown it all away for her. For Brinnie. Before Lana was even sure whether the enchantment wizards were right or wrong.

Impulsively, Brinnie grabbed Lana's hand, stopping her. Lana turned, head tilted. "What's wrong?"

"Thank you." Brinnie squeezed her fingers. "Thank you for everything. You're amazing, and I don't think I've told you that enough."

Lana's expression melted into a soft smile. "Battle partners, remember? We've got to look out for each other."

They combed the stacks for the next few hours. They had no trouble finding resources—instead, Brinnie wasn't sure what to read first. She tried to stuff as much knowledge into her brain as she could, and Lana shuffled through books to pass her the most relevant content. The two guards hovered nearby, expressions bored.

Lana slid another book into the "not helpful" pile and picked up a new one from the stack. "Do you think it's strange how . . . passive Castelon has been in this war?"

"They're idiots." Brinnie flipped to a new page, scanning its contents. "Cowards too, I guess."

Lana lowered her voice even further. "But don't you think it's weird how much they didn't want to hear it? How easily they're just . . . letting estates go? It's almost like they *want* Mordred to win."

Brinnie looked up sharply. "What?"

"I know that doesn't actually make sense, but they seem oddly complacent. As long as Castelon isn't being attacked, they're letting it happen. Bare minimum to the strongholds, no help to the estates." Lana shrugged, flipping through her book. "All I'm saying is that if an Allied estate was being attacked, Mordizan would be there in an instant. A threat to one is a threat to all of us. It's weird to me that the enchantment wizards don't operate the same way."

Lana had focused on her book, but Brinnie gazed across the room, thoughts far away, conflicting plans and ideas running through her mind.

Finally, she huffed. "We need more information. I do know one thing—I don't trust Scott. Someone on that Council must be up to something. Sheer ineptitude only goes so far." Her eyes narrowed. "I think we're facing a wolf in sheep's clothing—and maybe more than one."

CHAPTER TWENTY-SEVEN

Brinnie bit back a yelp as Lana pulled on the strings of her dress.

"I'm sorry!" She dropped the laces.

"No, it's okay, keep going." Brinnie squared her shoulders. "It will probably be good for the wound, honestly. Some support."

Lana picked up the strings again, tugging much more gently. "You know, this is the second Masters' Gathering I've helped you get ready for, and the second one where you have ulterior motives." She gave a light chuckle. "You sure know how to have a good time."

Brinnie's mind traveled back to her last big ball, the Mordizan Masters' Gathering, with Marcus as her date. The chaos of trying to find Mordred's key, meeting Ignatius, speaking in code with Dad . . . the moment in the garden she and Marcus had realized they were more than just allies.

"Whatever happens . . ." she'd said.

"We're in it together," he'd finished.

Something wet trickled down her cheeks. She reached up to brush it away and realized they were tears.

"Oh, Brinnie. I'm sorry. I didn't mean to remind you." Lana gave her a gentle hug.

Don't break down. If you start, you'll never stop. "I'm fine." She took a shuddering breath. "Sorry."

"Don't be. You're grieving." Lana's brow remained furrowed, one hand on Brinnie's shoulder. "I'm here if you want to talk. Or if you don't." She sighed. "Whatever you need. Only, please don't keep killing yourself like this."

She opened her mouth to argue, but Lana was right. She'd spent the past two days furiously researching, barely eating or sleeping, preparing for this gathering of Masters, heirs, and estate representatives. Much like the gathering at Mordizan, this one began with a ball of sorts, followed the next day by hours of meetings. *Keeping the party bit seems a little insensitive given the situation.* Unfortunately, with Lana glued to her side, she hadn't been able to pursue her other research, but she doubted she would have had time anyway.

"I have to keep moving forward." She shifted her skirts uncomfortably—black again, but with accents of blue. She'd read blue inspired trust. She made herself meet Lana's gaze, willing her to understand. "If I'm not killing myself, I'll die."

Lana didn't speak for a moment as she finished tying the laces in back before returning to the front to place the intricate belt. "The first time I saw you awake again was at that trial," she said finally. "I hardly recognized you." Moisture welled in her eyes. "*You* have always been your greatest strength. Not your power or your cunning or your bravery. Just you." She adjusted Brinnie's skirts, and they finally fell right. "Who you are is the one thing they can't take from you. But I feel like you're trying to destroy yourself."

Brinnie clenched her jaw, holding in a rollercoaster of emotions. "Brinnie Lane was weak," she said finally. "I'd like to think she died at Wraithwood."

Lana straightened and met her eyes. "And I pray to God she didn't. Because that's the Brinnie I was willing to risk my life for." She turned and headed for the door. "I'll call for your mom so you two can go together."

Soon, Brinnie was riding in a shadowy floating chair next to Mom as they headed for the gathering, two guards trailing Brinnie, as usual. For the evening, Lana had been given the night off from watching Brinnie's back. With Mom there and Brinnie on alert, they didn't feel the need to make a case for allowing Lana into the exclusive gathering.

Mom cleared her throat. "Are you ready to socialize and strategize?"

Brinnie groaned but softened the reaction with a grin. "How long did it take you to think of that catch phrase?"

"Remember. We're being civil. Making friends."

"No insulting anyone besides Scott. Got it."

Mom sighed. "I'll settle for that, I suppose."

Mom led the way through the halls of the castle to a ballroom. That shouldn't have been surprising, but for some reason Brinnie had envisioned everyone gathering in the Council Chamber, the Council scowling down on the party like a brood of disgruntled vultures. Brinnie dismissed her shadowy ride a few feet from the door. As they stepped in, the herald announced them. "Lady Eira Ludovic-Drakon and Lady Brynna Ludovic-Drakon."

Brinnie's gaze rose to the soaring ceiling of the immense ballroom, where light orbs glowed as they floated in the shape of chandeliers near the many vaulted arches of light gray stone. Soft music bounced around the columns lining the room, drifting from a quartet on a corner stage that had clearly been magically amplified to carry throughout the hall. Across the floor, wizards in fine costumery chatted, sipped from delicate glasses, and roved about the room.

Brinnie's heart clenched, heat rushing up her neck. How could they stand to socialize in such opulence when at this very moment, people were fighting and dying? How could anyone bear to continue life as normal when around the world, destruction advanced?

A mirthless smile twitched her lips. *I suppose that's no different than usual.*

"Eira!" A woman in a deep rose dress lined with fur accents took Mom by the arm. Her eyes sparkled as she spoke rapidly in what sounded like the ancient language.

Another hiccup in this plan. The lingua franca here was not English, and her mastery of the ancient language went no further than being able to recognize when it was being spoken.

She tried to tune in and catch any words that she could. Something niggled at the back of her mind. Wasn't that one of the powers wizards could have? Not one useful in battle, so she hadn't paid much attention to it in classes, but she thought she remembered something along those lines. *Lingua wizards or something?*

She searched her inventory. *Fire, water, flora, fauna . . . wait, what's this?* She felt something shift in her ears.

"You probably don't remember me," the woman was saying, "but we used to play together at gatherings as little girls."

"Nina Gordislov! Of course I remember." Mom took her hands, a brilliant smile lighting her face. "How are you and your family?"

Brinnie raised an eyebrow. *Right. Mom had a whole life here at one point.*

Mom appeared to be quite fluent in the ancient language despite her many years in the human world.

"We are well." Nina's warm brown eyes crinkled. "My brother took over as Master of Grignak five years ago."

"Little Viktor. It's hard to imagine him all grown up."

"It's been a long time." Nina pointed her chin toward a man in forest green shaking hands with another man not far from them. "He even grew into those gangly legs."

The two of them chuckled, and Brinnie held back a sigh. *Patience.* If Nina was the sister of a Master, she could be a valuable ally.

"I was so sorry to hear about Wraithwood." Nina squeezed Mom's hands. "I know it must be hard losing your beautiful home."

"Thank you. I'm just glad we escaped with our lives."

Not all of us.

Nina released Mom and turned toward Brinnie. "And this must be your daughter, Brynna. A pleasure to meet you."

Brinnie's impatience began to melt at Nina's warm, open expression. She smiled and hoped the magic worked for speaking as well as hearing. "The same to you."

Mom shot her a surprised stare. Brinnie tried to send back an "I'll explain later" look.

Nina tilted her head, eyes searching Brinnie's face. "I couldn't make it to your trial, so I only heard from my brother about the events." She gave a sharp nod. "I think you take after the Ludovic side. Not the Drakons."

Brinnie bit her tongue. *She's not trying to insult Dad and Ms. Tynsdale . . . Aunt Lydia? That feels weird.* "Thank you."

"Your support means a lot, Nina," Mom added.

Nina sighed. "For what it's worth, I wish we were helping the estates under attack. Viktor won't listen to me, of course. He didn't tell me about Wraithwood until it was already too late." She pressed her lips together. "Just as stubborn as our father was."

"I understand."

After they finished their conversation with Nina, who was called away by another wizard, Mom turned to Brinnie. "Since when do you speak the ancient language?"

"Since right now. Another surprise power." She scanned the room. "I have some ideas for who we should talk to next based on my research, but I don't know what they look like."

Mom's eyebrows slowly rose. "That's what you've been doing in the library."

Brinnie glanced toward where members of the Council stood hobnobbing. "The Masters may not listen to us, but they have wives, sisters, daughters . . . As archaic as this patriarchal system is, we can work with it. Win the hearts of the women, and we have a line to the ears of the Masters." She shrugged one shoulder, a mischievous smile twitching her lips. "Plenty of the women are generals, governors, and warriors in their own right. If we can stir up a little insubordination, all the better."

Mom regarded her for a moment without speaking. Finally, quietly, she said, "This world suits you."

Brinnie blinked. Did it?

She loved libraries and quiet streams and snuggling with a big goofy dog. She loved cracking jokes and making pancakes and watching the rain while curled up with a good book and spending time with the people she cared about. Certainly, she did love the subtle magic and otherworldly charm of the world of wizards. But *not* facing crowds or the threat of death or the fate of the world on her shoulders or making choices on who should live and who should die.

The Mistress of Shadows, however . . . *she* could navigate this world. So Brinnie needed to take a back seat for a while.

They spent the next two hours conversing with various Masters' wives, sisters, and daughters. Mom never addressed the situation directly, but rather maintained cordial conversation, dropping hints about how terribly the other estates were faring. Brinnie forced herself to do the same. Strategic moves in this game of chess. No charging forward, just setting up the pieces.

Many of the wizards danced, but the young men in the crowd carefully chose any partner but Brinnie. *Chickens.* They weren't the only ones she caught eyeing her, as if worried she would turn on them all. *Good. You should be afraid.*

As the thought ran through her mind, who should come bounding up but Nathan, golden curls bouncing. "Brynna!" A gigantic grin split his cheeks. "Wonderful to see you here! Do you want to dance?"

She tilted her head, considering. He had the energy of an overly enthusiastic Labrador, but if he was related to Scott, perhaps she could use that. "I need to be careful, but maybe for one song."

"We'll dance slowly and carefully." He held out a hand and led her onto the dance floor.

They joined a slow waltz and were soon three-stepping around the room—much more gracefully than Brinnie had first done with Marcus.

Her heart panged so hard she almost gasped in pain. What she wouldn't give to have Marcus here instead, plotting with her, making snide remarks about the Council.

"I love dancing," Nathan was saying. "Besides dogs, I think dancing might be my favorite thing. I have a dog named Sloth. He's a terrible dancer, but maybe you could meet him sometime."

There was something almost endearing about his oblivious bubbliness. "You're not much for war and politics, are you?"

His head tilted. "Is anyone? Except dark wizards, maybe." He looked at her earnestly. "But I don't think you're dark at all. I think you're right. We should be helping the estates."

This was turning out to be an even more helpful night than expected. "Really? Will you talk to your grandfather about it?"

He shrugged. "I can try. He doesn't listen to me much, though."

I can definitely see that.

The song changed to a more upbeat tune. Nathan paused. "Do you think you're up for it?"

Her abdomen ached. Probably best not to rip stitches again doing something stupid like dancing. "I don't think so."

"Then I have an idea for something I think you'll like." He grabbed her hand and darted off. "Follow me!"

"Whoa, slow down." She hurried after him as he dragged her along through a door in the side of the ballroom. They made their way through twists and turns. "Where are we going?"

"You'll see."

They emerged into a moonlit courtyard and passed through an archway into a broader yard. Nathan led the way to what looked like a barn. "Over here." He cupped his hands around his mouth and shouted, "Sloth!"

A massive, shaggy dog came galloping out of the barn, tongue flapping. It jumped, putting its paws on Nathan's shoulders, and licked his face as he laughed, rubbing the dog's sides and scratching its ears. "This is Sloth, my best boy."

The dog jumped down, circling with his tail wagging.

"Hey, bud." Brinnie held out her hand, and the dog snuffled her fingers, leaning into her pets.

Nathan placed his fists on his hips like a proud father. "He's our stable dog. Looks after the horses like a regular stable hand. Isn't that right, boy?"

Sloth bumped into Brinnie's legs, tail zooming. She thumped his side and ruffled his ears. Her throat ached from unshed tears. Was Bruno okay? Ami?

Nathan's brow knit. "What's wrong?"

"Just reminded of our dog back at Wraithwood." She swallowed. "I don't know what happened to him after we fled."

He shifted uncomfortably. "I bet he'll be waiting for you when you come back. Even dark wizards must like dogs."

When you come back. As if that was a possibility. She straightened. "We should probably return. My mom will be wondering about me. Especially after that assassin scare."

"Right. Follow me."

They said goodbye to Sloth and made their way through the castle to the ballroom.

The crowd had begun to dwindle. Mom turned toward them. "There you are, Brinnie. I was thinking we might turn in."

She nodded, the ache in her gut intensifying in response to the prospect of rest. She turned to thank Nathan for introducing her to Sloth, but he was gone.

As she and Mom headed back toward their rooms, Mom massaged her temples. "I'm not used to this sort of thing anymore. Reconvene on intel tomorrow?"

"Yes, please." Brinnie leaned her head back against her shadow chair.

In Brinnie's room, Lana roused from the bed they had brought in for her and stretched. "Well? How was it?"

Brinnie shrugged. "Some possible allies. And some interesting bonding time with Nathan Castelius."

Lana stepped in to help as Brinnie pulled at the strings of her dress. "Oh?"

"No one wanted to dance with me, of course, but then he did, and he took me to see the stable dog." Brinnie reached for one fastening as Lana undid another. "He's a bit irritating, but he might be helpful, as someone close to Scott."

"Hmm."

Lana finished loosening the bodice to the point Brinnie could breathe more easily, and Brinnie managed to undo the ties on her overskirt.

"This might be a little soon, but you seem to attract men in power. One heir after another."

Brinnie's lips twitched. "I'll admit, I do seem to be collecting." Guilt immediately pummeled her in the chest. Was this lightheartedness disrespectful to those she had lost? To Mrs. Winslow and Marcus?

"Hey. Stop that." Lana flicked her in the forehead.

"Ow!"

"You don't need to feel guilty for life going on. They would want you to be happy."

Brinnie squinted at her. "How did you know what I was thinking?"

"You're not hard to read. Really, Brinnie. I don't know how you made it as long as you did as an infiltrator."

Finally stripped down to the shift under her dress, Brinnie sat on the edge of the bed and sighed. "Life *is* going on. That's why I'm cozying up with all these wizards."

Lana bit her lip. "Okay."

Brinnie stood with a groan and reached for her pajamas, heading for the bathroom adjoining the room. "I'll be back."

She wasn't supposed to soak in a bath with her wounds, though the idea of hot water soothing her muscles sounded glorious. Instead, she washed her face, hoping cool water would soothe the prickling heat behind her eyelids.

It didn't. Her chest heaved in a hiccupping sob.

Images of Mrs. Winslow's still body flashed before her mind. She was dead. Gone. And Brinnie knew exactly how it happened.

But what about Marcus?

How had he died? Painfully, slowly dying of hunger and thirst? Had they been killed by someone in the past? Perhaps torn apart in the portal?

He's not dead, part of her whispered.

She pounded her fist against the sink. *No. Stop it.* That voice that kept telling her to hope needed to die. She couldn't live like that. She had to accept this and move on.

Because if he was still alive, she knew what he would say. He would tell her not to go forward with the plans she had been making in secret. He would do anything to keep her from her plot.

And she couldn't let that stop her.

CHAPTER TWENTY-EIGHT

"Am I battle-ready yet?"

The healer gave Brinnie a look that wasn't amused. "It's looking better, but it would heal faster if you didn't exert yourself so much."

After her checkup, Brinnie changed into an uncomfortable outfit appropriate for the upcoming meeting, a slight alteration of the dress she'd worn to her trial. She'd claimed black as her signature color. As the de facto representative of Dirklon, she had a seat at the table, unlike at the Mordizan Masters' Gathering.

Lana hovered, dark circles under her eyes.

"Hey." Brinnie caught her attention. "You were up all night keeping watch for assassins. Make sure you sleep while I'm gone."

She offered a wan smile. "I will. I can't help but think of all the people who might want to take you out before the meeting."

"As long as I'm conscious, I can protect myself." A knock at the door interrupted their conversation. "Come in."

Mom stuck her head inside, blonde hair neatly curled. "Are you ready?"

"Absolutely, representative." Brinnie threw a mock salute to Lana. "We'll be back."

They made their way to the Council Chamber, where Brinnie would, for the first time, be occupying the benches rather than the stand. Dirklon had been placed next to Wraithwood, meaning she could stay close to Mom as well.

They ascended the stairs and took their seats as the Council began its opening grandstanding and formalities. Brinnie rolled her eyes. This time, all of the boxes housed at least one estate representative. From what Brinnie understood, each Master was only required to show up in person every ten years and could usually send a representative in their stead. However, this meeting appeared to hold high stakes. As she scanned the gathering, connecting faces to her reading, it seemed most Masters who weren't actively fighting Mordred's forces had made a personal appearance.

The formalities droned on. In a monotone, a herald read a report on the condition of estates all over the world. Nothing Brinnie didn't already know as far as martial developments, but her eyebrows rose at the amount of time dedicated to trade, financial, and agricultural statistics. *Important, I guess, but we have more pressing issues.*

When the herald seemed to be winding down, Scott Castelius slipped him another stack of papers, which he dutifully continued to read.

Is he trying to filibuster? Did he hope if the updates ran on long enough, they wouldn't have time to debate?

Sorry, Scott, but if necessary, I will sit here all day.

Finally, the herald finished reading the last paper and sat down.

Brinnie immediately shot to her feet. "On behalf of Dirklon, may I bring an order of business to the floor."

Master Castelius gave her a startled look as the words in the ancient language left her mouth. She held back a smirk. *Thought I didn't understand any of that, didn't you?*

His mouth pressed into a thin line. "Permission denied. You may put in a request to be listed on the docket."

Brinnie flashed a smile. "I did. I believe if you check the agenda, you will find it is the first on the list."

His gaze dropped to the sheet in front of him, his eyes widening, then narrowing. "Very well. Permission to speak."

They had Miss Burtle and her paperwork skills to thank for that. Brinnie didn't know all of the rules of what made it onto the agenda or what strings had to be pulled, but the prickly secretary had made it happen.

"As you read in the report this morning, Dirklon has lost a quarter of its troops. Meanwhile, Vanderhill has fallen, establishing a clear pattern of Mordred picking off the smaller estates one by one, working his way up. Pulling back from these estates only hastens his march to Castelon."

His voice remained flat. "I suppose you have a solution."

"In fact, yes. Why be complacent and let Mordred come to us, when we could bring the war to him?"

Murmurs arose around the room.

Lana's voice from their time in the library echoed in Brinnie's mind. *"All I'm saying is that if an Allied estate was being attacked, Mordizan would be there in an instant. A threat to one is a threat to all of us."*

"Allies of Mordred can send as many warriors forward as they want without worrying about keeping a defensive force, because they aren't afraid of a counterattack. Why are we letting that happen? Why not split their forces? Keep them on their toes and spread them thin." She offered a wicked grin. "Attacking just a few estates will put all of them on the defensive, since they won't know where we're headed next."

One of the Council members looked down his nose at her. "I hardly think we're in a position to make counterattacks, Miss Drakon."

She pretended not to notice the blatant disrespect of "miss" instead of "lady," keeping her shoulders straight. "You're right, we're not in position anywhere, are we? Because all we do is fall back."

"You are out of line." Master Castelius tapped his gavel.

"It makes sense." One of the defeated heirs rose. "If we can spare a few units, just enough to stir up a bit of trouble, we might be able to cut down on the numbers on the enemy's offensive."

Brinnie made a mental note of Artor Ronan, the heir speaking. She had been correct in thinking he would be an ally.

"The Council has already voted against counterattacks unanimously in a previous session." Master Castelius picked up the agenda. "We shall move on to the next item."

Mom stood. "If I may."

Even from the distance, Brinnie could see his jaw twitch. "Yes."

"Do we not have a law that states if all Masters or estate representatives outside the Council vote against the Council's ruling, the ruling is considered null?"

"Yes, that is a rule, but it has never happened before in history. To our next point—"

"I move that we bring the debate to the floor and take a vote," Mom said.

"One movement is not enough. Now—"

Artor Ronan stood. "I second the motion."

"As do I." Brinnie raised a hand.

"And I will kill this motion before we waste any more time." Viktor Gordislov rose to his full considerable height. "I will vote with the Council's ruling. You won't receive a unanimous vote. I will not send my warriors off to fight battles on another continent. I'm keeping them at Grignak to protect my people."

Not if Nina has anything to say about it.

Master Castelius nodded. "Do you rescind your motion, Lady Ludovic?"

"Yes, my lord." Mom bobbed her head graciously and returned to her seat.

The session continued with plans on which estates to stock with troops. Brinnie watched with interest as shouting matches erupted over abandoned estates. Everyone appeared to want their own protected . . . but few wished to come to the aid of others.

So proud to be on this team, everyone. Really feel like the good guys right now.

A small, spiteful part of her wanted to let them all crash and burn.

Eventually, the session let out for a recess. Mom caught the attention of their friends in the gallery and gave them a wave. Instead of joining the Masters and their entourages for lunch, they had decided to take a break from the drama by meeting with the Wraithwooders.

Brinnie's heart gave a pitter patter. That was almost even more nerve-wracking. She'd hardly spoken to them since they had arrived at Castelon—and she didn't have any good reason for that other than being a coward.

They emerged in a small courtyard for a picnic lunch around a stone table. For once, the sun had made an appearance instead of the usual English drizzle. Quentin and Maddy arrived first, and Maddy plopped a picnic basket in the center of the table, beaming. "Kitchen raid successful."

Mr. Winslow and Miss Burtle approached more slowly. Brinnie's heart rate sped up as she met Mr. Winslow's eyes. Did he look okay? He seemed more tired than usual, but he greeted them with a smile and a, "Howdy there."

"You look dramatic as usual, Brinnie." Maddy flopped onto one of the benches around the table. She gestured to her own tunic and pants. "I wanted to be fancy, but Quentin said this was good enough."

"You'll look silly wearing ball gowns." He rolled his eyes, reaching for the basket. "Let's see what you managed to find."

Brinnie let the others carry the conversation. Quentin and Maddy threw grapes for each other to catch while Brinnie clapped at their successes and Mom dodged their misses until Miss Burtle threatened to take their food away. Mr. Winslow gave a low chuckle that squeezed Brinnie's chest. *He can laugh. That's good.*

Quentin stood. "I have an announcement."

"Is it that your aim stinks?" Maddy chucked a grape at him, hitting right between his eyes. "We all know that."

"You're on your last warning, young lady." Miss Burtle shielded herself from the rebounding grape.

"The *news*," Quentin said, raising his voice, "is that I'm leaving tomorrow for Dirklon. I'm going to join the fight."

Mom nodded. "Good for you."

"Hold up!" Maddy stood as well. "You stink at fighting even more than throwing. You're going to get yourself killed."

He scowled. "Thank you for that vote of confidence."

Brinnie hid a smile behind her hand. "I think what she's trying to say is that she's worried about you and she'll miss you."

Maddy crossed her arms. "Just saying maybe you should stay here."

"I've made up my mind." He firmed his jaw. "You're right, I am lousy at fighting. But even if I'm lousy, I'm another person Mordred has to get through to take over the world, and that's got to be worth something." He glanced at Brinnie. "Some people can do something just by being here, but me? I can't just keep sitting here and hoping that chatting with some people is going to bring around a change of heart to send fighters. I need to *be* a fighter."

His words and the resolute tilt to his chin struck Brinnie. They had all come a long way since those early days at Wraithwood. "Well put."

"No ideas until you're healed." Mom pointed a finger at Brinnie. Then she turned back to Quentin. "I'm proud of you, young man."

Miss Burtle cut into a sandwich with a fork and knife. "I'm starting to dislike you less."

He grinned. "That was like a giant hug coming from you."

She pointed the knife at him. "Don't get used to it."

Brinnie basked in the good-natured bickering. She managed to eat more than usual without her insides aching. As they began to disperse to return to their respective places—her and Mom in the boxes, the rest in the gallery—Brinnie hung back with Mr. Winslow.

She cleared her throat, words tight. "How are you doing?"

"Well as can be expected." Though rimmed with tiredness, his blue eyes shone with warmth. "She would be proud of you."

Tears pricked her eyes and she blinked rapidly. "I'm sorry," she whispered.

He rested a large, callused hand on her shoulder. "Now don't go blaming yourself. You did everything you could." He gave her shoulder a light squeeze, then dropped his hand. "'Sides, I reckon I'll see her soon enough, and she'd give me a talking to for letting you mope around."

She cracked a slight smile. "I can't say I would be handling this nearly as well in your shoes." Her smile faded as they reached a crossroads in the corridors where they would need to part. "Are you . . . really okay?"

He stopped at the intersection and turned to face her. "We both knew it was bound to happen to one of us. We made peace with that a long time ago. Don't mean it doesn't hurt, though." Though his eyes looked wet, his expression remained resolute. "You hang in there, missy. It'll get better."

"It will." As they parted ways, she straightened her shoulders. *I'll make sure of it.*

After the end of the long and utterly useless Council session, Brinnie told Mom she was heading back to her room to rest.

Instead, as soon as she rounded a corner into an empty hallway, she shrugged on a shadowy cloak of invisibility and headed for the library.

She would prefer to sneak about at night under the cover of darkness —and when she could change out of this dress—but Lana remained vigilant then. For now, her bodyguard slept soundly, relieved of her duties while Brinnie was awake and capable of defending herself.

"That's such a neat trick."

She whirled around and snapped back to visibility. "Nathan?"

The Castelius boy stood in the hall behind her, grinning. "Turning invisible. I wish I could do that. I can only levitate. But that's fun too."

She shook off the uneasy prickling sensation on the back of her neck. How hadn't she noticed him behind her? *You need to focus more on your surroundings.* "Yeah, it can be handy."

"Where are you headed?" He bounced into step beside her.

Should she say? If Castelon was anything like Mordizan, the resources she needed might not be open to the public. Nathan might be useful in the search—and easier to dupe than Lana. "I'm headed to the library. I need to do some research on Mordred."

"Oh, I can help." He started walking. "I don't like to read much, but I know where most things are. My tutor made sure of it."

Perfect. "That would be amazing. I have a bit of an oddly specific request." *Here it goes.* "I have reason to suspect Mordred might be using dark magic. I need to do research to figure out what kind he might be using."

For a moment, something glinted in Nathan's eye, and Brinnie worried she had gone too far.

Instead, he tapped a finger to his chin. "Hmm, dark magic. They don't really leave that out in the open—kind of dangerous—but my grandfather has books about it in his private library. He lets me use it whenever I want. I'll show you!" He darted off in another direction.

Brinnie scurried to keep up, wincing at her twinging side. *Definitely overdoing it today.* But Scott's private library . . . She smirked to herself. *I'm sure he would be delighted to know I'm raiding his space.*

Nathan led her through parts of the castle she'd never seen before, the halls and windows wider, the ceilings higher, the tapestries more intricate than those of the wing where she was staying. She got the feeling the slight against her family was intentional.

They reached an archway manned by two guards, but Nathan passed them by with a nod. Beyond, ornate carpets covered the stone floor of the wide corridors, walls interrupted by windows of stained glass and glossy wood doors. A woman holding a duster whom Brinnie presumed was a maid or housekeeper offered a slight curtsy to them and scuttled by.

Nathan blazed a trail to a pair of carved wood doors and turned the brass handle on the left, pushing the door inward. "After you."

She stepped inside, the smell of leather and old books wrapping around her. In the center of the room, an ostentatious solid wood desk shone in front of a massive hearth, over which hung a painted portrait of what appeared to be Scott Castelius and family, his children with their spouses and children. Shelves lined the walls, with free-standing bookcases making up a couple of rows on either side, most of the books beautifully bound, many accented with what appeared to be gold leaf.

She spun slowly. "These are beautiful, but they don't strike me as books about dark magic."

"Oh, these aren't." He strode past her, heading for the wide stone hearth behind the desk. He walked right in, ducking only slightly, turned to the right, and was gone.

Brinnie's eyebrows shot up. She followed, peeking around the corner of the fireplace. Beyond the initial line of stones, a tunnel led back several feet.

They emerged from the tunnel into what felt more like an archive than the display library in front. Old books and scrolls were carefully labeled on well-organized shelves.

Nathan headed straight to the back of the room and gestured to one of the bookshelves that housed both scrolls and tomes. "These might help."

She gathered her skirts to better navigate the narrow rows. She leaned over the shelf he had suggested, squinting at the labels, all in the ancient language.

She took a deep breath and rubbed her eyes. If magic allowed her to speak and understand the language, it should help her read it as well.

She opened her eyes and squinted at the lettering. Mental translation felt unwieldy, like reading her high school Spanish books, but she could understand enough.

One word stood out—*dywledrith*. Dark magic.

"Thank you, Nathan. These should be quite helpful."

The one type of magic even Mordred wouldn't touch. Which meant he would be powerless against it.

In the end, you were right, Keilrie.

She could almost hear the old woman's cackle.

CHAPTER TWENTY-NINE

Brinnie cast off her invisibility and knocked on the door. The hinges creaked softly as a figure opened it inward, ushering her inside.

She stepped across the threshold and turned to Nina Gordislov. The ancient language felt cumbersome in her mouth, probably due to her lack of sleep. "What news do you have?"

"Viktor is spending an extra couple of days here in Castelon. Just enough time."

"Good." She hesitated. "What will your brother do to those who disobey him?"

"Nothing, once he knows I was behind it." The woman squared her shoulders. "As far as the troops know, the orders will be coming from Viktor himself."

Brinnie debated asking what he would do to Nina, but that wasn't her concern. Nina had made this decision herself. She handed the woman a folded piece of paper. "This is a map, with details to the port. Artor Ronan will be there with a ship, big enough to accommodate two score of your warriors, human or wizard."

Nina tucked the paper into her sleeve. "They'll be there."

Brinnie slipped out of the room, turning invisible once more. She hurried down the halls, making her way to the other side of the castle.

She had received word that one of the Masters wanted to speak with her—unusual, considering most of her contacts operated at lower levels, under the noses of the Masters. She could only hope it wasn't a trap. *Well, if it is, the whole plan has been compromised. And I need to find out.*

Another dark hall, another knock on the door. She stepped in as the bearded wizard inside held up a light orb, illuminating the visage of the only member of the Council who had voted in her favor at the trial. "Brynna. A pleasure to see you."

"You as well, Master Ragnulfsen." She eyed him. "I appreciated your support in court."

His wrinkled countenance drooped. "You are the last person I know of to have seen my great niece and nephew, Anika and Dawson." His head bowed. "I know better than to hope they survived, but I am grateful for your valiant attempts at Riverdell."

Her throat squeezed. *More people left behind.* She searched for words. "They were both fierce, and brilliant."

"And we can't let their sacrifice be in vain." He held out his hand, and after a moment's hesitation, she responded by holding hers out as well, palm up. He dropped a small object into it—a signet ring.

"I don't believe in this foolishness about abandoning 'lesser' estates," he continued. "We are only hastening all of our demise. Unfortunately, I am outnumbered, and any act against the Council upon which I sit would be considered an act of treason." He closed her fingers around the signet. "If you were to deceive my forces, pretending to be acting under my authority with this ring, my steward would not be difficult to fool. A brilliant commander in battle, but very, very trusting." He winked. "She might be persuaded to lend a third of our forces. Not that I could be held responsible for such a thing."

She fumbled for words. "Certainly not." She slipped the signet into her pocket, heart pounding. This didn't feel like a trap, but she didn't feel inclined to trust anyone on the Council. "Of course, I don't know why you would think I might undermine the Council's edicts either."

His mischievous expression melted into seriousness. "Because you are brave enough to do and say what the rest of us fear to voice."

She was brave? As if she had a choice in any of this? *I'm just trying to keep this world from collapsing.*

She mustered some of her swagger and shrugged. "The other members of the Council are too scared out of their wits to be threatening."

"Fear is a powerful force." He opened the door once more. "Be careful."

She had one more stop before her night of subterfuge was over. Within a moment, she had transformed herself into a nondescript man of average height and few distinguishing features. Then she threw down a portal.

She emerged from the mist onto creaking wooden boards that swayed beneath her feet. Water sloshed beneath the pier, the harbor sending up a smell of salt and fish.

A man sitting on a crate jolted and cursed as she appeared. "Was starting to think you weren't coming."

She could just make out his words through a thick brogue. "You spoke with the other man over the phone? The ship will be ready?"

He raised an eyebrow at her. "'Course. Long as you can pay." He held out a hand the size of a baseball mitt. "Other feller said you have the money."

She pulled a small pouch full of wizard currency out of her pocket, knocking against the signet ring. "I can pay." She hefted the bag in her hand. "But can you keep your mouth, eyes, and ears shut?"

He grinned, revealing yellowed teeth. "I don't care what you're doing, long as you're paying."

She handed over the purse. "No questions. You know where to have the ship ready."

"Sure, sure." He peered into the bag, seemed satisfied, and closed the drawstring once more. "I know how you magic folk are. I won't be telling your secrets."

"Magic isn't real."

He winked at her and shook the bag of coins. "It sure ain't."

She left him on his crate swigging beer as she smashed another portal and returned to the gates of Castelon. She mounted a shadow eagle and swooped to her bedroom window, hopping inside and landing with a roll, grimacing at the strain to her wound.

As she stood, brushing herself off and dropping her covering of invisibility, Lana shot to her feet from where she'd been sitting on her bed. "Well?"

Brinnie shrugged off her light jacket. "No issues. As a bonus, Eringaard is with us." She held up the ring. "And we have the key right here to a third of their forces."

Lana's mouth dropped open, then she slowly shook her head. "I can't believe you've managed all of this in a week."

She hardly could either.

I can, her dry eyes screamed at her. *Do you even know the meaning of sleep?*

"It took a lot of socializing, but it paid off." Hours and hours of acting like some court lady versed in diplomacy, instead of an exhausted teenager on the brink of screaming at everyone to pull their heads out of the dirt.

She flopped on the bed and winced as her developing scar stretched. "I'm wiped."

Lana perched back on her bed, legs crossed. "Does your mom know about this yet?"

"Our allies? Sure. My nighttime escapades? Not so much." She stared down at her boots, still on. Was there a way to use magic so she didn't have to sit up again? "She seems to think I'll die if I breathe wrong. You would think Nathan was taking me bungee jumping instead of to the library."

"Bungee jumping?" Lana turned the words over in her mouth like a foreign language.

"Right. Um, it's where humans strap themselves to stretchy cords and jump off tall things and free fall on purpose."

"Just . . . for fun?"

"People seem to think so." She hoisted herself up to reach for her boots.

"Humans are weird." Lana smothered a massive yawn. "Sorry. You didn't stay out with Nathan as long yesterday. I didn't get as good of a nap before you came back and started being noisy."

Yank. One boot off. "I'm not noisy."

"Not you. Him." She began braiding her hair. "Don't get me wrong, I do love a good library, but I don't usually have that amount of energy bubbling out of me after however many hours you two spend in there." Lana raised an eyebrow. "Assuming you two are engaging in normal library activities."

Her shoulders tensed. *Does she know? How could she know? Most people don't just guess their friend is researching dark magic.* Boot two popped off. Brinnie kicked the shoes under the bed to deal with later and sprawled out, trying to act casual. She forced an easy laugh. "What else would you do in a library?"

Lana's eyebrow rose higher. "Some University students in the study rooms had ideas."

The words took a moment to process. Brinnie's eyes widened. "What —I, that's not—"

"I imagine he would be considered good-looking, in that, like, puppy dog kind of way."

Brinnie sat up. "That is not what's happening. He's nice and he's helpful, so he assists me with my research."

Lana leaned forward, hands folded in her lap, sympathy written on her face. "Marcus would understand, Brinnie. It's okay to move on."

Her eyes threatened to pop out of her head. "What! We weren't—I was not . . . *with* Marcus." She could feel her face flushing.

"Okay." From the tone of the word, Lana obviously didn't believe it for a minute. She resumed braiding. "For two brave warriors, you both were awfully big chickens about your feelings."

Both? *Not both. Just me.* She pushed the thought away. In retrospect, maybe Lana believing she had a thing for Nathan wouldn't be bad. That could excuse Brinnie's long absences—without having to explain why she needed Scott Castelius's grandson to sneak her into the Master's private library. "Maybe. But . . . I am enjoying my time with Nathan." She picked up speed on the lie. "It's the one semi-normal thing in my life right now. This is what normal high schoolers think about. Not war and the end of the human race."

"I get it." Lana winked. "You keep having fun with him. As long as you keep kicking butt in secret."

Brinnie returned a playful smile, but as she rolled over to fall asleep, the expression faded to a grimace. The perhaps most dangerous of her secret stunts would occur tomorrow night.

After a morning debrief with Mom where she had no choice but to admit to some of her activities—where else would she get the signet ring?—Brinnie spent the rest of the day gathering supplies for her nighttime adventure.

She slipped by the two Castelon guards easily enough by pretending to retire to her chamber and instead jumping out the window. Lana, luckily, was napping after her nighttime vigil, and wouldn't think much of Brinnie being gone—she usually had tasks to do during the day anyway. Escaping Lana tonight would prove more difficult, but for now, she was safe.

She was thankful for a chilly day that made wearing a hooded cloak appear normal. She didn't need a random person recognizing her. It might also hide her gawking as she made her way into the city of Castelon.

Unlike the dark stone of Mordizan, the buildings in Castelon seemed built with whimsy. Strange shapes poked toward the cloudy sky, bright colors decorating walls and rooftops. Like in Mordizan, some wizards led strange pets, both leashed and free, such as a boar and . . . yes, a skunk on a lead. A man with a floppy hat on a street corner sang while playing what appeared to be a hurdy gurdy as a group of children gathered around giggling. Meanwhile, wizards wearing every sort of style imaginable shopped at eclectic storefronts from bakeries to a potions shop. Brinnie worried she might actually stand out in the very normal loose dress that came to mid-thigh, comfortable leggings, and shoes without heels she had chosen.

She turned, glancing at the light stone of the castle rising behind her, like some sort of Disneyland scene. Even on this somewhat blustery day, the setting felt far too whimsical for a city at war, presided over by an uncaring idiot of a Master. Like any city, she was sure less savory areas lay hidden beyond this vibrant marketplace, but she struggled to curb her anger. *How can anyone live like this, knowing what's happening?*

Or maybe this shows why there's something worth fighting for.

She stopped in her tracks. Giggling children. A couple walking by hand in hand, exchanging blushing smiles. A teenager slipping what appeared to be an ice cube down the back of his friend's shirt, and the whole group of them, including the pranked boy, guffawing.

If everyone lived in subdued misery, why bother stopping Mordred at all?

She felt her tight jaw loosen. Normal people, going about normal lives. Wizards enjoying magic.

This is why I have to do this. To protect the good in this world.

She continued down the street. Now that she was looking, she could see the signs of stress. Adults exchanging pensive looks, speaking in low tones. A hand clasped to a shoulder in comfort. The amount of people strolling down the wide street seemed small for the number of shops. And several appeared to be closed. Gone fighting? Hiding? Dead?

She spent hours tracking down the shops she needed. Her concept of wizard currency values was rudimentary, especially since her experience had been with the apparently different currency used by Mordizan and the Allied estates, but if she overpaid the shopkeepers, at least she was stimulating a wartime economy while looking stupid for not knowing what a tence and a quarter was.

Finally, she lugged a bag full of supplies back to the castle and dumped them in the alcove she had coordinated with Nathan. He would have an easier time evading questions about a mysterious sack of odds and ends than she would.

As she rounded the outer castle courtyard to fly back to her window, she felt a shadow pass over her. She whirled, looking up.

None other than Nathan swooped past her, cawing like a bird while gliding on . . . bat-like wings sprouted from his shoulder blades?

He circled and touched down next to her, wings kicking up wind as he stumbled into a standing position, a grin plastered across his wind-reddened face. "I hoped I might see you."

She stared at the wings. "Sorry, that's a new one for me. You can *fly?*"

He chuckled and pulled a corked vial out of his pocket. "Not usually, but the potions master on Circus Row gave me a prototype of his product. It's a new brew, very revolutionary, that takes several different kinds of magic to make. It gives you wings for up to an hour."

Giving the Master's grandson a prototype sounded like asking for a legal case. "I didn't know potions could be that powerful."

"Here." He held out the other vial to her. "Try it."

"I think I'm good, but thank you."

His expression dropped. "Oh. All right. I asked for two so we could try it together."

I feel like I just kicked a puppy. She hesitated a moment. *The potion didn't kill him, at least.* "Oh, well, I guess I could give it a try."

His grin returned as she uncorked the vial, tipped back the contents, and immediately felt a warm fuzzy feeling on her shoulder blades. With a force that shoved her a few stumbling steps forward, enormous wings sprang from her back, sending her cloak flying over her head.

Nathan belly laughed as she untangled herself from the folds, unable to hold back a giggle herself. "Should have thought to take that off first."

"I'm glad you didn't." He pointed to the sky. "Onward and upward! I imagine I only have about thirty minutes left."

Strangely, she could feel the wings like an extension of her own body, like arms attached between her shoulder blades, but requiring no real muscles to move. She flapped, and her feet left the ground, stealing a gasp from her lungs. *If they fail, you'll make a shadow bird to catch yourself.* With a few more powerful flaps, she rose into the air, her stomach plummeting to her feet in an exhilarating rush. "To be honest, I do like this better than a broomstick."

"Oh, much better!" Nathan tucked in his arms and legs and attempted a clumsy front flip, wings flapping and fluttering to keep him aloft. "This invention is perfect. I wish I could fly all the time. Want to take a pass over the city?"

Cold wind hitting her teeth made her aware of her wide smile. "I have time."

They soared over the buildings, a few people pointing as they passed. *Very subtle, Brinnie. Hopefully no one figures out it's you and that you're slipping parole.*

Nathan led the way in a controlled dive toward a high, grassy hill overlooking the city. They touched down in a stumbling run, both laughing.

Brinnie looked up, across the bright rooftops of Castelon, and her heart twinged. "It really is a beautiful place, once outside the castle walls."

Nathan's wings flapped in the breeze, and he wrestled them into a folded position. "Don't you just love being a wizard?"

Her smile faded. "Sometimes. When I can think about something besides war."

"But we have magic. Imagine being a human and dealing with international politics and disease and world wars and nuclear threats without magic." He chuckled at Brinnie's surprised look. "I do *know* about the human world. My grandfather keeps up to date on what's going on there, too. It's good policy to be informed."

"You make a valid point. Magic is an advantage."

"Exactly. You just have to see the bright side. Like flying, and, wait, what's this?" He pulled something out of his deep pocket with a grin. "Oh, it's a small something for you."

Her eyebrow rose as he held out a thin, plain gray cuff. *Is that just . . . an iron band?* "Thank you." She accepted the gift and watched his reaction as she slipped it onto her wrist. He smiled, so she must have been correct in her assumption that the object was indeed a bracelet. The ring shrank to fit her wrist exactly. "Oh! That's cool. I appreciate the gift." She hesitated. "What's the occasion?"

He shrugged. "Friendship, I guess." He started down the hill with a spring in his step. "We should probably walk back so the wings don't wear off and drop us out of the sky."

She followed, not quite sure about his fashion taste, but oddly touched.

His wings faded by the time they reached the bottom of the hill. Brinnie stopped. "We probably shouldn't go in together. I snuck out, and I'd prefer the guards not realize."

"Oh, definitely." Even standing still, he bounced on his toes. "I'll see you tonight. You got everything?"

"I dropped it where we planned."

"Then I'll see you at midnight." He winked and bounded away.

"See you at midnight," she said to his retreating form. She felt the last remnants of her wings dissolve as she turned her face toward the castle. If all went well, this might be the last lighthearted romp she would experience in a very long time.

CHAPTER
THIRTY

Lana smirked as Brinnie straddled the windowsill, ready to leap out. "Have fun."

"I told you, it's just a late-night research session. Nathan didn't have time until now."

"Uh-huh." She raised an eyebrow. "Be smart."

Brinnie rolled her eyes, turned invisible, and hopped out the window onto her waiting eagle.

Her hands trembled as she brushed away the loose strands of hair the breeze blew into her face. If Lana saw her nerves, hopefully she attributed them to what she thought was the true nature of Brinnie's late-night rendezvous with Nathan.

Her stomach hurt from the tension of lying to Lana by pretending to lie to her. *I'll tell her the truth later. After it's done.*

She stepped off the eagle in a shadowy corner of an inner courtyard and slipped inside the castle, heading downward, for Castelon's dungeons.

Nathan had given instructions, and she hoped she could actually follow them, considering that getting lost seemed to be her trademark move. She pulled out the piece of paper with directions and followed the written list and crude map into ever-narrowing dank tunnels. Finally, she spotted a flickering light ahead.

She rounded the corner into a roughly circular room with a domed ceiling. The stone walls looked ancient, some of the rock crumbled away, the floor uneven.

Nathan stood waiting, holding the bag in one hand and a torch in the other. "Good, you found it."

She rubbed her wrist. The bracelet he'd given her earlier was beginning to irritate her skin. *I'll take it off after this.* "For me, a miracle."

She took the bag from him and crouched to the ground, beginning to pull out the necessary items, and, of course, the vellum scroll that contained the most important information of all.

Nathan set the torch in one rusted sconce dangling precariously from the crumbling wall. "Can I help?"

She hesitated. "I don't know if it's safe for you to be here while I do this."

His face fell. "I know I couldn't convince my grandfather of anything, but I was hoping I could at least help you with this."

Her heart softened. He had been instrumental to get to this point. At first, she'd been reluctant to share her plans, but once she did, he'd responded with his characteristic enthusiasm. *"I bet you can control it just fine. I believe in you."*

"Okay." She handed him the tallow candles. "You can place and light these where I say."

Drawing chalk lines on the rough floor took what seemed an eternity, especially as her healing scars protested the repeated bending and standing.

Nathan dripped wax from one candle onto the floor to affix the other tall, skinny candles in place. The flickering torch seemed to make the chalk lines move and dance as Brinnie copied the designs and inscriptions from the scroll, careful not to step on any of the lines.

Finally, after checking several times, she was satisfied with her work. The books they'd read had detailed all sorts of terrible things that could happen from incorrectly drawn lines.

"Okay, let's light the candles and get the incense going." She reached for the bag. "Make sure you stay outside the edges of the circle."

Her heart beat faster as they lit sticks of incense at the four cardinal points, and she hoped their compass was accurate. The sickly sweet smell reminded her of Keilrie's creepy room under the fortress. Of so many dreams where she resisted the darkness with everything she had.

This is different. I'm not Keilrie.

The old woman's cackles echoed in her head. *"Mistress of shadows. Creature of darkness. Vessel of the dark ones. Those are your names. You will join us."*

Not the same. I have to. To defeat Mordred, I have to.

So much magic groaned inside of her. So many powers. All powers Mordred had. All powers he could combat.

Except for this. *Dywledrith.*

She laid out the elemental stones. Prepared the ceremonial silver knife. Nathan backed away, standing in the doorway.

She lifted the bundle of herbs, set it alight, and began the chant in the ancient language, placing her feet on the first line.

The words had taken painstaking hours to memorize, careful not to utter them aloud. The movies that depicted Latin as some mystical language for rituals were close, but they used the wrong ancient tongue.

And they weren't uttered by a wizard.

She followed the spiraling paths of chalk, chanting as the fragrant herbs burned down to her fingertips. Part of the instructions, which luckily didn't actually hurt her, due to her resistance. The fumes, however, nearly blinded her, her head spinning, eyes watering. The dried bunch burned to ash in her hands, which she scattered as she walked.

The spiraling paths led her to the middle of the circle. Though she knew she remained in the underground room, she felt as if she had descended, floating in some sort of dream state. The whispers began around her. The hovering presence of shadows not her own. Goosebumps broke out across her skin, and a voice deep inside shrieked for her to stop, to run.

But an even stronger force seemed to pull her to the end of the chalk path, where she knelt in the center of all the markings, still reciting, still speaking the words.

She lifted the ceremonial knife, pure silver, and bared her right forearm. "Power requires sacrifice," she recited in the ancient language. "Blood must be spilled in gain and binding."

Only two more steps. Two more steps, and this ritual would be complete, for good or ill. She slit just above her wrist.

As blood welled, as if from afar, she heard Nathan shout something. Her head turned toward him, visible through flickering smoke and flame, and she saw his finger pointed toward her.

No, not toward her. Toward the cuff on her other wrist.

The band tightened and bit into her skin white-hot. She cried out, dropping the knife. The world around her darkened. Darkened, like in the dungeons of Mordizan, where her magic had been suppressed.

She tried to summon fire, shadows, something, but nothing happened. Instead, the darkness around her seemed to rumble. She stumbled to her feet. "Nathan, what—"

"I'm sorry, Brynna." He took two steps forward, and his head tilted. For once, he stood with utter stillness. No grin lit his features, and instead of a sparkle, she could only detect a hard glint in his eye. "I did like you. And it was entertaining to watch you interact with the dunce you thought I was. The dunce everyone thinks I am. Alas, we can't let you destroy the world we've worked so hard to build."

He stalked forward, one foot scuffing through one of her chalk outlines.

A physical pain shot through her head like lightning. She gasped, almost falling.

Around them, the swirling shadows hissed, darting faster.

"Nathan, please, you're making them angry." She clutched her head. "You're going to get us both killed."

He snorted, glancing where her panicked eyes followed the ominous shapes. "I don't see anything but smoke and flames."

Another scuff. A pain shooting through her chest. This time, she did fall.

"Dramatic." Before she could recover, he grabbed her hair and yanked her head back, snatching up the ceremonial knife in his other hand. A cold smirk grew across his lips. "Your magic is tethered by that cuff. You're wounded. You're weak." The smirk grew to almost a snarl. "Isn't it a shame that you killed yourself attempting dark magic? An irreparable stain on your cause." The knife flashed toward her exposed throat.

A bright light popped, and a wind rushed through the room. Near blinded, Brinnie ducked out of the way of the sweeping knife as Nathan's hand loosened around her hair.

But there was no swipe with the knife. His wide eyes met hers, glanced down. She followed the trajectory of his stare to the point of a blade protruding from beneath his sternum.

His mouth opened, closed. Then he fell beside her face-first with a thud.

She looked up.

Behind him, holding a bloody sword, stood Marcus.

CHAPTER
THIRTY-ONE

Brinnie stared for only a moment. Then she was on her feet, a strangled sob choking from her chest as she threw her arms around him. Really him, solid, alive, right here.

"Whoa." Marcus hugged her back with one arm, sword still ready in the other as he scanned the room. "Is he the only one? Are there more attackers?"

"Just him, we're fine." She raised one hand to his face, still not sure he could be real. "Marcus." Her voice cracked. "Please tell me you're not dead."

Apparently satisfied there were no further threats, he finally looked down at her, meeting her gaze in the darkened room. Half the candles seemed to have blown out. "I'm fine." He took hold of the hand she'd lifted to his cheek and held it out, looking at her wrist. "Are you? What is this?" He scanned the room, and his grip tightened, expression darkening. "What happened here?"

She yanked her hand away and took a few stumbling steps backward. "You were gone for *weeks*." Her breath shuddered. "If anyone should be asking what happened, it should be me. We all thought you were *dead*, Marcus." A sob hiccupped in her chest. "*I* thought you were dead."

He stared at her, brow furrowed. "Weeks? Brinnie, we left yesterday."

She could barely force the words out. "Not for me."

He dropped the sword, and before he could even take a step forward, she was leaping into his arms, clinging to his neck as sobs wracked her body.

I was so alone.

"I'm so sorry. I'm here. I can't imagine."

The comforting warmth of his voice in her mind only set the tears flowing faster. *Alive, alive, alive.* She didn't know how, or why, but he was here, and instead of selling her soul to otherworldly entities she found herself in his arms.

"Hey." He brushed tears from beneath her eyes. "Remember to breathe, okay?"

She took a shuddering breath. Movement caught her eye, and her gaze shot to a figure behind him. "Ignatius?"

He waved one hand, the other holding the Case of the Master Key. "Hi. I'm here too. Do I get a hug?"

She relinquished Marcus from her bear hug, but held on to his arm, afraid to let him go, as if he might disappear again. "For you two . . . it was only one day?"

"That's correct." Marcus looked down at Nathan. "Clearly a lot happened here. Where are we, and who did I just kill?"

"We're at Castelon, and uh, you just killed the Master of Castelon's grandson."

His eyebrows shot up. "That's politically unfortunate. Why was he trying to kill you?"

"I wish I knew." She stared down at the limp, bloodstained form of the once bubbly young man. "Just yesterday, I thought we were friends, but I've made plenty of enemies here."

"Second question." Ignatius strolled forward. "Why are we at Castelon and not Wraithwood?"

She swallowed. "Wraithwood fell a few weeks ago. We fled." She squeezed her eyes shut and gripped Marcus's arm. "Mrs. Winslow didn't make it."

He drew her closer, his jaw tight. He didn't need to say anything.

After a moment, Marcus cleared his throat. "I would guess we ended up here with you rather than at Wraithwood because the portal anchored on your connection to the Case. Traveling through time, I suppose it's not odd that a day in the past might be weeks or even months here."

Brinnie glanced between the two of them. "Did you find Excalibur?"

"We did." Marcus hesitated.

"But we couldn't pull it from the stone," Ignatius finished. "No amount of brute strength or spellcasting."

"Of course the portal took you to a time when the sword was in the stone." She rubbed her temple. "Not any of the many years when it had already been pulled and was easily snatchable."

"I think we have a lot to catch up on." Marcus nodded to the messy scene, ritual incense and candles overturned, blood splattered, chalk smudged. "Especially this."

She couldn't meet his eye. "Everything is worse than when you left," she said quietly. "We've had to make some difficult choices."

Her heart sank, taking in the failed ritual. With still no Excalibur, this might have been their only hope. She would need to visit the shops again, redo the spell work . . . she was lucky Nathan's interruption hadn't killed them both. And that whatever flash had occurred from the portal seemed to have scared off the angry shadows.

"Brinnie."

She squeezed his arm tighter.

"This wasn't his spell work, was it?"

"We'll say assassins killed him," she said aloud to both of them. "First of all because we don't need you on trial, Marcus, but secondly because we need to stage this somewhere less . . . incriminating for me. I've already had one assassination attempt, so we'll say they killed him while trying to get to me when we were hanging out together, and then ran before we could catch them."

"You're not going to answer me, are you?"

Let's have this conversation later, after we take care of the immediate issues.

He sighed. "I'll grab the body. Let's go stage a botched assassination attempt."

In the end, Marcus and Brinnie left Ignatius lurking beneath the castle and staged the murder in a study room of the library, Nathan's back to a window.

Brinnie surveyed the scene. "We need more blood. His leaked out down in the dungeon."

Marcus pushed up his sleeve. "We can use mine, and you can heal me after."

"Before you do that." She held up the cuff on her wrist, blisters ringing the piece of metal. "This is suppressing my magic somehow. I don't think it's completely gone, but this gives me a good singe if I try to use it." She pulled, wincing as the bracelet dug into the burns. "I can't seem to get it off."

"Maybe there's a catch." Marcus gently took her hand in his, running his fingers across the surface of the cuff. "How did he slip this on you?"

Her cheeks felt red. "Um, he gave it to me as a gift, I put it on, and it shrank to fit."

He stopped for a moment. "A gift of a handcuff?"

"Okay, looking back on it, I know it's obviously a handcuff and not an ugly bracelet, but wizards are strange sometimes, so I thought he must just have a terrible sense of style, or maybe this sort of thing is *in* here." She rolled her eyes as he held back a smirk. "Yes, feel free to laugh at me."

He continued to prod the cuff, squinting at the rough surface. "There has to be a button somewhere."

She missed that line between his brows when he concentrated. The way his eyes danced with amusement. The timbre of his voice. Everything.

"Marcus." She hesitated. "I may have fallen apart a little bit without you."

He ceased his investigation and waited for her to continue, holding her hand between his.

"It was my spell work," she whispered. "I didn't care what it would do to me—I was willing to try *dywledrith* if I could kill Mordred for taking so many people away from me."

He still didn't speak. Just listened.

"I'm not sure if I regret trying, though."

"I can't imagine what these weeks have been like." He squeezed her hand. "Something even worse than how I felt when you were in Mordizan's dungeon. I don't know what decisions I would have made." He sighed, cupping her cheek in his palm. "But your soul is worth far more than what vengeance could bring you."

She closed her eyes and leaned into his touch, her tears trickling onto his fingers. There was the truth of it. Regardless of saving humankind, or anything else, revenge on Mordred had outweighed everything. And she hadn't cared who she became to do it. "You might not like this version of me."

"I love every version of you."

Her eyes opened at that. Her lungs felt squeezed in her chest. "Don't leave me again," she breathed. "Ever. You said you wouldn't leave me here alone if the world depended on it, and maybe I should have believed you, but everyone said there was no way you could survive . . ."

"You're right. New promise." His words seeped into her mind. *"From now on, no solo missions. We'll stay together."*

She nodded and leaned into him. He rested his forehead on hers, and everything finally felt right in the world again. *I love you, Marcus Vorath. And I won't let you die without telling you.*

"Did you mean to share that thought?"

She hesitated for only a moment. "I did." Her heart rate picked up speed, but she met his eyes. "I'm not taking any more chances."

She could feel his heart racing in his chest, matching hers. "I know we've kind of been forced into this close connection, so I never want to take advantage and overstep—"

"Overstep." She held his gaze. "Whatever step you wish you could take. Take it." Tears welled in her eyes. "Or one day you might be staring at ruins and wish you had."

He took in a breath. Then one hand was cupping the back of her head, another on her waist, his lips on hers. She tangled her fingers in his dark hair, softer than she expected, pulling him to her. Both of them splattered in her blood, Nathan's blood, chalk dust, halfway through staging a murder in a library study room, but for the two of them, she wouldn't expect it any other way.

"And I love you. I love Brinnie Lane and Brynna Ludovic and Brynna Drakon and everything in between."

Her thoughts were fuzzy, distracted by the electric feel of his touch. *How did you become so romantic?*

"Not my usual nature, so I believe you are to blame."

His hand brushed the healing scar on her back, and she gave a sharp gasp of pain, breaking the kiss.

"Are you okay?" He pulled back.

"I'm fine, sorry. I have an injury that's still healing from the battle at Wraithwood."

He raised an eyebrow. "You haven't seen a healer about it?"

"Well, yes." She hesitated, then lifted her shirt to show him her abdomen. "Mordred kind of made me a shish kebab with an enchanted blade."

He swore under his breath. "All the way through?" His eyes lifted to hers. "And you lived? That shouldn't be possible."

She laughed. "Are you disappointed?"

He snorted. "No. And honestly not surprised. I'm beginning to think you're indestructible."

She carefully guarded her thoughts on that subject. On what her dreams and feelings suggested about the magic radiating inside of her. Even with the cuff on her wrist, she felt the magic buzzing through her veins, like angry bees upset with being contained. Instead, she smirked. "You can't get rid of me."

"Nor would I try."

A beat of awkward silence prevailed, and she felt her cheeks reddening, heart beating far too fast at her own brazenness, at what had just happened. Flustered, she held up her wrist. "But let's get rid of this so we can cut you."

He guffawed, the awkward tension released. "Yes, ma'am. Did he say a command word to activate it?"

She wracked her brain, trying to remember what he'd said when she had been deep in the ritual. "Um . . . I feel like it was a nonsense word. I speak pretty much all languages now, by the way. New magic I discovered."

"I assume now isn't the right time to ask how to say 'Castelon is the worst' in twenty languages."

"We can do that later for sure." She rubbed her temples, trying to remember. "I'm just going to try saying a lot of things it could have been and see if it works."

For the next few minutes, she attempted to utter various sounds that resembled what she'd heard from Nathan. Marcus chimed in with similar-sounding nonsense words until she was giggling, which felt a bit inappropriate in the presence of a dead body. Finally, the cuff made a clicking sound.

Magic rushed through her, throwing off sparks. Marcus stomped out a possible flame on the ground while Brinnie yanked off the cuff and threw the offending bracelet on the table.

"Thank goodness." She breathed a sigh of relief and worked her fingers. "I should be ready to heal you now."

With Marcus's blood, they created the appropriate bloodstains. Afterward, Brinnie ran her fingers over the slice in his arm, and the skin knit back together.

She released his arm and handed him the paper Nathan had given her with directions. "Okay, can you find your way back to Ignatius?"

He tapped his temple with one finger. "If you could do it, I can do it."

"Rude." She stuck her tongue out at him. "I'll give you a few extra minutes to get out of the vicinity before I start running around screaming for help." She placed the back of her hand to her forehead and feigned a swoon. "How terrible that my secret lover was slain by assassins. Alas, too, that the shame of my nighttime rendezvous should be exposed to the castle."

Marcus's nose wrinkled. "Does he have to be your secret lover?"

"Well, I'm not going to *say* that he is, but people are going to assume. I'll make up some story about staying too long in the library, losing track of time . . ."

"Slipping past your guards to do so."

"Yeah." She winced. "There's really no *good* way to frame this."

"Maybe the truth, or at least, most of it." Marcus shrugged. "He tried to kill you, I killed him. I can stand trial."

"Yes, after you somehow slipped into the castle, considering we didn't tell them anything about the time travel, didn't announce your presence, and then stabbed someone." Brinnie drummed her fingers on the table. "The Council isn't going to find the heir of Mordizan innocent after murdering Master Castelius's grandson with only me, the shadowmaster under guard, as a witness that it was in fact an attempted assassination." She shoved a frustrated hand through her hair. "I can hardly believe he did it myself. Anyone who's ever met Nathan can probably attest that he was a caffeinated Labrador. His grandfather most definitely made him do it."

"His grandfather." Marcus snapped his fingers. "Can we get him alone and cut a deal? Clearly Castelius is behind these assassination attempts. We can bluff that we have incriminating proof that we'll reveal to the Council, bringing him down with us—unless he agrees to go along with a coverup. The story that you and Nathan met here in the library, assassins killed him instead of you, *and*—" he gave a dramatic pause "—Ignatius and I showed up just in time to scare off the assassins."

"So part of the deal is that Castelius will act like you two have permission to be here. No trial. No questions asked how or when you arrived."

"Precisely. He knows who I am already, but for good measure we'll pretend Ignatius is just a random friend."

"That does nicely explain how I somehow allowed assassins to escape while remaining unscathed, if they spooked from you and Ignatius wandering by." She felt a smirk blossoming. "I do like the idea of threatening Castelius. Okay, that's the new plan. You and Ignatius are good at sneaking—you both get to the study room while I go harass Scott. Then I'll meet you back here and start screaming." She took a step toward the door and stopped. "Oh. I did leave Lana under the impression I had a thing going on with Nathan, which is where she thinks I am right now. Couldn't let her find out about the dark magic. So, you know, you might want to play into the jealous lover a little bit around her."

"Whoa, two things." He held up a finger. "One, you're not going to come clean to her?"

She fidgeted. "I mean, I wasn't really planning to 'come clean' to anyone. This whole plot is a coverup so no one knows."

"So that *Castelon* doesn't know." He frowned. "Lying to friends doesn't tend to go well."

She sighed. "Fine. I'll . . . tell her if it comes up." She put her hands on her hips. "So what's number two?"

A mischievous glint sparked in his eye. "Two, why would I be acting like a jealous lover?"

"Um." She felt her cheeks heating. "Well. If I *was* seeing Nathan, Lana was pretty confident, that, you know, you liked me, and so, in her mind, you know—"

"Only Lana was confident?"

Now her ears felt red. "Well, I told her that was silly."

"Really?" He took a step closer.

"Well." She was stuttering, which only made his smirk widen. "Yeah so uh, we'll need to address what happened a little bit ago after this whole blackmail plot wraps up. You, ah, weren't *exactly* clear previously, so to be honest I wasn't expecting it to go quite like this . . ."

"I suppose I wasn't clear." She felt her back against the door as he reached out and brushed a lock of hair behind her ear. "I tried to show you in a hundred small ways, but I never wanted to pressure you or put a strain on our relationship. Especially with all you had been through, all that was happening . . . the last thing I wanted to do was cause you any more distress." His eyes held hers. "But if you would like me to, I would be happy to make my feelings abundantly clear."

A shiver ran down her spine. "You've got to stop pulling out lines like that."

He took half a step back awkwardly. "Sorry. I thought that's what we were doing here. I'm terrible at flirting—well, I would guess, I haven't really tried, definitely not successfully, seeing as you've never noticed my attempts . . ." He trailed off as she giggled. "I feel like I'm making a fool of myself here, aren't I?"

"You were doing *too* well—it was a compliment." She stood on her tiptoes and kissed his cheek. "I'll be back soon, and we can talk all of it over." She grabbed the door handle and darted out of the room before she could be further distracted.

His voice followed her in her head. *"Try not to cause too much trouble."*

The thought of Scott's face when he woke to her looming over him sent a smirk traveling across her face. *No promises.*

CHAPTER THIRTY-TWO

"Hello, Scott."

The man's eyes snapped open and he started to bolt up, but Brinnie pressed the flat of her blade against his throat.

"Shh." She smiled at him, his darting eyes reminding her of the dried blood on her face. "A very nice bedroom you have here." She leaned back slightly and surveyed the room, its heavy draperies and thick carpets. "Terrible security though." She pointed the blade directly at his bobbing Adam's apple. "We're going to have a little chat. You're not going to try to fight, or yell, because we both know that if you make me angry, you won't be leaving this room alive."

Marcus's voice chuckled in her mind. *"You are delightfully terrifying."*

Already spying on me?

"There are a lot of stairs in this castle. I need something to entertain me."

She watched Castelius's face darken to a vibrant crimson, but he gave a tiny jerk of his head in acknowledgement.

She raised her hand, and the knife evaporated into darkness. "Good. Here's what we're going to do."

Brinnie sniffled, wiping a nonexistent tear from her eye. "It was all so sudden."

The elderly coroner awkwardly patted her on the shoulder. "There there. Nothing you could have done."

Two wizards floated Nathan Castelius's lifeless body out of the library, covered in a white sheet. Now so late at night as to be early morning, the long day assisted by providing Brinnie with tired, watering eyes, perfect for appearing distraught.

Escorted by Marcus, she wove through the crowd of guards, statespeople, and curious bystanders who had been summoned to the commotion in the library. After what felt like hours, she walked away without a hint of suspicion placed upon her—or Marcus—as the murderer.

As they headed for the exit, Brinnie spotted Lana sprinting toward them, one hand holding the scabbard at her hip. The swordswoman skidded to a stop in front of them. "I came as soon as I heard. What *happened?*" Her attention turned to Marcus, and her mouth dropped open. "You're alive."

"We'll debrief back at our room." Brinnie bobbed her head toward the hovering wizards around them and lowered her voice. "They're both alive. Ignatius is grabbing the Master Key. We stowed it so Castelon wouldn't take it." She pulled both Marcus and Lana toward the door. "I'll tell you more when we have everyone together."

In the hall, she spotted a messenger and waved him over. "Do you have paper and a pen?"

After sending him off with messages to all of the Wraithwooders to meet at her room, the three of them started that way themselves. Brinnie's feet dragged, exhaustion tugging at her eyelids. She tripped on her own foot and stumbled.

Marcus caught her arm. *"You need rest."*

I'll sleep after we get all of this sorted out.

"Lana, tell Brinnie she needs rest."

Traitor.

"You can't even walk right." Lana put a hand on her hip. "I prescribe a short nap while we wait for everyone to arrive." Before Brinnie could protest, she held up a hand. "I promise, we'll wake you up once everyone gets there."

Once in the room, Brinnie looked from her bloody, dusty clothes, to the bathroom, to the bed, and stretched out on the floor. Washing up would take too much effort. "You two better wake me up."

The next thing she knew, a crick had formed in her neck, Lana was crouching next to her rubbing her arm, and she was on eye level with several pairs of feet. The crowd of family and friends had gathered around the two-person table near the fireplace. An ever-smaller crowd, with Uncle Merlin and Quentin both gone. No Ms. Tynsdale or Mrs. Winslow. No Marcie or Jerry or Anna or David or . . .

I can't think about that right now. Marcus and Ignatius had returned, bringing their little group total to eight. Seven other people packed into the room, all speaking in low tones. *I can't believe I slept through all of that.*

She sat up with a groan, rubbing her eyes. "Okay, good. Everyone is here. Time to debrief."

Marcus strode over and offered her a hand up. "We've covered what happened with Excalibur and time travel and that Nathan Castelius is dead."

She searched his eyes. *Did you tell them about the dark magic?*

"No. That's your decision on whether to tell. But we definitely got some curious looks about what you were doing with Nathan at two in the morning."

They can wonder.

She hobbled the few steps to the table, legs half asleep and abdomen aching. "Okay, thanks for joining us, everyone."

Mom gestured toward Brinnie's bloody clothes. "First question before you start—is any of that yours?"

"No. We'll get back to the fact that Scott Castelius is trying to have me assassinated, though. First order of business." She leaned her hands on the table, a bit dizzy. "Excalibur was in the stone. Marcus and Ignatius couldn't get it out. How are we getting Excalibur?" A slightly unhinged giggle bubbled inside her that she tried unsuccessfully to stifle. "Is it like Mjolnir? Were they unworthy?"

"It was never about worthiness, nice as that legend might be." Miss Burtle pursed her lips. "The sword was sealed in the stone with blood magic."

Maddy rocked on her heels. "That sounds spooky."

"Not particularly." Brinnie thought back to her studies. "Blood magic was performed by pre-Myrddin wizards as a way to make magical locks and seals only accessible to certain people by harnessing the power of bloodlines, restricting accessibility to only certain people or families." She wrinkled her nose. "I don't know why I didn't learn that's what happened with Excalibur."

"Most likely because it makes a very nice story that Arthur was the only one worthy enough or strong enough to pull it." Miss Burtle sniffed. "Not as dramatic as the sword having already been keyed to him."

"Bloodlines." Brinnie tapped her fingers. "So in theory, a descendant of the person could also unlock the blood magic?"

"Yes," Miss Burtle replied, at the same time Mom said, "Absolutely not."

Miss Burtle raised an eyebrow at Mom, then her expression smoothed. "Ah. I see. *Yes,* in theory that could be done. In practice, I agree with Eira. Going back in time again is a foolish idea."

"I didn't even *say* anything yet and you're shutting me down," Brinnie complained.

"We know you too well." Marcus offered a slight smile. "But we did only make it back to this time period because the Case was attracted to you. If we try again, with you this time, what will the Master Key be drawn to?"

Conversation swirled around her. Mom said something about going back herself, as another of Arthur's descendants. Someone else debated the wisdom of risking losing the Master Key to time. Brinnie tuned it all out, brain whirring.

"Not any time and place," she blurted. "Not any time the Master Key already exists. Only then, and only now."

The room went quiet. "Explain," Miss Burtle said.

She rubbed her temple, a sleep-deprivation headache forming. "To no one's surprise, I've been doing a lot of research. Such an overwhelmingly powerful object like the Master Key couldn't exist twice in one time without catastrophic effects. Effects we would know about, if we did go back in time and end up in the wrong place. It follows that if we go back in time, upon our return, the Master Key will only bring us to the time we left or later."

Maddy bounced on her toes. "So you're saying that if you were going to be unsuccessful, we would already know about it, because the two Master Keys would like, blow each other up or something."

"Something like that, yes."

"That makes two fairly significant assumptions." Miss Burtle held up a finger. "First, it assumes history is set in stone and can't be changed by your actions. Second, it assumes that you in the future *do* go back to the past—maybe there was no catastrophic effect because you decided not to go."

"I'm about seventy-five percent sure, from what I've been reading, that the history we know has already suffered the effects of anything caused by time travel. Anything we now know as the past is because it did in fact happen, regardless of cause." Brinnie continued to rub her forehead. "But we don't really have time for theoretical quantum mechanics. We don't have a choice. I need to go, and when it pulls me back to the present, it will probably pull me to Mordred."

Mom sighed. "Why Mordred?"

"I'd have Excalibur, and Excalibur is Mordred's bane. It would be attracted to him. Probably more strongly than the Case would be drawn to me, even." Brinnie stumbled toward the bed, leaned down, and pulled out a folder filled with papers from beneath. She slapped the file on the table, flipped it open, and leafed to the appropriate pages, sliding them across the table. "I've been sneaking around with Nathan Castelius—including at odd hours of the night—to get into books and records that aren't open to the public."

Marcus reached for one of the papers, squinting at Brinnie's scrawl. "You've been researching theoretical magic?" He glanced at her, voice echoing in her mind. *"I thought you were researching dark magic."*

Multitasking. "Maybe I didn't quite give up on the idea of a time travel rescue party." *Using dark magic to do it. Not that they need to know that.*

"Heard that."

You don't count.

She addressed the group. "As much as I hate math, I've been making —dare I say it—calculations. Magical pull of objects, kind of like the gravitational pull of celestial bodies. Time theory. Portal physics. I would say with about sixty percent confidence that if I go back in time and I pull Excalibur, the portal will take me straight to Mordred, just in time for the kill."

"And what's that other forty percent?" Mom scowled. "Utter disaster?"

Brinnie hesitated, shrugged. "It's worth a try."

"Not by you." Mom slid one of the papers back across the table. "I'm a descendant of Arthur, too. Let me take the Master Key and go back. If

I'm lost, the fight can go on without me. But Brinnie, with your skills, you're essential."

Brinnie took in the determined set to her mother's jaw, her straight shoulders. Willing to risk her life for this cause—and maybe . . . for Brinnie herself?

"Unfortunately, it should be me." Brinnie leaned a hip against the table. "If whoever goes back is going to end up near Mordred when we return to this time, my skills may be needed to get out of that situation alive. I can turn invisible. I'll cloak myself in shadows before I ever appear in the present, and Mordred will be none the wiser until I have a sword through his gut."

"And there's a forty percent chance you die." Marcus frowned at her. "Those are terrible odds."

"I mean, I'm not a calculator. The odds might be better." Probably a lot worse, but she carefully shielded that thought.

Ignatius spoke up for the first time. "Don't you all have a Council or something that sends task forces for these sorts of things?"

Brinnie and Marcus glanced at each other. "Not one we can trust." Brinnie turned to Mom. "Scott is actively trying to have me killed. It feels deeper than just retribution for courtroom antagonization. Nathan said something about not letting me destroy their world." Brinnie's foot tapped. "I already didn't trust the Council, but I think they're up to something."

A knock sounded at the door, and everyone froze.

Brinnie straightened. "Enter."

A breathless messenger pushed open the door, bowed. "Emergency meeting in the Council Chamber," he panted. "Mordred has attacked Arthrys. He's in Wales."

"Order." Master Castelius banged the gavel. "Order!"

The assembly crowding the Council Chamber quieted.

From the distance, Brinnie could see the red tinge to Scott Castelius's eyes. Exhaustion? Grief? Anger? But his voice remained all business. "It has come to our attention that an armed battalion, under the command of Mordred, has assaulted the castle at Arthrys, Castelon's closest neighbor in physical proximity."

"How did no one see them coming?" someone called out.

Marcus muttered, "Maybe because everyone here had their heads too far up their—"

Mom shushed him while Lana suppressed a snort.

Court protocol allowed Marcus and Lana in the boxes on the technicality of being members of Masters' families, if anyone decided to question Mom and Brinnie on why they'd allowed two former dark wizards into the meeting, but the wizards seemed preoccupied with more pressing concerns, for once.

She tuned back into the conversation as one of the Council members intoned, "Now the question upon the floor remains—shall we come to the aid of Arthrys?"

Brinnie's mouth dropped open. "This guy can't be for real."

"Thank you for your summary." Master Castelius turned his attention from the Council member to the crowd at large. "We must decide whether sending troops is worth the risk."

Brinnie couldn't keep her mouth shut. She amplified her voice. "What risk? Allowing Mordred a foothold in Castelon's backyard? Seems like a bigger risk than sparing some warriors to keep the fight off the front lawn."

A general rumble of agreement met her outburst.

"But what if this is only a diversion to lure our troops away so that he can attack the more prominent estates? Why attack such a small castle when he could have headed straight for Castelon and launched a surprise attack?" Master Castelius nodded as people began to whisper among themselves. "We wouldn't want to play right into his hand."

"Or maybe it's straightforward." Master Ragnulfsen raised his voice. "Maybe he doesn't have enough forces here yet to attack Castelon successfully, so he plans to start with a smaller target to establish a base."

"Mordred? Straightforward?" Master Castelius gazed out at the assembly. "That seems out of character. We can't be too hasty."

"Well, I have a simple solution." Brinnie stood, evading Mom's hand trying to grab her arm and pull her back down into her seat. "You sit back in comfort while I and whoever wants to join me go lend aid to Arthrys. Strictly volunteer."

Castelius glared at her. "Miss Drakon, I would be delighted if you went into battle."

She took his meaning. *I'd be delighted if you went into battle . . . and died.* "Good. Whoever is joining me should meet me at the gate in two hours." She waved her hand at the assemblage. "You all decide what you plan to do. I've made my choice, and I'll be waiting."

With that, she turned and headed for the stairs.

She didn't mind the rumble of voices around her as stalked across the floor of the Council Chamber, heading for the door, but when she felt a comforting presence to either side of her, she smiled. Marcus and Lana, flanking as a loyal entourage.

After they exited, Marcus took a step forward. "All right, highest marks on the theatrics. What do you have up your sleeve?"

She gave them both a look of wide-eyed innocence, still striding with purpose. "Me? Why don't you think I'm just valiantly going to defend our allies?"

"You know why Mordred wants Arthrys." Lana smirked.

Brinnie cracked a smile. "Glad we came to the same conclusion."

Marcus glanced between them. "At the risk of appearing stupid, I think I've missed something."

"I did too at first." Brinnie slowed her pace slightly, abdomen starting to ache—more than usual, anyway. "Mordred sneaks his way with an entire force of warriors to attack a base a couple hundred miles from Castelon, instead of Castelon itself. I asked myself what he wants with Arthrys. If he doesn't feel ready to attack Castelon, why would he risk being so close? And if Castelon is his next target, why waste time at Arthrys? He needs something."

"Excalibur." Marcus shook his head. "Of course. It's where Mordred was laid to rest. He knows he has one weakness, and he wants to find it before we can, or at least make sure that we never do."

"And Mordred doesn't know about the time travel. No one does, except our small Wraithwood group."

"Castelon might help if they knew *why* Mordred is attacking Arthrys," Lana said hesitantly. "If they thought they could find Excalibur there."

"That's the problem. I'm worried they might be able to."

They silenced for a moment while passing another wizard in the hall.

Once around the corner, Marcus spoke. "Merlin said it was destroyed."

"Yes, but we aren't *certain* pieces don't exist. If they do, I don't trust Castelon with them. Mordred might know something we don't. If we can find out where Mordred's looking, we can try to get there first." She clapped her hands together. "Two birds, one stone. Protect Arthrys, look for Excalibur shards."

"We need to pack weapons, armor, supplies." Lana began ticking off items on her fingers.

"We can use Ignatius's anywhere portals to get there," Marcus added.

Brinnie's heart warmed, watching them plotting.

We're back in business.

Despite the odds against them, a flicker of hope rose from what she'd thought were the dead ashes in her chest.

CHAPTER
THIRTY-THREE

Only five warriors met them at the gates of Castelon besides Ignatius and Mom.

"Honestly?" Brinnie held out a hand to the five. "No offense to you. I really appreciate you joining us. But out of everyone in that Council Chamber, we got five?"

A woman tightened her bracers. "I lost my home. I'm not about to sit in silence as more people lose theirs." Her eyes darkened. "I fear not many of us lived to tell the same tale and understand the gravity."

Brinnie's heart squeezed at the thought of so many who had gone down fighting.

The five wizards and Ignatius all looked ready for battle with rucksacks, weapons, and various articles of armor, but Mom remained in ordinary clothes. Brinnie cocked her head. "Do you need someone to lend you armor?"

"I'm not coming with you." She held up her hand, revealing a signet ring in her palm. "I'm headed to Eringaard to hopefully bring reinforcements to Arthrys."

Brinnie blinked. The confident tilt to Mom's shoulders, her determined jawline, her planning and initiative . . . After years and years of hiding, Eira Ludovic had truly returned.

"Good. We could use all the help we can get."

Ignatius reached into his pockets and pulled out several orbs. "I made an overabundance of these with Master Ludovic. Basically, a stockpile. We can use one for Arthrys, if anyone's been there, and a couple for you for Eringaard." He handed two portals to Mom.

Impulsively, Brinnie hugged her. "Be safe."

"You too." Mom returned the hug, gently, but it felt . . . sincere.

Then she stepped back, smashed the portal, and was gone.

"I've been to Arthrys," a man said. "Just tell me how to work this portal."

A few moments later, mist swirled around their group of nine. Brinnie held onto Marcus's arm, trying not to dig her fingers in too hard as the magic swirled around her, making her bones ache.

As the mist cleared, Brinnie heard a shout. She turned to a sword pointed straight toward her.

Before she could react, Lana's hand swept out, hitting the broad side of the sword and slapping it away. "We're allies, stand down."

The young man's sword trembled in his grasp. Now that the mist had receded, Brinnie took in their surroundings. A stone courtyard, near what appeared to be the gates to the castle keep. Through the open gates, she could see the outer walls across the green and the shapes of warriors lining the walls. So the fighting hadn't yet reached the keep. A relief there, at least.

She returned her attention to the young swordsman. "Our apologies for barging in. We're from Castelon, here to help. We need to talk to your lord."

The man led them toward the keep, rough gray stone rising against a slate sky. This castle was old—older than Mordizan, than Dirklon, than Castelon.

When they stepped inside, Brinnie blinked. Gone were the harsh lines of the exterior, replaced by ornate vaulting on the ceilings, decorative wall paintings, and shining wood floors. *Fancier than Castelon. Impressive.* It wasn't hard to be fancier than Mordizan's sprawl or Dirklon's austere militant presence, but this castle felt like something tourists would love.

The young man led them to a wide room dominated by a massive table. The thought crossed Brinnie's mind that he shouldn't have trusted their word so easily—someone should talk to him about blind acceptance.

Her attention diverted to the man with a long, gray beard pointing to locations on a map spread on the table, consulting with five other wizards while a few more darted in and out, presumably to relay orders. She vaguely remembered him—he had been present at some meetings of the Council, though not at the most recent. She bit her lip. Lord Faughn, Steward of Arthrys, had the build and mannerisms of a scholar, not a war leader.

Though protected by a cloaking spell from human eyes, Arthrys wasn't considered an estate. Rather, it had served as supposedly neutral turf housing Mordred and other remnants of pre-Myrddin times. As such, the castle had no Master, no double space, no city or town. More a museum or library than a fortress.

Until now.

"Lord Faughn." The young man gave a shallow bow. "Visitors from Castelon."

The Steward of Arthrys looked up, eyes running over the newcomers, making Brinnie painfully aware of how their group must look—four wizards clearly under the age of twenty, followed by five others in assorted beat up armor. Not an impressive delegation, but given he was a museum curator forced into warfare against a ransacking force, he could use all the help he could get.

She stepped forward. "Brynna Ludovic, my lord. We heard about Mordred attacking Arthrys and came to help."

His eyes widened at the name. "I thought you were under guard at Castelon."

Oh, yeah. I had guards. Whoops.

"I told them they were no longer needed while you were finding equipment. For some reason, they believed my story about Master Castelius sending us off."

I love you.

"Not anymore. We've come to offer some extra hands in battle." She hesitated. "And if I may, I would like to speak with you privately about an angle Arthrys might provide against Mordred."

He glanced at his companions, then waved her toward a corner of the room. "We can speak here."

Fair enough. Why should he trust her?

She followed, leaving the rest of her group behind. She kept her voice low. "We think we know why Mordred has decided to attack here. We think he's looking for Excalibur, or remnants of it. Is there anywhere in this estate where they might be found? Even information pointing toward the possible location is helpful."

He rubbed his beard. "His proverbial bane. I've had my scholars looking for anything that might help, and so far, we've turned up nothing. But if Mordred thinks it's here, he would probably have a better guess than we do."

"Could we look around? The warriors can help you in battle, and a couple of my companions will help me search."

He shrugged one shoulder and gave a short laugh. "Why not? Castelon has abandoned us. Might as well let you wander the place before we're overrun."

"I wouldn't give up hope yet." She glanced around the room, at the intricate paneling that anything could be hidden behind. "Any suggestions on where to start?"

"The crypts." He pointed downward. "Mordred was kept there." He sighed. "Back before Arthrys was forced to give up its historic standing as a landmark and instead choose a side in this infernal war."

"I wish we could help more with bringing forces. But . . ." She gestured. "This is all we could muster. We may have reinforcements on the way, though, if one of our plans pulls through."

He rubbed his face. "We have a standing guard for old time's sake, but most have never seen battle until now. Anything helps."

They returned to the table. Brinnie glanced out, toward where the walls and fighting must be, torn. She could help. Her presence in battle could make a difference.

But if anyone had a better chance at finding Excalibur, it would be a descendant of Arthur.

She sighed. "Marcus, with me. Lana, you can take care of directing our group into helping where needed?"

"You got it."

Ignatius made a pouting face. "I'm not in charge? You wound me."

"You definitely aren't in charge." She held back a glare. *We're friends now. This is good-natured banter. What friends do.* Even if any sudden movements from him still made her flinch. "Behave for Lana, or she'll put you in your place."

He glanced toward Lana and raised an eyebrow. "Oh, really? I wouldn't be opposed to—oof!"

Lana had unstrapped a shield from her back and shoved it into Ignatius's chest. "You're on shield duty. I imagine you're useless as an archer."

Brinnie left the group to be led away by one of Lord Faughn's men. She and Marcus followed another to the crypts.

She shot a guilty thought to Marcus. *I know it would make more sense for Ignatius to help me search, considering he's the least useful in battle, but . . .*

"I understand." While the scholar leading them chattered away about the history of the castle, Marcus gave her hand a squeeze. *"It's not fair to expect you to be alone with him, especially in the crypts."*

Her shoulders relaxed. *I know it's dumb and I should be a better tactician.*

"You're also a person, and keeping your sanity is a tactical advantage."

His slight encouraging smile as he looked down at her, his hand still around hers . . . even though she felt her cheeks redden at her own actions, she wove her fingers through his. *Thank you.*

They did need to talk—talk about what happened in that study room, how they'd kissed, what that meant . . . perhaps she shouldn't have done it, shouldn't have said anything. Not in wartime, when they shouldn't be distracted. Maybe both of them were overcome with intense emotions, and he didn't really feel that way about her . . .

No, he definitely did. And apparently had felt that way for a long time. She wasn't sure if that was better or worse. They couldn't do this anyway, right? Heirs weren't supposed to be together, and she was the heir to not one, but *two* estates. And the only heir to Wraithwood.

So I can't do anything because several decades or even hundreds of years from now I might inherit an estate?

Or any day. We're at war.

Wraithwood is conquered anyway. Your Mastership would mean nothing.

It would mean Marcus wouldn't be eligible for Mordizan.

Only if you married *him. Is that where you're going right now? You kissed him* one *time.*

Her brain leaked the thoughts that she had been trying so hard to suppress.

You may not live to inherit an estate anyway. Even if Mordred is defeated. Even if there is a happily ever after.

Not with the weight of so much magic clawing through her veins.

"These stairs lead down to the crypts." The scholar's words interrupted her mental turmoil. "Feel free to wander, but try not to touch things unless absolutely necessary. These vaults are ancient."

"Thank you for showing us the way." Determined to keep her mind on the task at hand, Brinnie let go of Marcus and headed for the stairs.

Partway down the rough, uneven steps, Marcus summoned a ball of fire and held it up to light the way. "Reminds me of sneaking around Mordizan together."

"The same amount of dust." She tried to keep her tone light.

He glanced at her out of the corner of his eye. "I, uh, was sensing some pretty spiraling thoughts earlier. I didn't listen in, but if you want to talk about it while we poke around a bunch of tombs . . ."

She avoided eye contact. "Not sure it's a pressing issue at the moment. I'm fine."

She could sense that he didn't buy it, but he didn't push. The stairs emptied into a stone room that smelled of dust and a hint of mildew, the ceiling low and held up by pillars. Candelabras, crates, and strange statues crowded around what appeared to be stone sarcophagi filling the room as far back as the eye could see.

"A historical attic, but underground." Brinnie rubbed her nose, tickled by dust. "Oh. I guess that's a basement."

"Start at one end and . . . poke around?"

"That's the best plan I have."

They pushed and tapped against the walls, checking for hidden cubbies or rooms. They levered crates open and rustled through objects nestled in straw that hopefully weren't cursed. *This is going to be like looking for the proverbial needle in the haystack.*

With guilt, she realized she didn't much mind the methodical pace, Marcus beside her, hardly needing to speak to work in tandem. She watched him heft a stack of crates. *He's really back.* A broken edge inside her had been pieced back together.

He brushed his hands and looked over toward her with a little smile. Caught staring.

"I missed you, okay." She plunged her hands into another crate of straw, ears burning. "It's just good to see you alive."

"I didn't say anything." He set down a pile of crates, moving to pry open the one that had been beneath, lips twitching. "You don't need to justify yourself." Now he really was smirking. "In fact, I didn't think anything of it until you started blushing."

Her face felt even warmer. "I don't blush."

He laughed. "Your cheeks and ears turn all pink."

"Blasted ghost-white genetics." She clapped her hands over her cheeks, then coughed from the dust that stirred up, wiping her face on her shirt. "That was a mistake."

"Care to explain the source of the blush?" He held up a goblet from the crate as if he hadn't a care in the world, put it down, reached back in.

She heaved a gigantic sigh, then winced as her wounds protested. "I guess if we're going to be down here forever, we might as well talk."

He sobered. "I'm listening."

She took a moment, opening another crate. "So, in that study room . . . I . . . may have been a bit brash. The shock of you being alive . . . I. Well. You know me. It's unusual for me to be so . . . forward."

"I have no complaints about you being 'forward.'"

She gently shook out the scrolls in this crate, in case a sword fragment might miraculously fall out. "So um. I don't know if that was just an, uh, emotional moment for the both of us, and I totally understand if you want to move on and pretend it didn't happen."

He paused, expression carefully neutral. "Do you want to pretend it didn't happen?"

No. "I'm trying to say that if you don't actually feel that way, it's okay, like I won't be offended, and I know that could make things complicated with Mordizan—"

"Brinnie." He huffed an incredulous laugh and straightened. "I told you I love you."

"Yes, well," she stuttered. "I mean, of course we love each other, we're best friends, but—"

"I didn't mean it like that." He strode over to her where she stood next to the stacked crates of scrolls. "Do you really still not know that?"

She bit her lip. "I didn't want you to know that I felt like this. Not in wartime. Not when it would make things so complicated."

"I don't think it has to be complicated." He gently took her hand. "We've always been at war, and we may always continue to be. There is no *good* or *safe* time to wait for. I care about you more than I've ever cared about anyone. If you want to keep our relationship as friends only, I won't bring it up again, but I don't think you should decide based on what you think you should do or what duty obligates you to do."

She couldn't help thinking of Ms. Tynsdale and Uncle Merlin, the grief on her aunt's face as she explained that they had kept apart, ultimately for no reason.

But we are both definitely *heirs. One day Mordizan* will *be his . . . unless I mess that up.*

Tears pricked the back of her eyes. "This is a bad time to be selfish. Besides, assume we did. If something happens to me . . . I don't want to do that to you."

He held her gaze. "If something happened to you, it doesn't matter what our relationship is. I still can't imagine anything worse. It didn't matter for you when you thought I was gone." He held her hand tighter. "Which is why I'll be right here, no matter what. We can figure anything else out as we get there."

What did I ever do to inspire this kind of loyalty? "This isn't a silly romance novel. They make it seem like love can always work out." She looked down. "And sometimes, it can't."

"Maybe they are silly. But maybe they're also right . . . if you want them to be." He slowly released her hand. "I won't pressure you, Brinnie. I want you to be happy."

"Being happy is a choice." She turned back to the scrolls, avoiding making eye contact. He might see the moisture gathering there. "We . . . we have to do the right thing."

He stepped away. "So be it."

He returned to the crate he was searching, the heavy silence punctuated only by rustling and clinking from the straw and artifacts. She glanced at him a few times, but he didn't look her way. Not arguing, but not cracking jokes or changing the topic either.

She knew she shouldn't say anything, but she heard herself blurt anyway, "If I didn't say no . . . What would that make us? I feel like we're a bit past the point of get-to-know-you coffee dates."

The heaviness lifted a bit as he gave a slight smile. "You're right, we've done this all wrong." He rubbed the back of his neck in a show of exaggerated distress. "I should have formally invited you to the next feast after you'd been vetted by my father's advisors as an appropriate match. I have bungled the rules of courtship."

"Of *courtship*?" Her lips twitched at that. "Oh, please no, that sounds terrible. Do they really make you do that?"

"All very public and political, yes." He shifted a crate aside and began poking around the base of a statue of some ancient wizard. "I tried not to think about my impending doom or try to guess when my father would decide it was strategic to put me on the market."

Brinnie raised an eyebrow. "You poor soul, forced to court the most beautiful and powerful women in the land. How would you have coped?"

He made a face at her. "You mock my suffering, you heartless woman."

"So what *would* we be? If, you know, it wasn't completely off the table."

"I suppose I would be your suitor, my lady." He gave her a slight bow.

"Ew, no, I hate that." He bowed with an even deeper flourish, and she stuck her tongue out at him. "I'm going to challenge you to a duel if you keep that up."

"Would you prefer 'boyfriend' like the humans say?" His brow wrinkled. "Why do they call it that? Because they're a boy, and your friend? It's such a strange way to refer to your, ah, significant other."

She felt a mischievous smile spread across her lips. "You know what. I don't think I would call you any of those things." She smirked. "I would call you my sig other."

"Sig other?" He screwed up his face. "That's the worst one yet. Do people actually *say* that?"

"I would give you the choice of that or 'boo,' final options."

"I'm starting to think I was saved from a terrible fate after all. The human world equipped you with methods of torture unknown to wizard kind."

"Whatever you say, sig other."

The banter continued as they rooted through crates and knocked on walls, the mood lightened—mostly. Her cheeks began to ache from chuckling at the irreverent absurdity of it all, cracking dumb jokes while searching for the object that might save them, a battle raging somewhere overhead. *But the war never ends, and life must continue regardless.*

Precisely. Which is why you should tell him you were wrong.

No. He won't push me, but I have to be strong for both of us. He might be willing to risk giving up Mordizan, but she couldn't let him do that.

Not for her. He would find someone else eventually, someone appropriate.

She ignored the way her heart stabbed at that thought.

They searched for hours. Her eyes began to burn. Her nose itched from the dust. They had only covered about half the room, and she felt antsy.

"What if I snuck into Mordred's camp and assassinated him?"

"No."

"What if I challenged him to a duel, David and Goliath style?"

"No."

"What if I swooped in on the back of an eagle like a bomber plane and—"

Marcus straightened, stretching his back. "Do you want to start from the other side of the room for a change of pace?"

"Yes, please."

The farther back they went, the more the stone had crumbled, and crates gave way to loose piles of everything from armor to currency she didn't recognize. "We'll never comb through all of this. It could take days. Weeks."

"We could ask Faughn for any spare scholars, maybe those too old or otherwise unable to fight." Marcus stepped over a sword—not Excalibur—that had fallen onto the floor. "Let's see how far back this goes."

The dust and cobwebs increased as they reached the other end of the vault. There, a barred door like from a jail cell hung open, revealing a smaller room. Brinnie glanced questioningly at Marcus, then stepped inside.

In the middle of the cell, a stone coffin had been cracked open, the lid resting against the side at a forty-five-degree angle. The etchings in the sarcophagus appeared ancient, perhaps Celtic. She peeked inside to confirm—empty.

She looked back at the barred door and the open lock, now deemed unnecessary by whoever had placed them there. Nothing else but the coffin sat in the small room. Goosebumps rose on her arms. "Mordred's tomb, you think?"

"I would say so." Marcus knelt next to the coffin, brushing dust from the decorative marks. "Some stylized script from the ancient language here. It appears to be the story of how Mordred fell. Nothing we don't already know."

Brinnie circled the coffin, looking for clues. "Maybe the remains of Excalibur were buried with him, under the coffin or something."

They poked and prodded at the markings, just in case any hid secret compartments. Marcus grunted, hefting the stone lid. "This is definitely solid."

Hesitantly, Brinnie stepped into the sarcophagus and tapped around on the bottom, but she found nothing. She straightened and brushed her hands together, clapping off dust. "It doesn't *seem* to be here, but . . . how mad would they be if we smashed this, just to be sure nothing's inside?"

They both stared down at the coffin. Over a thousand years of history . . . but what would it be worth if the world came to ruin?

"Okay. I think I saw some war hammers back there somewhere."

Before Brinnie could step out of the coffin, something boomed above them. Streams of dust, dirt, and tiny pieces of rubble showered from the ceiling.

She met Marcus's eyes. "Hold that thought and go investigate?"

They took the stairs up two at a time. Brinnie led the way into the room where they had first encountered Lord Faughn, but the maps on the table lay abandoned. Marcus motioned toward the doors, and they hurried out of the keep.

Faughn and several others stood outside, staring out toward the walls.

"What was that?" Brinnie asked breathlessly.

Faughn nodded across the green, expression grim. "War machines. One of the projectiles made it through and hit the keep."

Brinnie exchanged a glance with Marcus. *We're running out of time. Do you think Mordred knows something we don't?*

"Hard to say, but at this rate, they'll break through before we can search through even half of it."

New plan. You search, I'm heading to the wall to help.

"You're still injured."

She made a shooing motion. *I'll be using magic, not swinging a sword. I'll be fine.*

Before he could say anything else, she turned to Faughn. "Where are the projectiles coming from?"

He pointed in three different directions. "I believe they have multiple machines, there, there, and there."

"Okay." She tightened her ponytail. "I'll take out the war machines, then get back to searching. You think your forces can hold the wall once the catapults are out of the way?"

His eyebrows shot upward. "Er, yes, I suppose, but how—"

"Great, I'll be right back." She took a few steps to the side, summoning a shadow eagle and hopping on. "I'll find you in the crypts, Marcus."

Before any of them could protest, the eagle took off.

CHAPTER THIRTY-FOUR

Brinnie found Lana on the outer wall, armed with a crossbow and picking off invaders below manning what appeared to be an approaching battering ram.

Brinnie dropped next to her, waving the eagle away and crouching below the crenellation. "A battering ram too?"

Lana didn't skip a beat, ducking and loading another bolt into the crossbow before standing again, sighting, and releasing. "I don't know how they built this many siege engines so quickly. Even with wizards enhancing tree growth to produce timber and whatever other magical advantages various people can offer, there's no way such massive structures should be built yet." She cranked the bow. "Battering ram at twelve, catapults at ten and four, trebuchet at two. Battering ram is the only one close enough for me to pick off."

She stood again, sighted, released, then dropped once more. She jerked a two-fingered point to the left and right of them. "We have about a dozen wizards on anti-missile duty trying to blast the projectiles out of the sky before they hit, but success rate isn't great."

Lana shot to her feet, yanked a horn from her belt to her lips, and shouted down the wall. "Grappling hook to your right, Paulo. Charis, Malena, reinforce the right battlement." She ducked as an arrow flew over her head, tucking the horn away. From the way it magnified her voice, Brinnie assumed it was enchanted.

Brinnie's eyebrows rose. None of those three had come with them from Castelon. "You're in charge?"

She shrugged, loading another bolt. "Eh. Filling in some gaps in leadership."

For a moment, a different version of Lana's future ran through Brinnie's mind. Lana graduated from the University, a force to be reckoned with, probably quickly rising through the ranks to become a respected war leader.

Instead, she was here, fighting a losing battle on a losing side.

"What's the worst of them?" Brinnie nodded in the general direction of the war machines.

"Trebuchet." Lana aimed, fired. "Longest range. Aimed at the keep."

"Got it. See you later." Brinnie formed another eagle and hopped on.

Lana paused and looked at her fully. "Hold on, Brinnie, what are you—"

"Don't worry about it." With that, she took off.

Trebuchet at two. She turned invisible and kept the eagle as ethereal as she could while still remaining solid enough to carry her. Hopefully it could pass as just another bird to those who saw—an admittedly abnormally large bird. With evening approaching, hopefully visibility would slowly decrease as well, although she wouldn't be able to tell.

Now past the wall, her heart skipped a beat looking out over Mordred's forces. He'd brought an army.

The enemies ringed the outer wall as far as she could see, outnumbering defenders ten to one, magic blasting back and forth, grappling lines sailing upward only to be cut, shield formations on the ground blocking projectiles from above. How long could Arthrys hold like this? The defenders had thrown every able-bodied person on the walls, while rank upon rank of attackers waited to relieve their comrades should the first waves grow tired.

The trebuchet would be hard to miss. Even as she flew closer, the massive war machine released, the monstrous beam, probably thirty to forty feet long, swinging upward, whipping around a sling that launched a rock the size of a beach ball soaring toward the castle keep.

How? None of that fit through a portal. How did they build a complicated war machine so quickly?

"Allies on the ground? Maybe the machines were already mostly assembled."

Oh, hi there.

"Hi. Still haven't found Excalibur. Smashed up the sarcophagus, so hopefully I won't be burned at the stake by scholars. Remember once you torch one war machine, they're going to be on guard and expecting it with the others. And Mordred will probably guess it was you."

She didn't know what to say to that—she couldn't just ignore the other machines. So she deflected.

How did you know torching them was the plan?

"From one pyromaniac to another I say, is there any other way? Be careful."

She touched down several yards away from the crowded ground around the trebuchet and waved away the eagle. Invisible, she crept toward the siege engine, dancing around the warriors preparing the machine for its next launch.

She wriggled beneath the body of the machine, touching her hands to each of the supporting beams. She hesitated, then scurried up the ladder. What could be harder to replace than a forty-foot beam?

She clambered down its length, fingers teasing a smoldering flame inside the wood. At the end, she hopped a few feet down to the ground, where another rock waited.

The flame should work within at first. Squinting, she could make out little trails of smoke. By the time anyone noticed, the structure would be compromised, and it would be too late.

So she waited, watching the wood smolder until someone finally shouted, pointing to a creeping lick of flame.

An aqua wizard hurried to the scene, spraying water over the fire, but even as he did, Brinnie brushed her fingers along the beam, encouraging the flames.

They sprang to life, hungry. She slipped away as chaos developed, content to watch from a distance. No fiery projectile, a slow burn . . . they had no reason to suspect the fire had been intentional. At least, not yet.

A crack split the air, and she smiled to herself as the massive beam split, part of it snapping forward under pressure, counterweight smashing against the ground, the entire structure undermined. She sent the image to Marcus. *See, stealth is my middle name.*

His chuckle echoed in her mind. *"Ah yes, I'm sure they haven't even noticed something is wrong with the trebuchet."*

Fun's over, back to work for me. She concentrated, her imagination returning to that day at Castelon, when Nathan Castelius had shared the potion with her, causing them to sprout wings. She needed a low profile, smaller than an eagle. Why not wings of her own?

She gave her shadowy new wings a few flaps before launching into the sky.

"That's a new one."

Are you focusing on your search?

"Multitasking is my *middle name."*

She snorted, wheeling toward the next catapult.

Even the sensation of flying couldn't quite rid the frown from her face. Marcus could search night and day and never find anything. Even with her sabotage of the siege engines, they were drastically outnumbered. If Excalibur wasn't to be found, then for what? They should evacuate everyone, not lose lives.

If anyone knew, Mordred did. Mordred, who lurked somewhere behind these lines.

She could find him. Sneak into his war tent, go through his records, figure out what he knew.

She carefully hid those thoughts from Marcus. First, the catapults needed to be decommissioned. Then she could recklessly sneak into the heart of the enemy encampment and try to spy on the one wizard she knew she couldn't beat in combat. Good plan.

The first catapult went up in flames about the same as the trebuchet, but as she neared the second, it was clear someone had tipped them off. Fires and light orbs guarded against the impending night, a squad of warriors standing around the catapult, eyes on the sky and surrounding area as well as watching the machine, likely awaiting any telltale signs of smoke. So much for subtlety, then.

She wheeled, her back turned, as she built a white-hot ball of fire between her hands. Then she turned, ball expanding. A shout went up, but too late. She hurled the fireball down toward the center of the catapult, flapping her wings as hard as she could to soar away from the damage as arrows and other projectiles shot toward where she'd hovered less than a second before.

Then she turned outward, away from Arthrys, and toward the tents and campfires of the enemy.

Remarkably, she didn't hear any comments from Marcus, though to be fair, she hadn't sent him any mental "footage" in a while. She thought about checking in but cast the idea aside. He would want to know what she was doing.

She touched down behind a few trees near the regimented rows of tents. They extended from a collection of central, larger tents like spokes on a wheel. From the flag flapping above one, she didn't have to do much sleuthing to determine which was the command center.

She slipped through the camp undetected, coming to a halt outside the slightly parted flap of the door, just enough to see figures within, but not close enough to see faces without stepping inside and disturbing the flap, perhaps giving away her presence. Good enough. She paused to listen.

"I'm sorry, my lord. Only the battering ram remains, and they're picking off our men as quickly as we can send them forward."

"We were promised four war machines for this venture." Mordred's voice. "Now, because of lax security, we must reconfigure our approach. This is a significant delay."

"The walls can't hold for long, my lord." A third voice. "They are far outnumbered."

"Thank you for making the obvious plain. I am *peeved,* commander, because I now must expect you and your incompetent troops to make up the time we have lost to return to schedule. Send a force to construct a second battering ram for the northern gate."

"Yes, my lord."

Brinnie stepped to the side as a man scurried away, then ducked inside before the flap swung closed.

Mordred stood at a large camp table, two men and a woman with him.

"Do you think the machines were attacked by the shadowmaster, my lord?" the woman asked.

Mordred's eyes flashed. "I did not expect you to begin stating the obvious as well." He shifted a map on the desk. "I want your forces on that second battering ram. Select strong shield bearers, and levitation wizards to assist with the ram."

"Yes, my lord." She gave a curt bow and left.

Brinnie crept toward the table, trying not to so much as move a blade of grass. Mordred and the two men continued discussing plans and tactics, but she didn't tune in. Instead, she scanned the maps and papers. *Please have some sort of information.*

"Brinnie? Where are you?"

Shoot. *A bit busy at the moment, but I'll get back to you.*

She leaned closer, squinting to make out text in both English and the ancient language. Lists of forces, diagrams of battle strategies, maps of Arthrys and the surrounding area, maps of what she assumed were other estates, world maps and country maps with estates and strongholds labeled, handwritten letters . . . She froze, eyes racing over the contents of the letter before her.

Marcus. You were right about local allies providing the siege engines. A little too right.

"What do you mean?"

Castelon. Someone inside Castelon has been colluding with Mordred. Someone who might even be on the Council. Her heart beat faster, scanning another letter, another.

"How do you know? Who?"

I can't tell. Whoever wrote these letters knows what the Council members discuss in private as well as in the Council Chamber. They have access to everything, including underlings who don't question building siege engines and leaving them near Arthrys. She nudged the stack of papers enough to read the pages beneath, and her heart leapt in her throat. *They've been keeping Mordred updated on me, too. This one has the trial results. And this one has the fact that you're back. Nathan's death, with the details way closer to the truth than anyone should know . . .*

His voice came through stern. *"Brinnie. Where* are *you?"*

She ignored him for a moment. An insider, presumably a high-ranking insider, and maybe more than one, was colluding with Mordred. Almost everyone had to be a suspect.

She glanced between Mordred and the papers, ensuring he and his men were distracted, and gently shuffled the letters. The words detailed estates' forces and vulnerabilities, all the events that had occurred in Castelon concerning her. The one thing they didn't include—time travel. Mordred still presumably didn't know about the only way to retrieve Excalibur. Which, judging by the lack of concrete evidence in any of the maps and papers suggesting Excalibur's modern location, meant he would be pursuing that option if he knew.

Castelon was compromised. Mordred was poised to win, with or without Excalibur. He had someone watching her, she couldn't be sure who, but they knew intimate details, like the fact that Marcus killed Nathan, not an assassin.

Mordred possessed nearly all the information. The only piece she held over him was the location of Excalibur. How long before the spy, whoever they were, found that out as well? Her mind buzzed with calculations and possibilities before hitting on a plan that made her wince. Poor Marcus. He would understand, later.

I'm in Mordred's command tent. I will be attempting something truly stupid.

"Brinnie—"

Sorry, need to cut off communication to concentrate.

She closed a mental door on their connection and circled the table, positioning herself behind Mordred. She extended her fingers, wriggled them. She had one chance if this did work.

If Excalibur was Mordred's bane, her actions in the next few seconds shouldn't be successful—but on the off chance they were . . . she hesitated.

She may have killed in battle. Never intentionally, though she hadn't pulled punches either. But assassination, stabbing an unsuspecting victim in the back when they weren't attacking her, couldn't defend themselves . . .

It's Mordred. He is *attacking you. And the entire world.*

He's still a person. A terrible person, one who couldn't be reasoned with, as hard as she'd tried at times, but the only difference between him and any other confused, destructive individual was that his continued existence caused the deaths of thousands, soon to be billions. She didn't have time or the ability to capture him, imprison him. No matter how much she understood his pain, how much he'd lost.

She couldn't save him and save humanity.

A shadow sword wouldn't work on him, immune as he was to her magic. Instead, she eyed the blade strapped to the hip of the man beside Mordred. Could she pull it fast enough? *Lana would be so much better at this.*

Her arm darted forward. She yanked the shortsword from its scabbard, the screech loud as she pulled from the wrong angle. Mordred turned as she swung for his neck.

The blade made contact with flesh just as his hand shot out and grabbed her invisible wrist and twisted. She tried to stifle a yelp as her fingers released the blade. Blood trickled from a two-inch gash on his neck, but before her eyes, the slit sealed, healed almost immediately.

Mordred jerked her to him, whipping out his enchanted blade and finding her throat quicker than she would have thought possible. The scar on her arm burned cold. "You really thought you could assassinate me?" The blade stung, pressing into her skin. "Brynna. You should have known better. My blade informed me of your approach long before you arrived in this tent."

The two men with him took up defensive stances, their eyes wide, darting to find her. Afraid. If only Mordred had any of that fear.

"Fine." She dropped her invisibility. "Kill me quickly and get it over with."

"Not yet." The hand gripping her wrist released, clutching the hair at the back of her scalp instead, the glowing blade never wavering. "We have things to discuss." In her peripheral, she could see him jerk his head toward his companions. "Leave us. I have the situation under control. Tell Aleksa to bring me the items. She will know of what I speak."

They hesitated but bowed. One exited as the other picked up his sword and then followed suit.

"Are we going to talk like this?" Her teeth gritted as the movement pressed the sharp edge harder against her neck. "I think polite conversation dictates we at least face one another."

He gave a short, mirthless chuckle. "Though I would undoubtedly win, I have no desire to begin a fight with you today. I shall keep my blade here, and if you move, I will not hesitate to slit your throat." The edge slid slightly along her skin, almost a tickle if not for the raw spot it had already nicked. "You are of little use to me now, Brynna Ludovic."

"That can't quite be true, if I'm still alive."

His clawed grip tightened in her hair. "You know of Excalibur."

"Obviously."

"And you know where it is."

She stared ahead at the canvas wall of the tent. "I have suspicions."

"Then you will share those suspicions with me."

She barked a strangled laugh, as much as she could manage without slicing her own throat. "Why? What leverage do you have here? Either I tell you, you kill me, and you find Excalibur, or I don't tell you, you kill me, and you continue your search for a needle in a haystack. You have no bargaining chips."

He twisted her around to face him, tip of the blade pointing toward her esophagus, but she kept talking. "What are you going to do? Torture me? That didn't exactly work before, did it? Or are you going to kill people until I give in?" Her expression hardened. "That won't work this time. I've cut down plenty of wizards myself. War changes your perspective. Your morals. Blood and death won't move me anymore."

They stared at one another, his flinty eyes glaring into hers. She could tell he knew she spoke the truth. However many lives he could end now, they paled in comparison to the price of his victory.

"How very similar we are, shadowmaster."

"If so, I'm only the monster you've created."

Something flashed in his eyes, then. Not quite sorrow. Not quite regret. But perhaps a tinge of wistfulness for what could have been.

"You still have one final use to me." The flash of strange emotion returned. "I had wished something better for you, Brynna. You could have been so much more."

The tent flap rustled, and a woman stepped inside bearing heavy chains and manacles. "As you asked for, my lord. The enchanted restraints. It would take a magic hot as the sun itself to melt through them."

"Good." He nodded toward Brinnie. "Please cuff the prisoner. We will be bringing a bargaining piece to Arthrys." He smiled slightly. "What do they value more—a hub of scholars, or the enchantment wizards' mightiest warrior?"

Brinnie submitted to the cuffs and didn't try to run or escape as six soldiers surrounded her with spears, escorting her out of the camp, Mordred nearby. Two of the soldiers held the chains to her manacles, pulled tight enough to either side that in theory, she wouldn't be able to lunge toward any of them—and if she did, she would only be throwing herself onto the point of a spear.

She focused on steady breathing. *It will be quick.* Assuming she was correct about her abilities. Although, even if she was wrong, it would still be swift. Swift and unfortunate.

From the number of torches and light orbs surrounding them, Brinnie guessed night had fully fallen as they approached the walls behind a herald with the flag of ceasefire, just out of range of any reasonable projectiles.

"Where is Faughn?" Mordred called, his amplified voice echoing over the walls. "I have come to parley."

Lana's voice drifted down to them, faint without magical amplification despite her loudest shouting. "If you aren't here to surrender, Mordred, I suggest you crawl back into the latrines and parley with your fellow roaches."

Brinnie snorted. A sensation at the back of her mind distracted her from Mordred's reply. Something like a knocking. She lifted the guard over her mind.

"Brinnie, I've been reaching out for the past half hour. What's happening? I heard Mordred is at the wall."

Hello again. I'm sorry I shut you out. But you would yell at me, and I needed to concentrate.

"I don't yell at you. I'm heading for the wall."

No, please don't do that. She bit her lip, glancing toward Mordred. *I may have gotten myself captured, but I have it under control. For real.*

Silence for a moment. *"I'm not yelling, but I am asking. How?"*

I tried to assassinate Mordred. Unsuccessfully.

Another pause. *"So am I correct in assuming Mordred is at the wall trying to bargain for your freedom?"*

That would indeed be correct.

"I'm coming."

She sighed to herself. She couldn't stop him, even if she told him the truth. *Okay.* She watched Mordred, who currently waited for Lord Faughn to arrive at the wall. *Hey. I love you.*

"I don't like the sound of that."

Rude.

"Don't do anything crazy. We've been in worse situations. Let's hear Mordred's bargain."

She didn't argue. This part of her plan would be cruel. But no one could guess what she intended, or the plan would be futile.

A gray-haired form with a long beard appeared on the wall. She could just make out what appeared to be a breastplate now strapped over his scholarly robes, a shield bearer flanking him on either side. "What do you want, Mordred?" His voice carried, unlike Lana's.

"Look what I found." Mordred gestured toward Brinnie, and her guards yanked her chains to the sides, splaying her arms as if to better display her. "Brynna Drakon." His lips twisted in a smirk. "What price would you pay to have Castelon's fiercest warrior returned to you?"

She couldn't make out any facial expressions from here, but Faughn's tone remained steady. "What price are you asking?"

"It's simple. Turn Arthrys over to me. You and all of your people can go unharmed. I only want your fortress. Simply surrender to me, and I will let her and everyone who fought with you live."

"Don't do it!" Brinnie's voice boomed with magical amplification. She couldn't risk anyone not hearing her. "I'm not worth this entire fortress."

Another figure surfaced on the wall, running. Dark hair, broad shoulders—Marcus. Lana's blonde ponytail flashed as she darted from behind a merlon and grabbed his arm, pulling him back into shelter with her. Good. Despite the ceasefire, Brinnie didn't trust any of these wizards not to take a cheap shot at an unarmored enemy.

"Do *not* make this deal!" Brinnie repeated.

One of the soldiers stabbed the butt of his spear into her spine. She gasped, stumbled, but kept her footing.

Mordred didn't even glance toward her, still addressing Faughn. "You will fall soon enough. Take this deal, and you will at least spare your lives."

The distant form of Faughn spoke. "I know what you're after, Mordred. I was told of your desire for Excalibur. We will fight to our dying breath, but we will not give up this fortress to you."

"Very well." Mordred pivoted toward Brinnie and her six guards. "Her death, and all of your deaths, will be on your shoulders."

"Now is a good time to enact whatever escape plan you have, Brinnie."

She raised her face toward where she could see both him and Lana peering over the wall, even if he couldn't tell she was looking at him. *Marcus. I don't have an escape plan.*

A pause as he seemed to grab Lana's arm, presumably relaying the information. *"Fight, Brinnie. Fight with whatever you have. We're finding a weapon that can reach you."*

The guards behind her parted, chains still taut, allowing Mordred to step toward her.

I'll do what I can.

She was chained. Surrounded. None of her magic was a match for Mordred. But Brynna Ludovic would never go down without a fight.

As Mordred approached, she twisted and yanked at the chains, flashing in and out of visibility. The guards only pulled harder, wrenching her arms, her shoulders, stretching her still-healing wounds. She yelped but exploded into flame. Shadow wolves leapt at Mordred, at the guards, but except for one soldier, all remained unscathed, immune to her shadow magic.

Mordred grabbed her ponytail, yanking her head back, and placed his glowing blade to her throat. "No need for such a scene, Brynna. Both of us know you cannot escape."

A crossbow bolt hit the ground several feet in front of them. Mordred dug his blade into her throat, and she gave a gasping choke, warm blood wetting her neck. "I wouldn't suggest trying that again," he projected toward the wall. "You have one final chance to change your mind."

Her vision flickered for a moment, Faughn in front of her, Marcus's voice in her mind—no, her ears. She was seeing through his mind. "My lord, can't we at least fake a surrender? Buy us time to think? We can rescue her, I know it—"

Faughn's voice cut through both her mind and her physical hearing. "Mordred, will you allow us time to consider the offer?"

"No." She could hear the smirk in his voice. Arthrys would fall regardless. "You have ten seconds."

"Mordred." Her voice rasped, neck stinging. "I wish things could have been different."

His hold lightened, just a touch. "As do I, Brynna. However, I cannot allow you to live."

"I know." She took a shuddering breath, trying to calm her racing heart. "I know I have no room to bargain. No reason you should listen. But . . . can I make a final request?"

A beat. "You may."

"Let them retrieve my body." She squeezed her eyes shut, a tear leaking down her cheek. "For my family."

She could sense his consideration. Could almost hear him turning over in his mind the even greater emotional damage it would likely inflict upon Marcus, her family, all of them, to see her cold and drained of blood, throat gaping open. She felt the moment he decided to grant her foolish request. "I will have your body deposited at the gate, should they be brave enough to retrieve it."

"Thank you." She relaxed her tense muscles, taking slow, shallow breaths, preparing herself.

"Your time is up." His amplified voice echoed. "She will now die." Softer, so only she could hear, he added, "You have been a worthy opponent, Brynna."

She felt the freezing lightning of the blade across her neck. Heard Lana's scream, Marcus's yell, both in her ears and in her mind. She felt the hot blood splash down her neck and chest like someone had thrown a bucket of warm, sticky water. Her bones jarred against hard ground as she fell.

And then all went dark.

CHAPTER THIRTY-FIVE

The scream in his throat was raw, wordless, guttural. He dropped to his knees, pain ripping through his chest.

"Lana." His words came out in a growl. "Give me that crossbow."

Beside him, sobs shook the warrior's body. Arms limp, she dropped the crossbow in front of him, bolts clattering beside the weapon. "They won't reach." Her words repeated, like a chant. "They won't reach. They won't."

He snatched up the crossbow, shoving in a bolt, priming the weapon, cursing it under his breath for being such a clumsy weapon that took too long to load.

He took aim, angling for the distance, and pulled the trigger. The bolt landed somewhere far in front of Mordred.

Mordred's smug voice carried to them. "What will you do without your strongest warrior? What will you do now that she's dead?"

The two men holding the chains attached to her arms dragged her forward. Not bothering to lift her. Trailing her bloodied form along the ground.

The sound Marcus made wasn't one he could describe.

"A gift," Mordred continued. "We will leave the body at the gate, should you choose to retrieve it. I suggest you don't attack my men unless you wish to forfeit this offering."

Hands shaking, Marcus lowered the crossbow. Ten years seemed to pass as they dragged her limp form toward the wall. Bloody. Motionless. Messy hair covering her face.

He couldn't seem to draw in breath. This had to be a horrible dream. Not like this. It couldn't end like this.

The body dropped, face-first on the ground. The guards removed the cuffs and chains. Then they turned and walked away.

"Who has a rope?" He scanned the wall. "I have to get her."

"It may be a trap." Lord Faughn's face was pale. "They'll be attacking again soon."

"I don't care if it's a trap. Someone lower me down." He turned toward Lana. "Do you have rope?"

"I know where to find some," one of the nearby soldiers spoke up. He glanced toward Lord Faughn. "Permission, my lord?"

The steward nodded once. "Hurry."

The man ran. Marcus couldn't tear his eyes from Brinnie, her crumpled body so small in the expanse of the no man's land. His vision swam as if he might pass out.

When the soldier returned with a length of thick rope, Marcus tossed aside his sword and immediately lashed the rope around a merlon in the crenellation, tying the other end into a rough harness around himself. Lana grabbed the end around the merlon. "I've got you."

He gave a sharp nod and began his descent.

The rope burned his hands from the speed of his climb, racing down the wall just slow enough not to send himself swinging and bash into the stone. When he reached the end of the available line several feet from the bottom, Lana let out slack, lowering him the remaining distance to the ground. He unwrapped the rope around him, fingers clumsy with haste.

Neither side moved as he dashed to Brinnie, falling to his knees beside her. He cradled her into his arms, supporting her head as it lolled. Her eyes remained closed, as if sleeping. Like this, as long as he didn't look down to her neck, he could pretend she'd only passed out asleep after a long day and might wake up and smile at him at any moment, maybe make some comment about him being a weirdo for watching her sleep.

One of his tears splashed onto her cheek, reminding him of where he was—in the middle of a battlefield. He brushed the tear away and scooped her up, carrying her back toward the castle.

He lashed the two of them together with the rope to be sure he didn't drop her, shuddering at her blood seeping into his clothes, sticking to his skin. He'd been covered in blood more times than he could count, but not *hers*.

His breath came too quickly, and he forced himself to calm down. One hand in front of another, one foot at a time, back up the wall. The rope pulled at him as well, with more strength than he would have thought Lana alone could possess.

At the top, multiple pairs of arms reached over, pulling him and Brinnie to safety. A glance showed him two soldiers had joined Lana on the rope. She dropped the line and rushed to his side, helping to untangle the knots around Brinnie.

Now that he'd made it back, his body felt numb. Someone else joined Lana in detangling the harness—Ignatius. Not a hint of a mocking smile. When he caught Marcus's eye, he only gave a grim nod.

The rope fell away, leaving Marcus holding Brinnie close, so heavy and so light at the same time.

Then the projectiles began to batter the walls once more.

No, no. Those are his thoughts. His actions. Not mine.

She was not him. She was her. Watching, feeling, through his eyes. She needed to remember that. Death was far too comfortable, and she couldn't lose herself.

Brinnie drifted through Marcus's mind, watching as he retrieved her body, listening to his whirling, anguished thoughts. An idle part of her wished she could scale a wall like that. She'd probably fall to her death within five seconds.

Death. Right.

Her heart ached for him, his blurry eyes and the vise clamped around his heart begging her to speak up. But she couldn't. Not yet.

This floating sensation . . . she hadn't realized just how much pain she'd grown accustomed to in her mortal form. The pressing weight of gravity, the ache of magic in her bones, the stabbing pain of still-healing wounds. She felt none of them, only glorious lightness, and if she tuned in, the strength of Marcus's form. With so little effort, she could slip away and never feel the pain again . . .

No. Focus. She needed to focus.

They decided to bring her body to the crypt for safekeeping while the battle raged. Faughn offered a couple of soldiers to bring her there, but Marcus insisted on going himself.

Raging tears streaming down her cheeks, Lana snatched up the crossbow. "You take care of her. We'll take care of these monsters."

Brinnie's thoughts wandered. He descended the steps to the crypt, her in his arms. No, she descended. No. He. She forced herself to focus.

She couldn't feel anything through her own body. She didn't see anything beyond his eyes. The darkness of the crypt made him squint and reach for a torch, lighting it with a touch.

He gently laid her body propped against a stack of crates next to a sarcophagus that lay empty. He bent over the stone coffin, brushing away dust and grime, as if her dead body needed a clean place to rest.

"Just for now," he murmured. He turned to Brinnie's body, taking one of her cold hands in his. "I will bring you back to Wraithwood. We'll find your favorite spot in the rose garden." His voice cracked. "I'll burn every invader to a crisp if I have to. But I will take you home."

How did you know my favorite spot is in the rose garden?

He jumped, stumbling backward. "Brinnie?"

Okay, I'm super sorry, don't freak out, and be very quiet about this because it's a secret, but I'm not dead.

He knelt, peering into her face. "Are you . . . pretending somehow?"

Oh, my body is very much out of commission at the moment. Whatever is . . . me . . . is currently hanging out in your head, seeing what you're seeing. You're very good at climbing walls.

He ran a hand through his hair. His thoughts swirled so quickly she couldn't keep up. "Okay. Explain to me."

First, just mindspeak to me. There's a spy—or more than one—in our ranks. We need them to think I'm really dead. Right now, I don't trust anyone other than you, my family, and the Wraithwooders.

"Got it." He took a deep breath. *"So, how are you not dead? Your throat, it . . ."*

I took a bit of a risk. I can't heal myself, but I know the sleeper's curse doesn't work the same way as normal healing magic.

He swore under his breath. *"You planned this."*

Correct.

She felt the rush of anger burst inside him. *"For the love, Brinnie, I thought you were* dead. *I saw you die. Do you know what that . . . how that . . ."* He trailed off.

If she had a body, she would have winced. *I know. I was there for all of it. And I'm so sorry. But I don't trust* anyone *right now. Not even Lana. Definitely not Ignatius. It had to be real.*

"And you didn't know if it would work."

A pause. *And . . . I didn't know if it would work. Yes.* She sent a sigh. *If it didn't work, I didn't want you to know it was my own fault. I would rather you think it was unavoidable, that I died trying to be brave rather than doing something stupid.*

"Attacking Mordred in his own camp is still pretty stupid."

Fair point. She hesitated. *I really am sorry.*

He rubbed a hand over his face. *"I forgive you, but from now on, please, no more self-sacrificial shenanigans. You've given me enough heart attacks for a lifetime."*

Deal. So here's what I'm thinking. I'm dead. Mordred will inevitably conquer Arthrys. In the chaos, you will disappear and hopefully be presumed dead. Then we go back in time and pull Excalibur from the stone.

"Hold on. You're under a curse. How are we going to do that?"

Hopefully I only need to physically be there. You can make my hand grab it and pull it out.

He was quiet for a moment. *"You don't have a plan to wake up."*

No.

"So for all intents and purposes, you might as well be dead."

The pain in his voice zinged through her. *Marcus. I can't curse someone else to take my place. This was my decision. We'll pull that sword. Then I'll leave your mind. It will be up to you to kill him.*

Anger again. The force of it surprised her. "Why are you so eager to play the martyr?" he growled. "You're not some pawn or trump card to be strategically discarded. You're a *person.* Your life isn't worth less than anyone else's."

Mirroring anger sparked in her. *Then let me make it worth something. It's too late now, isn't it? We have a job to do.*

"No." He stood. "You're already worth something. You don't have to buy some sort of tactical advantage with your own life to excuse your existence. None of us would *be* here without you." His fists clenched.

"Your mother is an idiot, and so is everyone treating you like a resource instead of a human being. You don't *owe* any of them anything. You can choose to be a hero, but even if you didn't, even if you walked away from all of this . . ." He knelt again, as if she could hear him better if he was on the same level as her unconscious form. "I would love you the same, and you wouldn't be worth anything less."

Emotions were strange without a body. What might otherwise move her to tears served as only a strange, nebulous feeling. Which, perhaps, was a good thing. *I appreciate it. But without giving away the ruse, how do you intend to do anything about this?*

He stood. *"Ignatius has mastered abilities that spellcasters have been experimenting with for centuries. If someone can figure something out, maybe he can."*

Absolutely not. Ignatius is the last *person I trust.*

He reached for his hip, where his sword usually rested, but he'd left it on the wall. *"I'm willing to risk it. If necessary, I'll kill him myself."*

Before she could argue, he scooped up her body, laid it in the stone coffin, and swiveled toward the stairs.

I'm upset with you.

"Ditto."

We don't have time for this.

"We absolutely do." His jaw tightened. *"You made me promise not to leave you, Brinnie. You don't get to do the same thing to me."*

She didn't say anything as they emerged from the keep . . . into the shouting, clashing chaos of battle as attackers on the grounds streamed from the north, met by defenders not ten yards from the keep itself.

The back gate. They must have breached it. That was faster than I expected.

"Then we better find Ignatius fast."

Make sure Lana has a portal to get out of here safely.

"She does. More than one." He scanned the walls, the grounds. *"So do I, and of course Ignatius. We passed them around while you were . . . well, probably while you were snooping in the enemy camp."* He stopped. *"There."* His eyes locked on a figure on the wall shooting a crossbow down into the enemy throng.

Great. He's on the other side of the battlefield. Let's just go, we need to get the Case and Key too. Which, by the way, I think I missed where you all decided to stow them since I was napping at the beginning of the meeting.

Marcus ran for the wall, dodging, weaving, and shooting off balls of fire as necessary. *"Right. We gave it to Maddy."*

To Maddy? *Why on earth would you do that?*

"Because of that exact reaction." A knife winged toward him, and he narrowly dodged, still running. *"Castelon wouldn't expect the teenage human to have the world's most powerful magical object. I believe she planned to hide it beneath the bathroom sink."*

Her incredulous laugh floated through his mind. Fair enough. With their group, she shouldn't be surprised.

Marcus headed for the stone steps leading up the wall, taking them fast enough to make Brinnie nervous he might fall over the edge. Someone should really install guard rails. "Ignatius," he called. "Where's Lana?"

Ignatius turned, crossbow pointing away and primed. He gestured downward, toward the throng. "She said she's better in hand-to-hand combat. They breached the gate, as I expect you've noticed. Arthrys is doomed. I suggest we all portal away while we can." He patted his pocket. "I have enough extra for a few others as well, if you have suggestions, though I'd rather not use all of them before I have a chance to make more with Ludovic."

Marcus scanned the mass of fighting until a familiar blonde ponytail whipped into view, Lana's sword spinning and striking. "We need to tell her to portal." He turned back to Ignatius. "But I need you for something else in the keep before we go anywhere."

Ignatius gave him a strange look, but nodded. "All right. Let's fight our way back across the green, I guess." He bobbed his head toward a soldier slumped against the wall, presumably dead. "I think he has a sword if you need one."

Marcus retrieved the man's weapon from his grasp and hefted the blade, getting used to the weight. "A falchion. Interesting choice." He waved to Ignatius. "Let's go."

Brinnie wished she could do something as the two of them ran, slashed, and blasted their way back toward the keep. *We don't have time for all this. We can't trust Ignatius. We need to get the Case and go.*

Marcus grunted, ducking a broadsword and plunging the much shorter falchion into a gap in the man's armor. *"I don't think you meant to send that thought to me, but if you did, this isn't a great time."*

Nope, sorry. Please continue. Don't forget Lana.

The two of them hacked their way to where Lana fought, throwing light into the eyes of attackers before dispatching them. "Lana!" Marcus shouted. "Portal out of here."

She slashed one foe with her sword and slammed her hilt into the face of another. "Not yet. We still have the keep to retreat to."

"Arthrys is going to fall, and we need to live to fight another day." Marcus threw a ball of fire at a man who ran toward them. "Take some of the defenders with you if you want. Ignatius and I are heading to the keep. We'll follow soon."

"With Brinnie." Lana's sword slashed, blood splattering, and she gave Marcus a hard look.

He swallowed. "I would never leave her." Not a lie—but when Lana returned to Castelon and neither of them ever appeared . . .

She gave a sharp nod. "I'll see you soon."

Marcus's heart pumped hard and sweat beaded his brow by the time they reached the ring of Arthrysian forces around the hill on which the keep stood, defending the final wall while others shot down from the ramparts high above. Ignatius gasped for breath, bright red. Evidently the defenders recognized Marcus, because when he nodded to them, they allowed the two to slip through and dash into the keep itself, the heavy door and portcullis not yet shut, though Brinnie had no doubt the defenders would fall back behind them soon.

Marcus led the way down the stairs into the crypt. Ignatius followed until they stood panting beside the stone coffin where Brinnie's blood-soaked body still rested.

Ignatius glanced at the body, then back at Marcus. "What are we doing here?"

I still massively disagree with this.

"Brinnie doesn't think I should tell you this, but, you know me." He gave Ignatius a hard look. "If you betray her, I will never let you know a moment's peace. You will not be allowed to die. I will force you to live in cruel and unabated agony. Understand?"

Ignatius put his hands on his knees, still panting. "That seems a bit extreme and uncalled for. I thought we were friends again."

"Nate . . ."

"Fine, yes, agreed."

Excuse me, Nate?

"We were best friends for years, remember? I wasn't going to use his stupidly long name every time we talked." Marcus cleared his throat. "Brinnie isn't dead. She's under a sleeping curse. She faked her death for important reasons, and we need to wake her up without anyone knowing."

Ignatius stared at her limp form for a moment, then barked an incredulous laugh. "Of course she isn't. I don't blame you for falling for her, but she sure does keep you on your toes. She must make it worth it."

The flash of anger and protectiveness that swelled through Marcus warmed Brinnie's ethereal heart. "If you're going to be obscene, we're done here. The question is, can you do anything for her? Your spellcasting abilities . . . if anyone can figure something out, you can."

Ignatius shook his head, straightening. "You don't think I would have done something about the Ludovic/Tynsdale situation if I could? You'll need a curse swap. It's the only way."

I'm not curse swapping. And now Ignatius knows about it.

"I'll curse swap with you and have him do it."

Don't you dare. Then you'll just be in my head, and I swear I will sing every obnoxious song I can think of over and over in my mind until you wish for death.

Ignatius raised an eyebrow. "You in there?"

"Yes. Sorry." He let out a long breath. "Brinnie is both adamant about not curse swapping and upset with me for involving you."

Traitor.

Both of his eyebrows rose. "You're talking to her?"

"She's in my head."

Ignatius nodded, like head-hopping was a normal activity. "I imagine she's threatened to murder you should you inflict the curse on someone else. What's her end goal? Pilot you like a puppet to destroy Mordred while she pretends to be dead for whatever reason?"

Brinnie would have clenched her fists if she had them.

"She wants me to take her lifeless body back in time and use it to pull Excalibur and kill Mordred. There's a spy somewhere on the inside, so she faked her death to get them off the trail."

She screamed in frustration internally, wherever internally was. *You are ruining the entire point of this.*

"Sounds suitably self-sacrificial and foolish, as is her typical way."

Ignatius rolled his eyes and sighed. "Well, I'm not the spy. But I suppose it's up to me to take the curse."

Both Brinnie and Marcus were struck speechless for a moment.

"How do you figure?" Marcus finally managed.

For the first time in the conversation, Ignatius's swaggering persona ebbed, an almost sincere, sad half-smile in its place. "She won't let you pass it to anyone else. Other than Mordred, I don't know who she could hate more than me. I do want to do something worthwhile to stop Mordred. She's our best shot, and she needs to be awake and alive to do it."

"I . . ." Marcus's thoughts swirled. "It's irreversible once transferred. I can't ask you to do that."

"You never asked." The sad smile quirked again. "It's not just about her. We've hurt each other enough, Marcus. We were children when this all started. I hurt her to hurt you. It all needs to stop. And as much as your girlfriend drives me insane, she saved my life, and she's our best shot to change all of this so no more kids are forced to torture each other."

Marcus pressed his lips together. Brinnie couldn't think of anything to say, struggling to make sense of swirling gratitude, defiance, guilt, and confusion toward the man who had hurt her.

"I won't stop you," Marcus said at last. "If you want to do this, I'll let you." He gritted his teeth. "But it's not because I hate you and want this to happen."

Ignatius clapped a hand on his shoulder. "I know. You were always the better man." He let the hand drop. "I hope I'll be remembered as a good man too. Or at least, one who tried, at the end."

"We'll have to make it look like you died in battle," Marcus warned. "Secrecy is the whole point. We can't let Mordred know how Excalibur can be found."

"I know." Ignatius drew his own, thinner sword and handed it to Marcus hilt-first. "I'd prefer this to that machete you swiped from the wall. A good stab instead of hacked to pieces."

"However you want it done." Marcus accepted the blade. "Are you sure about this?"

He huffed a short laugh. "I don't have much to live for, do I? At least I have something to die for."

"There's always something new to live for. Death isn't meant to be an escape."

"Always the philosopher." Ignatius nodded to the sword. "I'm ready."

It felt wrong. She couldn't let this happen, even to Ignatius. Especially after he and Marcus seemed to have made up. *You're not going to bro-hug it out?*

"That was never really our style."

I can't let this happen.

"You can. Because he wants to—and because the world needs you, *not your disembodied voice floating in my head."*

She remained silent for a moment. *I didn't mean for anyone else to get hurt by this.*

"No? Just all of your friends and family, mourning your death? You don't think that will devastate them?"

Devastate? *I don't think I expected anyone to . . . care that much.*

Marcus reached out and clasped Ignatius's hand. "Thank you. From all of us. But especially from me."

Ignatius gave a faint teasing smirk. "Make sure the history books paint me as a hero, got it?"

Tell him thank you from me too. And that I'm sorry, and I forgive him.

Marcus relayed the message. Ignatius stared at a point above Marcus's head, as if Brinnie might be floating there. "Kill Mordred, and we'll call it even."

Brinnie drifted away as Marcus prepared to plunge the sword into Ignatius, causing enough of a bloody wound to make him appear dead once the curse had been transferred. She would wait in her body, ready to come back. Ready to make the final play against Mordred.

After a moment of quiet, a dizzy feeling, darkness, her eyes blinked open, staring at a stone ceiling. The deep ache in every cell, penetrating her bones. The pain of all the magic roiling inside her, reminding her that even this extension of life was temporary.

But for now, Brynna Ludovic was once more truly alive.

CHAPTER
THIRTY-SIX

The blood on her neck flaked as she sat up, parts still wet and sticky, her shirt clinging to her. Marcus held out a hand and she took it, standing shakily.

She put a hand to her neck, tracing where the blade had cut. Only a long, smooth scar, slightly raised. In half a daze, she lifted her shirt, revealing long silver scars where her previous wounds had still been healing. No doubt if the wounds to her neck and torso had been left by a normal blade, nothing would remain.

"I didn't expect to be in this body again," she said, her voice a croaking whisper. After the brief reprieve, the burning in her veins felt hotter than before.

Marcus gathered her to his chest, holding her. "I'm so glad you are. Even if you can't forgive me for bringing you back."

She looked down at Ignatius on the floor beside the stone coffin, completely still, blood covering his abdomen. "No. You were right. And . . ." She stepped out and knelt beside Ignatius, touching a hand to his shoulder. He could never hurt her again, but she didn't think he would have. In the end, he'd been willing to sacrifice for her. "Maybe I was wrong to trust no one. I never would have expected this."

Marcus rested a hand on her back. "You inspire loyalty, Brinnie. A lot of people care about you."

She had known that—in a way—but the way Lana screamed, the way Marcus fell apart and even Ignatius sobered and gave his own life . . .

Faking her death had been even crueler than she had imagined it would be. For reasons she couldn't quite understand, people cared about her regardless of her abilities.

She stood, unexpected tears pricking her eyes. "We need to stage the body, then we need to go."

Marcus easily carried Ignatius to the bottom of the stairs, where he dumped him unceremoniously as Brinnie winced. "Sorry." He cringed. "Bodies naturally fall in strange positions. If I just set him down it wouldn't look right." He didn't take his eyes from Ignatius, expression tight.

"I know." She took his hand. "Are . . . you okay?"

He let out a breath. "He was my closest friend for a long time. No matter what happened afterward."

"I'm sorry." Her heart clenched. Another way someone she loved was hurting because of her.

"But that is the way of war, and he gave his life honorably." Marcus squeezed her hand, pulling out a portal with the other. "As you've told me, we need to get that Case." He handed the portal to her.

A way of distracting himself, keeping them moving forward, but she didn't protest. She didn't let go of his hand as she smashed the portal, glad she had visited Maddy's room once, holding the image in her mind. Maybe someday they could retrieve Ignatius's body, give him a proper tomb. For now, they couldn't risk Mordred's forces finding him lying nicely in a stone coffin, looking closer, and discovering him under a curse. They couldn't risk Mordred putting the pieces together, figuring out Brinnie wasn't dead.

We will come back for you.

The mist of the portal receded to reveal a small room with a full-size bed in the middle, art prints Maddy must have somehow found in Castelon's shops hanging from the walls. Maddy herself lay sprawled in bed, mouth partway open as she emitted soft snores.

Perfect. With luck, we can grab the Case without her even knowing we were here.

"Agreed. After you."

Brinnie released Marcus's hand and led the way to the tiny bathroom leading off the bedroom. She opened the wooden cabinet beneath the sink and stared at the contents for a moment.

Extra toilet paper. A bar of soap. A folded towel.

But no Case.

"Great," she muttered. She whirled back toward the room and headed for Maddy.

She gently patted the girl's arm, trying not to startle her. "Hey, Maddy. It's Brinnie. Wake up."

Maddy's eyes blinked open, her brows crinkling as she squinted at Brinnie. Sleep slurred her words. "Um. Hi? What are you doing here?"

"Where's the Case?" Marcus asked, coming to stand by Brinnie.

Maddy rubbed her eyes, sitting up. "Assuming I'm not dreaming, this is pretty strange considering Brinnie is supposed to be dead."

"Maddy, we're in a hurry." Brinnie clenched her fists at her sides. "Where did the Case go?"

"Taken." She gestured toward the door, keeping her voice at a whisper. "And now we all have guards too. I guess your mom started some sort of mutiny at Eringaard, and they searched all of our rooms and put us under house arrest basically."

Brinnie began to pace. "Scott probably has it under constant guard. Any idea where?"

"None. But uh, hey, you're not dead, so that's good?"

"And you can't tell *anyone* that." Marcus fixed her with a hard look. "Not her family, not your friends, no one. No matter what anyone says or how much you want to. Especially now that Castelon has that Case." He turned to Brinnie. "If the infiltrator figures out what it can be used for and takes it . . ."

"I know." She ran a hand through her hair, halting her pacing. "We can't go after it. We don't have time to search the castle or to come up with some sort of heist." She took a deep breath. "I think we need to rely on Excalibur's pull on me to direct us there."

Maddy crossed her legs. "I'm bad at math, but I feel like that probably makes your odds of success a little lower."

Brinnie turned to Marcus, but he didn't speak, lips pressed together. Because he knew. Knew she was right, and she needed to do this.

"I'll go alone." Brinnie squared her shoulders. "No sense in risking more than one person."

"Absolutely not." Marcus stepped forward, as if afraid she would disappear then and there. "You never know when you might need backup. I'm coming."

She thought about arguing, but they had argued enough over the past twenty-four hours. "Okay."

He blinked, appearing surprised at her acquiescence, but quickly recovered. "Let's go then."

Maddy flopped back down in bed. "I never saw you. I might actually just think this was a weird dream by tomorrow morning."

"Thank you, Maddy." Brinnie hesitated. "Take good care of our family."

For once, the girl sobered. She gave a solemn salute. "You have my word."

Marcus held out a portal to Brinnie. "I have more for getting back."

She nodded once and accepted the orb. With her other hand, she took his and gripped it tightly. Then she smashed the portal.

Mist swirled, like it had so many times. Brinnie fought the instinct to step forward, to imagine a destination, to do anything but simply stand clutching Marcus's hand. For a moment, she worried their feet would never leave the floor of Maddy's room, and they would end up exactly where they began. Then her legs wobbled as the ground beneath her dissolved and they floated in nothingness.

Not nothingness. Colors churned, exploded, flashed, and melted over one another, like the day she had gazed into the Master Key. A force like wind blew through her hair. The assault of sensations, sights, rushing sound, a myriad of scents, bombarded her so that nothingness was instead everythingness, and she struggled to grip Marcus's hand and remain rooted to something, anything.

Then the shapes began to coalesce into recognizable forms, just flickers at first. Dark hair, red blood—her. The scene became more clear, and she saw herself almost dying by Mordred's hand, the blade slashing across her throat, but this time close up and in high definition in a way she hadn't seen through either Marcus's eyes or her own.

The image disappeared and another took its place. She lay on the ground, Mordred above her, blade swinging down for the second strike, right as Uncle Merlin dove forward, deflecting the hit. He knelt, reaching for her, soon to take them away from Wraithwood—and the scene shifted again.

The images kept flashing backward, faster and faster—the fight at Riverdell, Castelon's dungeon, the Council Chamber, the plane. Then back at Mordizan. She saw herself in Ignatius's torture chamber, screaming as his bloody instrument glinted. She saw herself dancing with Marcus at the Gathering, laughing with him in the library, dashing through the hidden passageways. She watched the affectionate looks he cast her way when she wasn't looking, the occasional blushing smile. All the cues she'd missed.

Her life continued to rewind like an old VHS, through her time in the human world, trying to fit in, trying to give up magic. She watched a much younger version of herself charge into the Maze for the first time, set on rescuing Bruno. Saw her wide eyes when she first witnessed Uncle Merlin disappear through the door with Anika and knew for certain that magic existed.

Her lifetime flashed before her eyes in reverse, even the parts she couldn't remember. She saw Mom crying when she looked into Brinnie's eyes as a baby for the first time—not tears of joy, but anguished tears because her unwanted child was a wizard.

The images raced too quickly for her to make out more than brief snippets—a clash of blades in battle, an explosion, dances, weddings, funerals, sunny meadows, cool forests. They flashed faster and faster until all became a blur. She clung to Marcus with both arms, squeezing her eyes shut against the whirlwind of time bearing down on them.

Until finally, the force slowed.

She opened her eyes, head spinning and trying not to retch. She blinked, vision adjusting to the green and yellow tones of a sun-dappled wood as the mist slowly receded, leaving them standing, arms wrapped around each other, surrounded by the quiet sounds of birdsong and rustling leaves.

Slowly, she peeled herself away from Marcus. Her voice came out in a rasp. "Is this the right place?"

He nodded toward a thinning in the trees in front of them. "There."

Her feet nearly floated over fallen leaves. The forest floor didn't crunch beneath her feet. She kicked at the debris, but nothing moved. "We're like ghosts." She reached for his hand, reassured by a presence she could actually touch. "I understood theoretically the matter paradox, and that we don't exist in this time. But I don't think I realized how . . . odd it feels."

"Nothing we do here can affect the future. It's a strange sort of freedom." Marcus reached out, and his hand passed through a leaf drifting to the ground. "But we don't know how long is passing in our time while we're here."

"Right. We have to be quick." She tried to rein in her wonder, her desire to test every hypothesis. Time travel worked. In theory, they could witness any event in history without worrying about messing up the future. As long as they managed to get back to their own time before they died of hunger or thirst—which could prove difficult without a tether.

She tugged Marcus forward, jogging through the trees, until they reached the small meadow, where she froze.

In the center of the glade sat a small, rounded boulder, perhaps the size of an oven. No anvil here. And from it protruded the hilt of a sword, glinting in a ray of sun.

The birds ceased chirping, the woods falling silent, almost as if they knew the gravity of this moment. Brinnie took a slow step forward.

The hilt shouldn't be so beautiful. The shining bronze, the twisting knotted designs, came from a smith of what must be legendary skill. The design was undeniably Celtic rather than Roman, suggesting a Celtic longsword with the small, u-shaped crossguard, but with a rounded pommel like a traditional gladius and a longer grip that deviated from the usual one-handed longsword of the Celts, suggesting the sword could be wielded with one or two hands.

She could feel Marcus in her mind, appreciating her knowledge of historical weaponry—knowledge that far surpassed her practical skill in wielding them. From his view, she could tell the hilt seemed well-balanced, the six inches of the double-edged blade protruding from the stone wickedly sharp.

She took another step forward, her heart beating faster. The famed Excalibur, the sword of legend, known and revered even by humans. Her feet led her to the stone, eyes glued to the weapon. "How can I pull it?" she breathed to Marcus. "We can't affect anything in this time."

"Maybe it's different for you." He kept his voice low. "It's your destiny. 'Mordred's bane, his final doom, the heir of Arthur doth supply.'"

The heir of Arthur. The words sounded ridiculous. She was just some kid from Arizona. *And one of only three living magical descendants of the king of legend.*

She reached out, her fingers wrapping around the hilt. As she closed them, they rested on the solid handle, not passing through. Her hold tightened on the wrapped grip, just above the crossguard, and she slowly lifted.

The sword slid against stone in a smooth glide, revealing the long, double-edged blade, short enough to be carried at the hip of a tall man, but longer than a Roman spatha, once more a beautiful blend of Roman, Celtic, and something else altogether. As the tip arced from the stone, she felt the perfect balance of it, the weight of the hilt. She held up the sword, and the sun glinted off the metal in a way that made Excalibur seem to radiate with its own internal flame.

For a moment, everything felt right. She had never been adept with weapons, her magic serving her far better, but the way the blade felt in her hand, almost as if it spoke to her bones . . .

"*Caledbwlch*," she whispered. "That was its name, originally, when Artorius carried it. Or, that will be, when he does."

Marcus's wide eyes shone with awe. "You're his true heir. Fifteen hundred years later."

An insect tickled her cheek, and she brushed it away, not letting a bug distract her. They would defeat Mordred with this sword. The confidence flowing through her made her certain.

Then she froze. A bug. Landed on her. Her arm drooped, Excalibur's tip nearly hitting the dirt. "Marcus. I affected the timeline."

"I know." He chuckled. "I watched. We'll bring it back as soon as we're done. It's tied to this stone."

"No." She gestured toward their surroundings at large, wherever the insect had gone. "A bug. It just landed on me. And I brushed it off. I touched it."

His eyes widened. He crouched and ran his fingers through the grass. The blades moved at his touch.

He looked up slowly. "We've changed the timeline. We're part of it now."

"What are we going to do?" She clutched Excalibur to her chest. "Who knows what we've messed up? We could erase ourselves from history."

"We don't need to panic yet." He stood. "We haven't done anything yet except remove Excalibur and touch a bug. We'll bring the sword back, and I don't think one insect will change the course of world history."

Or maybe that bug had been meant to start a chain reaction that would affect all of Europe. She tried to calm her racing heart. "We should go, quickly. Before we disturb anything else."

Marcus reached into his pocket for a portal, but before he could pull one out, rustling sounded from the underbrush. *"Quick, hide."*

The two of them darted for the trees, ducking behind a thick trunk and leafy underbrush. Brinnie peered around the foliage, squinting toward the clearing.

Her eyes widened, and she grabbed Marcus's arm. *It's you.*

A broad-shouldered young man trudged toward the stone, coming into the glade from the same direction they had a few moments ago. Brinnie saw no noticeable physical differences between this Marcus and the one beside her, but he wore bloody armor covered in dust as if from an explosion. He seemed to have come straight from a battlefield. He came alone, Excalibur clutched in one hand, hanging by his side.

He raised the sword and plunged the blade into the stone with a broken yell, buckling to his knees. His head remained bowed, face buried in his hands.

Without quite realizing she'd moved, Brinnie stepped forward, but the Marcus beside her held her back. *"We can't interfere. Who knows what that interaction will do to the timeline?"*

She didn't protest, placing her hand over his on her arm. *What happened? You brought Excalibur back . . . so why are you upset?*

"I don't know." Concern etched his brow as he watched his future self.

Do you think it didn't work?

"If we didn't succeed, why would I bring it back?"

Maybe to preserve history, even if we couldn't save the future. She scanned the tree line. *Where is future me?*

His expression seemed too carefully neutral. *"You probably stayed behind as the anchor point for me to come back with the Case."*

She nodded toward future Marcus, still kneeling beside the stone. *He doesn't have the Case.*

"Maybe we figured something out where we don't need it anymore."

She stared at the future Marcus. He hadn't moved. Nausea coiled in her gut. Something had gone wrong. Very wrong.

"Maybe I'm linked to you, you know, through the whole mind thing. I'm sure he'll go back soon." Marcus released her arm and reached for a portal. *"We should go. We shouldn't be seeing this. It may affect our actions."*

Instead, Brinnie darted from the trees, heading for the stone. *Maybe that's what we need. We need to prevent this.*

"Brinnie, wait."

She didn't listen. Instead, she called out to future Marcus, sliding to a stop next to him. "Marcus. What happened?"

His shoulders tightened. He stood slowly and faced her, wet eyes glancing at Excalibur before fixing back on her face, as if he couldn't risk looking away. "I remember this moment." He reached out as if to touch her but dropped his hand. "You were so determined."

That empty expression . . . "Please. What happened?"

He clutched a fist to his heart. "Nothing you can stop. Nothing you can change." A shuddering breath ripped from his lungs. "I can't tell you more than that. We've already done enough to the timeline." He backed away. "I believe in you, Brinnie."

She clutched the hilt of Excalibur, glancing over her shoulder as her Marcus, present Marcus, stepped up behind her and put a comforting arm around her shoulders. "Isn't there anything you can tell us?"

Future Marcus hesitated, then nodded. "One thing. Stay here for about five minutes. There's someone who wants to talk to you both." He gave a whisper of a chuckle, eyes never leaving her face. "And I have some theories about who he is now." He stood unmoving for a long moment. "Goodbye, Brinnie."

An awkward half-laugh burbled out from her. "Goodbye, Marcus. Uh, tell future me hi."

Without a word, he turned and strode away into the forest until he was swallowed by the trees.

She leaned into her Marcus. "I hope he'll be okay," she whispered.

He didn't speak for a moment. She tried not to pry into his swirling thoughts, but she knew what he was thinking.

She was going to die.

She hadn't slept in so long. Too long to dream of Keilrie, of portents of her demise. But the overwhelming magic continued to eat at her bones. Even if the sleeper's curse had reduced her external wounds to silvery scars, it didn't suck the magic from within her. She continued to live on borrowed time—but she'd imagined that time would be a bit longer.

She changed the subject. "So, someone's going to come talk to us."

He glanced around the clearing. "All of this feels dangerously close to causing a time paradox."

"*But* if we had caused a time paradox and imploded the universe, it would have already happened, therefore we're safe." Brinnie shot him a finger gun.

He rubbed his temple. "I'll take your word for it, oh paragon of excessive research."

"My studies were quite inconclusive, but we might as well be optimistic."

Marcus's gaze lifted toward something behind her, and she heard a deep voice speak. "Pardon me."

She turned to see an elderly man emerge from the trees, white beard reaching to mid-chest, leaning on a long staff of twisted wood as he made his way toward them. He wore a rough wool tunic that reached to his ankles tied with a cord at the waist, somewhat like a monk might wear, though he didn't sport the tonsure of clergy, and his words were in the ancient language.

"Myrddin?" Brinnie ventured.

The man laughed. "Not Myrddin. I'm not nearly such a strapping young man anymore." He came to a halt in front of the two of them. Something almost fond sparkled in his brown eyes. "But you don't have much time. I have something for each of you, Marcus and Brynna."

Marcus's fingers twitched as if ready to fight. "How do you know our names?"

"I know many things." He nodded to Marcus. "First you. You need to know, though it won't make a difference in your actions. You can't travel to a time or place without magic."

"I'm not sure I understand what you mean." His brow wrinkled. "Magic is everywhere, and always has been."

The old man didn't acknowledge Marcus's response, instead turning to Brinnie. "And you." He reached into the folds of his robe and pulled out a small brown package. "Don't open it until after the date written there."

She accepted the rectangular parcel, running her fingers over the brown, oiled paper tied with twine. A card attached to the twine displayed a date a few months away. "That's my birthday."

"So it is." He stepped back, nodding to each of them. "Here I bid you goodbye. It's time for you to return to your own time and place."

He turned and made for the trees once again, steps slow but even.

"Wait," Brinnie called. "Where on earth did you get brown paper in this time?"

He looked over his shoulder and smiled. "Who said it came from this time?"

She glanced down at the parcel in confusion. By the time she'd looked up again, the old man had melted back into the forest.

She turned toward Marcus. He stared after the old man with an almost dazed expression. He looked back at her, jaw tight. "None of that seemed good."

"It will be okay." She struggled to tuck the package into the pouch on her belt with one hand, but it didn't fit. Marcus took Excalibur to free up her other hand, and she strapped the package into her belt instead. Once she'd stowed the mysterious parcel, she returned her attention to him. "All of that was strange, but . . . we're about to go kill Mordred, right?"

"Right." He turned the sword over, examining the blade. "We'll kill him, and this will all be over."

She linked her left arm through his right. "We're off to kill the wizard," she said in a sing-song. He wouldn't understand the reference, but the jitters ramping up in her chest required a dumb joke.

He handed Excalibur back to her. "Are you ready?"

"Definitely." She hefted the blade, holding tight to his hand with the other so the portal wouldn't rip them apart. She could do this. She could kill him. She could finally end this war, or at least, throw the enemy into such disarray that they would take years to rise up again. Years during which she could solidify her allies, Marcus could gun for the Mordizan Mastership, and Lana and others could turn their estates to the side of the enchantment wizards.

And even if she didn't make it until the next battles began, they would be ready, with or without her.

Marcus pulled a portal from his pocket, tossed the orb to the ground, and stepped on it.

The portal smashed, and mist swirled around them.

CHAPTER THIRTY-SEVEN

The mist didn't swirl for long before it began to clear. A figure became visible through the fog—a sandy-haired, blue-eyed boy staring at them with his mouth open.

She tugged on Marcus's arm. *Back up, farther into the portal. It took us to Arthur.*

Thankfully, Arthur faded away. History played out before them, warriors battling with spears giving way to riders on horseback, to working men in a factory. Space seemed to warp as well as time, showing various climes from desert to high mountain.

Until everything slowed. Stone materialized beneath their feet, a courtyard coming into focus.

And directly in front of them stood Mordred himself.

Brinnie met his gaze and their eyes locked. Behind him, warriors in battle gear stared, frozen in surprise. She had no idea where they were, even when they were, whether it had been days or months. She saw Mordred's gaze drift to the sword, watched his eyes widen as understanding dawned. Fitting that they should meet in an unknown time and place, frozen with destiny between them.

She lifted the sword. "Checkmate."

Then she plunged the blade into his stomach, thrusting upward.

He bent, gasped, choked.

Brinnie heard commotion behind her, yells as Marcus defended her from warriors running to apprehend her. She twisted the blade, driving it deeper before a massive man slammed into her, knocking her aside. She skidded on cobblestone, skin scraping, but she kept her eyes fixed on Mordred, waiting. *Let it be over. Let us have won.*

Mordred clutched the hilt protruding from his stomach, blood pouring from the ragged wound. Someone yanked Brinnie's hands behind her back, but she couldn't be bothered to notice.

Slowly, Mordred pulled the blade forward, more blood falling as he grunted with pain. Finally, the sword clattered on the stone.

He still stood.

How? He should be dead. Any moment now, he would keel over, right? He had to.

Two wizards darted to his side, pressing their hands against the wound. Healers. He placed his own hand to his stomach, closed his eyes, and muttered under his breath. The tension across his brow eased. He opened his eyes and looked down at himself. The laugh that fell from his mouth seemed incredulous, yet pleased. He smirked at Brinnie. "You thought you could kill me?"

Her mouth worked. Her eyes darted to Marcus, who had been brought to his knees, similarly restrained. Beyond him, rank upon rank of warriors waited in the courtyard of the unfamiliar fortress. The only words she could manage were, "That was Excalibur."

"Oh, I recognize it." He kicked the sword across the stone. "Looks like the prophecy was wrong. It's just another sword after all." He pulled out his own blade and stalked forward. "I don't know how you faked your death, but I should have suspected when no one found your body." He whipped the tip of the blade underneath her chin. "You share the weakness of all post-Myrddin healers. You can't heal yourself. I will hack you to pieces this time to ensure your death." He glanced toward the crowd of warriors. "Perhaps a bit of a demonstration for my newest troops before we set out."

"Where are we?" Marcus nodded slightly toward the walls around them.

Mordred's smirk grew. "Ah, you wouldn't recognize it. Welcome to Artema. Meet my army of former enchantment wizards. It seems they would rather serve me than die."

Brinnie fought the urge to crumple. Castelon's greatest fighting force. She had bet everything on Excalibur—only to fail. The prophecy was a lie.

She struggled to pull air into her squeezing lungs. "You may have Artema. But Dirklon and Castelon and all the others will still defeat you."

He raised a brow. "What others? Eringaard? Grignak?" He slid his blade back into its sheath. "Wherever you've hidden for the past three months, you must not have been paying attention. I've conquered them all, even Dirklon. Only Castelon remains."

No. It can't be.

"And what do you mean to do with us?" Marcus growled.

"You two?" He tapped a finger to his chin. "I thought I already killed you, but I suppose I can do it again. In pieces, this time, to diffuse any doubt. We can hold the execution in front of Castelon right before we attack." He looked at Brinnie. "That way your mother can watch *you* die, as well."

A sick feeling stirred in her gut at his smug expression. "As well?"

"Of course. I execute every Master, you know, and every one of their descendants, to make room for my newly-appointed governors." He leaned forward. "She will watch you die the same way she watched your father perish as I cut off his head in front of her."

"No." Brinnie yanked against her captors. She tried to form a shadow sword to fight her way out, but her arms were twisted behind her. She sent wolves after him, but they only passed through. She sparked with fire, and one of the warriors holding her yelped, but another stepped in, this one evidently immune to flame. "You didn't." Her vision blurred, and she gritted her teeth. "I don't believe you! You're lying."

"Ah, Brynna. You should have stayed dead." He showed his teeth. "As it is, I will display your head beside your father's, spiked above the gates of Dirklon."

A feral screech tore through her. She kicked and pulled, but before she could do anything else, something bashed into her skull.

A cold, rough material pressed against her cheek. Her head throbbed. As the ground wavered in and out of focus, a familiar voice she couldn't immediately place drifted from somewhere nearby.

"I don't know what sort of bargain you want to strike for her. It was good riddance when you killed her the first time."

Brinnie rolled over, barely suppressing a groan. Manacles on her wrists and ankles clanked. Her joints ached from the position she must have landed in when they tossed her . . . wherever she was. Solid walls and a metal door with a barred window suggested a cell.

"I believe she could still be useful to all of us." Mordred's voice. "When the fighting ends, the blood of Arthur may prove valuable. My father turned to blood magic often."

"Everyone thinks the kid is dead." Nimue? Why was she at Artema instead of Mordizan? "We'll make sure the troops that saw her today think we decided to just kill her in this cell. No one would even know she was down there. A win for everyone, and your people never have to know you were involved."

A heavy sigh. "I think she's better dead, but I suppose I could toss her down there. If I think we should kill her later, though, I will. And I won't ask permission."

Her mind moved as if the gears were clogged with molasses. That voice . . . Scott Castelius? But why would he be here, talking to Mordred and Nimue?

"These are fair terms." Mordred again. "I have already sent spellcasters to begin work on a similar holding cell at Mordizan, but it will not be ready for some time. She has thus far been immune to or barely affected by previous containment spells."

"What about the Vorath heir?" Scott asked.

"We will dispose of him." Mordred's tone grew annoyed. "He's too unpredictable to keep around as a puppet."

Brinnie sat up, careful not to let the chains clank too much. She tentatively tried to summon a shadow creature, but the manacles burned her wrists. They must have been enchanted in the same way as the cuff at Castelon. Not completely blocking her abilities, but certainly stifling them.

I'll burn my own hands off before I let them kill Marcus.

"I think he actually could be useful." Nimue interrupted Brinnie's destructive train of thought. "Not as an heir. As leverage if we ever need Brynna to do something. She can't stand to see him hurt."

Betrayal zinged through Brinnie's heart—not that Nimue had ever made any pretense of being on their side. But a spark of hope followed. Was Nimue protecting Marcus by keeping him alive? Perhaps she had more altruistic motives than it appeared.

Mordred sighed. "You are correct. However, we cannot keep him here. If his father discovers he is alive and we have him imprisoned, Vorath will cause trouble. Nothing I can't handle, but I would prefer not to deal with infighting."

"I'll take him too, then." Master Castelius cleared his throat. "If we have that settled, I would like to return to Castelon as soon as possible. I will be needed in the defense against your upcoming attack."

Her brain struggled to comprehend. Scott Castelius, the leader of the enchantment wizards, colluding with Mordred? To imprison her—that made sense, in a strange way. Scott hated her. But the two seemed so familiar with one another.

Finally, her mind caught up. The air sucked from her lungs.

The spy was the Master of Castelon. He had been actively undermining the enchantment wizards all along.

She had to expose him. She had to get word to the other Masters.

None of it matters. Excalibur didn't work. All the estates are gone. Mordred has won.

But her stubborn brain wouldn't listen.

She shoved herself up from the floor, holding her throbbing head. Leaning against the wall for support, she made her way toward the door.

The chains just barely allowed her to reach. She peered through the bars over the window into the dim gloom beyond. She imagined this dungeon was also warded against magic. Between that and the manacles —and likely a concussion—her vision struggled.

She reached out for Marcus with her mind. *Hey. Are you okay? Where are you?*

Nothing. At least she knew from the conversation outside that he was alive. He must be unconscious. Or too far away to contact. If so, he had to be at a different estate, considering their range could reach from Arthrys all the way to Mordred's camp before.

She grasped the bars and called out, her voice raspy. "Where is Marcus?"

Footsteps tapped on stone, heading her way. Nimue came into view, outfitted in a dark leather breastplate, a short sword strapped to her hip along with her knives. Her eyes flicked to the scar across Brinnie's neck, then back up. "I see you're awake."

Brinnie's fingers clenched around the bars, her throat tight. She tried to read any emotion on Nimue's face. Part of her had hoped Nimue was better than this. She *knew* Mordred had too much power. So why was she still helping him?

But none of that left her mouth. Instead, her words came out in a trembling whisper. "You let him kill your brother?"

Nimue's expression went hard, blank. "I am loyal."

Brinnie stared back at her. Loyal. Not to Mordred. Not when she helped them before.

Loyal to her family.

If Mordred cared for one living person in this world, he cared for Nimue. Would he truly have risked alienating her?

Hope lifted in her chest. She allowed the smallest flicker of a smile. "I believe that, Nimue Drakon."

Her aunt turned and directed her next words down the narrow corridor. "The kid's awake. I'll take care of Vorath junior." She strode away without another glance at Brinnie.

Mordred came into view, replacing Nimue. Brinnie snarled at him and attempted to thrust her hand through the bars, but the chains yanked her back.

"Calm yourself. You are being transferred. You can make this difficult or easy."

She smirked, teeth bared. "When have I ever made it easy for you?" She stepped back and crossed her arms. "Transferred, huh? Changed your mind about chopping me up into lots of little pieces?"

"That can still be arranged." He reached into the folds of his robe and pulled out a vial. "I imagine you know what this is for."

The chains clanked as she dropped her arms. "Why would I let you drug me?"

He sighed. "You will be transported either way. If you insist on behaving like a child, you will find another pommel smashed into your head, and I would rather not damage your brain any further than it already is."

Unfortunately, he had a fair point. She blew out a puff of air and held out her hand. "Fine. I could use a drink anyway."

Sassing Mordred felt like the only thing keeping her from plunging over the precipice of despair. Every card had been played. Even if she escaped, she couldn't hurt him.

Mordred's world order would be established, no matter her actions—and humanity would die.

He dropped the vial into her palm, too quickly for her to attempt to grab his wrist and cause problems, as much as she would have liked to be difficult. She removed the cap and held the small bottle between her fingers, lifting it in a toast. "To the end of the world. Congratulations. How does it feel to become the greatest mass murderer in history?"

"I am liberating the world, Brynna. Perhaps someday you shall see that." His lips pressed into a thin line.

"Ah, yes, genocide and liberation are definitely synonyms."

His eyes narrowed. "Humans have shunned us, exiled us, hunted us, all the while destroying this world during their short, greedy lifespans. I will rid us of a parasite. Those who choose a blight upon the world over their own kind, clinging to the old ways, unfortunately must be cast aside."

"You're so sure, yet you still feel the need to justify yourself to me." She raised the vial. "Cheers. You had me for a moment, but I know the truth. You couldn't bring yourself to kill Nimue's brother. You have a shred of humanity in you still, deep down. It's a shame your pain has made you ignore it."

Before he could say anything else, she drained the potion, sinking to her knees so she wouldn't have as far to fall. "I hope you're happy when the world is burning around you, and you realize there's nothing you can do to reverse what you've done."

CHAPTER
THIRTY-EIGHT

In stories, now would be the time for the hero to ride in, turning the tide.

In stories, the legendary weapon of old would be unearthed. The hero would rise with some strange new power to defeat the enemy. The great battle would commence.

But they unearthed the legendary weapon—and it failed. She had gained astonishing power—and it still wasn't enough. The final battle had begun—but the defenders were in league with the attackers.

Her eyes protested opening. She could feel cuffs around her wrists and ankles still, the weight suggesting they were attached to chains. The stone beneath her felt cold and damp.

Shivering, she forced her eyelids open, and for a moment wondered if she had actually succeeded. The darkness pressed in on her, an ominous reminder of her lack of magic.

She pushed herself to a sitting position and realized the stone was damp from her own dripping hair and clothes. Much of the crusted blood had washed from her garments, leaving behind only dark stains.

Shoving back wet hair, chains clanking, she squinted at her surroundings. *Marcus? Can you hear me?*

No response.

She scooted backward, feeling along the short length of her chains to where they connected to a ring in a curved wall. A circular chamber? Far above, a faint glow of light seeped from an unknown source, as if she sat at the bottom of a shaft. "Hello?"

An answering cough made her jump, then a rasping voice said, "It's been a while since I had a fellow prisoner down here."

She peered into the darkness and could just make out a human-sized shape. "Who's there?"

"No one, anymore." A form shuffled nearer, into the dim illumination, until Brinnie could see a man with an unkempt gray beard, tousled salt and pepper hair, and gaunt cheekbones protruding beneath dirty wire-rimmed glasses. His worn clothing suggested a long time in this cell.

Brinnie stood, pain shooting through her head. She grimaced, leaning against the wall, and squinted upward. The cell appeared to be about fifteen feet in diameter, rising until she couldn't make out details. "Where are we?" She rubbed her temple. "And how did I get down here?"

"Deep beneath Castelon, in a special prison for Master Castelius's most hated. Or Castelon's most dangerous. Depending who you ask." The man sighed, his voice monotone. "I believe it might have been a well once, but I have no idea. They let prisoners down with ropes, then they pull the guards back up again. In your case, they even clapped you in irons. They never bothered with that for me." He nodded toward the smooth walls. "No way up—trust me, I've tried. And from what I can tell, it's warded against magic. Either that, or you're not a wizard—otherwise you would have tried something magical."

"I'm a wizard." Fog clouded her brain, remnants from Mordred's potion. "Are you?"

"No. Just a human." He sat and leaned against the wall a few feet away from her. "I don't know what you did to make Castelius mad at you, but I must admit, it's nice to talk to someone again."

What had a human done to be put in Castelon's most secure prison? He hardly seemed dangerous, but as she knew from her own appearance, looks could be deceiving. "How long have you been down here?"

He shrugged. "Months? Perhaps a few years? Who's to say."

She sank into a cross-legged position, slumping over her knees. "If you're here for annoying Scott, I imagine we'll get along well." Her fist clenched. "The scum. I should have been more suspicious of how he hated me ever since I stepped foot in Castelon." She dropped her head into her hands. "Maybe I would have put two and two together and realized he's on Mordred's side, for reasons I'll never understand."

The man gave a wry chuckle. "Annoying Scott. Something like that." He shook his head. "Castelius isn't on any side but his own. He's obsessed with power. If Mordred can give it to him, I'm not surprised he would turn on his own Council."

Another way this wasn't like the stories. The good guys weren't supposed to side with the bad guys. For the heroes to win, they had to exist in the first place.

Castelon no more stood as a beacon of hope than Mordizan.

She leaned her head back against the wall, gazing up toward a ceiling she couldn't see. Above, a battle most likely raged. One she could do nothing about, even if she could escape.

She'd always imagined she would either die in battle, or witness the world's downfall. Not wonder about it in a pit. "I got in Scott's way and tried to kill Mordred. What did you do to get thrown down here?"

"I did some research he didn't like. I found a way to end the war. But he didn't want to hear of it."

She sat forward and stared at the unassuming man. "For real?" Had he also discovered Excalibur, or had he come up with something else entirely?

"Yes, a way to definitively end everything, in theory." He shrugged one shoulder. "In practice, I failed to execute the plan. It requires a very specific person, one who, to my knowledge, has yet to be born."

"Oh." She rubbed her aching neck. "I doubt it would matter at this point anyway. Mordred has taken over all of the estates. Castelon is the only one left, and he's attacking it right now, with Scott on the inside."

"So that's the end for humankind." His tone didn't waver, as if he had anticipated and accepted this fate long before. "At least I tried to do something."

Brinnie tilted her head. Who *was* this man? She hesitated a moment, then stuck out her hand, chains clanking. "Brinnie."

He took her proffered hand and shook. "Morton. Dr. Nathaniel Morton."

Why did that name seem familiar? Not that his first and last name were uncommon . . .

She froze, her arm still extended in the handshake. A newspaper headline flashed through her mind, an explanation from Uncle Merlin two years ago. "You're the NASA scientist who went missing. The one who stole the Master Key and gave the Case to Mordizan to throw us off the scent, starting the whole protection spell crisis." She retracted her hand, eyes narrowing. "You tried to have us all kill each other."

"That was never the goal." His eyelids squeezed shut for a moment. "If you would allow me to explain, I'm happy to share the truth of it, to at least one person in this world."

She shifted to rest her elbow on her knee and her chin on her fist, waiting for him to speak.

"I used to be the Keeper of the Master Key," he began, "back when it was kept here. My father and grandfather before me were the Keeper before the job fell to me. The Keeper has always been a human, since the Key can't hurt us. I didn't have any doctorates or fancy degrees then, but I was inquisitive. The Key intrigued me. Its power to dampen magic and take down something as powerful as protection spells . . . well, it didn't seem like such a powerful object would only have that one use." He ran a hand through his hair. "My friends told me to leave well enough alone. Nothing good ever comes from messing in the affairs of wizards. But research couldn't hurt anyone, I thought. So, I began to study the Case, the Key, and as many ancient scrolls as I could get my hands on."

Brinnie's lips twitched in a wry smile. She would have done the same, no doubt.

"In my studies, I soon learned that Myrddin was not a simple man, nor did he cast simple spells. He liked to hide a greater magic under the guise of a lesser magic. I began to wonder—if the Key was tied to all magic, what secret powers might it possess?" Even now, years later, his eyes began to light with passion, fascination. The research high. "I ran tests, kept reading. Eventually I came across a prophecy from the famed bard Taliesin, mentor of Myrddin. I translated it from the ancient language into an English approximation so I could ponder the words better." He closed his eyes and recited,

"The key to the destruction lies
Within the key to stability.
Myrddin's flesh and Myrddin's blood
Shall destroy the world he built.
The line of Myrddin here must die
Or all we wrought shall be in vain.
But Mordred, with his dread talent

Has cased himself in sleep.
But forever curses lasteth not
And one day even dead shall rise
And dark and light will mingle then
At the dawn of Albion.
Mordred's bane, his final doom,
The heir of Arthur doth supply
With sword Excalibur in hand
His magic to destroy."

He opened his eyes, and Brinnie stared back at him, mind reeling. The prophecy they had used to find Mordred's bane, but in its completed form. So many thoughts careened through her head, that perhaps the most ridiculous one came out. "Did you add 'lasteth' and 'doth' just to make it sound cool and medieval?"

She could have sworn his ears reddened. "I may be a scientist, but I also have an appreciation for the arts."

The absurdity forced a guffaw from her lungs, laughter echoing and bouncing around the stone pit. She could hear the hysterical tinge but felt powerless to stop it. Finally, she gasped out, "I know parts of that prophecy. We used it to discover Mordred's bane. But it didn't work."

He shook his head. "It didn't work for me at first either. I focused on the first two lines, 'The key to the destruction lies within the key to stability.' I became convinced this meant the Master Key. If it could be destroyed, so could all magic."

Her body went still. Even here in this prison, her bones still ached from the magic within them, never gone, just suppressed, locked away. What would that feel like? All that magic—gone?

Morton didn't seem to notice how his words had affected her. "I told Master Castelius my idea. I thought he would be delighted. A way to stop the fighting, once and for all. With no more magic, there would be nothing to fight about. Wizards would be no more than ordinary humans."

Brinnie gave a short, incredulous laugh. "You thought a wizard would be happy about the idea of destroying magic? Destroying their entire society, way of life? Not to mention one of the deepest, most integral parts of their identity?"

He frowned. "I was young. As you seem to have guessed, Castelius was not pleased. He told me my ideas were far-fetched, ludicrous, and warned me to keep my theories to myself. I rebelled. I wrote a pamphlet of my theories and attempted to distribute it in order to gain assistance in my research. He intercepted me and told me that if I kept up this nonsense, he would have me killed."

For a smart man, he didn't think that through very well. She kept her thoughts to herself.

"It's a long story, but when his assassins did come for me, a couple of friends helped me fake my death and told me to start over in the human world and leave well enough alone."

"You didn't."

"Of course not." He looked almost offended. "I dedicated decades to scientific research, trying to figure out a way to destroy the Master Key. As you probably know, it's virtually indestructible. Magical knowledge didn't seem to have the answers, so I thought science might. After years of theories, trying to replicate tests as best I could, I finally thought I had found a way by splitting—well, I won't get into the physics of it. I used my knowledge as the former Keeper to break into Castelon and steal the Key, right during the Decennial Masters Council." His chest puffed. "That was a work of genius, if I do say so myself—and making a deal with Mordizan to send them the Case? They were so busy blaming each other for the disappearance, enemy and ally alike, that no one thought to look for me."

And they all thought you were dead, so why would they look for you? She let him continue uninterrupted.

"I took the Key to my lab. But I was wrong. It doesn't function according to any normal law or science *or* magic. My attempts only caused fluctuations in the protection spells and even more fighting. When I was caught and dragged back to Castelon, Master Castelius conducted a closed trial and reported that I had been trying to take down the protection spells to get all the wizards to kill each other. Thus villainizing me, he threw me into this dungeon. Here I've remained ever since."

She shook her head slowly. "I'm sorry. If we had known, we wouldn't have let him do that."

"Really?" He gave her a sideways look. "I was trying to destroy magic. You wouldn't want to stop me?"

"Obviously you failed, but at least you were trying to do something." She pinched the bridge of her nose, closing her eyes. "Unlike Castelius. Even if you didn't figure out a solution, I salute you for trying."

"Oh, I did figure out the solution. I was just apprehended before I could do anything about it."

Her chains clanked as her hand dropped from her face. "What?"

"Like I said. The Master Key doesn't function according to any normal law of science or magic. I had been looking in the wrong places." He tapped his nose like an old-timey actor about to let her in on a secret. "Myrddin didn't use ordinary magic. He used *dywledrith*."

She sucked in a breath. "Dark magic." She had been right about the only thing that could defeat Mordred? But how could everything their society was built upon—the Master Key, the protection spells, the Masters, the estates—have been formed from a forbidden magic that even Mordizan kept locked away?

"I should have been researching *dywledrith* all along." She pounded a fist against the ground. "I don't know how I didn't see it earlier. No normal magic, no matter how powerful Myrddin was, could tether all of the magic in the world. Where did it all go? Where did he banish magic so that each wizard could only possess one kind? What gives Masters their powers, and why do those powers stem from their estates?"

Her limbs ached for movement, to do something. She stood, pacing as much as she could in the pit. "Dark magic always has a terrible price." She turned, facing Dr. Morton. "What enormous price did Myrddin pay to chain magic itself?"

"Other than his own life . . ." His voice remained low, almost reverent. "He fractured the very world in half." His words dropped to a whisper. "The double spaces around the estates are just pockets we can access through the Gates—portals, really, to a dimension we can only reach a fraction of. An entire world exists on top of ours."

"What are you saying?" Brinnie breathed.

"Every bit of magic that wizards possess is only tethered here through the Master Key, siphoned from another dimension. Once, fantastical creatures roamed this world. Once, the very air was full of magic. But all of that was stripped from our dimension. This is supposed to be a place for humans, a place for science, but Myrddin's Key holds on to that last bit of magic from the other world like a fisherman clinging to his pole even with his hook through a whale. Can't you feel your own being at odds with the very atmosphere around you?"

"Yes," she admitted. Yes, she had immediately felt the difference when she stepped back into Wraithwood after so long away. The estates felt different, but she assumed that stemmed from the protection spells, the Masters' powers. Not magic seeping from another dimension.

Not a human world she truly *didn't* belong in. Where her magic, the most comfortable, most *her* part of her being, evidently fought to exist.

"Magic doesn't belong to this world." His glasses flickered in the dim light, the glow from above reflecting like fire in his eyes. "Destroy the Master Key, and magic leaves this world forever. No more wizards. No more Enchantment."

"No more war."

"Precisely." He sighed. "Not that we can do anything about it now. I missed my chance."

"Then let's get out of here and destroy it. What does it take? Dark magic?"

"I appreciate the determination," Dr. Morton said, "but the two of us can't destroy the Master Key. The prophecy makes that clear."

Brinnie pressed her lips together to hold in a sigh. "Please explain."

"Blood magic. *Dywledrith* and blood magic pair well together. 'Myrddin's flesh and Myrddin's blood shall destroy the world he built,' and 'Mordred's bane, his final doom, the heir of Arthur doth supply.'" He stopped, as if that explained anything. When she kept staring at him blankly, he huffed. "You know, 'with sword Excalibur in hand, *his magic to destroy*.' Only the heir of Arthur can wield Excalibur, Myrddin's descendant will destroy the world he built, and Excalibur destroys Mordred's magic—by destroying the Master Key. Presumably Mryddin and Arthur worked together to come up with a foolproof safety net that only a descendant of *both* of them could destroy the new rules of magic, and they already had a plan to kill Mordred, so Myrddin would have no descendants." He shrugged. "And you need Excalibur, of course."

"Wait." Brinnie's heart beat faster. "But Mordred didn't die. And he had descendants. I'm one of them."

He shook his head. "Unless you can marry a descendant of Arthur and have a child before Castelon falls, I'd say we're doomed."

"No, I'm a descendant of Arthur, too." Her heart raced even faster. "I'm Brynna Ludovic-Drakon. My mom is a descendant of Arthur, and my dad is a descendant of Myrddin. I pulled Excalibur from the stone . . . a couple of days ago? We have everything available in this time. For the first time ever in history."

His eyes widened. "The heir of Arthur. The bringer of the Golden Age of Albion. *You* are the fulfillment of the prophecy."

The hairs on her arms stood on end, and the back of her neck prickled. "Remind me about this Golden Age."

"The foretold time of peace and unity that would be brought about by Arthur. It was said to be when wizard and human would live together in harmony, when magic would be reconciled to the world. Albion was an ancient name for the British Isle, and the poetic Golden Age of Albion suggested not only a time of peace between wizards and humans, but also a unified Britannia in a time of upheaval and war."

"Well, upheaval and war sound familiar." She straightened her shoulders. "You couldn't destroy the Master Key two years ago. But you didn't have me." Her jaw tightened as she surveyed their prison. "We're getting out of here. And we're stopping all of this once and for all."

CHAPTER THIRTY-NINE

Perhaps expecting to escape Castelon's most secure prison on day one was a bit ambitious.

The sheer walls indeed proved too slippery to scale, even with Brinnie trying to rough them up by banging her chains against them. Without magic—she had never felt a ward so strong before, and paired with the cuffs, she had nothing—she couldn't melt her chains, and resorted to searching them for a weak link she might slowly be able to pry open. No such luck. They had been welded shut. The bands set into the wall to which the chains had been attached were deeply embedded and would probably require days, if not weeks, of consistent battering and yanking to budge.

"If I were significantly stronger," Brinnie panted after fruitlessly scraping the stone around the bars, "maybe I could launch you out of here."

His brows rose. "Yes. Significantly. Considering we are at least thirty feet down."

She slumped against the wall, pinching the bridge of her nose and squeezing her eyes shut. *Marcus, please, if you can hear me, say something.* She assumed the telepathy was magical, but it had still worked in Mordizan's warded dungeons. Maybe they could communicate here too.

Or maybe she would die in this pit, finally knowing how to stop Mordred, but unable to do so. A cruel joke. Part of her wondered if Scott thought tossing her in here with Dr. Morton would be funny.

At least they were keeping Marcus alive, for now. Leverage against her.

She took a shuddering breath, struggling to hold her emotions in check. *I shouldn't have pushed him away.* She wished she had kissed him in that crypt. She wished they hadn't fought over her sacrificing herself. All her worries for the future seemed so stupid when they likely wouldn't have a future at all.

Everyone who loved or cared about her, everyone but Marcus and perhaps Maddy, thought she was dead. The two of them had spent most of their time fighting recently. And for what? For all of her plans to fail.

If she escaped this pit, no matter how short her life might end up being, she would find her family, her friends. Her grand plans to save the world might work, but they might not. In the meantime, she could only control one thing. How she treated those closest to her.

Marcus. I really hope this magic is different. I hope you can hear me. Not every magic could have been accounted for with these wards. Why would they guard against dark magic, for example, or blood magic? Ancient magics no one was supposed to know anymore.

She didn't have any materials to try *dywledrith*, and she knew better than to use it anyway. Blood magic, if it could even still be wielded, wouldn't be helpful. She wracked her mind for anything she possessed that might evade the wards.

The wards. The wards were spells, right? She was a spellcaster. Completely untrained in a magic that required more technical knowledge than any other branch, but she did possess that magic.

Could she reverse them?

"Are you all right?"

She startled and opened her eyes. She'd forgotten Dr. Morton was still there. "Sorry. Just thinking. I'm going to try to mess with the wards, if I can."

"Are you a spellcaster?"

"Yes." Among other things. "I don't know if that counts when magic doesn't work, but it's worth a shot."

She sat in a cross-legged position and closed her eyes again. She let her mind drift, sensing the magic around her.

All of the varieties within her roiled, as if furious to be contained and stifled. Even her shadow magic seemed subdued, almost pouting. She smiled at that. *Patience, we'll get free.*

Realization stabbed through her heart. She would get free . . . and rid the world of magic. Including her own.

No shadows to blanket her. Lonely darkness, her vision gone, so instead of friends the night would only hold hidden threats.

The magic deteriorating her cells from within would leave her, but so would her own magic, her identity, her shadows.

No time to think about that. I have to do the right thing, not what I want.

She pressed her hands against the wall behind her, attempting to feel the wards, difficult over the shouting of all the magic inside her. The sheer weight of these spells . . . multiple spellcasters must have created these wards, a twisting, convoluted weave of dampers, locks, and bindings. Regardless, if she could feel them, maybe she could untangle them.

She let out a deep breath. "This is going to take a while."

Hours passed. Her head ached, still tender from the blow she'd received, the intense concentration not helping. She wished Ignatius could help her. Her fingers twitched as if assisting her mind in unraveling the pieces.

Morton napped. He must have grown used to hours upon hours of silence, alone in the pit.

Another knot of magic fell apart, a large one she'd been working on for longer than she cared to think about. Her shoulders slumped as she took a break, cold sweat beading her forehead. How long since she'd had any proper rest? Two days? Three? *Well, technically months, I guess. A whole new level of jetlag.*

"Brinnie?"

She sat up straight. *Marcus? You can hear me?*

"Thank God, I've been trying to reach you for hours. Where are you? Are you safe?"

I'm locked up in Castelon, but safe for now. I've been trying to reach you, as well.

"Castelon is good. I believe that's where I am too."

She explained what she had overheard between Mordred, Nimue, and Castelius, and her current location and attempts to pick apart the wards. She decided she didn't have time to explain Dr. Morton right now. *I guess maybe that last knot I untangled allowed enough magic to get through for us to speak.*

"Or we're in range. Haven't found anywhere a pit might be located, but I'm still trying."

In range? *Hold on, aren't you imprisoned?*

"Not anymore. But I should probably hurry up this search before someone notices two guards locked in my cell instead of me."

She snorted aloud. *You're a regular escape artist. Have you* ever *been locked up for more than a day?*

"I don't think so, but granted, you're usually the one breaking us out. I think all of their competent warriors must be fighting, because they assigned a pair of idiots to guard me."

Hope buoyed in her heart. She had been acting like she was alone in this fight. She should have known her partner in crime would be causing his own chaos. *In that case, while you're searching for us, let me catch you up on some very interesting information I've learned.*

Once she had finished filling him in on the full prophecy and *dywledrith*, he didn't say anything for a few moments.

What are you thinking?

"Nothing." The words came too quickly. *"So. Destroying magic. Or, at least, banishing it from this world. I'm on board with you. We need to free you from wherever you are, then we need to get the Master Key from Castelius and Excalibur from Mordred."* A breathy chuckle floated through her mind. *"No big deal. Just taking on* both *armies to accomplish something both sides would probably kill us for trying to do if they knew."*

Just keeping it interesting. Wouldn't want you to get bored.

"That is one thing I have never been with you around."

Keep looking, and find some rope if you can. I'm going to focus on these cuffs. You can get us out of the pit without magic, but I don't think these manacles will come off by any normal means.

She turned her attention to the wards on the chains. Before, breaking the spells on the prison itself would have helped her to then remove the cuffs, but now, she might as well focus her energy on this smaller of the two tasks.

The manacles kept her mind occupied for what felt like another half hour to an hour. She resisted the urge to break her concentration by checking on Marcus. Her work on the prison wards did seem to have done something, since the manacles began to grow hot around her wrists, burning from expended magic from her tampering.

Muffled thuds, grunts, what sounded like weapons clattering, and then the noise of an object thwacking against stone sent her eyes flying open. She twisted, scanning until she spotted a rope dangling from far above.

"Found you. Finally."

Dr. Morton sat up, blinking as he slid his glasses up his nose. "What's going on?"

"A rescue." She flashed him a smile. "We've been busy."

Marcus rappelled down the rope and dropped to his feet not far from them. His clothes were a bit dirty and rumpled, and he sported a bruise at his temple and a scratch across his cheek, but otherwise he looked little worse for the wear.

Her own messy hair and damp, blood-stained clothes sprang to mind, making her cringe, but Marcus didn't hesitate. He wrapped her in a hug, pulling away instantly to scan her for injuries. "You're okay?"

She chuckled. "I'm fine."

"Good." He pulled her close again, his warmth warding off the dank chill of the prison. "I was worried when I couldn't contact you for a while that Mordred had decided to . . . you know."

"I know." Chains clanking and tangling around both of them, she wrapped her arms around him, burying her face in his chest. He brushed her hair back from her face, the gentle touch soothing, and she let out a shuddering breath. They were both still alive to fight another day.

To destroy this entire system . . . and everything that had kept them apart.

Dr. Morton cleared his throat. "I assume you knocked out the guards, so we should probably hurry before they awaken."

Marcus pulled back, looked at him, blinked. "Um. Knocked out. Right." He gestured toward the rope. "Are you any good at climbing?"

"Ah." Dr. Morton scanned the rope. "Probably not quite that good."

Brinnie waved toward their escape. "I have to keep working on these cuffs anyway. You haul him up, give me some time to keep messing with the spells."

"Yes, ma'am." Marcus flashed her a grin before scaling the rope.

Dr. Morton's eyes bounced between the two of them. "Did you . . . know he was coming?"

"A lot of long stories there. He and I communicate telepathically."

She closed her eyes. "I need to focus. Make sure you tie that rope around yourself well, and use your hands and feet to balance against the wall so you don't go spinning."

She shut out all sounds around her, concentrating on the cuffs. The more she fiddled with the spellwork, the more they burned into her wrists, until her eyes watered. A long time seemed to have passed, but she couldn't stop to think about what might have happened to Marcus and Dr. Morton.

Footsteps crunching on rough stone finally distracted her from her task. She looked up to see Marcus approaching with . . . "Where did you get a hacksaw?"

"Staying here is making me nervous, and I figured you could work faster if you aren't trapped in a no-magic zone. Morton knew about a maintenance closet." He gestured to her chains. "I would go for the cuffs themselves, but . . ."

"Yes, please don't accidentally cut my hands off. I approve."

She held the chains taut against the bars so he could attack the links several inches from the first manacle. She winced at the horrible shrieking, grating sound as he began sawing. With luck, once they were past the wards, Marcus might be able to melt the cuffs right off her wrists. The manacles suppressed her magic, not his.

As the saw's shrieks continued, she glanced upward. *Is this going to be alerting anyone up there?*

"We're so deep in the dungeons, no one should just happen by."

The first chain link snapped, the sudden release of tension sending his saw jerking downward and her nearly stumbling. They exchanged an awkward laugh, and Brinnie held up the chain attached to her second wrist, pulling it tight.

Marcus commenced sawing that one. *"And the guards have been taken care of."*

Dr. Morton probably had a rude awakening coming that real war didn't look like the movies. *Once we get out of here, we need to locate our allies and split our forces. I can't go anywhere near Mordred without his blade alerting him. That was my downfall last time. Someone else needs to go for Excalibur while I find the Master Key.* As much as she hated it, she had to admit that there was a part of this plan she couldn't execute herself.

The hacksaw broke through the second chain. This time, Brinnie was ready and had braced herself. Just two more. She took hold of the chain to her left ankle.

He knelt to continue. *"I'll take care of Excalibur. We can communicate and coordinate from afar if plans change."*

That did make sense, as much as she would prefer him by her side. *You'll need backup. Once we find my family, we can plot your approach and figure out if they know where the Master Key is.*

"And let them know you're alive." He glanced up to flash her a smile, still sawing. *"That's a morale booster if I've ever seen one."*

When the fourth and final chain link snapped, Marcus tucked the hacksaw into the back of his belt and stood. "Shall we?"

"Wait." She took a deep breath, nervously fiddling with one manacle. "The things I said in the crypt, and everything we've argued about—I'm sorry. I keep worrying far into the future about potential issues instead of solving problems right in front of us. I'm trying to stop that." She gave a short laugh. "I guess destroying magic forever to solve our problem right now is a bit of an extreme way to implement the new plan."

He offered a crooked grin. "You never do anything halfway." He sobered. "And I'm sorry for being overbearing at times."

"Sometimes I need it." She hesitated. "If we both make it out of the next few days alive . . . I'd like to, uh, take back some things I said about duty and selflessness and other noble-sounding garbage that was code for 'I'm scared.'"

His brow furrowed. "So . . . are you trying to say you're not scared anymore?"

"Oh, I'm terrified. But not of us." She could feel her cheeks reddening. Hopefully he couldn't see the color in the dim light. "This is one thing I'm pretty sure of. I'd hate for something to happen without me saying that."

His eyes were soft as his hand cupped her cheek. "I won't tell you this will all work out, the plan will succeed, we'll both make it to the end. But I will tell you I'm glad we get to do it together, however long that lasts."

She turned her head slightly, holding his hand in hers, and brushed a kiss on his palm. She could feel him freeze, hesitate.

I think you said something before about making your feelings "abundantly clear." She kissed his palm again, featherlight so that his breath caught. *Consider this permission, if you're so inclined.*

"Now who's pulling out all the lines?" He pulled her to him.

For one blissful moment, his kisses danced over her forehead, her nose, her cheeks, eliciting giggles until his lips captured hers and she lost her breath. All too soon, he pulled away, his face looking as flushed as hers felt. "Morton. Waiting for us. I think we should probably climb a rope now, but let's, ah, definitely revisit this."

She pressed one more kiss to his lips. "I fully intend to."

At the top of the pit, Marcus managed to melt away the cuffs without singeing her wrists too severely. The damper on her magic made her fire resistance spotty.

As soon as the cuffs fell away, she felt the magic rushing through her, rejoicing. She took a step back as shadows, flame, and electricity flickered through her for a moment, too strong to contain. With hardly a thought, she melted away the irons on her ankles herself, the metal pooling around her feet.

Dr. Morton stared. "I suppose that's why you're the heir of Arthur."

She grinned. "Let's get this show on the road."

CHAPTER
FORTY

A boom shook the wall. Brinnie stumbled, debris cascading from above.

Marcus steadied her. "You can stay in the castle if you want and communicate to them through me."

She snorted. "I don't think they would ever forgive me for announcing I'm alive like that."

They had sent Dr. Morton on a reconnaissance mission within the castle for where the Master Key might be hidden, since he knew Castelon the best, and set up a meeting place to report back. Meanwhile, the two of them had asked around to find the location of Brinnie's family. Just as she'd suspected, her father was indeed alive—along with Mom, Uncle Merlin, and Lana.

As they ran, Brinnie tightened the straps of her gauntlets, taken from a fallen warrior whose hands were bigger than hers. She and Marcus had armored up, her mostly with flexible leather, him with heavier chain and plate as well as a sword. She didn't want to die from something stupid like a glancing blow or lose her fingers in a clumsy clash of blades.

They ascended the steps to the top of the wall, near the gate. Unsurprisingly, sources had pointed them toward the worst of the fighting, right at the front. Shouts, screams, and explosions rang overhead. Twice, they pressed themselves against the wall as messengers darted up and down the stairs on swifter, more agile feet than theirs. Once, they dodged as a limp body plummeted from above.

As soon as they reached the top, Marcus ducked behind the battlements, pulling her with him. An arrow rattled against stone not far from where they had been standing. "Do you see them?"

She scanned the chaotic mix of archers, messengers, supply runners, wizards shooting magical projectiles, others cutting down grappling hooks and siege ladders . . . "Not yet. Not a great vantage point though."

Another barrage of missiles clattered onto the wall around them. In the split second after the volley, she peeked around the merlon and onto the field of battle below before ducking back into shelter again and gesturing for Marcus to join her. "Found Uncle Merlin."

They both peered through the nearest embrasure. Below, the roiling mass of battle didn't afford much view of individual characteristics, but the form appearing and disappearing, blipping across the battlefield in the blink of an eye to deal waves of destruction before vanishing once more, could only be one person.

Marcus let out a low whistle. "Especially with his other Masters' powers intact, traveling is quite the formidable weapon."

Brinnie pointed at a man in dark armor wielding a flaming sword, a woman with shards of ice flying from her fingertips beside him. "And there are my parents." Fire and ice, working in tandem, scything through the flank of the enemy forces. "Why are they down there instead of on the ramparts?"

"It's a little crowded up here. They're all better close-range fighters." He nodded toward the chaotic scene surrounding what seemed to be a fallen battering ram still a few hundred feet from the gate, fighters crawling over the smoking war machine. "Some defenders on the ground stunting attack measures, the rest on the wall defending."

"How did they get down there in the first place? Won't they be stuck?"

A flash of mist caught her eye, followed shortly by another a few yards down the wall, where a stumbling warrior fell to his knees. A healer rushed forward, hands going to the man's bleeding abdomen.

"The anywhere portals." She let out a breathless laugh. "Ignatius and Uncle Merlin must have made *hundreds* of them."

"Ignatius wasn't kidding about a stockpile." His smile held sadness. "I'm sure he would be bragging to all of us about it if he could." Marcus stood, bent to stay under cover. "Let's see if they have more."

Upon their request, the healer passed them two portals with little question. "Try to stick together so you don't waste portals." Then she scurried off to her next patient.

Marcus handed one to Brinnie, and she slipped it into an inner pocket. "Merlin is moving too quickly," he said. "Your parents are an easier target."

"Good, let's go."

He grabbed her hand, smashing the portal with his other. The mist swirled and cleared right as a fireball shot toward them, engulfing them both before continuing its trajectory.

Brinnie brushed a spark from her sleeve. "Hello to you too, Dad."

He froze, hand still raised from releasing the flame. Then he ripped off his helmet, staring. "Brin?"

Beside him, Mom whirled toward them and gasped, shards of ice falling to the ground around her. "Brynna."

"One minute." Brinnie made a circular motion with her hand, and a fiery whirlwind whipped around their group, shielding the four of them in the epicenter from any outside interference. The fire should take care of anything the wind didn't, and vice versa. Then she gave a nervous laugh. "Surprise. I'm alive."

A sob tore from Mom's throat, and she dashed forward, throwing her arms around Brinnie. "How . . . we . . ." Only disconnected monosyllabic words broke through her tears. She pulled back and held Brinnie by the shoulders, searching her face. "Is it really you?"

Brinnie held up a hand, a shadow dancing over her palm. "No trick. No shapeshifter. It's me."

Dad's arms crashed around both of them in a bear hug, their armor clanking together, as he let out a whoop. He squeezed the two of them until Brinnie was breathless and laughing. Mom fussed over her, and both of them peppered her with questions, which Brinnie tried to answer as rapid-fire as they came.

Mom took Brinnie's face in her hands and kissed her forehead. "You're safe," she whispered, repeating it again like a mantra. "I can't believe you're safe."

As Brinnie took in the tears spilling from the eyes of her parents, truth struck her hard in the chest. Just like for her friends, the tragedy of her death hadn't just been a tactical loss to her parents. No matter what happened, they mourned *her.* Even Mom. Not a shred of judgment or reproach in her eyes, only relief and joy as she squeezed Brinnie again.

Marcus had been right. Little as she could fathom the concept, the people who loved her wanted her alive and well more than they wanted anything else from her. Even if it took "losing" her for the usual hard edge to Mom's tone to disappear.

"I could *shake* you right now." Her grip dropped to Brinnie's shoulders and tightened. "Don't ever do something like that again."

There it was. The scolding—but somehow this kind only made her feel more loved. "I promise, no more faking my death." She glanced toward Marcus. "We have a plan, but we need Uncle Merlin and Lana too."

A form in light chainmail appeared beside Mom. Uncle Merlin pushed back his hair, damp with sweat. "What is going on in . . . Brynna?"

She grinned. "Hi! Not dead."

"Ha!" A matching grin accompanied his incredulous laugh. "I suppose I shouldn't be surprised your entrance was accompanied by a literal whirlwind of fire."

Mom glanced at him, a soft smile lighting her features. "Merlin insisted you were alive, all these months."

"We're a bit too similar, you and I." He winked at Brinnie. "I assume you've been up to something. Care to fill us in?"

Her heart swelled. Every time Mordred said they were alike, he had been wrong. She was proud to believe there was more of Merlin than Mordred in her.

"Right. We have a plan. Outside this circle, though, no one is going to like it, so the operation is on the DL." She bit her lip. "Those inside this circle won't like it much either, but I doubt Mordred will ever see it coming."

"Any plan is better than what we've got." Dad nodded to her. "We have your back, kiddo."

So she laid out the plot.

Scorch marks marred the silver gates of Castelon. Chunks of the wall had crumbled, even with spellcasters on the ramparts frantically casting magical reinforcements, terra wizards and levitation wizards assisting. The castle clearly rested on its last legs.

Which meant a last-ditch frontal assault against the enemy wouldn't be out of the realm of logical next moves.

Brinnie watched through Marcus's eyes as he surveyed the castle from the battlefield, showing her the damage. *"Looking rough."* A flashing sword interrupted him, and he turned to parry blows.

From the wall, she used her own vision to scan the unending hordes of attackers, like an undulating sea of black gnats. In the distance, outlined by beige tents, stood the red command tent of Mordred. The tent Marcus needed to reach.

She turned and gazed down on the other side of the wall at the gathering of defenders filling the courtyard, falling into ranks ready to storm out of the gates. They couldn't remove too much of a presence from the walls if they wanted the advantage of surprise, and the small force seemed pathetic against the formidable foe outside. Most weren't trained warriors—townspeople, refugees, humans, and faces Brinnie recognized who had no business in battle, like Mr. Winslow, Miss Burtle, even Maddy standing beside Quentin in armor too big for her, gripping a sword like a baseball bat. Brinnie had heard that even David and Anna had learned archery and manned another portion of the wall near one of the lesser gates.

Brinnie wanted to tell them to fall back, to protect themselves. But on the cusp of the end of the world as they knew it, she doubted she could convince anyone to stand down.

Despite her heart screaming to protect her loved ones, pride filled her chest for the ragtag band with their motley assortment of weapons. Humanity's last defenders, with determined sets to their jaws and a hard look in their eyes.

A woman approached her. "The troops are ready, my lord."

Brinnie nodded. "Good." Her voice came out deep, matching the body she inhabited—that of Scott Castelius. Shapeshifting into the slimy man felt like wearing foul rags dredged from a sewer. "At my signal, have the gates opened."

Uncle Merlin appeared beside her. "Those currently on the battlefield are moving into position. Drakon, Arion, Eira, and I are ready to lead the columns once they emerge from the gates."

"Make sure Vorath hangs back from the most prominent fighting. I leave the rest of the timing to your and his judgment."

A quick nod, then he disappeared again.

The troops below didn't know they were a distraction as Marcus invaded Mordred's camp. Uncle Merlin couldn't transport into the camp, as he hadn't been there before, and Marcus couldn't portal for the same reason, so they had to resort to old-fashioned sneaking. Since Marcus was supposed to still be in a dungeon—or dead—his lack of presence on the battlefield wouldn't set off the suspicion that Uncle Merlin's or others' might. Her most powerful allies were also the highest profile.

The time had come. She lifted her hand high above her head, then let her arm drop.

The gates creaked and rattled as they groaned, swinging open. Brinnie's army surged forward, ranks messy, but still present, flowing toward the four leaders of the quadruple-pronged approach. More moving parts to watch, more of a distraction.

And now the time had come for her to play her part.

She nodded to the woman beside her, one of Castelius's commanders who Brinnie had pretended to actually recognize. "I will be rejoining the Council. Keep me apprised."

A muscle in the commander's jaw twitched, but she nodded. "Yes, my lord."

Brinnie swept away, toward the stairs. She couldn't blame the woman for being put out by Castelius's supposed slight, entrusting the leadership of the troops to the likes of Ludovics and Drakons instead of his own trusted leaders.

As soon as her feet hit the stone of the courtyard, Dr. Morton scuttled out of the shadows, pushing his glasses up his nose.

Brinnie scanned the courtyard. The chaos of defenders on the wall, missiles in the air, and the gate straining to shut once more served to distract from any interaction she might have here. She shifted into the form of a woman of average height and build with mousy brown hair. "Did you find it?"

"Bad news." He fiddled with his glasses again. "The Master Key is in the Council Chamber, under the scrutiny of the Council. Of seven."

She huffed out a breath, not sure what to complain about first—that the Council sat on their butts under the guise of strategizing while everyone else fought, that they hadn't put the Key in a more convenient place . . . "Won't it weaken all of their powers like that? They're making themselves vulnerable."

"Contained within the Case, it shouldn't make too much difference. You'll be fighting seven with their full powers."

She ran a hand over her face. "Well. Nothing like a challenge, I guess."

A darting figure caught her eye. She watched a message boy sprint across the courtyard, toward the commander.

"That's trouble." She ran after him.

But she was too late. She reached the top of the stairs, huffing, in time to hear the boy finish, "Master Castelius and the Council didn't give the order. They want you to call back the troops." He ducked as a ball of fire hit the ramparts and splattered sparks around them.

The commander hardly moved at the disturbance. "Master Castelius was standing on the wall with me ten minutes ago." She ground her teeth. "I watched him give the order."

The message boy panted, his cheeks flushed. "I just came from the Council Chamber, ma'am. He was there the whole time."

After a second, the commander cursed. "Shapeshifter." She whirled toward the battlefield. "If they retreat now, the enemy will only follow them through the gates. That shapeshifter sent them on a suicide mission."

Brinnie glanced in either direction to make sure no one was watching and turned invisible, crouching with her back against the outer crenellation.

The commander continued to curse. "I'll get this sorted out." She shouted to a man farther down the wall. "You're in charge until I get back." He didn't have time to finish his salute before she smashed a portal and disappeared into mist.

Would her testimony to the Council implicate Brinnie? Surely their first thought at "shapeshifter" wouldn't be that Brinnie escaped the inescapable dungeon. She'd hoped for an element of surprise.

Later. For now, she tuned into Marcus's mind, keeping track of his progress.

She found him jogging over hilly terrain, taking cover behind trees and shrubs when he could, approaching the enemy encampment from the left. With all attention focused frontward, hopefully no one would notice a lone warrior approaching camp from the rear.

Nice day for a run?

"I can practically hear Mr. Gerd saying that he told me all those laps would come in handy someday."

She peeked over the wall. The four snaking prongs of defenders fanned out, then pressed inward again, as if trying to meet and form a wedge after their attempt at a flanking maneuver failed. The assault couldn't look *too* foolish, or Mordred would never buy it, but the on-field leaders had been instructed to cause as much erratic chaos as possible to keep Mordred and his war leaders occupied.

She shot a quick visual of the battle to Marcus and returned her attention to him. *ETA?*

"Five minutes until I hit the camp. Then things will slow a bit, since I'll need to walk like I belong." His footfalls kept a steady beat. *"How are things there?"*

Castelius impersonation worked, of course. The Master Key is in the Council Chamber, guarded by the Council. Timing is everything.

"Just keeping it interesting, aren't they? Any sign of Mordred?"

No. It's making me antsy. Something solid hit the battlements, and she nearly fell. *Finding a more secure location and heading in the direction of the Master Key. I'll keep you posted.*

"Ditto."

She looked over the wall one more time, scanning for Mordred, before she descended and headed for the castle, cloaked in shadows.

While concentrating as best she could on not getting lost on her way to the Council Chamber, she occasionally tuned in to Marcus, now entering the enemy camp, now strolling with purpose but without rush, face mostly covered by a standard-issue Mordizan helmet pulled from the battlefield.

Her legs begged her to run, to hurry to the Council Chamber. Her friends and family fought an impossible battle, and they couldn't hold out forever. But without Excalibur, attacking the Council would be pointless.

In Marcus's vision, the red tent came into view. He slowed only slightly, scanning the two guards patrolling the exterior. *"The camp is near deserted. I don't want to know what the battlefield looks like, but I won't complain about no witnesses."* He strode toward the closest guard and stopped a few yards away with a nod. "Message for Lord Mordred."

The guard stepped away from the tent, presumably moving where the conversation wouldn't disturb the occupants, and tightened her grip on her spear. "Lord Mordred is not here."

"Very well. I imagine his counsel may receive the message."

The second guard joined them and held out his hand. "We'll take it."

Marcus bobbed his head in deference. "The message is oral, sir. I've been ordered to deliver it personally by Lady Nimue Drakon."

Both Brinnie and Marcus held their breaths at the lie. If Nimue was already inside that tent, the game would be up.

But the guard nodded once and turned to stride toward the entrance to announce Marcus's presence.

With both of the guards distracted and so near to one another, Marcus's arms whipped out. Brinnie focused on the corridor in front of her for a moment, then tuned back in. Both guards lay on the ground, throats slit, their deaths quick and without screams. Marcus stepped over their corpses and approached the tent on silent footfalls, standing to the side of the entrance and listening.

Brinnie took a flight of stairs and tried to keep her thoughts to herself. The two sentinels had only been doing their jobs, but he hadn't had any good option to nonlethally incapacitate them in a quiet way. *Soon this will all be over. No more senseless killing.*

"I'm sorry." She could hear the guilt tingeing his voice—guilt not so much that he had killed them, but that he'd hardly thought twice about doing so while she cringed.

Different upbringings. Hear anyone in there? Luckily not Mordred, it seems.

They both kept quiet. A voice drifted from within, male, and too familiar.

Your father.

"Surprised he would leave Mordizan."

Not much of a threat anyone can put up right now.

"Not from Castelon, maybe. But people are always scheming."

Marcus slunk along the side of the tent and peered inside the flap.

Within, a large camp table held the usual battle maps and missives, with an array of portals in the labeled compartments of a box in the center. Vorath spoke to a soldier, who saluted and turned for the door.

Marcus ducked out of the way, barely out of sight as the soldier jogged away to carry out whatever task he had been assigned.

Leaving the Master of Mordizan alone with the most prominent object on the camp table—the shining blade Excalibur.

Why is he alone? Where is Mordred? And the usual bevy of advisers?

Marcus looked in again, eyes going to the blade on Vorath's hip as the Master shuffled through papers. *"That looks like Mordred's blade, the one linked to you. This feels like a trap to lure you in. Look at all the portals. They probably figure my father could hold you off at least long enough to take you to Mordred via portal."*

I'm a little insulted. One wizard?

A chuckle rumbled through his mind. *"The Master of Mordizan himself. No, he probably couldn't defeat you, but at the very least you wouldn't kill him instantly, giving him time to bring Mordred to you, if not you to Mordred."*

But as far as anyone knows, I'm still in that pit. She bit her lip. *Unless pretending to be Scott tipped them off. They know I'm free. Which means they'll know we're up to something.*

"Nothing for it but to keep going forward."

Right. She took a deep breath. *You should probably sneak around and—*

Before she could finish the sentence, Marcus pushed aside the tent flap and stepped inside. "Hello, Father."

Are you insane? You can't challenge a Master.

Vorath's hand went to the blade at his hip, then froze. "Marcus." He scarcely breathed the name. Almost imperceptibly, his fingers trembled over the hilt. "What are you doing here?"

"I could ask you the same." He didn't reach for his sword, or the two daggers he'd used to strike down the guards. "Who's in charge at Mordizan?"

Brinnie wanted to scream at him. What did that have to do with anything? Why was he *talking* with Vorath? Did he have a death wish? But she couldn't interfere, couldn't break his concentration. She had to trust that Marcus had a plan. He hadn't let her down yet.

"I left Nimue in command. Mordred has been monopolizing enough of her time." More information than he should have shared, but he almost seemed to be . . . babbling? Distracted? Vorath's gaze roved over Marcus, taking in the battle-worn clothing and piecemeal armor and gear, splattered with mud and blood. "You've been fighting."

"Clearly. And you're sitting here as part of a trap for the shadowmaster."

"Clearly." He hesitated. "It's good to see you, son."

Marcus huffed a sharp laugh. "Is it?"

"Yes." Vorath's hand dropped away from his weapon entirely. "I've missed you."

He raised a brow. "Missed my help, maybe. My skill as a warrior."

"No." Vorath took a small step forward, but Marcus stepped back. The Master halted, giving his son a long look. "I already lost your mother."

"You killed my mother." Marcus's voice rang flat.

He stood unmoving, staring at Marcus. "I never meant for that to happen."

"You? Not executing a spy? I find that hard to believe." His jaw clenched. "You raised your own child to be a murderer. A monster."

Vorath's voice took on a tone Brinnie never thought she would hear. Almost pleading. "Marcus, I understand. You love this girl. I *know* what it's like to love a woman who would be your downfall, but you don't have to follow her whims. We can talk to Mordred about keeping her alive. You can come back to Mordizan and—"

"You don't understand at all." He barked a mirthless laugh. "She does matter to me, but the *reason* I'm doing all of this isn't for her. It's because it's right. Mordred won't stop at just the human world. He'll destroy Mordizan. He'll take ultimate power."

"Magic is dying—"

"So let it die." Marcus took two steps forward, fully in the middle of the tent, but Vorath didn't make a move to stop him. "Mom always said she didn't need a title or magic. She didn't need anything but you and me to be happy. She could have had that. *We* could have had that. But your blasted war, your infernal ambition, killed her. Whether you meant to or not. Even with magic dwindling, we could have ruled Mordizan in peace for centuries to come." He pounded a fist on the table. "But now we're here. Either we stop Mordred, or he'll destroy us all. You think he'll let any Masters live? Any heirs? Threats to his power? Put yourself in his position. You'd murder them all without a thought."

Silence. Brinnie stopped in an alcove within view of the Council Chamber, waiting.

"So you propose that we kill him first," Vorath said finally. Mockery entered his tone. "Wouldn't that be grand? He's all but won this war for us, we dispose of him, and live in happiness the rest of our days. I think you fail to remember that the shadowmaster ran him through with Excalibur itself and he didn't fall. No one can take him, son. We must find a way to live in his world."

"We have a way to stop him." Marcus nodded to the sword. "If you'll let me take it, I believe we can bring about the Mordizan Mom would have wanted." His feet moved into a fighting position. "If you won't, then I'll have to kill you."

Vorath looked at him for a long moment, his gaze panning to the sword on the table, then back again. Finally, his shoulders slumped, and he sighed. "At least make it look like you bested me. A dagger to the back, perhaps. If you fail, we're in no worse position than before."

Marcus blinked, as if he hadn't expected his words to work. Then, all business, he spun his finger in a circle. "Turn around."

Vorath did, turning his back to the entrance. Marcus pulled one of the daggers from his belt and threw it, the trajectory of the blade clumsy, not built for throwing, but it did the job. The knife sank into his father's back, above the shoulder. Vorath fell forward onto his knees, then face down. Not a killing blow, not if someone found him soon enough, but one that would believably incapacitate.

Marcus stepped forward, removed the sword from his hip, and laid the weapon on the table. He picked up Excalibur instead and attached the sword in its place. "He always had a soft spot for family. The only soft spot the man had."

Brinnie didn't think training his son to be a torturer and killer constituted a soft spot. But he hadn't killed his traitorous offspring outright. It was all about perspective, she supposed. *Maybe he can start anew in a world without magic.*

"We need to make that world first." He retrieved a portal from his pocket. *"Just tell me when."*

Brinnie exited the alcove and strode toward the doors of the Council Chamber. Two guards manned the doors—guards who could have been out on the battlefield, fighting. *I suppose assassination attempts are still on the table. Pretty sure the Masters are a better defense than a couple of guards, though.*

She walked right past them, invisible, and shoved open one of the wide doors to the Council Chamber.

Within, the Council, for once, didn't occupy their seats. Instead, a massive circular war table graced the center of the floor, the Council sitting or standing around it, young messengers lining the edges of the room, ready to dart away with orders at a moment's notice. The Case, presumably holding the Master Key, sat in the middle of the maps.

Seven men at the table. Six Council members, Master Ragnulfsen of Eringaard noticeably missing. Six Council members . . . and Mordred.

His gaze rose from the table, where the blade sat glowing. She cursed her distraction. She'd hardly noticed the coolness in her scar. So much magic running through her veins had caused her to tune out most signals her body sent. The tip of the blade pointed straight toward her.

Which meant the blade Vorath carried had been a doppelganger. Brinnie could have retrieved Excalibur herself. Almost as if Mordred knew Brinnie would send someone else after the sword and would come to the Council Chamber.

Mordred's voice rang across the room. "Hello, Brynna."

Beside Mordred, Scott Castelius whirled toward the door, eyes darting as if by looking hard enough, he would see the invisible, but a smirk still painted his face. The smirk of someone who had been expecting her.

Movement caught her attention. Two soldiers led Dr. Morton forward, his hands tied behind his back. He grimaced at her. "They caught me spying. I tried to warn you, but they were watching me . . ."

Tried to warn her.

He'd said, twice, that the Key was under the supervision of seven. He knew Ragnulfsen had abandoned the Council, because she'd told him. She had assumed the two times he'd mentioned the number seven were because of the Council of Seven. But he'd been telling her. Six Council members, and Mordred.

She'd missed the hints.

Her whole body quivered with rage. Not just Castelius, but the entire Council had joined forces with Mordred? "So all of you are just standing here together, plotting, while your armies slaughter one another?"

"We are discussing terms," Mordred said calmly. "As you may have noticed, none of these Council members possess a Mastership in anything but name only. Every estate has fallen to me."

"All but Castelon," Scott added.

Mordred glanced at him, and even from the doorway, Brinnie could see the look of annoyed amusement cross his face at Castelius's blindness. "All but Castelon," he agreed.

"Do they know?" Brinnie turned visible so Dr. Morton could see her attention directed at him. "Did you tell them?"

Dr. Morton nodded morosely. "I didn't know what else to do. I told them what you were missing with Excalibur. That it had to be wielded in tandem with the Master Key to activate the magic."

The words took a moment to register. A lie. "And . . . and that's it?"

"Oh, no, he told us much more. He explained the full prophecy in detail when threatened with a return to the pit." Mordred chuckled. "As much as I would enjoy watching you attempt to juggle the Master Key while stabbing me with Excalibur, you will be doing no such thing."

Mordred had fallen for a ruse.

For once, he hadn't figured everything out before she did. For once, he hadn't dug deeper. Because to him, to everyone on the Council, the thought of destroying magic, of giving up everything to stop the war, would never even cross their minds. Why would *anyone* make destroying magic possible?

And why would anyone be crazy enough to do it?

She squared her shoulders. "Well, if you know all that, you know I can stop you. Stop this war." She attempted to make eye contact with each of the Council members. "Can you hold off six Masters and me?"

"When the end of the war is so close already, and the end of our cowering near at hand?" Mordred tapped his fingers on the table. "You would bring us back to a hidden existence of dying magic when we could rule this world? Simply for revenge against me? That seems a bit unreasonable, Brynna." He inclined his head to the Council. "As you may observe, everyone else here sees reason."

"I'm not seeking revenge." She clenched her fists. "That's the whole point. *You* are bent on revenge against humans who have done nothing to you. They don't have to die. We can all live."

"Slowly stripped of magic, condemned to fleeting lifespans?" He turned to the Council members, a mocking smile playing over his lips. "That sounds like death, not life."

"Massacring an entire planet of humans sounds even more like death."

He sneered. "Gods do not concern themselves with the fate of mortals."

Marcus appeared beside her, the mist of the portal swirling around him. She held out her hand, and he placed Excalibur in her grip.

"Then I look forward to watching the gods bleed."

CHAPTER
FORTY-ONE

The moment the first explosion rocked the Council Chamber, the messengers lining the walls fled. Even the soldiers holding Dr. Morton turned and ran.

No one was foolish enough to stick around for a battle to the death between the most powerful wizards in the world.

Brinnie turned invisible, diving out of the way of a slab of stone hurtling toward her. Even the graying old Masters stood, firing projectiles at her and Marcus. None had bothered to draw a weapon. They didn't need to.

Fire couldn't hurt her, water and stone she could deflect, but when three Masters blasted the room with light, her shadows shredded, revealing her racing toward the table.

A sonar blast sent her reeling, ears ringing. Hundreds of cockroaches skittered toward her, and she engulfed herself in flames to avoid the bugs. Flashing light and screeching sound rendered her near blind and deaf, but she continued stumbling forward, gripping Excalibur. She didn't need to defeat them. She just needed to reach the Key.

Suddenly, the blasting magic ceased, and energy drained from her own bones. She looked up, spots dancing in front of her eyes.

Mordred stood, the Master Key in one hand, the open Case in the other, directed at her.

"Are you mad?" Master Castelius demanded.

"Calm yourself." He stared Brinnie down. "You may not be able to wield your magic, but neither can she."

Her legs wobbled. Oxygen seemed to have left the air, her lungs crushing under the weight of the sudden loss of pressure from magic. "I can still swing a sword," she gasped out.

She would implode. Her cells would burst inward. But she continued pushing forward. One step. Two.

Then everything gave out, and she fell to her knees.

Mordred held out a hand to Master Castelius. "Would you care to do the honors? A clean beheading would be best."

"Gladly." She heard a blade whispering from its sheath.

Pressure in her cranium tunneled her vision. Where was Marcus? Had he survived the earlier barrage of magic?

From the corner of her eye, she spotted a limp form five feet away, face down, half covered in rubble, sword still clutched in his hand. Marcus. *No.*

Master Castelius's footsteps crunched toward her. Energy leached from her body. She fell forward, arms scarcely holding her up, as Excalibur clattered to the ground.

So this was how it ended. Not even on the battlefield with her friends and family. Kneeling, helpless, in front of a bunch of old men who couldn't care less about the world or its people, not even their own. Who cared only about maintaining power. In the end, fighting didn't matter when even the leaders of the "good guys" never cared at all.

She slumped sideways, the last bit of strength leaving her body. *If anyone lives to remember me, I hope they know I tried.*

Then Mordred cried out.

With monumental effort, she lifted her head. Mordred's wrist spurted blood from where a small knife had been embedded. A dagger, one not meant for throwing. And the Master Key fell from his fingers, hitting the ground, rolling.

Movement above her diverted her attention. Master Castelius's face contorted into a snarl as his sword arced, swinging down toward her. She couldn't move fast enough.

Then he halted with a grunt. A gurgle. His eyes drifted downward, to the tip of a blade protruding from his stomach.

The blade ripped away, and he fell. A hand shoved him to the side so he didn't land on Brinnie, revealing Marcus standing behind him with a sword dripping blood. "Like grandfather, like grandson, I suppose."

She shivered, trembling with pain, with exhaustion, but her fingers gripped Excalibur's handle, attention darting for the Key. The orb was only a few yards away, but Mordred lurched toward it.

Marcus darted toward the rolling Master Key, colliding with Mordred. Both of them went down as Marcus kicked the orb toward Brinnie.

The Master Key rolled, crunching over debris, a glowing sphere impervious to its surroundings.

With every ounce of strength left in her body, she raised Excalibur above her head, then brought it down with a yell.

Metal rang out on what sounded like glass. Splinters raced across the surface of the Master Key, colors exploding through the cracks, faster and faster.

Marcus rolled away from Mordred, and, inexplicably, away from a swirl of mist. The Masters ran toward him, but as light from the Key hit them, they dropped to their knees, screaming and clawing at their skin. Blood and dust stained their once-pristine black robes as the very room trembled around them.

"We have to go, now." Marcus reached for the Case he'd knocked from Mordred's grasp, scooping it up, the tether that would hopefully bring them back to the Master Key after they deposited Excalibur where it belonged. They had only seconds before magic deteriorated completely, rendering portals useless.

She pushed herself to her knees and reached for Marcus. "Come on. The portals."

He shook his head, holding out his hand. "Give me Excalibur, Brinnie."

Her chest tightened, alarm bells ringing in her mind. Something was wrong. Very wrong. "Give me your hand. We're going back."

He continued the slow shake of his head, holding out one fist and opening it to reveal a single portal in his palm. "Not we. Me. This is the last one. The others shattered when I collided with Mordred."

Her heart stopped. She had no more portals either. He had been carrying them. It took one portal to go back in time.

And one portal to return.

"Don't be stupid." Her voice wobbled, then gained confidence. "We'll find another one in Arthur's time. The Case can still get us back here."

"No!" Mordred screamed, his eyes wild. This time, he dove toward Marcus. Marcus dodged, but not before Mordred shot out a hand toward the Case, smashing a vial into it. Flames of a color Brinnie hadn't seen before shot out, engulfing the chest.

The oppressive force of the Case lifted from Brinnie's bones, a very bad sign. She scrambled forward, attempting to summon water to douse the flames. Marcus dropped the Case and beat at the fire but snatched his hands back with a cry. Burned. The flames burned him.

"Enchanted Greek fire," he gasped. "No one has been able to reproduce it since antiquity."

Brinnie watched in horror as the Case dwindled to ashes. The Key continued to throw off rays of color, cracks widening and spider-webbing along the surface.

"You're not returning that sword," Mordred snarled. "Arthur will never become king." He unleashed an unhinged cackle, tears running down his face. "I may have lost. But you lost, too." He lunged toward Brinnie.

Instinctively, she whipped Excalibur up into a ready position, as if preparing to parry a blow.

But Mordred wielded no weapon. Instead, his manic lunge plunged him straight into the blade, the wickedly sharp sword sliding through effortlessly until his body hit the hilt, sending Brinnie stumbling back.

He stared down at the sword, then back up at her. The tears, the wildness, the anger, all gone. Only stone-cold lack of emotion.

"Congratulations, Brynna." His familiar steely gray eyes looked into hers one last time. A goodbye, of sorts, only grim acceptance staring back at her. Acceptance, and perhaps, a hint of pity. "You've destroyed everything you love."

Then he slumped, and she jerked Excalibur back as he toppled.

Her skin prickled from his words. *No. Nothing is destroyed yet.* She whirled toward Marcus. "We'll figure this out. There has to be a tether. Something."

His expression was set. "You can't travel to a time with no magic," he repeated the old man's words softly, gaze fixed on Excalibur. "When we met my future self in the past . . . I wasn't devastated because you died." He lifted his eyes to her. "It was because I knew I would never see you again."

"No." Her vision felt blurry, something wet on her cheeks. Tears.

"One portal. No Case." His eyes were wet as he held out his hand. "Give me the sword, Brynna."

"No." She clutched the bloody weapon to her chest. "I'm going with you."

"We don't know whether we can survive in the past once Excalibur is back in the stone. We won't have affected the past anymore. We may be wraiths." He stepped closer. "There's every chance this is a death sentence. I can't let that happen to you."

"That's a risk I'm willing to take." Panic made her voice shrill. "I'm going. Don't leave me."

He lifted his hands to her cheeks. The light from the crackling Master Key played across his face like a kaleidoscope, the myriad of colors mocking her. "You have so much to live for. Your family, your friends." His thumbs wiped away her tears. "Let me go, Brinnie."

Sobs shook her body. He wrapped her in his arms, sword and all. "We'll see one another again. I promise. In this life . . ."

"I'm not finishing that sentence."

He pressed his lips to hers, and she clung to him, never wanting to let him go. Beside them, ominous cracking noises emanated from the Key. "I love you," she whispered against his lips.

"I love you." The tension in his limbs began to relax as he captured her lips again, and she thought maybe she had convinced him. Her grip loosened on the sword.

Then the hilt slipped from her grasp and Marcus broke from her arms, giving her a gentle shove.

She stumbled backward as he backtracked, Excalibur in one hand, the portal in the other. "In this life, or the next."

The portal smashed. The mist swirled.

A wordless scream tore from her chest. She stepped forward.

And the Key exploded.

A scalding blast of light and color threw her backward, slamming her into the ground. Prismatic light blinded her, scorching through her, scraping through her bones, ripping and tearing. She couldn't tell if the shrieking in her ears came from her own screams of agony or the force of the explosion.

Then it all ended, leaving only shattered glass clinking to the ground and ash drifting down in soft motes like gray snow as she stared upward, ears ringing.

She rolled over and pushed herself up onto her hands and knees, arms trembling. Blood dripped from her nose and trailed down the cracked and ruptured ground toward the twisted corpse of Mordred.

Silence filled the world. Emptiness. No hum of magic. No shadows calling to her. Not even the whispers of *dywledrith*.

She had ended the war. Forever.

So why didn't she feel like she had won?

CHAPTER FORTY-TWO

A pale-yellow butterfly fluttered in front of her as she knelt in the grass, a taste of spring even as the leaves of a few trees began to turn for autumn. The sun shone warm on her shoulders and dappled the ground through the branches, where birdsong filtered through the leaves.

Brinnie brushed her fingers along the carved letters, the stone cool from shade beneath her fingertips. Only a few letters out of so many names carved in stone. So many names that never would be, since everyone who knew them had died with them. Hundreds, thousands of innocent victims. All casualties of one man's hurt. Of one man's obsession with revenge and power.

She dropped her hand from the simple headstone, lifting her fingers to trace another. No bodies lay beneath this earth. None could be found in the wreckage. She almost preferred it this way. They weren't truly here, anyway. They were in a far better place.

The first stone. Elsa Winslow. A wife, a housekeeper, a lover of all. She had no children of her own, but everyone who came into her house became like a child to her.

The second stone. David Matthew. A husband, a doctor, a father, a fearless fighter for justice, even without magic. He fell defending the wall of Castelon, fighting side by side with Anna, and Brinnie hadn't been there to save him. He left behind a wife and son, but he left them in the safe world he had won for them.

Finally, a stone she could barely bring herself to look at. Marcus Vorath. Her best friend. The man she loved. He sacrificed his life to save them all.

Snuffling alerted her to another presence. Bruno shoved his head under her arm, demanding pets. With such lovable charm, she wasn't surprised he and Ami had survived the capture of Wraithwood just fine. She scratched his ears, turning at the sound of footsteps.

"Brinnie." Anna stood at the other side of the cemetery, holding Isaac's little hand. Her eyes shone with bittersweet, unshed tears, but her smile was genuine. "It's starting."

She nodded. "I'll be right there."

Anna left, Isaac babbling beside her. The little boy was too young to yet realize what it meant that David was gone. When he grew older, Brinnie would be sure to tell her nephew stories of his heroic father—though Anna would undoubtedly beat her to it.

Brinnie lifted her fingertips to her lips, then touched them to Marcus's name. Then she stood, dusting off the front of her dress. She patted Mrs. Winslow's headstone. "You'd be proud of us today. Especially Uncle Merlin and Lydia."

She walked through the woods, unhindered by the Maze. The hedges had gone, along with magic. She stepped out onto the lawns of Wraithwood, the grass still green, the sun bright. Rows of chairs faced a bower in the rose garden, most of the attendees already seated.

"I've never been in a wedding before." Quentin held out his elbow, adjusting the collar of his button-down shirt. "I think we're walking down together."

She looped her arm through his. "I believe you're correct."

Violin music began, played by none other than Miss Burtle. A hidden talent.

The wedding party took their places with the usual ceremony. Dad stood at the bower, a Bible in his hands, Uncle Merlin in front of him, looking even more dapper than usual in a suit of earth tones. Mom stood as the matron of honor, Mr. Winslow as the best man. Anna and Brinnie had been selected as bridesmaids—soon to be joined by Miss Burtle once she finished playing—Quentin and Jerry as groomsmen, and Isaac as the ring bearer. Bruno, however, made the best entrance as the flower dog—escorted by Maddy and Marcie on either side, who corralled him from licking the guests.

Brinnie looked out over the seats at the gathering, relatively small for a wedding, but bigger than what she was used to at Wraithwood. Many had been left homeless by the war, and some had begun to build new lives at Wraithwood, Dr. Morton included, now sitting among them.

Lana and her family had made the journey, sitting not far from Ignatius, awoken from his sleeping curse after the eradication of magic. Several former Masters or heirs joined them, a symbolic gesture of unity as the estates continued to work together to build new lives, new identities, for so many wizards made human.

Her heart ached for the faces that should be there—friends of her uncle like Oswald Goddensfeld, long dead. Nimue, who no one had seen.

Her disappearance wasn't uncommon. Two months later, former wizards still struggled to find family and friends in the chaotic aftermath of war, unsure if loved ones yet lived. If, like the surviving members of the Council, they had fled into hiding. She had yet to find Marcus's father. Yet to find kind souls like Miss Trish and Lord Faughn—but she had time. All the time in the world.

Lydia Tynsdale rounded the corner of rose bushes and Brinnie heard her uncle's breath catch. Lydia was still the most beautiful woman Brinnie had ever seen. She floated down the aisle, a vision of beauty in white, the gown Brinnie's grandmother had worn on her wedding day. As Lydia took her place, taking Uncle Merlin's hands, nostalgic tears filled Brinnie's eyes. She had never thought she would see her aunt conscious again. Never thought the curse would someday be broken.

"We gather today to celebrate the union of Merlin Ludovic and Lydia Tynsdale," Dad began. "And the defeat of Mordred and the end of war."

Cheers erupted. Even if only a few knew what really happened.

Rumors flew rampant, but a few threads remained the same. The Council had been traitors, making deals with Mordred. Brinnie had figured that out and had managed to kill Mordred. With his dying breath, Mordred had destroyed the Master Key out of spite, ripping magic away from them all.

All hatred and vitriol about the loss of magic thus directed at Mordred. At the Council. And Brinnie had been painted, if not as a hero, at least as the one who stopped the war. The destruction of their world wasn't considered her fault.

Because if the former wizards knew what she'd done, they would come for blood.

"Two months ago today," Dad continued, "Mordred fell. Because of that, we now have Lydia here with us. We may gather here to celebrate, peacefully, a union of love. A beginning of a new life, in so many ways."

The two hadn't been sure about hosting a wedding while the world still reeled. In the end, they decided the ceremony would be more than a wedding. It would be symbolic. Life moved on after magic. They all had a future. Uncertain, wholly different, but still bright. Still full of life.

A cool breeze made the sunny day comfortable despite the heat. The rose garden, though a bit scraggly after Wraithwood's long occupation, provided the perfect venue. Birds sang and a few lingering late-season bees buzzed as if they knew. War had ended. Humanity had been saved.

Brinnie danced at the reception, free from the pain of too much magic eating away at her bones. She cheered with the toasts. She even smiled as Lydia smashed a piece of the cake Brinnie and Mom had made into Uncle Merlin's face.

But her heart felt dead as a stone.

She encountered Ignatius near the drinks table, both of them nursing a cup of punch, gazing out toward the dance floor. "Hey."

"Hey."

They stood in silence for a few moments. Brinnie watched Quentin give Maddy a twirl, Anna bounce Isaac on her hip, Lana . . . Brinnie followed Ignatius's eyes and shook her head with a slight smile. Never one to sit around, Lana had set up a game of bean bag toss and gathered enough players for a match. Her toss swished right through the hole.

Ignatius kept his voice low. "I haven't found anything."

The smile faded.

The circles under his eyes hinted at many long nights awake, poring over tomes, searching for anything that might help someone travel to a time without magic.

Marcus had been his best friend, too.

"It isn't possible, Brinnie." He sighed. "We're only human, now."

If anyone could figure something out, it would be him, a former spellcaster, the one who had been able to make anywhere portals and revolutionize inter-estate travel . . . for a brief while before magic disappeared forever. So Brinnie had turned to him for answers.

His words should have struck deeper, but she found herself only nodding. "I know."

She'd known ever since the Key exploded.

Things had changed between her and Ignatius. He had given his life for her, never expecting to awaken. They weren't friends, exactly, not yet, but they shared a bond of mutual life debts. She could never repay him for what he'd done to bring her back. Because of Ignatius, she and Marcus had been able to defeat Mordred.

"Are you angry with him?" Ignatius asked softly.

Brinnie's eyes swept the horizon, lingering on roses and leaves fluttering in the trees. "Sometimes," she admitted.

Sometimes, when she felt so alone in her own mind, her head ringing empty as her own thoughts echoed. *You left.*

No one answered.

For a moment, she couldn't bring herself to say anything more. Finally, she took a shuddering breath. "He promised he would never leave me, not even if the world depended on it." A breathy laugh bubbled in her throat. "Then he left me . . . because the world depended on it."

"And that's why you're angry?"

"No." She felt a wry smile rise to her lips. "It's because I can't help but love him all the more for it."

Ignatius put a comforting hand on her shoulder, then wordlessly walked away.

The young women lined up for the tossing of the bouquet. Brinnie attempted to duck out, but Maddy pulled her in. Brinnie saw Lydia toss the flowers over her shoulder. She saw the bundle go up and get lost in the sun.

Then something smacked her in the head. The bouquet fell on the ground in front of her.

She stared at the flowers. A few awkward laughs rippled through the party.

Beside her, Lana scooped up the bouquet, sighed dramatically, and placed it in Brinnie's arms. "Looks like we'll be working on your hand eye coordination in the training ring tomorrow."

Brinnie forced out a chuckle, and laughter echoed around her, the awkward tension broken. With her eyes, she tried to convey her gratitude to Lana. *Thank you.*

"No problem," she whispered. She clapped a hand on Brinnie's shoulder and squeezed before striding away calling out something about "cranking the tunes." Exposing Lana to human slang had been a mistake.

The party continued long into the night, the celebration as much to do with the wedding as the giddy feeling of being alive. Alive, without weapons in hand. Without the threat of Mordizan or Mordred or anyone else looming over their heads. Their new greatest concerns involved forging identities and learning to do taxes.

Long after everyone else had gone to bed, Brinnie sat at the kitchen table, twisting a flower back and forth in her fingers. She didn't bother to turn on a light. She never had before. Only now, she couldn't see a thing.

She hated the dark.

A shuffle of movement sent her jumping to her feet, whirling, a knife raised, only to face Miss Burtle's impassive expression. Miss Burtle stepped around her and reached over the table to turn on a lantern. "Thought I'd find you here."

Brinnie slumped back into her chair, sliding the knife back into its hidden sheath. Mom would scold her for carrying weapons at a wedding. "Sorry. Still jumpy."

"I doubt that's a habit you'll lose anytime soon." She sat across from Brinnie, holding a teacup filled with something that did not look like tea. "Have the nightmares stopped yet?"

Brinnie gestured to the dark, empty room. "I'm certainly not staying up for the rousing social interaction. Present company excluded, of course." Then she blew out a puff of air, deflating until her head rested in her hands. "What is wrong with me? We won."

"And *you* lost." Miss Burtle sipped her drink. "People. Purpose. Magic. The last one is hard in itself."

"How would you know?" she blurted. Then she rubbed her temple, realizing what she'd said. "I'm sorry. That was rude and uncalled for."

"I understand." Another sip, a deeper one this time. Definitely not tea. "My parents were wizards."

Well, this was new information. "They were?"

"Neither were full-blooded, obviously, considering I didn't inherit magic. We lived here, at Wraithwood. One day when we went to visit family at Habrin, we were attacked on the way." She stared past Brinnie.

"I watched my parents die. I never wished I had magic more than at that moment."

Pain stabbed her heart. Suddenly, so many pieces of the puzzle that was Miss Burtle fell into place. "I'm so sorry."

She returned her gaze to Brinnie. "I understand what it's like to grow up with magic, and then not to have it. I would imagine it's worse for you. I never had magic in the first place, only the expectation that I someday would. You were the world's most powerful wizard."

Brinnie twirled the flower in her fingers. Back and forth, back and forth, until the stem snapped. "I don't know who I am anymore without magic," she whispered. Her breath shuddered as the admission left her mouth. "Sometimes I wish I'd gone back with Marcus. If only because then I would know what I'm meant to do next."

"It's hard to figure out what to do next when you never thought you would live this long in the first place." Miss Burtle drained her cup.

"Yes." Brinnie's head tilted. "I think you put it into words." She nodded toward the teacup. "Do you have any more of that tea somewhere?"

"Not for you. I'll make you dust the library top to bottom if you suggest it again."

Brinnie scowled and changed the subject. "Any luck tracking down what happened to people in the double space when magic left?"

"None." She traced her finger around the rim of her cup. "Numbers are still sketchy, but it looks like about a quarter of the population was in the double space when the Key was destroyed. And the double space is well and truly gone."

Brinnie rubbed her forehead. Miss Burtle was one of the few who knew the truth of *dywledrith*, of the magical dimension. "They should be fine. They have their cities and towns, and a whole world no one could previously access."

"True."

Neither voiced the many, many flaws in the logic. How many people were permanently separated from their families? How many unknown magical creatures might now threaten those in the mirror world?

"Real life doesn't have a perfect solution," Miss Burtle said finally. "Sometimes you have to choose the least bad thing, if you'll excuse my terrible grammar."

"You think this was the least bad thing?"

"I do." She rose and gave Brinnie a quick pat on the shoulder before heading for the door. "And I think with work, and time, it might even become a very good thing."

Brinnie drifted up the stairs a few moments later. She might as well stare at the ceiling in the comfort of bed instead of a hard, wooden chair.

Dark stairs. She tripped halfway up, barely catching herself. No shadows. Only darkness.

For two months, she had attempted to focus on the tasks at hand. Reuniting friends and families. Assisting her parents and Uncle Merlin in their efforts of leadership, the Masters of the estates still de facto leaders of the former wizards, using knowledge and resources formerly spent on armies to help people return to their homes or build new ones, sculpt new identities in their respective countries. Those with skills like Miss Burtle's became invaluable.

Work to do kept her sane, and everyone seemed happy to allow the heroic slayer of Mordred to help. Relationships between former dark estates and former enchantment estates remained frigid, but their mutual hatred of Mordred for destroying magic linked them together enough to occasionally collaborate. Hatred that would be directed at her, if they knew the truth.

So she worked herself to the bone, and usually, it worked, keeping her from nightmares and flashbacks and panic attacks that threatened, especially in the dark.

But mostly the work kept her from dissolving into a puddle of grief.

The moment Marcus smashed that portal played on a loop in her head. She replayed the events of the conflict in the Council Chamber over and over, trying to think of what she could have done differently, how she could have secured another portal. Her imaginings tortured her, wondering if he had survived in the past, or died a wraith.

I can't keep living like this. Living in the past. I'm seventeen. I have an entire life ahead of me.

She stopped abruptly at the top of the stairs. Seventeen. Her birthday had come and gone.

She darted down the hall and burst into her room without knocking. In the bed, Lana startled, rubbing her eyes. With so many guests like Lana's family, Mom and Dad, and others coming to stay for the wedding, they had run out of space, and the two hadn't needed any convincing to be temporary roommates again, just like old times.

"I need to go to Artema." Brinnie's words came out breathless. "I left something important there."

The car bounced and jerked over a rough road not designed for vehicles. Lana gripped the handle on the roof above the passenger seat. "Maybe we should go a little slower."

Brinnie maintained a white-knuckled grip on the steering wheel. "I'm already only going twenty-five. This road is a mess. I blame the war."

A contact near Artema had provided them with the vehicle, an old, beat-up car with crank windows, but anything was better than having to explain to a driver why they wanted to go to the middle of nowhere.

Lana held the map Miss Burtle had provided in one hand. "We should be able to see the fortress around this bend."

Sure enough, a thick wall of smooth stone came into view. The ramparts had crumbled in many places, and the remains of the gate hung inward, abandoned. As a primarily military outpost, few wizards had homes in Artema, and those who did hadn't returned.

Brinnie pulled the car over and turned off the ignition. Her heart galloped in her chest. "It might not even be here," she said, more to herself than to Lana.

"We won't know unless we look." Her friend reached over and squeezed her hand.

They entered the courtyard, stepping over crumbled stones and scorched earth. The idle thought of what humans would make of Artema drifted through Brinnie's mind. The true miracle was that none of the estates had been discovered yet. Archaeologists and historians would no doubt lose their minds trying to figure it out. She could just imagine the tabloid headlines about aliens or Illuminati. Assuming former wizards didn't abandon self-preservation and leak the story.

She and Lana spread out, sweeping the outer courtyard. Somewhere around here, she had stabbed Mordred with Excalibur the first time.

Somewhere, she had dropped the small package from the old man from the past in the scuffle. She could only hope no one had picked it up, or that it hadn't been destroyed.

She tried to calm her rapid heartbeat. *What do you think this will change? You're setting yourself up for disappointment.*

But at least I might have the slightest bit of closure.

"Over here," Lana called.

In a corner filled with debris, dirty from trampling feet and wrinkled from the rain, lay the package. Brinnie inhaled sharply. "That's it."

They sat on a chunk of fallen battlement shaped almost like a bench. Brinnie balanced the package on her knees and slowly, carefully, peeled away the paper to reveal a layer of oilskin beneath. "Thank goodness," she breathed.

She unfolded the oilskin, unveiling a thin sheaf of yellowed pages covered in script handwritten in ink. Modern English script.

Lana stood. "I'll sweep the perimeter, just to be safe. Call if you need me."

Brinnie nodded, hardly registering the words. No sweep of the perimeter was needed, but she recognized Lana's attempt to give her some space.

She began to read.

Brinnie,

I hardly know where to begin. First of all, it's me, Marcus, writing this. I'm alive and well.

Second, I love you. I always have. I can't apologize enough times for what I did, tricking you, pushing you away. Your eyes filled with horror haunt my dreams. I would do it again, for you to be safe, but I will never forgive myself. And I am so, so sorry.

Like we both saw, I ended up back at the stone of Excalibur. I returned the sword to the stone. When I saw you there that day, I wanted to tell you everything. I wanted to tell you I loved you, hug you one last time. But I couldn't. If I revealed the future, I risked causing a time paradox, destroying everything. If I warned you, I might ruin it all. So I said nothing.

I wandered in that time for a while. Eventually I found Myrddin. He was still a somewhat young man at the time, but he was skilled enough to craft several portals for me. I used them all trying to get back to you, but with no control over where they took me, 1863 was the closest I reached. One of them took me to ancient Greece, to the famed wizards of Mt. Olympus. There, I learned from their studies of the nature of magic. I learned that according to their calculations and theorems, magic cannot be brought into a time where it does not exist, just as we were warned.

I tried to cheat the rules. I figured if I just used one portal and brought none with me, I wouldn't be taking magic into a time without it. Instead, it simply took me longer to find a wizard with the skill to craft me another portal.

Eventually, I ended up back in the time of Myrddin, mere days before his creation of the Master Key.

If everything works as it should—which it does, because I witnessed Taliesin hand you this parcel—this information will reach you.

Myrddin is about to split the worlds. Pockets of the mirror world, what we grew to call the double space, will be accessible through the Gates as long as the Master Key lasts. However, there is a failsafe.

The mirror world is not completely separated from our world. It never could be, as it is a reflection of our own. The Master Key tethered magic artificially in our world, but even in a world without magic, there are weak spaces. Thin barriers between the two worlds.

The Gates.

As of my writing, this is all theoretical. I haven't interfered with any of Myrddin's choices or actions. I've learned that any ways I've affected human history have simply been integrated into the past. I haven't changed anything, because those things have already happened. But magic, especially dywledrith, is different. It has the potential to create ruptures. I can't interfere. But from what I've learned, the Gates will always be weak points. At the four equinoxes, the barrier grows so thin as to be passable.

You can reach the mirror world.

My time grows short to pen this letter. Suffice to say, the year of Mordred's demise will be recorded in the mirror world. And on the autumnal equinox, the first equinox following Mordred's defeat, if all goes to plan, someone will be stationed at every Gate. I've included instructions below on how to make contact and establish a more permanent tether. This requires a person on either side of the Gate working together. On the autumnal equinox, someone will be waiting for you at any Gate. If you choose, you can create a link between the human world and the magical world. No magic will ever cross over—wizards will have no power in the human world—but people could pass between them.

Or, you may choose not to establish a connection. You can burn these papers. You may decide that magic should stay gone, that everyone should move on with their lives.

Whatever you decide, the choice is permanent. Once established, the tether cannot be severed, to my knowledge. If you decide not to establish a connection on the autumnal equinox, I have no idea if the people of the former double spaces, now the mirror world, will still be waiting. In fact, I can't guarantee they've heeded the instructions that we will be leaving for them at all. They may not even be waiting for you at the equinox. But I have hope that they will.

I love you, Brinnie. I don't know what will happen next for me, or for you. We well and truly burned every card in our hands and the table itself. We're playing a new game, one without any rules yet established. But that means we have the chance to create something new, and, God willing, something better.

I wish I could have been there with you to create that new world. Since it couldn't be, I've done the only thing I can.

Soon, I'm embarking on a new adventure in the mirror world. Maybe, in your time, soon you will be too. Or maybe you'll embark on an altogether different adventure, one no less magical for the lack of magic.

With all the love in the world,
in this time and yours,
Marcus

Tears ran down her face, blurring her vision and threatening the pages. She held them away so as not to ruin them. Then she shuffled the papers, reaching the instructions Marcus had spoken of.

Only a page. Simple, yet detailed. She could do it, easily.

Her fingers fumbled and she almost dropped her phone in her scramble to pull it out from her pocket. She typed in her query with trembling fingertips.

When is the autumnal equinox?

Her heart nearly stopped as she sucked in a breath. What were the odds?

"Today," she breathed. "The equinox is today."

And Marcus, ridiculous, amazing, brilliant Marcus, had put the key to all magic in her hands.

Yet, she hesitated. Magic had given her purpose. Given her something to live for.

But these past days had shown that magic wasn't needed to live a life worth living. Life went on. People fell in love, got married. Family and friends gathered in celebration. Just in sight across the courtyard, her best friend patrolled for imaginary threats. A best friend who had unquestioningly hopped on a red-eye flight with her headed for a ruined fortress in hopes of finding a mysterious package that may or may not exist anymore, simply because it was important to Brinnie.

Perhaps what she had loved about Wraithwood, about the world of magic, what had made her feel alive for the first time in her life, had little to do with magic itself.

Perhaps it had everything to do with the passionate, vibrant people who populated that world.

Lana wandered back over. "You okay?"

She had eight hours left before midnight. Eight hours to decide if the worlds should align, or forever remain separate.

Brinnie took a deep breath. Smiled. "Actually. Yes. More okay than I've been in a long time."

It might not even work. There may not be anyone waiting on the other side.

But even if she couldn't establish the connection, even if magic was really and truly gone . . .

She was okay. They were all okay. Because they all had a future. Even those they had lost, though they might not meet again in this life, that only gave her more hope, more optimism, for the next.

If she walked away right now, she realized, that would still be enough.

She drummed her fingers on the stone. "If there's a chance to be even more than okay . . ." She fixed her gaze on Lana, expression serious. "If there was an opportunity to open up possibilities that are even better, would you take it? Even if there's a chance of danger? A possibility of making things worse instead?"

Lana tilted her head, considering for a long moment. "Well, that's the danger in any decision, isn't it? Something could always go wrong."

She gave a small smile. "But things could also go even better than you ever dreamed. I don't think any decision should be based on fear."

"I think you're right." Brinnie stood slowly and reached for her friend's arm, tugging Lana after her. "Come on."

As they walked, Brinnie picked up speed, excitement flowing through her. Soon, Lana laughed as they made a headlong dash to the Gate of Artema. "Where are we going?"

"Somewhere amazing, I hope."

Standing in front of the Gate, Brinnie held the instructions out for both of them to see, tucking Marcus's letter carefully inside her shirt. "You're better at the ancient language than I am."

Lana's eyes went round, scanning the lines. "This . . . this incantation, it says . . ."

"Exactly." Not *dywledrith.* Activation words. Words that read more like a prayer, a prophecy, a celebration of the miracle of magic.

No. A song.

Brinnie wasn't sure how she knew the tune, but the notes felt right. Beside her, Lana joined in, two voices harmonizing in the lyrical cadence of the ancient language.

Hand in hand, they stepped forward. Toward the Gate. Toward what lay beyond.

For a moment, nothing happened.

That's okay. Magic or not, her family and friends waited for her back at Wraithwood. Mom would still hug her, Dad would still crack dumb jokes, Uncle Merlin would still suggest a game of Wizard's Chess that broke all the rules and drove Quentin crazy while Miss Burtle pretended not to chuckle behind a book. Some members of her family might be gone, but those who remained, though they would forever remember the ones they had lost, were building a new life. Just like those in the double space would. Like all wizards would.

But then, a wind rippled over her. A wind so *alive.* Energy washed over her skin, her bones. A joyous dance that her heart echoed.

Magic.

And from beyond the Gate, a third voice joined their song.

ACKNOWLEDGMENTS

Certain stories hold your heart. They haunt your mind, your life, seep into your very bones. When the final page is written, the last line complete, you hang in limbo, not quite sure it can truly be ended.

Even three years after the original publication of this final installment, *The Wraithwood Trilogy* is that story for me. Now, at the end of the trilogy, with these stunning new editions from Torchflame Books, I find myself with so many people to acknowledge and thank.

To my family, who were there first.

To my happy beginning, my wife, my love, the one who knows me best.

To the family I found, from the Skittles to the Goose clan.

To the animals I loved and who joined my writing sessions, from Merry and the Roat dogs to my black cat babies, Kookoo, Zibby, Dewey, and Violet.

To all those who made this journey possible—Linda Taylor, Hope Bolinger, Miralee Ferrell, Jenny Mertes, Tim Pietz, Teri Rider, and Jori Hanna.

To you, young Alyssa. You who made it here. Who didn't give up. You may not even be able to fathom this, but there is so, so much more out there for you, if you are only brave enough, like Brinnie, to set the cards on fire, move beyond the way things "have to be," and start anew. Thank you for still writing, still fighting, even when you didn't know that. Things are so much brighter on the other side.

And thank you to the readers, to all of you who have followed Brinnie's journey from beginning to end—or at least, the end for now. Thank you for the messages and posts and reviews and demands for the final book. Thank you so much for going on this adventure with me. None of this would be possible without you.

May your world be filled with magic, with dreams, with adventure, with hope.

ABOUT THE AUTHOR

Alyssa Roat is an award-winning multi-published author and has worked in a wide variety of roles within the publishing industry. She has four black cats who allegedly have never been fed in their lives and occasionally help her write by walking across the keyboard. Her name is a pun, which means you can learn more about her at www.alyssawrote.com or on social media @alyssawrote.

THANK YOU!

Thank you for reading! The team at Torchflame Books hopes you've enjoyed this book and might consider leaving a review on Amazon, Goodreads, BookBub, The Story Graph, or anywhere else you like to track your recent reads. Alternatively, you could post online or tell a friend about it. This helps our authors more than you may know.

- The Team at Torchflame Books

Follow Torchflame Books for news about our authors and upcoming new releases @TorchflameBooks.

Find your next great read at torchflamebooks.com.

THE STORY CONTINUES...

WRAITHWOOD

Sent to Wraithwood Estate to live with an uncle she never knew, Brinnie Lane's quiet life takes a thrilling turn. The eerie mansion hides secrets of a hidden war, a tragic event, and ties to Arthurian legend. As Brinnie uncovers her family's mysterious past, she must confront the impossible: what if magic is real?

MORDIZAN

When Brinnie's sister is captured by the ruthless Mordred, she returns to the dangerous world of magic she thought she'd left behind. To save her, Brinnie goes undercover in Mordizan, seeking a prophecy that could destroy Mordred forever. How far will she go to defeat him? And how much of herself will she lose in the process?

CASTELON

Brinnie races against time to stop Mordred's reign of terror. With magic consuming her and the legendary weapon to defeat Mordred still lost, she must face war, political betrayal, and the allure of forbidden power. Only one man holds the knowledge of the weapon that could destroy Mordred forever—a man they already buried.

Get your copy at torchflamebooks.com/authors/alyssa-roat/

MORE FROM ALYSSA ROAT

DEAR HERO

Teen superhero Cortex and teen supervillain Vortex meet on Meta-Match, a nemesis pairing app for heroes and villains. But when darkness from the past threatens them both, they may need each other for the fight to come. Can a hero trust a villain to do the right thing? And can a villain trust a hero not to screw her over?

DEAR HENCHMAN

Kevin and Himari didn't plan to be heroes. Henchmen and sidekicks are supposed to brew coffee, take pics of their hero or villain for social media, and stay in the background. But when a taxidermy-collecting villain robs Kevin's hero of his powers and leaves Himari's villain wounded, it's up to the sidekicks and henchmen to save the world regardless of whether they have superpowers or not.

DEAR HADES

Freshly resurrected as 21st century teens, Medusa and Tiresias seek a second chance amidst meddling gods, murderous heroes, and a classic Greek bet. With pressure building on all sides, they must work together to save mortals and monsters alike.

Get your copy at torchflamebooks.com/authors/alyssa-roat/

www.ingramcontent.com/pod-product-compliance
Lightning Source LLC
LaVergne TN
LVHW050919080826
845145LV00001B/132

* 9 7 8 1 6 1 1 5 3 6 2 0 1 *